P9-DDR-504

Alexa was *crying*.

In public. In front of Benjamin. Because she was pregnant and because she had to tell him the truth. It was terrifying.

She pulled away from his touch, comforting—disturbingly so—as it was, and reached into her bag for a tissue. She found one, mopped herself up and sternly told her hormones she wouldn't stand for tears again. When she was certain they'd got the picture, she downed the rest of her tea, lukewarm now, because of the tears, and looked at him.

His expression was inscrutable. She didn't know if that made her feel better or worse. But she couldn't rely on him to make herself feel better. So she took a deep breath, held it for a few seconds, then let it out. It was shaky at best, hitched at worst. She did it again, and again, until it came smoothly. Then she said, "I'm pregnant."

Surprise Double Delivery

THERESE BEHARRIE
&
KARIN BAINE

Previously published as *Her Twin Baby Secret*
and *Their One-Night Twin Surprise*

If you purchased this book without a cover you should be aware that this book is stolen property. It was reported as "unsold and destroyed" to the publisher, and neither the author nor the publisher has received any payment for this "stripped book."

ISBN-13: 978-1-335-61747-7

Surprise Double Delivery

Copyright © 2021 by Harlequin Books S.A.

Her Twin Baby Secret
First published in 2020. This edition published in 2021.
Copyright © 2020 by Therese Beharrie

Their One-Night Twin Surprise
First published in 2019. This edition published in 2021.
Copyright © 2019 by Karin Baine

Recycling programs
for this product may
not exist in your area.

All rights reserved. No part of this book may be used or reproduced in any manner whatsoever without written permission except in the case of brief quotations embodied in critical articles and reviews.

This is a work of fiction. Names, characters, places and incidents are either the product of the author's imagination or are used fictitiously. Any resemblance to actual persons, living or dead, businesses, companies, events or locales is entirely coincidental.

This edition published by arrangement with Harlequin Books S.A.

For questions and comments about the quality of this book, please contact us at CustomerService@Harlequin.com.

Harlequin Enterprises ULC
22 Adelaide St. West, 40th Floor
Toronto, Ontario M5H 4E3, Canada
www.Harlequin.com

Printed in U.S.A.

CONTENTS

Being an author has always been **Therese Beharrie**'s dream. But it was only when the corporate world loomed during her final year at university that she realized how soon she wanted that dream to become a reality. So she got serious about her writing and now writes books she wants to see in the world featuring people who look like her for a living. When she's not writing, she's spending time with her husband and dogs in Cape Town, South Africa. She admits that this is a perfect life and is grateful for it.

Books by Therese Beharrie

Harlequin Romance

Billionaires for Heiresses

Second Chance with Her Billionaire
From Heiress to Mom

Conveniently Wed, Royally Bound

United by Their Royal Baby
Falling for His Convenient Queen

The Tycoon's Reluctant Cinderella
A Marriage Worth Saving
The Millionaire's Redemption
Tempted by the Billionaire Next Door
Surprise Baby, Second Chance
Her Festive Flirtation
Island Fling with the Tycoon

Visit the Author Profile page at
Harlequin.com for more titles.

Her Twin Baby Secret

THERESE BEHARRIE

For Grant, who would pretend to be
in a fake relationship with me so I can save
face in a heartbeat. If we weren't already
married, I mean. I love you.

For the online friends who've become my
community. I didn't ever think you could exist,
but I'm so grateful you do.

Prologue

Alexa Moore had never thought the pressure her parents had put on her her entire life would result in this. She barely contained the squeal of excitement tickling her throat.

Her father was sitting beside her in the car, her mother at the back. Both were staring at their phones. They were either checking their emails, replying to emails, or writing their own emails. Leighton and Karla Moore were simple in that way. Work came first; everything else, second. They'd reconciled having a family in light of those priorities by treating their children as though they were work. That was why Alexa and her younger brother by a year, Lee, were raised to function much as their parents did: work was the most important thing. Being Leighton and Karla's children, they had to work harder than anyone else.

Who needed a loving, emotionally supportive family anyway?

But that wasn't for today. Today was for happiness and new beginnings. She wasn't stubborn enough not to acknowledge her parents' contribution to this moment. It was part of why she'd brought them with her. They were the ones who had suggested—instructed—her to start working as soon as she turned sixteen. They'd told her to give them half of what she earned, and because she was their child she'd asked them to help her invest the other half. On her graduation from her Honours degree in business, they'd gifted her with a policy they'd taken out with that money. It had been an impressive nest egg. And it had kept growing while she attended culinary school.

She'd got a bursary to study at Cape Town's Culinary Institute. She was lucky. If she hadn't, she would have had to use that nest egg and she wouldn't be able to move forward with her dream. Her parents had paid for her studies in business on the condition that she got distinctions for all her subjects. She had, though not easily, because she knew she'd already disappointed them by not taking the mathematics bursary an elite tertiary faculty had offered.

But her dream was her dream. A business degree helped her get to that dream—and helped her please her parents more than culinary school had. Their disappointment was worth it for this moment though. She had no student loans, four years of business knowledge, two years of culinary knowledge, and two years' experience in the industry. She was finally ready. This was the last step.

She pulled up in front of the property, letting out a happy sigh before she got out of the car. The brick façade of the building was as appealing as it had been the first time she'd seen it. As the first time it had encouraged her to take a chance on it.

'This is it.'

She clasped her fingers together behind her back to keep from fidgeting.

'This?'

'Yes.' She straightened her spine at the disapproval in her father's voice. 'It's an up-and-coming neighbourhood.'

'It looks unsafe, Lex,' Karla said.

'Oh, it's fine.' She waved a hand. 'You know how Cape Town city centre is. The fanciest road is right next to the dodgiest one. Besides, there are so many people around.'

As if proving it, a group of young people walked past them. They were most likely students; not exactly her target clientele. But everyone had to start somewhere, and students meant lecturers and parents and more mature people who would come to the classy joint in the dingy neighbourhood for the feel of it. She jiggled her shoulders.

'I'm going to call it In the Rough, because this place is a diamond in the rough.' She grinned. 'It's going to be—'

'Lee, darling!'

The world either slowed at her mother's exclamation, or Alexa's heart was pumping alarmingly fast. Why was her brother here? How much of what she'd said had he heard? Would he use it against her?

'What are you doing here?' she asked, her voice cool, a reaction to mitigate the heated emotions those questions had evoked. She would not show them that vulnerability. 'I didn't tell you about this.'

'Dad did,' Lee said, taking their father's hand in a quick shake. 'He told me about a week ago you were planning on showing them a property. Gave me the address and everything, so I could check it out myself.'

'Why would you want to?'

'I can't check on what my big sister is doing with her life?'

No, she wanted to answer. She would have, if their parents weren't there—they would disapprove. Somehow, after years of trying and failing to obtain their approval, she still wanted it. After years of her brother using that desire as a weapon to compete with her, she was still offering it to him.

'To be fair, I'm not doing this with my life yet.' She was trying to be civil, like she always did. Because she was still trying to be a decent person with Lee, too. When would she learn her lesson when it came to her family? 'I wanted Mom and Dad to see this place before I put in an offer.'

'I know.'

'Did you want to see it, too?'

'Oh, I already have.'

She frowned. 'Why?'

'Because I made an offer.' He shoved his hands

into his pockets, his smile catlike. 'The owner accepted it this morning. This place is going to be mine.'

There was a stunned silence. Her parents broke it by asking Lee why he'd bought the place. Bits and pieces of his answer floated across to her. He wanted to secure the place as a surprise for Alexa. It was a smart business decision to invest in property, particularly in a neighbourhood that was fast becoming one to watch. If he and Alexa worked together, there was less chance of failure. The Moores could become a powerhouse in the hospitality industry.

Lies. Lies, all of it.

Lee spoke to them as fluently as he did his other languages. His linguistic skills were as impressive as her mathematical skills. He knew five of South Africa's eleven official languages; he also knew how to fool their parents. They thought he was a good, supportive brother when in reality, he was a master manipulator. All for the sake of winning a competition he'd made up in his head where they were the only competitors and he the only willing participant.

'Alexa,' Karla called. 'You're daydreaming, darling.'

She blinked. 'Sorry.'

'Did you hear what your brother did?'

'Yes.'

'Aren't you glad?'

'Why would I be glad?'

Her mother exchanged a look with her father. Leighton took the baton.

'Lee's made the smart decision here. It's not a buyer's market at the moment, so you might not have got the property. He has more capital, and more clout, so he had a better chance of being successful in the purchase.'

'He didn't know about the property before you told him,' she said numbly. 'And he only has more capital because he's been working longer.' In the business sector, which was more lucrative. Even her nest egg couldn't beat that. 'The owner said she hadn't had much interest in the six months the property's been on the market.'

'She did sound thrilled with my offer.'

She turned at the satisfaction in Lee's voice. When she saw it reflected on his face, her heart broke. This didn't feel like the other times. When he'd race to the dinner table, turn back to her and say, 'I win!' though he'd been the only one running. Or when he would bring a test home from school, announcing that he'd beat Alexa's mark from the year before.

This was more malicious. It was…uglier. And it proved that she would always be a target Lee would shoot at, no matter what the cost.

Unless she did something about it.

'I hope you find a tenant soon, Lee.'

'Wait!' he said when she started walking to her car. 'I thought you'd rent it?'

'So you can pop in whenever you want? Make your presence known in my business? Pull the rug out from under me when I think I'm safe?' She shook her head. 'I appreciate the offer, but you'll have to find someone else.'

'Alexa, you're being foolish.'

'No, Dad, I'm being realistic. But this is a great neighbourhood.' Her voice cracked, echoing her heart. 'He'll find someone to rent from him soon enough.'

'Darling, your brother only wants to help.'

She took a deep breath before offering her mother a smile. 'I know.' Even after he'd punctured a hole in her dreams and her parents were defending him, she couldn't be blunt. 'I can't take his help or I wouldn't be making the Moore name proud, would I? It's all about achieving things we can be proud of. I can't be proud of this.'

Another breath.

'You should go to the restaurant I booked for us tonight with Lee. He deserves it.' She smiled at her family, well aware that it didn't reach her eyes. 'I hope you enjoy the food.'

She got into her car and drove away, leaving her heart and her dreams shattered behind her.

Chapter 1

Four years later

'Oh,' Alexa said flatly. 'It's you.'

Benjamin Foster couldn't help the laugh that rumbled in his chest. 'Yes, it's me.'

Alexa Moore, owner of the elite Infinity restaurant, and the woman who probably hated him more than anyone else in the world, glowered.

'You need to stop following me.'

'I'm not following you,' he denied.

'Are you sure? You seem to be everywhere I am.'

'Because we're in the same business.'

Her eyes stopped scanning the room and settled on him. Sharpened. 'You're here to offer Cherise de Bruyn a job.'

He tilted his head. 'How did you know?'

'You think I didn't hear about Victor Fourie being poached from In the Rough?' She smiled, but it wasn't friendly. 'It's terrible when karma does her thing, isn't it?'

'I'm not sure why she would get involved.'

She gave him a look. He allowed himself a small smile.

'Fine, I do know.' A few seconds passed. Something cleared in his brain. 'You're here to offer Cherise a job, too.'

She responded by ignoring him. He shouldn't have wanted to smile. It seemed rude to since he was the reason she had to offer Cherise a job. She hadn't confirmed that was why she was there, but he was fairly certain. When the thought of being rude did nothing to deter his amusement—apparently what his presence did to her tickled his funny bone—he turned to the barperson and ordered a drink.

'Can I get you one?'

'I don't want to owe you one, so no, thank you.'

He *tsk*ed. 'That's not very mature, Alexa.'

'Maturity is for the weak,' she muttered under her breath.

He didn't bother hiding his grin this time, but paid for his drink before he replied. 'I don't agree with that.'

'Why would you, Benjamin?' she said with a sigh. 'I said it. On principle, you can't agree with me lest *you* seem weak.'

'"*Lest*"?'

'It means to avoid the risk of.'

'I know what it means. I'm wondering why you said it.'

She sighed again, as though he were chopping up the last of her patience. Which was probably true. They'd known one another for eight years now. Or perhaps it would be better to say they'd known about one another for eight years. They didn't know one another, not by a long shot. They had only gone to the Culinary Institute together, the current venue of their meeting, and met on and off in the six years after that.

Whenever they did, they rubbed each other up the wrong way. It caused a friction so intense that sometimes Benjamin struggled to figure out how he felt about her. On the one hand, she never backed down, said interesting things like *lest*, and made him laugh. On the other hand, she was his greatest competition.

Who could be friendly with the competition?

Infinity was rated highly on all the important websites. He often heard whispers of the patrons of his own restaurant comparing In the Rough's food or ambience to Infinity's. It wasn't uncommon for patrons to do so; comments like that were part of the business. But her restaurant was the one he heard mentioned most frequently. It was also the one they preferred most frequently.

'Really?' she asked when he leaned against the bar. 'In this spacious, beautiful, but most importantly *spacious* place, you couldn't find someone else to bother?'

'Bothering you is more fun.'

Her reply came in the form of a glare. He smiled back, sipped from his drink, and didn't move. He did watch though.

She was right—the venue was gorgeous. It was nestled in the valley of one of the many vineyards in Stellenbosch. Bright green fields stretched out in front of them courtesy of an all-glass wall. The room they were in, usually a dining hall, had been transformed for the sake of the graduation. Chairs were set out in rows, a small stage had been erected on one side, and the opposite side housed the bar they were at. On the other side of the glass wall, accessed through a door on the side, were tables and chairs under tall trees.

He remembered sitting there many a lunch time when he'd been at the Institute. Hell, he remembered watching Alexa glower at him from inside the dining hall much in the same way she was doing now. He'd known even then that she was dangerous. How, he wasn't sure.

'What the hell is he doing here?'

The words weren't meant for him, but he heard them. When he followed her gaze, he saw the cause. Her brother, his business partner, was there. Benjamin didn't know why. Securing a head chef was more in line with Benjamin's responsibilities. But their partnership had evolved in the last four years, and their roles weren't what they initially were when they started working together.

Back then, Benjamin was the head chef and Lee's

management company dealt with the running of the restaurant. Benjamin had since taken over some of those responsibilities, which was hard to do without a head chef. It meant that Benjamin's time was still needed in the kitchen. For three glorious months after Victor Fourie had been persuaded to work for In the Rough, Benjamin had been able to explore more of the management side of things. As it turned out, he enjoyed running a restaurant more than spending all his time in the kitchen.

But Lee had been acting strangely when it came to this head chef thing. With Victor Fourie, Lee had actively encouraged Benjamin to go after the man even though he knew Victor worked for Alexa. It had started out harmlessly enough. They'd been out for drinks one night, discussing work, when the chef walked into the bar. It had seemed like a perfectly fair move to ask him to join them. After that night, Lee had told him to get Victor to take over some of Benjamin's responsibilities. Since it would take an immense amount of pressure off Benjamin, he'd done it, though he hadn't understood Lee's insistence. Now Lee was here…

'Ben!' Lee said when he saw them. His eyes flickered to his sister. Something Benjamin didn't like shimmered there. 'Fancy seeing you here.'

'Is it?' Benjamin asked, taking Lee's hand. 'I told you I was coming.'

'He has to pretend it's a surprise in front of me,' Alexa said, her voice emotionless.

He'd only ever heard her speak that way with her

brother. He would have thought, after his and Alexa's antagonistic history, she would have aimed that tone at him, too. But when she spoke to him, her voice was icy, or annoyed, or full of emotion, none of which he could read. He found he preferred it.

'If he doesn't,' she continued, 'it would be clear that he's really here because of me.'

'Not everything I do is because of you, Alexa.' Lee said it smoothly, but Benjamin could feel the resentment.

'I wish that were true.'

Lee didn't acknowledge that Alexa had spoken. 'What I am surprised about is finding you two together.'

'Why?' Benjamin asked.

'Don't you hate one another?'

He looked at Alexa; Alexa looked at him. For a beat, they said nothing. Her expression changed then, going from icy cool to warm. His heart thundered in response to her hazel eyes opening. They grew lighter when they did, so that he could see the green flecks in the light brown. In a way no grown man should experience, Benjamin's knees went weak.

Her eyebrow quirked, as if she knew, though there was no possible way she could. But the show of sassiness pulled the side of her face higher, softening a defined cheekbone. It was an extraordinary juxtaposition to the other side of her face, which was untouched by the expression. It was still hard lines and sharp angles. That had never applied to her lips though, one side of which was now quirked up—

much like her brow—in amusement. At him. He was amusing her.

Because he was admiring her full lips that looked as soft as dough. An interesting comparison, though not surprising since he regularly dealt with dough. What *was* surprising was that he wanted to mould that dough as he did in the kitchen. But with his lips instead of his hands, though he could imagine brushing a thumb over those soft creases...

He took a long drag from his drink, severely disappointed that it wasn't alcohol. He could have done with the shock, the burn of downing a whiskey. But no, he'd decided he shouldn't drink because he wanted a clear head when he spoke to Cherise.

How was this clear?

'Well, Lee,' Alexa said, her voice as smooth as the brandy he'd longed for. Or had he thought of whiskey? 'You know what they say: hate and love are two sides of the same coin.'

Lee's head dropped. 'What are you saying?'

'You don't know?' She turned to Benjamin. 'You kept your word. How lovely of you.'

Benjamin didn't know what was going on, but he understood he shouldn't say anything.

'There's no way you and Ben are dating.'

'You're entitled to believe what you want to, Lee. We don't owe you explanations.'

'You're dating her?' Lee asked Benjamin now. 'No. Of course not. You would have told me.'

'I asked him not to. Apparently his loyalties are

divided now.' She wrinkled her nose. 'I shouldn't have said that. It was insensitive.'

She grabbed Benjamin's hand. Good thing he was still numb from shock, or he might have felt that explosion of warmth from the contact.

'I'm sorry, Ben.'

Their eyes met again. Nothing he could read on her face gave him any clues to her feelings. No plea that he play along; no acknowledgement that this was strange. Or maybe there were clues, but he couldn't recognise them.

Then she smiled at him. Her mouth widened, revealing strikingly straight white teeth. Those lips curved up, softening all the lines and angles of her face. Even her gaze warmed, though he had no idea why or how. It was a genuine smile that both stunned and enthralled him. He couldn't look away.

'Oh, you *are* together.' Lee's voice penetrated the fog in his brain. 'Wow. I can already see the headline in *Cape Town Culinary*: "Rival restaurant owners fall in love".' He paused. 'Maybe we should get the photographer to take a picture of you two now for the article? I'll call her over.'

Both of them wrenched their gazes away from one another to stare at Lee.

Chapter 2

'I'd rather not,' Alexa said when she recovered from the shock. She set the water she'd been drinking on the bar, slid off the stool. 'If you'll excuse me, I think some fresh air would do me good.'

She looked at neither of them. Not the man who'd broken her heart too many times for her to count; not the man who'd helped her brother do it. Though now, of course, she was pretending that he was her boyfriend. She alone, because Benjamin had not once said a word about the elaborate tale she'd woven. He would now, of course. As soon as she was out of the way, he'd tell Lee that she was lying and they'd laugh at her.

Nausea welled up inside her. She hoped it didn't mean she'd throw up. She could already imagine

Lee's questions: *Rough night last night, sis? Or are you pregnant?* He would laugh, she wouldn't, and he'd know something was up. The last thing she needed was her brother discovering her secret.

She soothed the panic the idea evoked by reminding herself that Lee's presence in the last four years had generally made her queasy. That could be the answer now, too. The thought calmed her. Remembering she'd been feeling surprisingly good these last months helped, too. She took a breath, exhaled slowly. She was one week away from entering her second trimester. Once she got there, she'd tell her parents, and there would be no chance Lee could tell them for her.

It might have been a little paranoid—but then, it might not. She had a brother who was intent on ruining her life after all. Telling their parents she was pregnant before she could was exactly the kind of thing he'd do. She wouldn't get the chance to tell them the story she'd practised since she'd decided to do something about her need for a family. Not the broken one she currently had, but a whole one. A safe one. A family she could actually trust.

As usual, the thought sent vibrations through her. Pain, disappointment prickled her skin. She stopped walking, bracing herself against a tree as she caught the breath her emotions stole. She didn't get the chance to.

'You haven't seen me in months and this is how you treat me?'

She closed her eyes, put all her defences in place, and turned. 'I thought you'd get the message.'

'What message?'

'I don't want to see you, Lee,' she told him. 'I don't want you in my life.'

Something almost imperceptible passed over his face. 'We're family. You have no choice.'

'I'm aware that we're family.' She took a deep breath. 'That's the only reason we've seen one another at all in the last four years. Mom and Dad have birthdays, and there are special days, like Christmas and…' She broke off. She didn't have to explain anything to him. 'Anyway, we have to see one another at those occasions. But not outside of them.'

'All this because I bought a building you wanted?'

'You know it wasn't only a building,' she snapped. Pulled it back. But it was hard to contain. It sat in her chest like a swarm of angry bees, waiting to be let out. She could *not* let it out. 'You've insisted on making this about you and me, but really it's about you. It's always been. I want to live my life without you. You can't seem to live yours without me.'

He smirked. 'You're putting an awful lot of importance on yourself.'

'No, you are.'

She meant to stride past him, but his hand caught her wrist.

'I assume you're here for a new head chef. What happens if you don't get one, Lex?' he asked softly. 'You can't keep running Infinity and its kitchen. You must be spreading yourself thin since your last chef left.'

'He didn't leave. You stole him. You and Benjamin stole him.'

'Which makes me wonder how your romance bloomed?' Lee's lips curved into a smile that broke her heart. Because it was mean, and so unlike that of the brother she'd once thought she had. 'Were you looking for revenge? Maybe you thought you could make him fall in love with you, then break his heart? Or maybe use your body to—'

'Lee.'

The voice was deep with unbridled emotion. Both she and Lee looked in the direction it came from. Benjamin stood there, watching them with a glower she'd never seen on him before. He was usually effortlessly charming, which had been one of the reasons she didn't like him. No one could be that charming, certainly not *effortlessly*. Her conclusion had been that he was a demon, or some kind of magical being sent there to test her patience. The test was going smoothly. Her results were not as positive.

His disapproval should have been aimed at her then, considering their history of battling against one another. But it wasn't. It was aimed at Lee. A thrill went through her before she stomped it down viciously. She did a few more jumps on it for good measure.

'Ben,' Lee said with a smile. He tended to reserve the vicious side of his temperament for her. 'Didn't see you there.'

'I thought as much. I doubt you'd be talking to Alexa that way if you did.'

Benjamin's eyes met hers. She wasn't sure how she knew it, but he was asking her if she was okay. She angled her head. He looked back at Lee.

'You should probably get someone to help you if that's your perception of relationships.' He held a hand out to her. It took her a moment to realise he meant for her to take it. As if someone else were in her body, she did. 'Even so, I have to say I'm not thrilled with your implication. Alexa and I are in a healthy relationship. Neither of us is using the other. Unless there's something you want to tell me, Lex?'

Oh. He was keeping the pretence going.

Oh.

She shook her head.

'If I say something corny like "I'm using you for your addictive kisses", would you be mad?' he asked.

There it was, that effortless charm. It was kind of nice when it was being used for good. To help her instead of annoy her.

'You probably shouldn't say it, to be safe.'

He laughed. For a moment, it was just the two of them, amused at one another. A part of her wiggled with glee; another part told her to take a step back. This was confusing, and happening too fast. She wasn't even sure what 'this' was.

'Seriously?' Genuine confusion lit Lee's face. 'I thought this, you two, were a joke.'

'You were accusing Alexa of those things earlier

and you thought this was a joke?' Benjamin's voice had switched from charm to ice.

Alexa cleared her throat. She didn't want this turning into a full-on brawl. Even if the prospect of seeing Lee punched brought her more joy than it should have. She was strangely certain that would be the outcome if she didn't intervene.

'Ben and I agreed to keep business and our personal lives separate,' she told Lee. 'That's why no one knew about our relationship until today.'

'And you told *me*?' Lee asked. 'Now I know you two are lying.'

'You don't have to believe us, Lee.'

But she really wanted him to. Maybe that was why she went along with what Benjamin said next.

'He doesn't have to believe us, but why don't we show him why he should?'

When he looked at her, asked her permission with his eyes, she nodded. Told herself wanting to make Lee believe her was why she'd went along with what Benjamin did next. But all of that dissipated when he kissed her.

He'd never wanted to punch someone as much as he'd wanted to punch his business partner in the last few minutes. He wasn't sure if it was because Lee was acting almost unrecognisably, or if his instincts were tingling because he *did* recognise the way Lee was acting. It was the same way people in his past had acted. They'd need something from him, then act surprised, attacked, victimised when he asked them if they were taking advantage of his desire to help.

His instincts could also have been tingling because despite his past, he still wanted to help someone who needed him. It was clear Alexa did. It was his weakness, helping people. Not when the help was appreciated; only when the help was taken advantage of. He didn't know where Alexa fitted into that. It didn't keep him from kissing her though.

Not his best decision, though his lips disagreed. They heartily approved of the softness of Alexa's lips pressed against them. She smelled of something sweet and light; reminded him of walking through a garden at the beginning of spring. It felt as though he'd been drawn into that scene when her mouth began to move against his. His body felt lighter, as it often did after a long, dull winter and the sun made its comeback. He could easily imagine the two of them in that garden, surrounded by flowers, overcome with the joy and happiness a new season tended to bring.

The taste of her brought him sharply back into his body.

He hadn't intended on *really* kissing her. A quick meeting of lips was enough to convince her brother they were together—people who didn't like one another didn't kiss at all. He assumed. Before he started to kiss this woman he supposedly didn't like.

There was no time to think of it since his tongue had somehow disobeyed his desire to keep things simple. Instead, it had slipped between Alexa's lips, plunging them both into complicated.

But damn, if complicated didn't feel *good*. She was sweet, spicy, exactly as her personality dictated. The tangling of their tongues sent pulses through his body, settling in places that made him both uncomfortable and desperate. He used it as an excuse to rest a hand on the small of her back, pressing her against him. She gave a little gasp into his mouth as her body moulded against his, but she didn't pull away. She did the opposite in fact, reaching her arms around his neck and pulling herself higher so their bodies were aligned at a more pleasurable height.

It was that thought that had him pulling away. He wouldn't embarrass himself in public. More importantly, he couldn't embarrass Alexa. Both would happen if they didn't pull themselves together.

She didn't protest, lowering herself to her feet again, her gaze avoiding his. But then she shook her head and looked at him. Curiosity and desire were fierce in her expression, but it was the confusion that did him in.

Was it brought on by this little charade they were performing? Or was she surprised at the intensity of their kisses?

'Happy?' she asked.

He almost answered before he realised she wasn't talking to him. Good thing his brain had started working in time. He would have said something he couldn't take back if he answered. Something in the vicinity of a *yes and no* and maybe a few other statements.

Lee was watching them with a frown.

'You two really are together.'

'So you keep saying.'

'I mean it this time,' Lee said. His next words were directed at Benjamin. 'You've complicated things.'

No kidding. 'You didn't know about us for months.' *Because there was nothing to know.* 'We'll be fine.'

'I'm sure Cherise de Bruyn agrees.'

Benjamin thought that was a strange thing to say until he saw the jerk of Lee's head to the side. Cherise stood with her fellow graduates, watching the three of them with a bemused smile on her face. Considering he'd spoken to her first thing when he arrived, he was sure Alexa had, too. Now Cherise was watching the two people competing for her to work for them kiss, and was probably wondering what the hell would happen next.

To be fair, so was he.

Chapter 3

Alexa paused at her front door, wondering why she was doing what she was doing. No answer she came up with made her feel better about doing it, so she simply unlocked the door. She stepped aside to let Benjamin pass her, then closed it and resisted—barely—leaning her forehead against it. Alexa couldn't give in to her impulses any more. They were what had got her into trouble in the first place. If she hadn't pretended Benjamin was her boyfriend, she wouldn't be letting him into her home now to discuss the way forward.

It seemed particularly cruel that she had to do that here. Her home was *her* space. It was where she recovered from long, rough days. It was where she cried when the pressure of running a business got to her. It was where she remembered her complicated feelings when her sous chef had brought in her new baby.

Kenya had come in to show the baby around and had brought her mother, too. There had been so much love between the three of them. Alexa had watched it, her heart breaking and filling at the same time. When Kenya had handed her the child, that breaking stopped. She'd remembered all those times she'd thought family couldn't only mean competition and neglect. She hadn't seen examples otherwise, but she'd hoped. Then, between her studies, work, and her brother ruining her dreams, she'd forgotten that hope. Until she'd seen Kenya and her family. Until she'd held that baby.

She'd remembered that, once upon a time, her dreams had included having a family. A warm, happy family with people who loved and respected one another. She thought about how she had no one to go home to at night. How the idea of dating and trusting someone so she could have someone to go home to made her feel ill. A new idea had popped into her head then. One year later, whoops, she was pregnant and there was no going back.

It wasn't so much *whoops* as going through vigorous fertility treatments and being artificially inseminated twice. But *whoops* was what she planned to tell her parents. Rather their disappointment that she hadn't been careful than tell them she didn't want anyone in her life who could hurt her the way they had.

She was clearly in a very healthy mental space.

'Nice place,' Benjamin said, breaking into her thoughts.

'Thanks.'

It was more invasive than she'd anticipated, having him look at her stuff. But they needed privacy, her place was the closest, and it was better to be here than at Infinity. There was more of her there, and with their baggage, it had felt wrong to take him there.

It wasn't that she wasn't proud of her home. Everything in it had been put there for a reason. The beige sofas were comfortable and expensive, the first items she'd bought for the flat. The restaurant had still been a baby, so it had taken most of her disposable income to buy them. She had slept on them for four months. They weren't as comfortable as a bed, but then, she hadn't been sleeping much anyway. She had been fuelled by the desire to succeed, and three to four hours of sleep were more than enough in those days.

The coffee table had come next, then the dining room set, both made from the most gorgeous stained wood. The fluffy carpet had been an indulgence considering she still hadn't had a bed, but filling the open-plan lounge and dining-room had been more important to her. It had made the flat feel like a home.

Her priorities had then shifted to her bedroom, which took her six months to complete. Last was her kitchen, separated from the dining room by half-wall, half-glass, with an opening on the right. The style somehow managed to give the impression of being open-plan, but offered privacy, too. She hadn't had the money to do what she wanted in the kitchen for the longest time, which was why she'd left it for last. Besides, she had everything she wanted at her restaurant, and that was enough.

After a year and a half, her kitchen was exactly what she had imagined it would be. Her appliances were top-of-the-range. Shelves were strategically placed all over the room; spices near the stove, fresh herbs near the window. Cupboards were filled with the best quality ingredients, and close to where they were needed. She'd added colour with fake plants, because her energy was mostly focused on keeping the herbs alive and there was too much competition for the light. And her utensils! Those were colourful, too, though pastel, which made her feel classy and grown-up. Heaven only knew why.

'I didn't expect it to be quite this…warm.'

She threw her handbag onto the sofa, shrugged off her coat. 'Because I'm so cold-hearted, you mean?'

'Not at all.'

'Then what did you mean?'

'It's just…' He looked around, as if to confirm what he was about to say. 'It really is lovely. Everything fits. It's like you selected each thing on purpose.'

'You didn't?' she asked. 'In your own home?'

'I don't have my own home.'

'What do you mean?'

'I live with my parents.'

She stared at him. She didn't know how long it was until his lip curled.

'You have an opinion on that?'

'No,' she replied. 'I don't.'

'You have an opinion on everything. Also, your face is saying something different.'

'You're right. I do have an opinion. But I don't want to share it.'

It was pure stubbornness, since sharing her opinion would have been the perfect segue into the questions she had. Why was he, a successful adult, still living with his parents? She knew he was successful because In the Rough was her main rival, according to reviews and social media, and she was pretty damn successful, despite the forces working against her.

It still smarted that they were succeeding with a restaurant that had been meant to be hers. The location, the property, the name—Lee had stolen it all from her. Then he'd gone and recruited Benjamin to work with him. Lee could have chosen *anyone* else. Actually, she was sure that Lee had specifically chosen Benjamin because the man annoyed her so much, though she wasn't sure how Lee would know that. Either way, Benjamin annoyed her more now that he was in cahoots with her brother. At least before, he'd annoyed her on his own merits.

He'd singled her out their first day at the Institute. She had no idea why, since she minded her own business. For some inexplicable reason, he'd decided she was partly *his* business, and he began to compete with her. She'd instantly recoiled; she had enough competition in life. She hadn't cut Lee out of her life and minimised her contact with her parents, only to replace them with a negligible man-child.

Now she had to work with the man-child.

'Would you like some alcohol?' she asked after a deep sigh.

His eyes flickered with amusement, contrasting the tighter lines on his face. 'Anything you want to give me is fine.'

She bit her tongue before she could reply. She hadn't thought of anything to reply with, but her tongue was often quicker than her brain. She didn't want to take the chance of saying something inappropriate. Such as how what she wanted to give him was another kiss to see if the spark she'd felt was a fluke...

She poured him a generous glass of whiskey from a bottle that was still three quarters full and settled on water and peppermint for herself.

'You're not having any?' he asked, accepting the glass from her.

She leaned back against the counter on the opposite side of the kitchen. 'I'm on an alcohol fast.'

'Why?'

She rolled her eyes. 'Does it matter?'

'You're annoyed because I asked?'

'Yes, actually. It's rude.'

Plus she didn't have a good answer for him. She hadn't anticipated him asking why she was fasting from alcohol. She should have known he wouldn't be polite and leave it at that though.

'Sorry.' His lips twitched. 'So...'

He didn't say anything more. She didn't speak either. The silence stretched between them like a cat in the sun. Then, as a cat would, it stared Alexa in the eyes, unblinking, until she sighed.

'This is what dating you is like?' She didn't wait for an answer. 'How disturbing.'

How she knew exactly what to say to get under his skin was what was really disturbing.

But then, disturbing seemed to be the theme of the night. What with the fake relationship, the kiss, being in Alexa's home. He'd offended her by noting that her flat was homey, but he couldn't help but be honest. She'd done an amazing job turning what would have been a trendy, but not particularly special place into something he could imagine coming home to.

Well, not him, exactly. He had his own home. With his parents. Which she had an opinion on, but wouldn't tell him about because she was stubborn. He couldn't be upset by it since he was stubborn, too. If she'd asked why he still lived with his parents he wouldn't have told her.

Not that any of it was important now.

'Cherise saw us.'

'I know.' She drained her glass. Her gaze rested on his, before it rose to his face. Something about it made his body feel more aware. 'Would you like some more?'

He glanced at the glass. Empty. Strange. He didn't remember drinking from it. Except for that one time when he'd taken a long, deep gulp and—

Ah, yes. He remembered now.

'No, thank you.' Probably best with all the disturbing stuff happening.

'Tea, then? I'm making myself some.'

'Anything to avoid having a straight conversation with me?'

'What is this we're having, then?' she asked, filling the kettle with water. She took out two mugs, despite the fact that he hadn't answered her. 'A skew conversation? Diagonal?'

'Funny lady.'

Amusement flickered in her eyes. 'I try.'

'To annoy me, yes,' he muttered.

The amused light danced in her eyes again. He felt an answering light in his chest. He didn't care for it. It made him think the tables had turned.

'I know we have to talk about this.' She took out ginger from the fridge, sliced up some pieces and threw it in one cup. She looked over at him. 'Tea? Coffee?'

'Coffee. Please,' he added as an afterthought.

She began to make his coffee, expression pensive. 'I suppose I wanted to make the conversation easier. Less awkward. A discussion over hot drinks seemed like something that would help with that.'

His mother would like her, he thought before he could stop himself. Usually, he was more careful when it came to comparisons between his mother and people he wasn't related to. Hell, people he was related to, too. It tended to evoke protective feelings in him when he did. He blamed it on the fact that he felt protective of his mother, so when he recognised something akin to her in someone else, those feelings bled over. It had too often in the past, and he'd been hurt because of it. Which should have made him more careful. It usually did. Except now, apparently.

'How did I manage to upset you with that?' she asked, more resigned than curious.

'You didn't.' A lie. Or half-lie. He'd upset himself, but because of something she'd said.

Her eyes narrowed, but she finished his coffee, slid it over the counter towards him. She finished her own drink with a teaspoon of honey, then leaned back against the counter as she had with her water.

'Okay, so let's talk straight.' She bit her lip, then straightened her shoulders. 'I'm sorry for pretending you're my boyfriend. It was an impulse.'

'Why did you?'

She tilted her head, as if considering his question. Or perhaps considering whether she'd answer it.

'My brother is a jerk.'

He stared.

'You can't possibly not have noticed,' she replied at the look. 'He's entitled, and competitive, and generally unkind. I wanted to push him off a cliff. Since literally doing so would send me to prison, I settled for figuratively. You were the figurative.'

He took a minute to process that.

'He's normally a decent guy.'

'Maybe to you. But since you said normally, I think you recognised that he wasn't decent today.' She paused, her lips pursing. 'He normally isn't decent with me.'

Lee's behaviour today didn't encourage him to disagree with her. So he didn't.

'It's weird that you pretended *I* was your boyfriend. You hate me.'

'You were the closest person,' she said coolly, not denying his statement. 'Also, you're his business partner. Best cliff.' She shrugged.

He took a steadying breath. He didn't like being used. He'd had too many instances of it in his life. His last girlfriend, his father's colleague, his cousin. Those were but a few, but they were the most recent. Remembering them had him steeling himself against Alexa's charm—or whatever it was that kept him standing there.

'I don't like being used.'

'I'm sorry.' Her voice and expression were sincere. 'I'm sorry for putting you in a position to be used. For using you.'

It was that sincerity that had him saying, 'Apology accepted,' when he wasn't entirely sure he meant it.

'Thank you.' There was a brief pause. 'So maybe now you can explain why you decided to go along with the charade. Maybe you can apologise for that kiss, too.'

Chapter 4

The expression on his face was comical. But, since she'd asked him a serious question, one she would very much have liked an answer for, she decided not to give in to the smile. To wait.

His expression became more comical. His mouth contracted and expanded, as if he were mouthing what he wanted to say, but not quite. Emotions danced in his eyes, though she couldn't put her finger on what they were. But really, it was that tick near his nose, which she'd never before seen, that amused her the most.

Still, she didn't smile.

'I thought… I mean, he was… I wanted to…'

His stammers made resisting the smile harder. It was strange. She had never before spoken with him long enough to have to resist any of her emotions. Usually, those emotions ranged from irritated to downright angry. Amusement generally didn't feature; not unless it was tainted with satisfaction. This wasn't. This was simply…amusement.

An alarm went off in her head.

'You wanted to *what*?' she asked, her words sharp, marching to that alarm.

He cleared his throat and met her eyes. His expression was now serious.

'I wanted Lee to stop acting like a jerk.'

'Well.' It was all she said for a while. 'You succeeded, just for a moment.'

'But at what cost?'

His eyes bored into hers, and her face began to heat. Was he asking how she'd felt about that kiss? If he was, he'd have his answer in her blush.

Because it had embarrassed her, she assured herself. Her fingers lifted and slipped under the neckline of her dress. She lifted it, let it fall, sending air down her body, which had suddenly become clammy. For some reason, her skin was itchy, too. It was exactly how she felt on a summer's day in the kitchen. Hot and sticky, but satisfied at what she was cooking up.

Wait—satisfied? Where had that come from? What was happening to her?

Embarrassment, an inner voice offered again. She clung to it. Ignored the fact that her memories of that kiss, of how she'd felt much as she did now while he'd been kissing her, were vehemently disagreeing.

She took a deliberate sip of her tea. She'd put

enough ginger in it that the flavour burned her throat. She relished it. Then met his eyes.

'A high cost,' she told him. 'It means Cherise thinks we're dating.'

He was watching her closely. She hoped to heaven he hadn't developed the ability to see into her head. 'And now she's confused about our opposing offers.'

'I tried to tell her the same thing we told Lee,' she said with a sigh. 'The whole "we're dating, but we're keeping our personal and professional lives separate" thing. I don't know if she bought it. She's certainly confused by it.'

'Me, too, to be honest with you.'

He gestured, asking if she'd like to have a seat in the lounge. She would have, desperately, since her body was aching from a day of standing. Her baby apparently didn't like that kind of strenuous activity. But it felt too intimate, sitting with him on the sofas she'd bought and slept on for months. A twinge in her back urged her to reconsider, and she spent hopelessly too long trying to decide. In the end, she strode past him without answering, as though it had been her idea all along.

Man, pregnancy was making her *stubborn*.

It was definitely the pregnancy. She didn't possess a stubborn bone in her body normally.

She sank into the sofa as soon as she sat down, a sigh leaving her lips immediately. His brows were raised when she looked at him.

'Why didn't you say something?'

'About what?'

'Needing to sit down.'

'I didn't need to.'

'So what you did now wasn't you finally relaxing and your body thanking you for it?'

'I have no idea what you're talking about.'

He shook his head, but the sides of his mouth were quirked. 'Stubborn isn't an appealing quality.'

'I don't care if you find me appealing.' She didn't give herself a chance to figure out why that felt like a lie. 'Besides, it's been a long day.'

'You get stubborn after a long day?'

'That's what I said, yes.'

'Is it because you're tired?' He was outright smiling now. Taunting her, really. 'Or is it a physical symptom? Aching legs, sore back, stubborn personality?'

'Yes.' It wasn't an answer, but it was all he'd get. 'Now—what are we going to do about Cherise?'

The smile faded, but the twinkle in his eyes didn't. He was sitting beneath the light fixture, which could account for that twinkle. But it didn't; she'd seen that twinkle before. It appeared whenever he was amused with her. It was frustrating to know. More frustrating was how attractive that amusement made him.

It danced in his brown eyes, crinkled the skin around them. That forced his cheeks up, which spread his full lips—lips she now knew had objectively impressive skills. None of that factored into how the angles of his face were affected. Warming them, softening them; perhaps a combination of the two. Either way, it dimmed his arrogance, that self-assured *I know I'm successful and handsome* edge of his. That edge was as devastating as it was irritating, particularly as it always seemed to be directed at her.

'What were you planning on doing about Cherise before all this happened?'

She snorted. 'Wouldn't you like to know?'

'Yes,' he deadpanned. 'That's why I asked.'

'You asked so you could outdo whatever I planned to do.'

'I wouldn't dream of it.'

'Like you wouldn't dream of stealing my head chef? Who was already working for me, I might add. Happily. For months.'

'That can't be true if he left,' Benjamin pointed out softly. 'It didn't take me much to convince him either.'

'Are you defending *stealing* my chef?'

'I didn't steal him. I…gave him another option.'

'You stole him,' she said flatly. 'Probably at the behest of my brother, because, as I mentioned before, he's a jerk.'

He hesitated, which gave her the answer. And disappointed her, strangely. Why, she wasn't sure. It might have been because he'd defended her in front of her brother and hadn't freaked out completely when she'd pretended he was her boyfriend. But one day's experience couldn't erase years of experience to the contrary. That experience had taught her that Benjamin Foster could be just as much of a jerk as her brother.

'I think you're on the right track though,' she powered on. If she did, it would help get him out of her house and she'd finally be able to rest. 'We do what we intended to do and let her make the decision as she would have without this complication.'

'We're not continuing the charade?'

She thought about it. 'We have two options, I suppose. One is that we do, but only verbally. If she asks, we'll talk about one another lovingly. Affectionately. Then, in a few months, we break up.'

'And the other option?'

'Tell her the truth. We were playing a joke on Lee.'

He went quiet for a few seconds. 'But if Lee finds out, we both look foolish. We'll have to answer why we were so…' he hesitated '…*invested* in proving we were together.'

'There's that,' she said slowly. She didn't want him to know she'd thought about that, too. Not to mention she hated the idea of Lee discovering the truth. He'd take such pleasure in it. He'd probably hold it over her head every time she'd have the misfortune of seeing him. 'There's also the implication that we're friends. Why would we play a joke on Lee if we weren't?'

'You're worried about people thinking we're friends, but not that we're in a relationship?'

'Well, yeah. At least there's a physical aspect to a relationship. People would think I was distracted from your personality because you look the way you do.'

He frowned. She could almost see his brain malfunctioning. Mostly because she was pretty sure that was what was happening to hers.

'Is that a compliment?'

'No,' she answered immediately.

But it was. She couldn't figure out why she'd said it.

She vowed there and then never to admit she found him attractive again. She wouldn't even *think* about his broad shoulders and full lips. He certainly wouldn't kiss her again either, so she'd have no reason to. And if she did think it—and he did kiss her—she'd remind herself there were high stakes involved.

She laid a hand on her belly, feeling the slight curve. At this stage it could have been a good, generous meal as much as a baby, which amused her. She stroked her thumb over the curve, mentally assuring her child that she'd protect it. She paused when she saw him watching her.

What was it about being in his presence that made her lower her guard?

She moved her hand.

'Fine. We'll pretend to be together,' he said curtly. 'But only because Lee deserves to think it, after how he treated you.' He paused, as though something had just occurred to him. The frown deepened. He was scowling when he continued. 'We'll do whatever we intended to do with Cherise. I'll keep talk of our relationship with your brother to the minimum. We should both do that, to whoever we meet.' He downed the rest of his coffee and set the cup on the table. Stood. 'And in a few months, our fake relationship will end. It'll be as clean as this situation allows.'

'Er…yeah, sure.'

She set her own mug down, confused by the change in his temperament. But that was the least of her problems. She'd just realised her pregnancy wouldn't be a secret for much longer. People would have questions about the paternity of her baby. If she said it was Benjamin, she would be dragging him down an even more convoluted path. If she said it was some random guy as she'd planned to, people would do the calculations and accuse her of cheating on Benjamin.

Oh, no.

She really should have thought about this earlier.

'Benjamin, I think we need to talk about—'

'We've talked about everything already, haven't we?' he interrupted. His eyes were sharp, and she almost shivered from the intensity of them. So she just nodded.

'Great, then we don't have to see one another again for a while.'

'Okay.' Numbly, she followed him to the door.

'Thanks for the drinks.'

'Okay.'

'Good luck with Cherise.'

'Thanks.'

And then he was gone, leaving her to think about the extent of the mess she'd created that day.

The resolution he and Alexa had come to regarding their fake relationship went up in flames the moment he walked into In the Rough the next morning.

'You're dating my sister?' Lee asked, sitting arms folded at a stool in front of the bar. Apparently, he'd been waiting. 'What the hell, man? Do you have no boundaries?'

It wasn't early in the morning. In the Rough only opened from lunchtime, so generally he worked from home for a couple of hours when he woke up, then made his way to the restaurant at about nine. His staff would start trickling in then, too, most of them there by ten, and then it would be a bustle of activity until they closed at eleven at night. This morning, he'd been particularly grateful for the quiet so he could figure out what the hell had happened the night before.

One moment he'd been deciding whether to let Alexa's backhanded compliment slide, the next he was watching her stroke her stomach and his gut had clenched with need. It made no sense, but that gesture had seemed somewhat protective. It reminded him of the times he'd seen pregnant women do the same thing. Though Alexa probably wasn't pregnant, it had made him think about a life he'd never wanted. He was too busy taking care of his parents to even consider it.

Not that he minded; not in the least. His mother was lovely. Sharp and charming and the kind of mother who made sacrifices for her children. Except there were no children, only him. And that sharpness and charm and kindness didn't negate the strain of her illness.

They'd had no idea what caused it for a long time.

His mother had been his father's admin help at the panel-beaters' company his father owned and ran. For ten years, almost, until she'd started complaining about the pain right after she'd had Benjamin. Aches that felt like they were all over, restricting her movement, making simple tasks hard to carry out. Doctors had prescribed ibuprofen, diagnosed her with the flu, told her she'd strained a muscle, or pushed too hard, or that she needed to take a break.

But even when she took a break, the pain would continue. Sometimes, if she stayed in bed and rested, it would make it worse. The doctors maintained they could find nothing wrong. It was the eighth doctor she'd gone to in four years who had diagnosed her with fibromyalgia.

His life hadn't changed dramatically, or at all, with that diagnosis. His father had simply sat him down and explained as best he could to a four-year-old that his mom was sick. Frank Foster had told Benjamin to try not to bother his mother as much when she was in bed. Maybe Benjamin could even help out a little more at home. He hadn't known the difference between that and what he'd done before, except now it came with the weight of verbal responsibility.

But she was his mother, and he wanted her to be happy. As he grew older, he thought having him couldn't have helped with his mom's pain. Because she'd made sacrifices for him at the cost of her own health, physical and mental, he would do the same for her. So he had. For the past twenty-odd years he had helped his parents. Now he cared for his parents. There wasn't really room for him to consider caring for anyone else in that situation either.

That pulse of need he'd felt with Alexa the night before? A fluke. There was nothing more to it. And he didn't engage with it any more because something more significant had occurred to him when he'd been talking with Alexa.

Now might be the time to confirm it.

'Did you hear me?' Lee demanded.

But maybe not before he'd had another cup of coffee.

'Mia,' he said to the tall woman behind the counter. 'Is the machine on?'

'You know it,' she replied with a sympathetic grin. It made him realise she'd heard what Lee had said. 'The usual?'

He unclenched his jaw slowly. 'No. Double espresso, please.' Her brows lifted, but she only nodded. He looked at Lee. 'Can you wait for me in the office? I'll be there in a second.'

'Mia, could you please add another cappuccino to that?' Lee said. 'And bring it to Ben's office when it's ready?' He shook his head. 'Or have someone else bring it. Sorry. It slipped my mind.'

Her smile didn't waver, but something on Mia's face tightened. It probably wasn't because Lee had been referring to her disability—the limp that Benjamin hadn't once asked about because it was none of his business—but because Lee had done so poorly. Benjamin wouldn't have expected it from him; Lee handled most things smoothly. Then again, he hadn't expected Lee to be a jerk to his own sister, so maybe he didn't know his business partner as well as he thought.

'Yeah, sure,' Mia said.

'Thank you.'

Lee gestured for Benjamin to lead the way. After one last glance at Mia to make sure she was okay, Benjamin walked away from the enticing smell of coffee to his office. It was a simple room. Not very big, but there was enough space for his desk and cabinet, and the large windows gave it an airy feel. Unfortunately, those windows looked out onto a car park with a busy Cape Town road just behind it. But that was the price he paid to be in a central location.

At least, that was what Lee had told him when he'd been courting Benjamin. Over the years, Benjamin had begun to believe him. Was he a fool to do so?

'This isn't your only business,' Benjamin noted, taking off his jacket and slinging it over the chair. 'Surely you have better things to do than to wait for me to talk about something that isn't business.'

'Except this affects our business,' Lee said with none of the charm, the ease Benjamin had once been privy to. 'Honestly, Ben. There are millions of women in South Africa, but you decide to sleep with my sister?'

'Watch it,' Benjamin growled, though he had no reason to defend Alexa. Apart from their fictional relationship. Which was not, as the title stated, real.

'She's already changed you,' Lee replied with a shake of his head. 'You weren't foolish before yesterday. Hell, the last time we spoke, you knew how important getting Cherise de Bruyn to work with us was. But now you're letting your head be messed around by your—'

'Be careful about what you say next.'

Lee's jaw tightened. 'This isn't going to work.'

'What isn't?' he asked coolly, leaning back in his chair. 'This partnership? Or my relationship with your sister?'

Lee opened and closed his mouth several times before he said, 'The relationship.'

'That hardly seems like any of your business.'

'It's literally my business.'

'No, my relationship has nothing to do with this business.' He paused when one of his waiters brought in their coffees. 'Alexa and I have been able to keep our relationship under wraps for months. It hasn't affected the way I've run things around here.'

'And yet here you are, snapping at me.'

'Because for some reason, when it comes to your sister, you change, too, Lee.' He downed the espresso. When it seared his stomach, he remembered he'd forgotten to eat breakfast. 'I don't like the way you treat her. I don't like the way you treat me when it comes to her.'

It was a warning.

'I thought this wouldn't happen.'

'What does that mean?'

'I thought working with someone who competed

with my sister meant *I'd* be working with someone who competed with my sister.'

And there it was. Confirmation of his suspicions. When he told Alexa he wanted to continue the charade because of how Lee treated her, he realised there was more to it. It was because of how Lee had treated him, too. Lee had used him. Much as so many other people in his life had.

'My relationship with your sister doesn't have to affect the way we do things around here,' he said coldly. 'It won't for me. I'm perfectly capable of working with you and dating your sister. Since you two don't have a relationship, it shouldn't matter to you anyway.'

Lee's face was tight. Benjamin couldn't read what caused that tightness, or what was behind it. All he could see was a complicated mess of emotions. Since he had enough of those himself, especially after Lee's little bombshell, he didn't need to figure Lee's feelings out.

'We won't let your involvement with my sister affect the business.'

Benjamin gave a tight nod.

'What about our friendship?'

Benjamin didn't know how to answer that. He didn't trust Lee any more. How could they still be friends?

'See?' Lee said. 'You're already treating me differently.'

'I've explained why.'

He'd use Lee's treatment of Alexa as the scapegoat

here. He was sure she wouldn't mind. They were in this together after all.

Lee exhaled harshly. 'Fine. We'll just pretend you're not dating my sister.'

'What?'

His mother stood in the doorway, eyes impossibly wide.

'You're dating Benjamin Foster?'

Alexa's feet stopped working. That meant she was standing in the doorway of her office, frozen by both the words and the stare of accusation from Kenya.

'Who told you that?'

'You should have.'

'How did you find out?'

'A friend of mine was at Cherise's graduation yesterday.' Kenya leaned back in Alexa's chair. 'She asked me why I didn't tell her. Apparently, you and Benjamin were hot and heavy yesterday and it was the talk of everyone there. *And I didn't know.*'

'It hasn't been going on for very long,' she grumbled. *Like, less than twenty-four hours.* 'Besides, I didn't want people to know. It's new.'

And fake.

'Am I still people, Alexa?'

The question was serious enough to make Alexa blink. When she recovered from the shock, Kenya was watching her, waiting for an answer.

'I... I didn't tell anyone.'

Kenya stood, nodding slowly as she did. 'Yeah, why would you tell anyone? Least of all someone

you've worked with for four years. Least of all someone who considers you a friend. Clearly that doesn't
apply to how you consider me, does it?'

It would be so easy to get through this. If Alexa
told Kenya the relationship was fake, contrived when
she'd been desperate and in a panic to get away from
her brother, Kenya wouldn't be upset with her.

She opened her mouth, but nothing came out. Not
a single word.

What would happen if she told Kenya the truth?
She'd look like a fool, for one. But Kenya might tell
her friend, who might tell their friend, and before she
knew it both her and Benjamin's reputations would
be ruined. Not to mention that her brother would
find out. And she couldn't face Lee's smirk when
he heard she'd made up the entire thing for his sake.

'You can't even dispute it,' Kenya said, hurt thick
in her voice. She strode past Alexa. Alexa wanted to
say something, but her phone rang before she could.
Picking up the landline, she barked, 'Yes?'

'Benjamin Foster's on the line for you,' came the
voice of one of her waiters.

She bit back a sigh. 'Put him through.'

'Alexa?'

His deep voice was even more disturbing over
the phone. Now she had to imagine his face. And
for some reason it came without the arrogance that
usually put her off.

'You called for me, didn't you?'

'Yes, I did, darling.'

'Darling? Really?' She looked behind her to ensure

no one was there. 'You realise we're on the phone, right? No one else can hear what we're saying.'

'I'm here with my mother.'

'Your mother?'

'She'd like to meet you.'

'She'd like to… Wait, I'm missing something, aren't I?'

'Yes.'

It was the first time she felt as though he was answering her properly.

'Are you free for dinner tonight?'

'I'm not, actually. I'm working. As are you, considering we run restaurants.'

'I'm sure you can take an evening off for this *very important date.*'

She rolled her eyes. Belatedly, she realised he couldn't see her. She let the disappointment pass through her.

'Look, Benjamin, I don't know what's going on, but there's no way I'm going to meet your mother.'

'She would like to meet you.'

She could hear he was clenching his teeth.

'Is she giving you a hard time, Benny? Let me talk to her.' There was a short pause where Alexa could swear she heard Benjamin apologise. 'Alexa? This is Nina, Benjamin's mother.'

She closed her eyes. 'Hi, Nina.'

'Is it possible for us to meet?'

'Mrs Foster.' Alexa cleared her throat. 'I, um, I'm not sure.'

'Be sure, dear.' There was admonishment there,

but Mrs Foster spoke again so quickly Alexa barely had time to process it. 'This evening might be too soon, considering your commitments. How about tomorrow evening? Could you arrange for someone to take care of things then?'

'I…um… I…don't know…'

'I just wouldn't want to meet you at your restaurant, dear.' Mrs Foster gave a sparkling laugh. 'You'd have to come out and speak to me in front of your employees and… Well, I don't need to tell you how awkward that might end up being.'

'No,' Alexa said numbly. 'You don't.'

'So it's settled, then! I'll see you tomorrow.'

'I… Yes, you will.' She cleared her throat. 'Could you please put Benjamin back on the phone?'

'Of course.'

There was another pause, then a, 'Yeah.'

'I have an hour for lunch today and clearly we need to talk. Can you meet me at St George's Mall at one?'

'Yes.'

'It wasn't a real question, but I'm glad you agreed. It makes things easier.'

Chapter 5

'What were you *THINKING*?'

It was the first thing Alexa said when she saw him. A bit rude, in his opinion, but he allowed it because she'd made a good impression on his mother. Nina had murmured her approval and patted his cheek in affection. All this came after she'd read him the Riot Act for keeping his relationship a secret.

'Hello, Alexa,' he said calmly. 'Would you like to have a seat at one of the coffee shops? It is lunch, after all. And I haven't had breakfast. A busy morning,' he added, taking her elbow lightly and steering her through the crowds of people milling about. 'What with speaking to your brother about our fake relationship, having my mother find out about it, and then, of course, my actual business, which is open, but why would they need the manager and acting head chef there for the lunchtime rush?'

'I have responsibilities, too.'

'And yet here we are, gallivanting in the middle of the day.'

'It's not gallivanting.'

But she said it under her breath. He took it as agreement. How could he not?

St George's Mall had once been a busy street in Cape Town, but it had been reimagined for pedestrians. Now people walked through the bricked area lined with green trees and yellow umbrellas without the bother of traffic. There were three men playing drums a little way away from them, a boy who couldn't be older than nine dancing to the beat. Tourists browsed through the stands selling jewellery and African-inspired crafts. Residents walked with purpose to get to where they needed to be, or stopped at one of the cafes to grab something to eat. Police presence was heavy, but quaint, since they monitored the area on horses.

It was one of his favourite places, just fifteen minutes away from his restaurant. It screamed with the vibrancy of Cape Town, which was one reason he loved his city. He wasn't sure why Alexa had suggested it, since it was further away for her than for him. Could she have been considering him? Or was she merely trying to minimise the chances of someone she knew seeing them together?

He would have related to that, except his mother already knew, so his father would, too, and they were the main people he cared about. It was too late for keeping secrets for him.

'Hey,' she said, snapping her fingers. 'Can we sit here? Or should I ask another time?'

'Sorry,' he muttered, and gestured for her to sit.

They took a few minutes to look at the menu. At least, he did. She'd glanced at hers quickly, then set it down and was now watching him.

'You must be thinking it's a pity you don't have X-ray vision with how you're staring at me.'

'Hadn't considered it before, actually. Just like I hadn't considered having to talk to your mother and be manoeuvred—quite expertly, I might add—into having dinner with your family.' She slapped her hand against her leg under the table. *'I'm not even your girlfriend.'*

He exhaled, hoping the nervous energy in his body would escape from his lungs. No such luck. It stayed in his chest, bouncing around as though it were being chased by a happy puppy.

'Let's get something to drink.'

'Why would you let your mother think we're in a relationship?' she asked, ignoring him. 'This turns something that could easily be solved into something so much more—'

'Alexa,' he interrupted, his voice slicing through her panic. 'Let's get something to drink. We can talk about it afterwards.'

Her jaw locked, but she nodded. The waiter came over. He ordered sparkling water—he needed a break from the coffee. It was probably the cause of the ner-

vous energy. Probably—and Alexa got rooibos tea.
When the waiter left, Alexa stared wordlessly at him.
To emphasise her displeasure, she folded her arms
and leaned back.

He took a deep breath.

'My mother being under the impression we're together wasn't my fault,' he said slowly. 'Lee am-
bushed me this morning—' that was more aggressive
than what Lee had done; or maybe not '—and when
he was talking about the relationship, my mother
walked in. I'd forgotten some papers at home and
she thought I might need them.'

He could hardly be upset with her for being sweet.

'Anyway, she found out, and since I've never told
her about any of my relationships, she kind of latched
on to the information. I couldn't tell her it was a lie
without…' He grasped on to the first thing he could
think of. 'Without your brother overhearing it.'

'Couldn't you have told her when he left?'

'No.' Anger made the word choppy. 'She was excited. I couldn't disappoint her.'

'People survive disappointing their parents.'

The words were so unexpected, so cool, his anger
fizzled.

'Is that what happened to you?'

'It doesn't matter.' Her features softened, but the
lines around her mouth were still tense. 'What's
going to happen when she finds out we're not really
together, Benjamin? You don't think she's going to
be disappointed then? You don't think she's going
to hate knowing that you lied to her? That you don't

have a girlfriend?' She blushed. 'I mean, I'm assuming. I don't care about your romantic—'

'Of course I don't have a girlfriend,' he said, affronted. 'Do you think I'd be pretending to be your boyfriend if I did? Do you think so poorly of me?'

She stilled, though her eyes, big and bright, remained steady. 'You want me to say no, but experience has taught me I can't say that without reservation.'

He had no reply to that. What could he say? But it left a bitter taste in his mouth that she thought that of him. He didn't deserve it. The only thing he'd done that was morally ambiguous was offer her chef a job at In the Rough. Even then he'd done things above board. Victor Fourie had accepted Benjamin's offer without a comment about what he'd left behind. In the same way he'd left In the Rough behind when he'd moved on a couple of months ago.

Then again, he could see why she'd have that opinion of him. He worked with her brother, a man she had no relationship with. A man who treated her poorly, and apparently went out of his way to do so. Lee had used Benjamin to that end, too, and he'd unwittingly become a tool to hurt Alexa with. Frankly, he was still working out how he felt about it. Especially since he'd considered Lee a friend until all this had happened.

His fake relationship had thrown everything into upheaval. Including his relationship with his mother. He wasn't proud of it, but he couldn't bear to break his mother's heart. Up until today, he hadn't even known his mother wanted him to be in a relationship. But the happiness in her voice as she questioned him about his girlfriend—his first, according to her—told him otherwise.

He couldn't tell her it was all fake. He loved her too much. And yeah, maybe he'd get over disappointing her. But in that moment, it hadn't even occurred to him.

The waiter interrupted his thoughts, and when the man walked away, he sighed.

'I'm sorry. About my mother. I wasn't thinking. Or I wasn't thinking properly.'

She held the mug in her hands as if to warm herself, though it was a typical summer's day.

'I've been there,' she murmured. Then she set the mug down and took her head in her hands instead. 'I was there—yesterday. Because of my stupid brother, I caused this mess and—'

She hiccupped. An actual hiccup that was most likely the precursor to a sob. His hand shot out of its own volition, grasping her arm and squeezing in comfort. A hand left her head and rested on his hand.

And just like that, he knew he was in trouble.

Of course, he'd known that before. The entire thing with Alexa was, as she said, a mess. But before, he'd still had some control over his actions. He wasn't helping her because she needed help. Well, not *only* because she needed help. He also wanted to help her with his own free will. The moment she showed him vulnerability, though, that free will had waved goodbye and jumped on the nearest plane to anywhere but his mind. Because now he wanted to help her because she *really* needed help. She was distraught, and things needed to be fixed, and he was the ultimate help when things needed to be fixed.

He'd done it with his mother and father for most of his life, more so as an adult. He'd done it with his last girlfriend. His cousins. Friends. And he would do it now, with Alexa.

He curled his free hand into a fist.

She was *crying*. In public. In front of him. Because she was pregnant and because she had to tell him the truth. It was terrifying.

She pulled away from his touch, comforting—disturbingly so—as it was, and reached into her bag for a tissue. She found one, mopped herself up, and sternly told her hormones she wouldn't stand for tears again. When she was certain they'd got the picture, she downed the rest of her tea, lukewarm now, because of the tears, and looked at him.

His expression was inscrutable. She didn't know if that made her feel better or worse. But she couldn't rely on him to make herself feel better. So she took a deep breath, held it for a few seconds, then let it out. It was shaky at best; hitched at worse. She did it again, and again, until it came smoothly. Then she said, 'I'm pregnant.'

He stared at her.

She cleared her throat. 'So, you see, you have to tell your mother the truth or she'll think the baby's yours and things will get more complicated.'

He still stared at her.

'I wouldn't have told you if I didn't have to. I went over it in my head a million times last night, and again, after that phone call with your mother.'

He didn't say a word. She pursed her lips when they started to shake.

No, she told the tears that were threatening. *I had you under control. You can't disobey me.*

'I didn't want you to know,' she said, thinking that speaking would distract her. 'I didn't want *anyone* to know until I had no choice but to tell them. No one knows besides you. Because somehow, my decision is now going to reflect on you.'

He kept staring, but his mouth had opened. She had to wait a while longer before he said anything.

'You're pregnant?'

She nodded.

'We have to tell people the truth.'

She clenched her teeth when the statement brought a fresh wave of heat to her eyes. She would *not* cry in front of him. Not again.

'Okay.' Her voice broke as she said it. Damn it.

'They'll think the baby's mine, Alexa,' Benjamin said, his voice pleading. 'My mother and your brother and everyone else. We can't just break up then.'

'Why not?' she asked desperately. 'Who cares what they think?'

'I do.' His face was stern. 'It'll be my reputation on the line.'

'It doesn't have to be,' she said, desperation once

again taking the wheel. 'You can tell them I cheated on you.'

'*What?*'

'Make me the bad guy.' She hated the thought of it, but it was her only option.

'You'd rather have everyone think you cheated than tell the truth?'

'I don't care what everyone thinks,' she said heatedly. 'If Lee finds out I made this up because of him...' She met his gaze. 'He took my property and my restaurant years ago and he had no reason to. If I give him this, it'll fuel him for years.'

'What do you mean, your property? Your *restaurant*?'

She scoffed. 'Please don't pretend you don't know what Lee did. It's an insult to you and me both.'

'I have no idea what you're talking about.'

He seemed genuinely confused. Though that could have as easily come from the news that she was pregnant as from this. She sighed.

'I found the building for In the Rough. Came up with the name, too, because of the neighbourhood. I was determined to turn that place—*my* place—into a diamond.' The memory of it curved her lips. 'I went through hundreds of listings to find it, and I was so excited because it was *finally* time. I'd spent eight years working towards that moment, and finally...' She trailed off when a wave of sadness crashed over her. 'Anyway, I was supposed to take my parents to see it. I mean, I did take my parents to see it. But I made the mistake of telling them where it was when

I scheduled the event with them a week before. We always had to make plans in advance with them.'

She shook off the resentment that she'd had to schedule the meeting with her parents in the first place. Second, but not by much, was that they'd told Lee.

'They told Lee, and he bought it out from under me. He offered to rent it to me. I declined. He would have never allowed me to do what I wanted to do.' She waved a hand. She wasn't sure what it was meant to signify. 'And then I heard you two had become partners. It made sense. If my brother was the devil, I suppose I considered you a demon. My dreams had turned into my own personal hell.'

It was as funny as it was heartbreaking. She was sure the small smile she hadn't been able to resist conveyed both.

'I knew none of that.'

'Would it have changed anything if you had?' she asked, wanting to know.

A complicated array of emotions danced across his face. She supposed she could understand it. It was a good business decision to be a partner with Lee. He came with property, a smart name, business knowledge, and experience. He also came with baggage: her. She had no idea whether Benjamin cared about that, but what she'd told him now didn't reflect well on Lee regardless. Unless he shared Lee's opinion of her, and her brother's lack of scruples, in which case it wouldn't change anything.

But he wouldn't look this tortured if things hadn't

changed for him, would he? Or was she grasping at straws, desperate for someone, anyone, to finally be on her side instead of Lee's?

'It's smart to be in business with Lee,' came the careful answer. 'He's a good businessperson.'

'You still think so after what I told you?'

The stare flickered. 'He's been good to me.'

She licked her bottom lip before drawing it between her teeth. Then she nodded. 'I suppose that's fair.'

Disappointing, but fair. But it helped sharpen her idea of him. She'd been faltering on what she thought of him because he hadn't deliberately set out to hurt her with the restaurant. But after what had happened with her chef, and now, with his opinion of Lee remaining unchanged... It was best if she didn't think he was someone he wasn't.

'If we tell my brother the truth, he'll use it against you, too,' she said.

His lips parted, as if he hadn't considered it. Or maybe he didn't believe it was possible.

'It's too complicated to continue this lie, Alexa.'

She exhaled. 'Okay.' It was time to leave. She needed to recover from all this in private. She needed to prepare, too. 'Give me a few days. It shouldn't make a difference for you, but it'll help me figure some things out.'

He gave a slow nod. 'Then I guess I'll tell my mother.'

'Let me.' She had no idea why she said it, but it was too late to take it back. 'I'll come to dinner tomorrow. I'll tell her I dragged you into this and that you were being the perfect gentleman. I'll explain to her what happened with my brother, and how you couldn't come clean with him near by. We'll make you come out of this smelling of roses.'

'Why?'

'It's the least I can do after the trouble I caused.' She took out money and tossed it on the table. 'Call Infinity with the details about tomorrow.'

She hoped he couldn't see her shaking as she walked away.

Chapter 6

He offered to pick up Alexa at her flat. Partly because his mother had taught him to be a gentleman, and partly because he felt bad about the way things had gone the day before. He blamed it on his shock. She was *pregnant*, and he was the only person who knew. It seemed significant. It shouldn't have. She hadn't told him because she wanted him to know, but because it made their lie infinitely more complicated. Though he wanted to help her, he couldn't see how to. And he'd disappointed her because of it. But rather her than his mother.

Nina's reaction to the news that he was in a relationship had been surprising. After her shock and the millions of questions that had come with it, she told him how happy she was that he was dating.

'You're always taking care of us, Benny,' she'd said. 'I was worried it stopped you from living your life. But now you have someone!' She had clasped her hands in glee. 'I can't tell you how much I've wanted this to happen.'

He could only imagine how she'd react if she thought he was having a baby. He was worried enough about telling her the truth.

He took a shaky breath and rang Alexa's doorbell. Tried to keep his jaw from dropping when she opened the door almost immediately.

She wore a light pink dress, cinched below her breasts and falling softly over her stomach. He thought it might be a wrap-around dress considering how the material crossed over her body, parting in a slight V at her legs, ending in two different lengths. The V revealed two gorgeous legs, toned, sliding down into heels that matched the exact shade of the dress. There was another V, though he kept himself from looking at that too closely, since it appeared at her chest.

He *had* looked closely enough to notice that her breasts had become fuller with pregnancy.

Not that he had anything to compare them to. He hadn't looked at her breasts before. He'd simply…noticed they were there. She was an attractive woman, and, since he was attracted to attractive women, he'd noticed. And now he noticed that her breasts were fuller. It was all scientific. There was nothing more to it.

He noticed the style of her dress was somehow

both highlighting her pregnancy and hiding it. Or did he only think that now because he knew she was pregnant? She wasn't showing apart from the fuller breasts and the slightest curve of her stomach. The dress flattered her body shape, which even before pregnancy had been a glorious mixture of full curves and lean muscle.

She'd always dressed for her body. Sometimes in dresses that made her look demure and saintly; other times in skirts and shirts that made him think she wanted to torment every person in the room around her. Though this dress seemed to fit with her general style—flattering, understated, seductive—at the same time it somehow didn't. It was warmer, softer, though he'd bite his own tongue off before admitting it.

'Are you going to say hello or keep staring?'

He instantly blinked, as if his body was trying to tell her he wasn't staring. But that was undermined by the blush he could feel heating his face. It got hotter when he realised he hadn't looked at her face since she opened the door. If he had, he wouldn't have spent such a long time contemplating her dress or her style, but trying to get his breath back.

She'd left her hair loose. He couldn't remember ever seeing it that way before. It was long, wavy, flowing past her shoulders and stopping halfway to her elbows. She'd parted it so that most of the thick locks had settled on the right side of her face. The rich brown of it bled into the lighter brown of her skin, as if folding dark chocolate into milk chocolate for a deliciously sinful dessert. Just at the beginning stages, before they mixed and created a brown that was more like his own skin tone.

Her lips were painted the same colour as her dress, her checks dusted with some of that colour, too. Her eyes, which were watching him speculatively, were somehow more pronounced, more emotive than usual. He guessed that also had something to do with make-up.

'Keep staring, then,' she answered for him. 'Okay.' She reached behind the door to somewhere he couldn't see, bringing a coat back, which she handed to him. 'Could you at least make yourself useful, please?'

He took the coat without a word, stepping back when she closed the door behind her. Then she looked at him.

'Honestly, Benjamin, this is an overreaction, surely.'

'No.'

'No, it's not an overreaction?' she asked. He nodded. 'You've seen me dressed up before. Mixers at the Institute. Graduation. Ours and Cherise's.'

'Not like this.'

'This is because I'm pregnant and I didn't feel good in anything else.' She straightened her shoulders. 'I know it's probably more formal than tonight required. It's just… The shop assistant told me it suited me.' She lifted a shoulder, though it wasn't as careless as he was sure she intended. It was defensive. 'I thought the dress deserved more effort from other parts of me.'

'Your hair's loose.'

'It has been before.'

'I've never seen it loose before.'

She frowned. 'Well, it's not my preference.'

'I know. That's wearing your hair in a bun.'

'I… Yes.'

She lifted a hand, tucked some hair behind her ear.

'A ponytail would probably be your next option.'

Her lips parted.

'Either on top of your head, when you're working, or at your nape, when you're dressing up.' He had no idea why he was doing this. It felt as if he was seducing her. But surely seduction couldn't happen without him intending it? He kept talking. 'Sometimes you plait your hair in two, then twirl the plaits around your head and pin them like a crown.'

Breath shuddered from between her lips. He swore he heard her swallow. Then she said, 'Only in the kitchen.'

He lifted a hand, pausing before he could do what he wanted. 'Can I touch it?'

'Can you…? My hair?' she asked, her eyes dipping to where his hand hovered above the strands on her shoulder. He nodded. 'Okay.'

'You're sure?'

'Yes.'

She sounded annoyed that he'd clarified. It made

him smile. So did the strands of her hair, which were curly and soft and just a little wet.

'I like it like this.'

'In that case, I'll wear it this way more often,' she said dryly. 'It's incredibly practical for someone who owns a restaurant.'

He laughed. Gave in to the urge to tuck her hair behind her ear as he'd seen her do earlier. 'I wouldn't say no.'

She exhaled. 'What are you doing, Benjamin?'

He dropped his hand, looked at her face. 'I don't know.'

'You do know.'

'No, I don't.' He smiled. Almost as soon as he did, the smile vanished. 'Except for right now. Right now, I'm contemplating how to get you to kiss me again. I'd say it's an appropriate response to how incredible you look.' He shook his head. 'I was staring earlier because I didn't have anything to say. You're so beautiful. And so is this dress…and your hair, your face…' He shook his head again. Offered her a wry, possibly apologetic smile. 'I'm sorry. I think the last couple of days have officially caught up with me.'

Her expression was unreadable, but she said, 'It's been a rough couple of days.'

'Yeah.'

'Because of me.' She paused. 'I'm sorry.'

'You don't have to apologise. You already have, anyway.'

'Right.' She leaned back against her door, which

he realised only now she hadn't moved away from. 'This hasn't been easy for me either.'

'I know.'

'A large part of it is because you get on my nerves. A lot,' she added when he frowned.

'That seems uncalled for, considering I just gave you a bunch of compliments.'

'You want acknowledgement for that?'

'A thank you would be nice,' he muttered.

'You're right.'

'Sorry—could you say that again?' He patted his pocket, looking for his phone. 'I want to record it for posterity.'

'This, for example, is extremely annoying. But at the same time, I can't stop thinking about the kiss we had the other day.'

He stilled.

'Which gets on my nerves, too. An interesting conundrum. Am I annoyed because I'm attracted to you? Am I annoyed because you annoy me but I'm still attracted to you?' She exhaled. It sounded frustrated. 'I don't have answers, but I keep asking these questions. Then, of course, you do something decent, like pretend to be my boyfriend even though you have no reason or incentive to. You stand up for me in front of my brother, which I found disturbingly hot. In the same breath, you act stupidly, and tell your mother—your *mother*—that I'm your girlfriend. Which, tonight, we have to rectify.'

She shook her head.

'Honestly, Benjamin, these last few days have

been the most frustratingly complicated of my life, and I'm an entrepreneur with a crappy family. And I'm *pregnant*, about to become a single mother. Complicated is the air I breathe. But you make things…' She trailed off with a little laugh. 'And still, I want to kiss you, too.'

It took him an embarrassingly long time to process everything she said. By the time he got to the end of it, the part where she wanted to kiss him, his jaw dropped. Trying to maintain his dignity, he shook his head.

'I don't need someone to kiss me out of charity. Especially not someone who thinks I'm annoying.' The more he spoke, the more indignant he felt. 'I'm only annoying because you're annoyed with everyone. Don't deny it,' he said when she opened her mouth. 'It was like that at the Institute. You had so many people trying to be your friend and you'd brush them aside. Draw into yourself. It's like no one was ever good enough for you.'

She tilted her head, the muscles in her jaw tightening and relaxing, one eyebrow raised. 'You're upset—and lashing out—because I called you annoying?'

'I'm not…' He clenched his teeth. 'This is exactly what I'm talking about.'

'Oh—was this you trying to be my friend? Is this me drawing into myself?'

'You know what?' he said, shrugging his shoulders in an attempt to shrug off the irritation. 'I don't need to do this.'

'No, you don't,' she agreed. 'You should have just kissed me like I asked you to and neither of us would be annoyed now.'

'When did you ask me to kiss you?'

She narrowed her eyes. 'You think I told you I've been thinking about our kiss for the fun of it? That I'm attracted to you because I was ranting?' She snorted. 'You spend an eternity staring at me, telling me you're trying to get me to kiss you, and when I give you permission—'

'That was *not* permission.'

'Yes, it was. I said, and I quote—'

'Shut up.'

'Excuse me?'

'You gave me permission?'

'I did. But if you think you can—'

This time, he shut her up by kissing her.

Apparently, he did think he could. And she wasn't mad about it.

Not about the way his lips pressed against hers with a force that had her pushing back against her front door. Not about the fact that they'd had a ridiculous argument that culminated in this kiss in the passageway of her flat. She had no idea what her neighbours thought. She liked the idea of them cheering her on. It wasn't what she'd be doing if someone was arguing near her flat, but she was uptight like that. Her neighbours generally seemed cool.

None of that mattered now, of course. Benjamin had teased her lips open—it hadn't taken much cajoling—and now their tongues were entwined, moving around one another like two loose strands of a rope longing to be tied. She blamed the inelegance of it on the passion. Their argument had fuelled it, though she suspected it was always there between them, simply because of who they were. She couldn't fault it when it created a hunger that could be sated like this. With his lips moving against her, allowing gooseflesh to take the place of her skin. With his tongue, sending heat to places in her body that had been cool for longer than she could remember.

As if he had heard her, Benjamin's hands began to move. They'd been on her waist, keeping her in place, she suspected. But now they skimmed the sides of her breasts, running along her neck, angling her head so he could kiss her more deeply. The throaty moan that he got in response was a soundtrack for his journey back down, although now he lingered exactly where she needed him to. His touch was gentle at her waist, his thumbs brushing her belly. She gasped. It was intimate, him touching her stomach like that. It felt as if he was claiming her. Her baby.

And that was more intense than when he reached her hips and pulled her against him, bringing the most aching part of her to where she needed him.

But that wasn't true any more. The most aching part of her was her heart now, his innocent caress of her stomach awakening things that she'd forced to sleep years ago. When he pulled back, she offered him a small smile of reassurance. It was okay, him kissing her. She was okay. She wasn't being threatened by the loneliness that always followed her. She wasn't overcome by the enormity of her decision to have a baby alone.

After the thing with Kenya and her baby had happened, Alexa had thought more seriously about having her own. She'd done so with her head *and* her heart. Her head had told her that she was thirty years old, and her ability to become a mother wouldn't always be as simple as it was now. It told her that her business was steady enough for her to take maternity leave, and that when she came back she'd be stronger for having had her baby. If her business took a knock, she was still only thirty, and she'd work her tail off—with even more incentive than usual—to make sure it was back on track.

Her heart had told her that she was ready. She'd spent her entire life examining what she shouldn't be as a mother; who she shouldn't be as a parent. She was ready to finally have the family of her dreams. Where support, love, inclusion were the norm. She wouldn't push her child to breaking point, or create an environment where her child felt they needed to compete for her love. No, she would create warmth and happiness. A home, as she'd done with her flat.

But that was before she'd lost her head chef. Now her business didn't seem nearly as stable as it had been before. And that was before this kiss with Benjamin. Suddenly she was thinking about whether she was robbing her child of having someone else to love them. If she was robbing herself of sharing the miracle of the life growing inside her; or the tenderness Benjamin had shown her.

'Hey,' he said softly, his thumb brushing over her cheek. 'It couldn't have been that bad.'

'What? No.' She shook her head. 'It's not—it wasn't bad.' She gave him that smile again. 'We should probably get to dinner.'

'Alexa—'

'I'm fine, Benjamin. I promise.' But she wasn't. She was promising a lie. 'We're fine, too.' That one she meant.

Because in her head, this would be the last kiss. Tonight would be the last night they spent together. Soon people would know their relationship was fake, a joke. Lee would know—but she would survive it. She would go on to court Cherise de Bruyn and focus on getting the chef, as she should have from the beginning. No one would distract her. Not even Benjamin.

At least that way, though her heart seemed to be unsure of her decisions, her head wouldn't be.

Chapter 7

'Really, Mom?' said Benjamin when they walked in. 'You haven't even said hello but already you have baby videos out?' His mother gave him a bright smile in return, and he couldn't even be mad. He rolled his eyes though. Looked at Alexa. 'Go ahead. Clearly my mother would like to start the evening with embarrassment.'

Alexa walked past him, wearing a smile more genuine than the last few she'd given him. He didn't know if he was relieved or annoyed. Neither. Both.

'I'm going to be very disappointed if there are no videos of him running around naked,' Alexa said. 'It's the only level of embarrassment I'll accept.'

'Well, then, you're in luck,' Nina Foster said with a smile.

'It's lovely to meet you, Mrs Foster.' Alexa held out a hand.

'I've already told you my name is Nina.' His mother ignored Alexa's hand, instead pulling her in for a hug. Alexa accepted with a small laugh. Benjamin released a breath he didn't realise he'd been holding. When his mother pulled back, she said, 'You can call me Aunty Nina, dear.'

At that, Alexa grinned. 'Perfect.'

'I take it Dad's in the kitchen,' Benjamin said to distract himself from the troubling warmth in his chest.

'Yes. He's almost done though. That man loves to cook.' Nina aimed that at Alexa. 'It's where Benny gets his talent.'

'In that case, I'm looking forward to dinner.' Alexa turned to Benjamin. 'Should I hang this up, or can I drape it over a chair?'

'Oh, I've got it.'

He took the coat, went to his bedroom and hung it on a hanger from his own cupboard. It was the least he could do, considering the coat had been collateral damage in their make-out session, when he'd tossed it on the floor. He wouldn't have bothered doing anything with her coat otherwise.

His mother would have scolded him, but only after he'd already set the guest's coat down somewhere innocuous. It was the approach he took with most of his clothing, as evidenced by the tornado that had gone off in his room. His parents refused to go in there. Since he helped with the household expenses, they had a y*ou're an adult, you deserve your privacy* policy. Except he didn't think they meant privacy in the form of someone—including, on particularly bad days, him—being unable to find anything inside the room.

He took another look at things, winced. It would be better if Alexa—

'Is this your room?'

He turned quickly, blocking the doorway with his body. She was a little further down the passage, so she hadn't seen anything. Yet. He would keep it that way.

'Er…no. I mean, yes.' He closed the door behind him. 'It's where I…do things.'

'Things?'

'Sleep.'

'Hmm.'

'Dress.'

'Okay.' She narrowed her eyes. 'Why don't you want me to see it?'

It was obviously too much to hope that she would be polite and ignore his reluctance. But no, not Alexa. She was too straightforward, too unapologetic to allow something like politeness to get in the way of information she wanted.

'It's untidy.'

She waved a hand. 'So was mine the other day.'

'*That* was untidy?' He rolled his eyes. 'Honestly, I have no idea what that word means with some people. My mother says exactly the same thing and the place is spotless.' He paused. 'I'm willing to bet she told you our place is untidy right now. And I know for a fact she spent the entire day supervising our cleaner.'

'I wouldn't take that bet.' She lifted her nose in the air before she grinned. 'Because she just did.'

He chuckled, but stopped when she took a step forward. 'I'm not like you or my mother.'

'What does that mean?'

'When I say something's untidy, I mean it.'

'Well, so do I. I have certain standards, same as in the restaurant. If I say it's untidy, it doesn't suit those standards.' Her gaze sharpened. 'I've never been to yours. Are you saying you keep a sloppy house?'

'Of course not,' he said, offended. 'I have high standards, too.' But he winced. 'That doesn't necessarily translate to my room.'

'So what you're saying is you live in a pigsty.'

'I would not say that.'

'Let me see it, then.' She folded her arms, baiting him.

Damn her.

'I'd rather not. Did my mother send you here?' he asked without waiting to hear her reply. 'I was barely gone for a minute.'

'No. I asked to use the bathroom. What with this situation happening…' She gestured to her stomach.

'You *told* her?'

'That I needed to go to the bathroom because I'm pregnant?' She pulled a face. 'Of course not. Why would I?'

'Oh.' He winced. 'I'm sorry. That was an over-reaction.'

She rolled her eyes. 'The bathroom?'

'That one.' He pointed to the room across the hall-way.

'Thank you,' Alexa said, and walked into it.

Benjamin stood there for a beat, feeling foolish as his heart rate went back to normal. He shook his head. He needed to put this lie behind him. It was making him skittish. But when he went back to the living room to do just that, his mother was sitting with her hands interlocked over her stomach. Her eyes were closed, and to someone who didn't know her, it would seem as if she was napping. To someone who did know her…

'Mom,' he said, lowering himself in front of her. 'Why didn't you tell me you weren't feeling well?'

She opened her eyes, the tight lines of pain in the creases around them confirming his suspicion. 'I'm fine. Stop fussing.'

'Do we have to do this every time? It's been decades.'

'Exactly. Decades and I still have to tell you I'm fine.'

'But you're not fine. You're in pain.'

'Just a little, from the excitement of the day.'

'Mom…' He trailed off, sighed. 'I wish you'd told me. We could have cancelled. You could have got some rest and not put so much pressure on yourself.'

'And miss the chance to meet Alexa?'

'Mom, Alexa's not—' He broke off. Mostly because he couldn't tell her the truth when she was like this. 'Alexa's not going anywhere,' he finished lamely. 'I'd have brought her the moment you felt better.'

'Would you have?' his mother asked, her eyes tired but sharp. 'I didn't even know about her until yesterday. You never tell us about your dating life. I assumed she's your first proper girlfriend, but I don't even know if that's true.'

'It's because—'

'I had to force you to bring her here,' she interrupted him. Her eyes were flashing now, pain mingled in with the anger. 'And she's pregnant, Benny. *Pregnant*. You hid that from us.'

'What? Oh, no, Mom. She's not—'

'Your bedroom isn't that far away, Benjamin.'

She'd heard them. Damn it. Why hadn't he thought about that?

'We can talk about it when you feel better. Let me help you to bed now.'

'No.' Nina straightened, though he could see she was doing her best not to wince. 'I want to have dinner with you and get to know that woman who's going to be in our lives from now on.'

'She's not…'

He broke off, his mind spinning with how to tell her the truth. Through it, he heard the memory of Alexa's voice asking him why he hadn't told his mother when she'd first overheard him. He should have. But he was caught by that excitement on her face, and he couldn't bear to disappoint her.

He was as much to blame for the situation they were in as Alexa was, he realised. At least this situation. And now, his mother was in pain because of him. Because of his lies.

He exhaled. 'Mom, Alexa's baby… It's not mine.'

She was intruding. She'd known it the moment she'd seen Benjamin crouching in front of his mother. When she'd heard them talk, the conversation so personal she'd had to rest a hand on her chest because her heart felt as if it was breaking, she told herself to walk away. Except she couldn't. She was too riveted by this tender side of a man she'd once called a demon.

She'd felt that tenderness during their kiss. It was what had turned the moment from a purely physical one into something emotional. So she shouldn't have been surprised that he had the capacity to be tender. But seeing it up close and personal, especially after *feeling* it up close and personal? It felt as if someone had walked into her body, gathered her emotions together and tossed them in the air like confetti at a wedding.

She was scrambling to get them back together again when his mother had told him she knew about the baby. Then he confessed it wasn't his, and said nothing about their fake relationship. She'd given him a moment to continue, to tell his mother *why* the baby wasn't his. He hadn't. He merely watched his mother gasp, lift a hand to her mouth, his face crumbling.

So Alexa threw the emotions she had just collected to the ground, and stomped over them to help Benjamin.

'Ben,' she said softly. He looked at her, his eyes ravaged with sadness. 'Let me.'

'We need to—'

'No, *I* need to.' She sent him one look to tell him to shut up, then looked at his mother. 'Benjamin isn't the father of my baby. He's just a decent man who… is decent.' She offered him a smile before sitting on the sofa opposite Nina.

'Mrs Foster… Aunty Nina… I found out I was pregnant pretty quickly. After about two weeks. Benjamin and I hadn't started dating yet, and, well… I got myself into a situation.'

She was keeping as far to the truth as possible. The fertility treatments meant she had found out she was pregnant early. When she had, she'd refused to come in to monitor the pregnancy as her specialist had advised. She wanted to have a normal pregnancy as far as possible. Since it had started out in an unusual way, monitoring things had overwhelmed her.

She also hadn't been fake dating Benjamin then.

'I didn't want to tell him when he asked me out because he seemed like a good guy. For once, I wanted a good guy in my life. I didn't tell him for the longest time. It was wrong, and selfish, and it hurt both you and him. For that, I will never forgive myself.'

She swallowed when her eyes began to prickle. Pressed a hand to her stomach because she felt alone in this deeply personal and strangely true tale she was telling Benjamin's mother. It comforted her, which sent another wave of prickling over her eyes, and she took her time before she continued.

'He hasn't known I'm pregnant very long. I think he was still deciding what to do when you found out about me. It put him in an impossible situation. He didn't want you to be disappointed, but bringing me here tonight makes it seem like he wants me and the baby, and he isn't there yet. He didn't tell you about me because he didn't want that, for either of us,' she said with a lift of her hand.

There was a long silence. Alexa didn't know if someone was waiting for her to speak, or if she was waiting for someone to speak. Eventually, Nina broke the silence.

'Knowing all this, you're still here?'

'It's an impossible situation,' she said with a small smile. 'But it's our normal. So...*normally*... I thought meeting his mother was important.'

There was another long silence. This time, Benjamin broke it.

'I'm sorry, Mom. It was never my intention to... to disappoint you.'

His mother heaved out a sigh. 'You haven't disappointed me. In fact, your behaviour with Alexa... I'd like to think *I* raised you to be someone who doesn't judge people by actions you don't agree with.'

'If it were really you,' Benjamin said slyly, 'you wouldn't judge me for my recent actions.'

Alexa bit her lip, but stopped trying to hide her smile when Nina laughed.

'You're too charming for your own good, boy.'

'I've always thought so, too,' Alexa agreed.

'Thank you,' Benjamin replied with a grin.

Nina gave them an amused look. Then she sobered. 'My son clearly cares about you, Alexa. That's enough for me.'

Alexa nodded, pressure she didn't realise was there releasing inside her. 'Thank you.'

Nina shook her head. 'I'm actually rooting for this to work out. Because at this pace, that baby of yours might be my only chance at a grandchild.'

They didn't have time to reply, as a tall man with a shock of grey hair walked into the room.

'Benjie, boy.' In the man's grin, Alexa saw Benjamin.

'Hi, Dad.'

Benjamin's father looked at their faces, frowned. 'What did I miss?'

Chapter 8

'This isn't my place,' Alexa said, as if only now noticing he hadn't taken her back to her flat. Which was surprising, as they hadn't spoken since they'd left his house, so she hadn't been distracted. In fact, she'd been staring out of the window the entire time.

'No, it's not.'

He didn't say anything else as he drove along the gravel road that led into the quarry. Handy, because if he had, he wouldn't have heard her small gasp when he parked. He couldn't deny that part of why he'd brought her was the wow factor. The quarry was spectacular at night; on a summer's night, even more so. There was no cool breeze to chill them, no dew glazing the grass that stretched out in front of the car park. The sky was clear, the full moon illuminating things enough that he didn't have to get out his phone's torch to guide them to the water.

And really, it was the water that was the star of the quarry. It was nestled in the hollow of the rocks, stretching out in inky darkness. The moon was reflected in it, the stars, too, and it made him wonder if perhaps this was all a little too romantic. But he wanted quiet, and the quarry was quiet. He went to the back of his car, and got out the camping chairs he kept there.

'You prepared for this?' she asked when she got out of the car. 'Were you intending on bringing me here?'

'No.' He carried the chairs to his usual spot beneath the tree at the edge of the water. When he heard her behind him he said, 'I keep these in my car.'

'For this reason?'

'Exactly.'

'You bring ladies out here a lot, then?' She gave him a sly look as she lowered herself into the chair. Then she frowned. 'You'd better be prepared to help me out of this chair. It's low, and being pregnant means I have zero control over my balance.'

'So what you're saying is that I could leave you here and you'd have to stay in the chair for ever?'

'Yes,' she replied, voice dry as a badly made cake. 'That's exactly what I'm saying.'

'Good to know.' He paused. 'Better watch your attitude.'

'You know what? I don't even need your help. The

grass looks pretty soft. I can tilt to the side, break my fall with my hand, and figure it out from there.'

'The grass is lower than the chair.'

'I said I'd figure it out.'

He couldn't help his laugh, though he tried to be respectful and kept it quick and low—until she joined in, which he hadn't expected. It was strange to be laughing with her, but he suspected they were relieving the tension of the night. There'd been an undercurrent during the entire meal. He didn't blame his mother for being reserved—both Alexa's news and her pain had probably occupied her mind and her body—but it meant that he'd overcompensated. The result was a strained meal where everyone pretended nothing was wrong and it was…draining.

When they stopped laughing, they lapsed into an easy silence; another surprise. But honestly, he was grateful for it. It gave him a moment to gather his thoughts, prepare his words.

'Thank you.'

'For what?'

'What you had to do with my mom. You made a difficult situation easier.'

She sighed. 'I lied.'

'Did you?'

She frowned. 'You mean, besides the fact that I kept our fake relationship going?'

'Yes, actually.'

It took some time for her to understand.

'Oh, you want to know if the stuff I said about the father of the baby's true.'

He did. But now that she said it, he felt as if he was asking too much. Maybe if he was honest with her, too…

'Look, I know I said the lies had to end. But…' He trailed off, sighed. 'At some point tonight I realised it worked for me to be in a fake relationship, too. It made my mother happy. Maybe I knew it would and that's why I let her think we were together in the first place.' It was something he'd have to think about. 'Your pregnancy complicated things, and I got scared. But your explanation made sense. Hell, it somehow made both of us look good.'

She looked at the water. 'I wouldn't say that.'

'I would.' He let it sit for a moment. 'I realised tonight the only people whose opinions I care about are my parents. So, we can keep this going for as long as we both want to.'

'You're not afraid of disappointing your mother when it ends?'

He heaved out a breath. 'I can't see an outcome that won't hurt her. I'd rather she think I tried and it didn't work out than know I lied to her.'

'Sneaky,' she commented.

'You're one to talk.'

She laughed. 'Touché.' There was a beat. 'Thank you.'

'This isn't only for you.'

For once, he believed it. He wasn't doing this only to help her. It helped him and his family, too. It might have been strained at dinner this evening, but there'd also been light. That light had been because of Alexa. Because of what she represented to his parents.

A future that didn't only involve taking care of them.

He'd sacrifice his reputation for his parents' peace of mind.

'I know,' she said softly. 'Still. Thank you.' Silence danced between them for a few minutes. 'To answer your earlier question, I don't know what kind of guy got me pregnant.'

His brain took a moment to shift gears. 'You don't know…if he's a good guy?'

'I don't know who he is.'

'Oh.'

Sure. That was fine. She was allowed her sexual freedom. If she didn't know who she'd slept with, that was her business. Except…

No, no exceptions. He wouldn't be a judgemental jerk.

'I was waiting,' she said into the silence, 'for some kind of bigoted statement about my sex life.'

'I wouldn't dare.'

She laughed lightly. 'You were basically biting your tongue.'

'It isn't my business.'

'No, it's not.' Her laughter faded. 'Which makes why I'm telling you I was artificially inseminated by donor sperm puzzling.'

'You were artificially inseminated?' he repeated dumbly.

'Yep.' She unclasped the hands that had been

locked around her knee. 'I wanted to have a baby and the available men were... Well, I suppose there were none. Whom I trusted anyway.'

'You have no male friends?'

'I don't have any...' She broke off. 'I don't have that many friends. Besides, could you imagine me asking a friend to be the father of my child?' She shuddered. 'That would be asking for trouble. Involvement. People don't tend to keep their word, so the promise that they would never encroach on the way I raised a child would be gone pretty quickly, I bet. Especially if the baby looked like the friend.'

He thought about it. 'Alternatively, you could have gone through this *with* someone. You wouldn't have to make decisions alone. You'd have support.'

'Spoken like a man who's had support his entire life.'

'Is that a criticism?'

'Not a criticism. An observation.'

'In return, then, I observe that you don't trust people.'

'An accurate observation. Trusting people isn't worth a damn.'

He tried to formulate an answer, but found himself at a loss for words. Not emotion though. He felt sorry that she'd lived a life that encouraged her to think this way. There was some rage, too, because it seemed completely unfair that he'd had parents who'd loved him and taught him the value of leaning on family and she hadn't. Or maybe it wasn't

so much rage as it was guilt, because he had something she didn't.

'Don't feel sorry for me.'

'I'm not.'

'Your mother wouldn't like you lying to me.'

His face twisted. 'Are you really using my mother
to make me feel guilty about this?'

'Yes. I am a smart woman who uses the tools at
her disposal.'

He chuckled softly. 'Can't argue with that.'

'Finally, you learn.'

She settled back in the chair, resting her hands
on her belly. It had the same protective tint as the
way she'd rubbed her stomach that night in her flat.
Now he knew she'd done it because she was pregnant. What he didn't know was why *he'd* done it.
Why, when they'd kissed, he'd grazed her stomach
and felt a rush of protectiveness he didn't know existed inside him. Need had joined so quickly and intensely that he'd had to pull back from their kiss to
deal with it. To try and deny it, as he'd done the first
time he'd felt that need.

'I don't feel sorry,' he said slowly, 'I feel sad.'

She didn't answer, tilting her head from side to
side.

'What?' he asked.

'I'm trying to figure out whether sad is worse.'

'And?'

She looked over, eyes shining with emotion he
couldn't read but knew meant something. 'It isn't.'

Without thinking about it, he reached out a hand.

She stared at it, at him, looked down, then slowly took his hand. He wanted to stand up and shout for joy. He wanted to thank her for letting him in. He wanted to pull her into his arms and kiss her. Sate the heat the contact sent through his body. Instead, he squeezed and let the quiet of the evening settle over them.

It surprised him by settling the twisting of his stomach, too. He was used to the twisting, since it came whenever his mother was in pain.

When he was young, he had thought he could do something about it. His mother would be in bed, curled up to favour whichever side of her was aching more, and he'd bring her tea. Make her food. Offer to run a bath for her, or cuddle her until she felt better. She'd never accept, and she'd apologise afterwards. She'd tell him the version of her who was in pain wasn't really *her*.

Throughout her illness, she'd tried to separate the person who was in pain and the one who wasn't. Which he understood. Her illness had been relatively unknown in South Africa when she'd been diagnosed, and even the dialogue with her doctors had separated those identities. But he knew, even as a kid, that the same mother who couldn't move some days was the mother who would spend hours reading to him. Or taking him to some exciting place he wanted to see. Or answering all his questions with patience and honesty. As he grew older, he realised his mother had separated who she was because she saw her body as her enemy during her flare-ups. It was separate for her; it was separate *from* her. It was betraying her.

He'd wanted to help her because he wanted her to remember he loved all of her, even if she couldn't do it herself. It was a big burden for a kid to undertake, even though he hadn't completely understood it. And it had evolved as he got older. Now, he tried to nudge instead of directly say. He tried to support instead of fix. It was navigating a minefield— a stubborn minefield—but since there weren't any explosions, at least not yet, Benjamin thought he was doing pretty okay. As long as he was there, he would keep doing okay.

'Is your mom going to be all right?'

He frowned, trying to remember if he'd spoken out loud and the question had been provoked. He was sure he hadn't, which meant Alexa was simply curious. He sighed in relief.

'Yeah, she'll be fine.'

'Is she unwell?'

He took a breath. 'She has something called fibromyalgia. It's a—'

'I know what it is.' At his surprised look, she rolled her eyes. 'People are more open about chronic illnesses these days.'

'But… I mean, it's not something you just know.'

'I didn't,' she agreed. 'Until I went to look it up after seeing an acquaintance talk about it online.'

He kept his mouth shut because if he didn't he was sure he'd make inelegant grunts she'd make fun of.

'It sounds tough,' she said softly. 'Living your

life in pain the whole time. I can't imagine.' There
was a short pause. 'I *can* imagine how hard it must
have been for you.'

He gave her a sharp look, dropping her hand in
the process. She didn't seem fazed, only folding her
hands over her stomach again.

'What do you mean?' he asked.

'Well, you're the kind of person who agrees to
be in a fake relationship with his mortal enemy because you were feeling protective. At least, I guess
that was how you were feeling? Maybe it was indignant at how Lee dared to act towards me. I can't tell
with you.' She shrugged. 'Regardless, you're someone who does things when other people seem vulnerable. I'm guessing you see your mother's pain as
her being vulnerable, which makes you want to do
something. Except you can't, because it's *her* pain.'

It was remarkably astute. Uncomfortably astute.
Which was why he said, 'No.'

The corners of her lips twitched. 'Hmm…'

'It's been fine for me.'

'Okay.'

'She's the one in pain.'

'Sure.'

'Is it hard for me to see her that way? Sure. But
is it worse for me? No.'

'That's not what I said though. I know it's worse
for her. Of course it is.' She paused. 'I might be off
base here, what with having a messed-up family situation myself, but I don't think it would be easy for
me to see someone I care about in pain.'

'It's…not.'

'I don't doubt it.' There was a long pause as the words washed over them. 'It's not an excuse for you not to pick up after yourself though. How do you even find anything in your room? It looks like the aftermath of a police search.'

As soon as the surprise faded—though he should have known she'd look—he started laughing. 'It's organised chaos.'

'Rubbish!'

'It's not rubbish.'

'You're telling me you know where every T-shirt is placed? Every shirt? Pants?'

'Exactly.'

'So if I hid something in there you'd find it?'

'Did you hide something in my room?'

She gave him a sly look. 'Maybe.'

'Alexa,' he nearly growled.

'What?' She blinked at him innocently. 'You said it's organised chaos. I'd just like to prove, once and for all, on behalf of everyone who's been sceptical about organised chaos, that that's nonsense.'

'You're trying to trap me on behalf of an entire group of people?'

'Sometimes your actions have to be bigger than yourself.'

He shook his head, but even his disbelief couldn't overshadow his amusement. Then he thought of something.

'How did you know I'd say organised chaos though?'

'Please. I've spent years trying to avoid interacting with you. It hasn't worked—' she sent him an accusatory look '—but at least I got to know who you are.'

He sighed. 'What did you hide in my room?'

'A handkerchief.'

'You carry a handkerchief?'

'Yes.' She sniffed. 'It's for the essential oils I carry in my purse, too. In case I have an overbearing bout of nausea.'

'Efficient.'

'Thanks.'

'Can you at least tell me what the handkerchief looks like?'

'Pink. Like my dress.'

'That should make it easier to find.'

'It'll be a breeze. You know where everything is, remember?'

She patted his hand, winked at his glare, and he turned away before he could smile again.

He couldn't say whether it was the teasing that soothed him, but the anxiety in his body had stopped humming. Except it couldn't be the teasing. She'd done plenty of that before, though it had lost its snarkiness at some point over the last few days.

As he thought about it, he realised it was that she understood. His position in his family had always made him feel alone, and finally he didn't feel that way any more.

He let it wash over him. Didn't even question that Alexa had been the one to make him feel that way—

or what it meant. Still, he couldn't let her get the upper hand.

'So,' he said casually, 'are we going to talk about that kiss?'

'What kiss?'

He snorted. 'There's no way you don't—'

'What kiss, Benjamin?'

At her tone, he looked over. Saw her determination. It made him laugh, which turned the determination into a glare. Satisfied that he'd won, he stood and offered a hand to help her up.

Chapter 9

Alexa walked into the restaurant and saw him immediately.

'You've got to be kidding me,' she muttered, pausing.

It had been a few days since she and Benjamin had had *that* moment. It wasn't a defined moment. She couldn't say—oh, this thing happened and things have changed. Besides the kisses. And the fact that she thought he might be nice, despite the whole stealing-her-chef thing. Or how kind he was with his parents; how eager he was to please them. All she knew for sure was that at some point at the quarry, things had shifted. She needed time to sort through it, and she had other things to do first.

Such as secure her chef before she went on maternity leave.

There was time. She was days away from entering her second trimester, so she had about six months. That was what she told herself logically. In reality, she was freaking out. Hiring a new chef was a nightmare. She knew because she'd done so months before and it had all gone to hell anyway. So she needed time to find the right person, make sure they worked well with the rest of her team. Train them to work for Infinity, with her and with Kenya. She had to be there to observe and make sure everything would go smoothly when she was away.

She only had six months to do so.

No wonder she had indigestion.

That could have been her pregnancy, too, but she had a feeling being stressed about the new chef didn't help. Or being at odds with Kenya, who'd stubbornly refused to talk about anything other than work in the last week. Usually, Kenya was a champagne bottle, shaken and uncorked and overflowing with personal anecdotes. Now she was a bottle of wine; one that was aging and still and not overflowing with anything.

It was hard for Alexa to believe she missed all of Kenya's energy and her much too personal stories about her life. But she did. And now she had to deal with realising she missed the connection of it, too, and think about how to fix it, and about why Kenya was really so mad at her. She did *not* need to face Benjamin and his kissable lips today.

She marched over to the table.

'You're stealing my appointments with Cherise now, too?'

He looked up, smiled at her, and did it all so slowly that it felt as though someone had pushed a button for that to happen. Her heart did a little skip at that face; her mind recognised that his surprise, his pleasure at seeing her were genuine.

'Hey!' He stood. 'You have an appointment with Cherise, too?'

'Too?' She looked at the table. There were only two seats. 'How can we both have an appointment with her?'

He shrugged. 'She called me the day before yesterday to ask me if I could meet her here.' He gestured at the restaurant. It was perfectly nice with black and white décor, some greenery courtesy of plants, and the faint smell of fish because of its position near the water of the V&A Waterfront. 'Said it would be a nice neutral space.'

Alexa huffed out a breath. 'Yeah, because that's what I told her. After I called her the day before yesterday to ask for this meeting.'

He blinked. 'You called Cherise after we spent the night together?'

'I'm not sure I'd describe dinner with your family as us spending the night together, but yes, I did.' She straightened her spine. 'You said we should continue with our plans as usual.'

'Yeah, but I didn't expect—'

He frowned. Shoved his hands into his pockets. Suddenly she noticed that he was wearing a shirt. She'd seen him in one before, but now he looked... different. His shoulders were broad, chest defined, the material clinging to all of it. She half expected him to move and tear through a perfectly good piece of clothing.

Why was a part of her cheering for that to happen?

'I guess she wanted to speak with both of us at the same time.'

'I did,' Cherise said from beside them. Alexa nearly jumped out of her skin.

'How long have you been there?'

'Just arrived,' Cherise replied. 'Sorry to spring this on you.' She narrowed her eyes. 'Although I was sure I wouldn't actually be able to do that, since you two are dating.'

There was a beat as Alexa realised she was going to have to pretend again. Fortunately, Benjamin spoke before she could say anything.

'We keep our personal and professional lives separate.' He smiled, oozing charm. Alexa nearly slipped on the puddle of it before she realised this was what he did. He charmed people. But *not* her. Especially not if she continued ignoring the fact that they'd kissed. 'Thought it for the best, considering we're in the same business.'

'I imagine that must help. Or make things more complicated, if you're meeting up like this.'

'It doesn't happen as often as you'd think,' Alexa answered Cherise. Cherise gave her a rueful smile.

'I thought it might be easier to discuss this together.' She paused. 'In hindsight, I suppose I was using your relationship to make things easier for myself. I wouldn't have to have two meetings about possibly the same thing. I'm blurring things for you,' she added with a frown.

'Don't worry about it,' Benjamin said smoothly. 'We're mature enough to handle it.'

He sent Alexa a look as if to say *I'm mature enough*. It took all of Alexa's willpower not to roll her eyes at him, or stick out her tongue. Or do anything really that would undermine her maturity. She could be mature.

'Should we get someone to add a chair to this table?' Alexa asked coolly. Maturely. She gestured to a waiter. 'I booked a two-seater.'

'This is the table I booked, actually,' Benjamin said, also gesturing to the waiter. When he looked at Alexa, she pulled a face. *This is you being mature?*

'Oh, I booked a table for three,' Cherise interjected. 'I just saw you two here and came directly to speak to you. I'll have the waiter take us.'

Soon they were sitting together and ordering drinks.

'So,' Cherise started, 'I know whatever either of you wanted to say to me today probably isn't going to work out because the other crashed the lunch.'

She and Benjamin exchanged a look. They hadn't *crashed* the lunch. Cherise had invited Benjamin to an appointment Alexa and she had agreed on. If anything, Cherise had done the crashing. By proxy.

Acid pushed up in Alexa's chest. She'd done a lot of research to find Cherise. Her first step had been to call her old mentor at the restaurant she'd worked at after the Institute. He'd recommended two people, one of whom was studying at the same institute she'd studied at—Cherise—the other of whom was still working for him, but was looking for something more, more urgently than what he could offer.

It had taken her a while to find out that Cherise wasn't studying at the Institute as a newbie who wanted to learn everything she could. No, Cherise had worked under the best chefs, her old mentor included, for almost a decade, and had decided to formalise her knowledge by getting an official qualification. She was interested in something new, which, after speaking with some of the people Cherise had worked with, including the instructors they had in common, Alexa was eager to offer.

Except now it seemed Cherise wasn't going to be that good a match after all.

'I thought I'd say some things to both of you instead,' Cherise said. 'One: I would be happy to work with either of you. I'm looking for something different to what I've done in the past, which tended to lean towards more traditional fine dining. Nothing wrong with it,' she added quickly, 'but I'd like to do something more creative than cauliflower purée. I'm eager to explore that creativity, and I believe your restaurants, both younger, trendier places, would give me the space to do that.'

Alexa rubbed the burning in her chest thoughtfully. It wasn't subsiding, though her doubts about Cherise were. Perhaps that was enough for now.

'Two: I have no idea which one of you I'd like to work for.' Cherise gave them a small smile. 'I've dined at both your restaurants. Both of them were amazing experiences, and each of your spaces I respond to. Yours is more traditional, with the wood and the partitions between each side of the restaurant,' she said to Benjamin, 'but there's something about it that makes me nostalgic. Yet I love how modern Infinity is,' Cherise continued, speaking to Alexa now. 'It's sleek, and so not where I'd expect to be served fine dining.'

'Thank you…?'

Cherise laughed. 'It's a compliment,' she assured Alexa. 'You've brought a younger crowd in by modernising your place, and I respect someone who can instil respect for good food in a generation that fast food was basically designed for.'

'Well, then, thank you,' Alexa said more firmly.

'The conclusion I've come to is that it will depend on who I get along with the best. The only way I can know that is to spend more time with you both.'

'Of course,' Alexa said. 'You can come to the restaurant any time you'd like. I can show you around, have you speak with some of my staff. I'm sure Benjamin would allow that, too.'

'Sure.'

'And I'd love that. But I was thinking of something a little different.'

'What?'

She wrinkled her nose. 'School.'

'Why do I feel like we were being interviewed?' Benjamin asked minutes after Cherise had left the restaurant.

'Not were,' Alexa corrected. 'Are. We now have

to take a three-day course at the Institute. Which I don't mind per se, it's just…' Her voice faded and she let out a huge sigh.

'Everything okay?'

'Fine.'

But she dropped her head onto a hand she'd rested on the table.

If his instincts hadn't already been tingling from that sigh, this would have done them in. In fact, it felt as though an alarm was going off in his head. It dimmed the sound of the inner voice warning him not to get involved. Things were already almost impracticably complicated between them; he didn't need to further complicate that by getting involved with her issues.

Except she looked so fragile, sitting there with her hand on her head. It was so different to how she usually seemed—abrasive, bull-headed, *strong*—that he had to fight harder than he would have liked not to ask. And then he found himself fighting against *that* because he did want to ask. Hell, he even wanted to make it better. Which was exactly how things usually went wrong. People would take advantage of his tendency to take over. After he'd had a 'friend' do it recently, he'd learnt his lesson.

He eyed Alexa.

'You okay?' he asked anyway, because he was a fool who hadn't learnt a thing.

'I've already said I'm fine,' she said, but there was no heat in the words. If she were feeling herself, there definitely would have been heat in the words.

'It's just that—' he tried not to show his surprise that she'd continued '—this is turning out to be a lot harder than I thought it would be. Everything is,' she said in an uncharacteristically small voice as she lifted her head. 'I wanted to get Cherise to work for me so I could go on maternity leave without worrying I was ruining my restaurant by having a baby. Leaving it vulnerable in some way. Maybe even to you and Lee. Now I have to do this course with you.' She looked up at him. Her eyes were gleaming, but sharp. 'No offence.'

He wondered if he should dignify that with a response.

'Why can't anything be simple?' she whispered now. 'Why can't I have a family that doesn't suck? Why couldn't my chef have stayed on so that I wouldn't have this stress during my pregnancy? Why couldn't…?'

She exhaled. Waved a hand.

'I'm fine.'

'Clearly.'

She gave him a dark look. He preferred it to the sadness.

'I can't help you with—'

'Any of it,' she interrupted. 'You can't help me with any of it. But I appreciate the effort.'

'I wasn't going to say that.'

'Oh, I know,' she said, straightening now. She took a deep sip of water, but kept her gaze on him. 'I know what you were going to say, Benjamin. It was going to be about what you could help me with.

You might even have been considering stepping out of this race with Cherise because things would be easier for me then.'

'I wasn't—'

She cut him off with a single raised eyebrow. And because, of course, he *was*.

'Where would it leave you, Benjamin?' she asked softly. 'You'd have to look for another chef. You'd have to answer to my brother. You're clearly letting your personal feelings override how you feel professionally.'

'There are no personal feelings.'

She looked at him strangely. The confusion cleared in seconds.

'Oh, no, I don't mean *for* me. Of course not.' There was a beat. 'I meant you're letting your desire to fix things for people cloud your professional opinion. Which should be that you should do that three-day course and fight to have her work for you.'

She grabbed her purse, threw some notes onto the table.

'That's what I'll be doing.'

Then she was gone.

He sat, bemused, until the waiter came to the table, saw the money Alexa had left, and asked if he wanted the bill. He said yes, stuffed her notes in his wallet, and paid with his card. Then he walked. Not to his car, where he probably should have gone. He had work to do.

But his thoughts demanded that he pay them heed, and he couldn't do that when he was driving, or working. So he walked. Away from the bustle of the Waterfront, where tourists shopped and locals ate. Down, past the docks, until he was simply walking along the edge of the Waterfront, waves splashing against the rocks beyond the railing.

The conversation he'd had with Alexa...

Well, he couldn't exactly call it a conversation. More a monologue, with the occasional pauses. He couldn't be upset with her though; she was right. There'd been a moment, and not a brief one, where he'd thought about giving up the fight for Cherise.

A lot about that bothered him. The first was, simply, that it was stupid. He'd spent a long time trying to find her. Speaking with his contacts at restaurants she'd worked in and at the Institute. Making sure she had the skills a chef in his kitchen would need.

He'd started out as the head chef, back when Lee had reached out to him years ago. Though that was tainted now with the knowledge that Lee had done it to get back at Alexa, Benjamin could still recognise his luck. Because Lee had been the one to help him make the transition once he'd discovered his passion went beyond the kitchen.

Since Lee had multiple businesses, he couldn't invest much time in the restaurant. So when Benjamin had decided to switch gears and spoken to Lee about his desire to branch out, Lee had offered to train him. For two years, they'd done just that. This was the first year he'd taken on the responsibility fully, and he wanted to make Lee proud. Hell, he wanted to make himself proud. Giving away his chance because he wanted to help out a woman who didn't need his help was definitely stupid.

The second thing that bothered him about wanting to was that she'd seen through him. She had the uncanny ability to do so, which she'd displayed at lunch today and at the quarry the other night. He could blame the ability on the fact that she didn't seem to want his help. Despite what he'd first thought about her, Alexa wasn't using him. If she was, she would have said it by now. She was disturbingly honest like that.

Which was why he couldn't be dishonest with himself when it came to her. She didn't see through him because she didn't want his help. Well, not only because of that. It was also because she knew him, could see him, and he didn't like it.

He had a persona to maintain. An important one. The moment his parents realised he felt responsible for looking after them, they'd stop him from doing so. The moment his mother saw that he'd seen another future for himself because of the fake relationship with Alexa, she'd do anything she could for him to have it.

But he couldn't have it. It wasn't compatible with living at home, helping his father around the house, spending time with his mother. If Alexa saw through him, she might see the things he didn't want anyone knowing, too. What if she mentioned it to his mother? To his father? And just because she wasn't using him now didn't mean she never would. Look at what his friends had done. His cousins.

They pretended to spend time with him, be his friend, but they only wanted things. Money, free food, help with an event. It was predictable in its consistency. As predictable as his ability to fall for it. Because they needed him.

He had reasons to stay away from Alexa. To not give in to the pull he felt between them. Good reasons. Professional *and* personal reasons. He only had one reason to see her: he had to get Cherise to work for him.

One more reason, a voice in his head reminded him. He almost groaned.

Yes, he had one more reason to see her. He was also supposed to be in a relationship with her.

Chapter 10

A fortnight later Alexa arrived at the Institute early, ready to get the first day of the course over with. Perhaps not a winning attitude, but the best one she could muster under the circumstances. She'd been to the doctor the day before for her thirteen-week appointment. Apparently, she'd been blessed with twins.

It did not seem like a blessing at that moment.

She'd known it was a possibility, of course. She'd read many articles about fertility treatments; her doctor had pretty much repeated the information to her verbatim. But she hadn't once considered that *she'd* have twins. Twins weren't for someone who needed to find a chef for her business so it wouldn't fail or be vulnerable to attacks by a sibling or for someone who didn't know how to raise one child, let alone two. *Two!* What had she done to deserve this?

Well, a voice in her brain said, quite reasonably, *you're at odds with your family. You're pretending to date a man and lying to the people you care about. Your only friend isn't talking to you because of the lie, and you refuse to tell her the truth. You also haven't told her you're pregnant—with twins—and you've pushed away anyone who could possibly come to care about you.*

It was a long list of her flaws. Surprisingly long, considering her own head had provided them. Although that the list was there at all wasn't a surprise. She wasn't perfect. The fact that she was prickly, bull-headed, and stubborn wasn't news. But since those characteristics had helped her survive her family and build her business, she could see the good in them, too.

So maybe twins were her punishment for her irreverence.

Not that her children were a punishment. Of course not.

'Sorry,' she murmured to them. 'I'm just surprised. And worried. What if I'm not a good mother to you? There are two of you now, so I'll be screwing up twice as much.'

She let out a huge breath, and sipped the herbal tea she'd bought before she'd left for the Institute. The warmth of it gave her some much-needed comfort. The rap on her window did not—nor did seeing who it was.

She opened the window. 'I'll be sending you my hospital bills.'

Benjamin gave her a half-smile, almost as if he expected her to give him a hard time. Almost as if he liked it. 'For what?'

'My heart attack.'

She grabbed her things, closed the window, and got out of the car. He hadn't moved far away, so when she turned, she found herself in his bubble. His musky scent didn't make her nauseous, as she'd expected it to, since it was in the window of her morning illness time. Maybe because her other body parts had woken up and decided to respond to it.

When she'd read that pregnancy would make her more…sensitive, she'd laughed. She hadn't been sensitive to anyone in such a long time. She couldn't even remember who the last person she'd been sensitive to was. And yet what she was feeling now was anything but amusement. She was incredibly aware of the smell of him. Incredibly aware of his body only centimetres from hers.

He looked delicious in his black T-shirt and jeans; his standard outfit in the kitchen, even when they'd been studying. Again, she noticed his shoulders, his chest. His body was muscular and strong and she wondered what it would be like if he scooped her into his arms. Would she feel light, even now, pregnant with twins? Would she be annoyed that he'd dare do it?

Or would she be amused, attracted? A playful

combination of both that would have her inching forward to kiss him…?

'Oh,' she said, and leaned back against the car.

'Are you okay?' he asked, moving even closer.

'Yeah. You're just…um…awfully close.'

He looked down, seemingly only noticing it now. His lips curved into a smile that had her heart racing. Not because it was sexy and sly. Of course not. It was because she knew what that slyness meant.

'Are you having a tough time because I'm close to you, Alexa?'

Oh, no. He was speaking in a low voice that was even more seductive than the smile.

'No.' She cleared her throat when the word came out huskily. 'I'm having a hard time because I'm pregnant. I need air and space and…stuff,' she finished lamely.

It was a pity. He'd believed her until she'd said that. Now he was smirking, which was quite annoying. But it gave her an idea.

'It's probably good that I'm close to you though. I'm so dizzy.'

She braced herself, then rested her head on his chest. The bracing didn't help. Not when his arms automatically went around her, holding her tighter against him. His heart thudded against her cheek, her own heart echoing. She closed her eyes as she realised her mistake.

'It's okay,' he said softly. 'I've got you.'

The words had a lump growing in her throat. She looked up, defiantly, she thought, because she didn't need him to *have* her. But she completely melted at his expression. It was soft and concerned and protective. Then he ran the back of his finger over her cheek, his gaze slipping to her lips, and she was melting, all right, but for the wrong reasons.

'I should…sit down.'

'Yeah,' he said shakily, stepping away.

He'd been as affected as she had.

She wrapped her hands around her cup. How was she still holding it? How hadn't she dumped it all over Benjamin? She began to walk over the strip of stones that separated the car park and the grass. They settled on the bench under a large tree metres away, and she sighed at the view of the vineyard. Bright green and dark green with the brown of the sand stretching out in front of them. At the very end of the vineyard rose a mountain; tall and solid, it enclosed the area and made everything seem private. With the quiet of the early morning settling over them, Alexa realised she hadn't come early to get the day over with as much as she'd come for this.

She could remember the days she'd done the same thing when she'd been studying. She'd still been living at home, paying her parents for the pleasure with the little she earned working part-time as a kitchen hand. She couldn't wait to escape to this beautiful place every weekday. Away from the attention her parents had lavished on her about her goals in life. Goals that weren't aligned with the ones they'd had for her life, which was why they had kept pushing.

Pushing and pushing, until she had been sure she would fall over from the stress of it.

'Is it better now?'

'Hmm?' She looked over at him. Blinked. 'Oh, the dizziness? Yes. Tons.'

He smiled, but apparently knew better than to comment. 'What distracted you just now?'

'I used to love coming here early. It's so beautiful, and peaceful.' She exhaled, forcing out the bad memories that came with the good ones.

'It really is something,' he agreed. Except he was looking at her. Intensely.

She cleared her throat. 'Is…um…is this why you're here so early?'

'You know what they say. Early bird gets the best view.'

'And maybe the station third from the front.' She laughed at his expression. 'We all know that one's the best.'

'Not true. Station seven is.'

'Station seven's left stove plate can't simmer.'

He laughed. 'How do you know this place so well?'

'You mean, how is it that you can't fool me?' She gave him an amused look. 'I pay attention.'

'Yeah,' he said softly. 'You do.'

Somehow, she didn't think he was referring to the stove. She sipped her tea instead of asking him, and nearly spat it out again when he said, 'You've grown.'

Swallowing it back down proved challenging.

'What do you mean?'

'Your stomach is bigger,' he said quickly. Which, of course, she'd known, but it was worth asking the question for that look of panic on his face. She hid her smile with another sip of tea.

'Yes. This happens when you're expecting.'

'It's only been two weeks. Is it supposed to grow so quickly?'

She laughed lightly. 'I hope so. But my doctor is happy with everything. I saw her yesterday. I guess growing fast is what happens when you're expecting two.'

Maybe a part of her had known he would react this way. Multiple blinks, mouth opening and closing, every muscle she could see frozen. He was in shock, and it felt like a vindication of her own reaction. It even made her want to laugh at her own reaction, which was probably as comical as his. No—most likely more. She was the one carrying the twins.

'Two? As in twins?'

She merely raised her brows in answer.

'Of course it's twins. Two are twins.' He stood, began to pace. 'You're sure?'

Though she hadn't quite anticipated *this* reaction, she nodded, eager to see where it would go.

'Man. Twins? *Twins.*' His long legs easily strode back and forth over the distance in front of the bench. 'I can't believe you're having two.'

'I couldn't either,' she said slowly, 'and I'll actually be the one giving birth to them. Raising them.'

It took him a few moments, but he seemed to

understand the implication. He stopped, gave her a sheepish smile.

'Sorry. I guess for a moment there I was…' He broke off, confusion crossing his face. 'I don't know what I was doing.'

'Maybe you imagined what it would be like if we really were dating,' she offered. 'Think about it. You started dating a woman who was pregnant, something you didn't sign up for, but you're too good a guy to let that keep you from developing a relationship with her. So, hey, maybe you can be a father to one kid if you liked one another enough. But two?' She gave a slight shake of the head. 'That would freak anyone out.'

'Even you?'

She laughed. It sounded a little deranged even to her own ears. Not that that kept her from answering.

'I always wanted a family. A good one, I mean. I realised about a year ago that I could only create that for myself. I couldn't rely on my own family for that.' She stared at that green in the distance, letting herself speak. She needed to say it out loud. 'I thought someday I'd have another. I'd teach them to cherish one another. To be each other's best friend, not competition. Not like my relationship with Lee. They would be different, how I dreamt siblings would be—always there for each other, so they would always know love.'

She rested her hands on her stomach. On the two lives growing there.

'But I would have time between them. Two right away? It's scary. What if I'm not cut out for this?'

She exhaled sharply; shook her head sharply. Now wasn't the time to have a breakdown. She'd only found out about the twins the day before, and clearly she needed to process. But she wouldn't do it now, in front of him. Well, *more* in front of him than she already had done. She wouldn't say anything about her fear of her restaurant failing. Or failing the people who relied on her there. Less because she felt it—although she did—and more because she knew he'd feel sorry for her. Based on his expression now, he already did. And her pregnancy didn't even involve him.

She inhaled now. Offered him a smile. 'But no, I'm not freaking out.'

He smiled back, because she was vulnerability wrapped up in fire and he wanted to burn himself so badly. He couldn't help it. The combination of her traits—traits that were polar opposites in everyone but her, that made her who she was—was so appealing. Fascinating. Intriguing.

Even as he thought it, he shook his head. How could he find her appealing? Fascinating? Intriguing? He'd just thought—seconds ago—that she was vulnerable. Vulnerability meant she would need someone. It put her in the perfect position to use someone. And that someone couldn't be him.

Mainly because something inside him, *everything* inside him, wanted it to be him.

He'd been trained for this, hadn't he? He'd spent years managing his mother's vulnerabilities. Not that they needed to be managed, he thought with a frown. His mother's pain wasn't a problem he needed to solve; he knew that. It was just… He'd had to manage his reaction to it. He had to be the person she needed during her bad times, which meant he couldn't take over and demand she do what he wanted her to, no matter how strong the urge. He had to support her without overwhelming her. It was the hardest thing he'd ever done. But he'd done it. He was good at it. Maybe that was why he was so attracted to Alexa— he could be good at managing himself with her, too.

'Good thing,' he replied, unwilling, or maybe unable, to dive into the mess of his thoughts. 'If you were freaking out about it, I wouldn't be able to reassure you.'

She gave him a bland look. He chuckled.

'There's nothing wrong with accepting reassurance.'

'But I don't need to,' she said, voice full of emotion, though she was desperately trying to control it, 'because I'm not freaking out.'

'A logical reaction to your news.'

'Hmm.'

'Not freaking out. Who would freak out, finding out they were going to have two children when they were expecting one?' He sat down beside her. 'I'm going to be honest with you: you don't have to worry about being a bad mother. There's no way.'

He wanted to reach out and take her hand, but it

felt too intimate. Then he did it anyway, because his gut told him to and he wasn't going to think about where that gut feeling was coming from.

'It's okay to feel jolted by this. I think anyone would. But your reaction now doesn't mean you'll be a bad mother.'

'I didn't think…' She broke off. Looked at him. 'I did.'

He smiled. 'I know. But you're strong-minded. Kind when it counts. Resilient. You'll get through having two.'

'You sound sure about that.'

'I am. You've built a restaurant from the ground up, Alexa. It's successful because of you. Surely raising two kids can't be much harder.'

He winked at her, and she smiled despite the emotion running wild over her face. Then it disappeared.

'What did I say?'

'Nothing. You were doing a perfectly adequate job of comforting me.'

He chuckled. 'As long as it was adequate.'

'Thank you.'

She squeezed his hand. Then, without warning, she leaned forward and kissed him. It was over before he could react, the only evidence it had happened the tingling at his lips.

She stood. 'You can't see that I'm pregnant, can you? I mean, I know *you* can, but as someone who didn't know?'

He opened his mouth. Closed it. Lowered his eyes because what else could he do? He tried to focus on her question. What had she asked him? Oh, yes, her clothes.

She was wearing… He didn't quite know what. It was a brightly coloured piece of material that was draped over her front from left to right. It did wonders for her cleavage, and he had to wrench his gaze away to answer her question. The material hung loosely over her stomach, and, paired with her tights and trainers, made her look both chic and comfortable. And not pregnant.

'You can't tell. It's loose enough that if I didn't know you were pregnant, I'd think…'

He broke off, but it was too late.

'You'd think what?'

He shook his head.

'You'd better say it, Foster.'

He shook his head again, this time more vehemently.

'You're saying that if people didn't know I was pregnant they'd think I was putting on weight?'

'I did *not* say that.'

'Only because you thought better of it.'

But her chest was shaking, and soon, sound joined.

'You think this is funny?' he asked.

'*You're* funny.'

'Wow. Thanks.'

She shrugged. Patted him on the shoulder. 'I appreciate that you wanted to preserve my feelings. But honestly, I don't care what people think of my body. As long as I feel good and everything works like it's supposed to, weight isn't important to me.'

He opened his mouth, then closed it when he realised he had nothing to add to that. It was a healthy way to think of the body, and, because he knew how prevalent weight-watching was in their culture, very enlightened.

'Yeah,' he said. 'You don't have to worry about being a mother, Alexa. You'll do fine.'

Her surprised look made the compliment well worth it.

Chapter 11

He'd been cooking his entire life. It started because he wanted to be exactly like his father when he was younger. It continued because he wanted to make his parents' lives easier after his mother's diagnosis. She couldn't work at his father's business for periods of time, and during those periods his father had been overwhelmed at work. At least until he realised a temp could solve his problems. In any case, Benjamin had taken the opportunity before his father had realised that to make himself useful in the kitchen at home.

He hadn't known much at that point, and dinner had often been some form of a sandwich. Then he'd moved on to pasta, which had seemed doable for a boy under ten. He began to study his father more seriously, helping with the harder tasks. By the time he was a teenager, he could fry a steak with the best of them. Soon after, he was adding sauces and presenting meals he saw on the cooking shows he'd come to love. When he had to decide what he wanted to do with his life, it seemed natural to go into professional cooking.

Except he didn't get into culinary school the first year. Or the second, or third. Competition was steep, and he had nothing to give him an edge. He spent the years he wasn't cooking getting a degree in financial management, thinking he could at least help his father out if he couldn't have his dream. When he graduated, he'd pretty much given up on the Institute. Until his parents sat him down and told him he deserved to give it one more try if it truly was what he wanted to do with his life.

He spent the two years after that in kitchens of different restaurants, wherever would have him. Sometimes he got work as a kitchen assistant; sometimes he washed the dishes. But he always, always tried to learn from those in charge. And eventually, the fourth time he applied, he got into the Institute.

And not once in all that time, and during all those experiences, had he thought baking was for him.

Today proved that.

'I didn't realise the course was going to be about decorating,' he said casually.

Cherise was beside him, putting buttercream into several separate bowls so she could colour them for her rainbow cake.

'Yeah,' she said, 'I thought it would be fun. And, since it's the Institute's only short course, it worked.' She looked at him. 'Are you having trouble?'

'Not at all.'

He'd already coloured his buttercream, which he knew would be the easiest part of his day. He hadn't done anything more than that because it would have entailed showing his weaknesses, and he preferred not to parade those if he could help it.

Cherise smiled. 'This isn't a test to see whether you can decorate a cake. I'm aware you probably don't need those skills at the restaurant.'

He took a beat, then realised it was best to be honest. 'It's not that I don't need the skills. It's that I don't have them, no matter how hard I try.'

Her smile widened. 'Well, then, today should be fun for you.'

'Not sure that's the word I'd use.'

She laughed and her focus went back to her cake. He sighed and did the same with his. But not before he sneaked a look at Alexa, who stood on the other side of Cherise. She was already on the second layer of her cake, and looked as comfortable with the task as she did with any other. It was part of the problem he'd had with her when they were studying together. Nothing seemed to faze her. No task, no matter how ridiculous, pulled the rug out from under her.

Back then, he hadn't appreciated how easily she found everything. It had simply seemed unfair that she would have skill with everything in the kitchen.

Now, at least, he could admire that skill. Except he saw that Cherise was admiring it, too.

It frustrated him, almost as much as it had in the past—except now feelings were creeping in.

He tried to tell himself he was just a sucker who couldn't resist someone who needed his help. It was clear Alexa did, even if she didn't think so. And he could easily be like her brother, using his vulnerabilities, his desires, to get what she wanted.

A voice in his head told him he had it all wrong. He didn't listen, instead focusing on getting his cake decorated as best he could. It took much more concentration and precision than he would have liked, but when he was done, he was proud of what he'd created.

'Nice job,' Cherise commented.

'Thanks.' He wiped his forehead with an arm. 'It was hard work.'

She laughed. 'Worth it though, don't you think, Alexa?'

Alexa peered past Cherise, appraising his cake before looking at him. 'It looks good.'

That's it. That's all she said. There was no judgement, no praise. Just an honest statement and yet somehow, it made him mad. He was sure she'd decorated her cake with a fraction of the effort he had put into his own. And now she had the cheek to tell him his looked good?

He wasn't being logical. A part of him recognised it. But he leaned into the irrationality of his thoughts, letting it fuel him for the rest of the day. He worked through lunch, though he knew it was silly, considering he was there to get to know Cherise. As far as he could tell, though, it seemed as if Cherise was more interested in chatting with him during their working sessions. Alexa was oddly quiet, though when he glanced out of the window during lunch, he saw her and Cherise laughing about something.

He gritted his teeth, did what he had to do, and at the earliest moment he could he walked out of the doors. Seconds later, footsteps followed him.

'Hey,' Alexa said. 'Wait up.'

He kept walking.

'Benjamin,' she said, her voice exasperated. 'I'm pregnant. There are two people growing inside me. Please don't make me run after you.'

That forced him to slow down, but he didn't stop. He was afraid of what would happen if he stopped. He was well aware he was in a mood. He also knew his mood was tied up in her, in both good and bad ways, except he couldn't discern between the two at the moment. It didn't bode well for their conversation. So when she caught up with him, he decided to stay quiet.

'Cherise wanted to know what's wrong with you.' Alexa rubbed her stomach. 'She asked me like she expected me to know. But I didn't know, and I had to pretend to, because we're together and when you're in a mood, apparently, I need to be able to explain that.'

'What did you say?' he couldn't help but ask.

'That you're competitive. And a perfectionist.

When you put the two together, it can be a damning combination.'

'So you bad-mouthed me.'

'Not entirely,' she said easily, ignoring his bad temper. 'I also said it makes you a hell of an entrepreneur. You want to give your patrons the best. It makes you serious, disagreeable perhaps, but it also makes you one of the best people she could work for.'

He took several moments to reply. Even then, he could only manage a, 'Why?'

'Because it's true.' She shrugged. 'Because I don't blame you for a being a good chef and leader.'

He narrowed his eyes. 'Sounds like you're implying something.'

'Why would I?' she asked sarcastically. 'It's not like I gave you a compliment, spoke highly and fairly about you to a potential employee, and you're choosing to focus on the negative in all that.'

All fair points and, consistent with his mood, that annoyed him. He bit down on his tongue. After a few seconds, she sighed.

'Look, I get that you're in competition mode, or whatever, but I'm not going to keep defending you for acting boorish. If you want Cherise to get to know you, you should show her who you are. Unless, of course, you *are* boorish, and the man who was kind to me this morning and this entire time actually doesn't exist.'

She sounded tired, defeated, and his heart turned. But he couldn't tell her that he was going through something. How could he? He didn't understand it himself. It had to do with her, and with him not trusting himself around her, and that sounded like…like admitting that he was still the same fool who had let the people in his past take advantage of him.

'Yeah, I thought I might have been fooling myself,' she said softly. She closed her eyes before he could see any emotion. When she opened them again, they were unreadable. 'Cherise asked if we'd be interested in having a drink with her after work. I said yes, but now I'm not so sure.'

She turned on her heel. It took him a beat before he could move after her.

'You're not going to go?'

'No, I'm going.' She didn't stop walking when he fell into step beside her. 'I'm just not speaking for you. If you want to go, you can tell her yourself.'

It took him all of the way back to Cherise to decide that he would be going, too. In the mood he was in, heaven had better help him.

'You're not drinking?'

'Oh. Um…no.' Alexa had prepared for this in the car. But there was something about actually being asked about her pregnancy, even indirectly, that made her freeze up. Probably the fact that she had to lie. 'I'm driving.'

'One drink wouldn't hurt,' Cherise said kindly.

There was nothing Alexa wanted less than kindness at that moment.

'She's a lightweight,' Benjamin cut in. 'One drink

and she's about as tipsy as I am after four. So, to answer your question—one drink *would* hurt.'

If she went by Benjamin's tone, it wasn't kindness
that inspired his words. But it wasn't malice either,
and he was saving her from having to think about
a more intricate lie. She gave him a half-smile in
thanks, but looked away before she could see whether
he smiled back. He was acting weird, and she didn't
want to be hurt by whatever mood he was in.

Because you're already hurt.

No, she told the inner voice. She wasn't hurt by
Benjamin's attitude. So what if he was acting like
the old Benjamin? The one who was reluctant and
competitive and reminded her more of her brother
than of the person she was beginning to think of as
more than an acquaintance?

If anything, the problem was that she had begun
to think of him in a friendly manner. He wasn't her
friend—she wouldn't make that mistake—but she'd
confided in him and kissed him. No wonder she was
feeling a little out of sorts now that he was acting
like someone she hadn't confided in or kissed. She
should have anticipated it, and she hadn't, and that
was partly why she was feeling this way.

Benjamin had always been so competitive in
class. She hadn't known him before, so she'd assumed he was just a competitive person. Working
with her brother, stealing her head chef... Those
things seemed to prove it. Then he'd pretended to
be her boyfriend in front of Lee. She'd seen him
with his mother, he'd offered to give her Cherise...

Those things didn't seem like a person who was inherently competitive, but simply someone who liked competition.

There was nothing wrong with that. Hell, she was even willing to be in the competition with him. But that was before today had happened. Before she'd seen him watching her as she worked and she could all but feel the frustration radiating off him. He glanced at her so many times that she knew he was comparing. It was common sense as much as it was experience; she'd spent her entire childhood knowing what that comparison looked like. Lee had done it to her. And she had no desire, none, to be a basis of comparison again.

That was what this empty feeling in her chest was. Annoyance that Benjamin saw her as someone to beat. Someone to be better than. She didn't think better or worse had anything to do with Cherise's choice; it would be the person Cherise got along with best. Except it was clear Benjamin didn't see it that way. So she was annoyed. Maybe a little disappointed. But that was it.

'He's right,' she said with a quick smile. 'I've never been able to hold my alcohol well.'

'Fortunately we don't have that in common,' Cherise said, lifting the glass the bartender set in front of her. She downed it, hissing as she slammed the glass back on the counter. 'I can drink with the best of them.' She grinned. 'I probably shouldn't tell potential employers that.'

'Why not?' Benjamin asked. 'It's not likely we wouldn't find out.'

'I don't intend on drinking on the job. Or coming in hungover.'

'The longer you spend working with us, the higher the possibility of a fun night out. Or some kind of event.' Benjamin shrugged. 'We would have found out during the second or third drinking game of the night.'

'You play drinking games with your staff?'

Benjamin raised his glass and tilted it to her. 'We're not of the belief that there should be all work and no play.'

'That happens at Infinity, too, Alexa?'

'Oh, no,' Alexa said with a shake of her head. 'I let my employees have their fun on their own time. Making sure they have that time is more of a priority to me.'

'What about team morale?' Benjamin asked her.

'Created through good pay cheques and a healthy working environment.' She waited a beat. 'In the Rough should try it.'

'Ooh,' Cherise said with a smile. 'Harsh.'

'And probably undeserved.' Alexa smiled back, but didn't look at Benjamin.

'Probably?' he said.

She directed the smile at him, but it wasn't genuine. Nor was the teasing tone of his voice.

'You guys are really cute together,' Cherise said. 'You've never thought about one big business?'

'Oh, no,' she said at the same time Benjamin chuckled with a shake of his head.

'Why not?' Cherise asked. 'You're both skilled. Can you imagine what you could create together?'

'You're only saying this because we're both so wonderful and you'd rather not choose,' Alexa teased, trying to ease the tension that was settling in her stomach. 'If we joined forces you would be our second in command, and you're drunk on the prospect of such power.'

'Well, you're not wrong.'

They laughed. The tension unfurled. Then there was a tap on the microphone. They turned to a small stage at the opposite end of the room as a tall woman with tattoos up and down her arms cleared her throat.

'Thank you all for coming to Wild Acorn tonight.'

There were cheers from who Alexa assumed were regulars. They sat at a table in the front, all still fairly formally dressed as though they'd come straight from work. She could see that happening. The bar was down a quiet road in Somerset West near the Institute, and they'd followed Cherise to get there. There was no way they would have found it by themselves, and yet it seemed popular.

'As most of you know, tonight is karaoke night—' she paused for another round of cheers '—and for those of you who don't, I thought I'd go over the rules.'

'There are rules for karaoke?' Alexa said under her breath.

'One,' the lady continued, seemingly answering

Alexa, 'you have to take this seriously. No making anyone uncomfortable with a bad rendition of some famous ballad.' There was a beat. 'Just kidding! The only rule is that you have fun. Sing from the heart, dance if you will, and the best performer tonight has their tab taken care of.'

'Nice prize,' Benjamin commented. He looked at Cherise. 'Did you bring us here thinking you could make us sing?'

His smile faded when she answered, 'Hoping to.' She looked from Benjamin to Alexa. 'Who's going to go first?'

Chapter 12

'I feel like I shouldn't be watching this.' He was about to reply, but Cherise's voiced cracked on a high note and he winced instead. Alexa looked at him with a wrinkled nose. 'Yeah, we definitely shouldn't be watching this.'

'It's a bar. Where are we going to go?'

'You're saying we're trapped.' She took a long sip from her drink, studying Cherise as she executed some dance moves. 'I didn't think we would see how Cherise responds in a disaster at such an early stage.'

'And she responds—' he waited for Cherise to finish moonwalking '—poorly, apparently.'

Alexa gave a laugh. It wasn't the first time she'd done it that evening, but it sounded like her first genuine one. He couldn't be critical of it, of her, when he knew he was the reason she wasn't enjoying herself. And he felt terrible because of it.

With each sip of alcohol, he'd gained clarity. By the end of his second glass, he'd realised he was conflating his insecurities about trusting himself with his insecurities about trusting Alexa. He didn't know if she was fooling him; he didn't know if he could trust his gut when it told him she wasn't. His third glass told him he had been a jerk today, trying to figure it out. He started ordering water instead of alcohol, and was now wondering what the best way was to apologise.

'Look, Alexa—'

'Your turn!' she exclaimed, cutting him off.

He narrowed his eyes. 'I didn't say I was going to go up there.'

'You didn't say you weren't either.' She lifted a shoulder. 'I'm not the one asking you to go on stage.'

She tilted her head, gesturing to Cherise, who was eagerly waving at them.

'That wave could be for you, too.'

'It could,' she acknowledged, 'but since you're volunteering…'

'I'm not—'

In a movement quicker than he could have defended himself against, she stuck a hand underneath his arm and poked his armpit. Hard. The result was both surprise and amusement—he'd always been ticklish there. It was also a hand which popped into the sky, making it seem as though he were volunteering.

'Clever.' He stood, walked until he was so close to her he could smell the mint on her breath from her virgin mojito. 'But I'm clever, too.'

She tilted her head up, her eyes cool. 'Not everything is a competition.'

'No, it's not.' He lowered slightly, bringing their faces close. 'This isn't me competing. It's getting revenge.'

'Revenge?'

'You're going to do this with me.'

She smiled. It was mocking and unconcerned and—though he had no idea how or why—incredibly sexy.

'Oh, no, Benjamin, I will not be doing this with you.'

'Except—' he lifted a hand and tucked a stray curl behind her ear '—you are. Otherwise this would seem like a seduction to anyone looking.'

She pressed up on her toes, bringing their faces closer. 'Isn't it?'

'No.' It was though. And somehow he was being seduced, too. 'It's a request to do a duet.'

'I'm not doing a duet.'

'Not even for your fake boyfriend?'

Her lips parted. He brushed a thumb over it. When hot air touched his skin, he inhaled sharply. Then exhaled, because it felt as though he'd inhaled a copious amount of desire for her, too. His brain scrambled trying to remember what he'd intended when he stood up. To make it seem as if he was asking her to join him? To touch her and remind himself that she was the person she seemed to be, independent and not manipulative and certainly not who his fears made her out to be?

She took his hand, pulled it away from her face. 'This isn't going to happen.' The statement was ambiguous enough that it made him wonder what she was talking about until she clarified. 'I'm not making a fool of myself up there.'

He swallowed. Right. Of course she was talking about the singing and not…whatever had just happened.

'It'll be fun.'

'How?'

'We'll sing together. We'll both sing poorly together, I mean.'

'Yet another reason not to do it.'

'We're not auditioning for a singing competition,' he said, frustrated now. 'We're only singing.'

'No, I meant that if you sing badly, I refuse to sing with you.' She stood, emptying her glass as she did. 'I will not let my perfect soprano be tarnished by you.'

He couldn't even argue with that since he'd said he sang poorly. Then he realised she was moving to the stage, and he blinked. Why had she been arguing with him if she intended on singing? Was he really that awful that she didn't want to be on stage with him?

Yes, probably, he thought, sitting back down and offering Cherise a weak smile when she joined him. He'd been terrible to Alexa all day—save for that morning. But that morning had felt as though they were in a bubble, and once things had got real, the bubble had popped and he...

He'd fallen hard to the ground while Alexa somehow stayed afloat, looking down at him in pity. Disappointment. Could he even blame her?

'I thought you were going to go up with her.'

'Me, too.'

'Your seduction didn't work?' Cherise gave him a sly grin. He smiled back weakly.

'Apparently not. I'm going to have to work on it.'

'Probably,' she said, bringing her beer to her lips. 'She doesn't seem like the type of person to fall for the usual stuff. She's tougher, but that kind of makes it mean more, in my opinion.'

He thought about it as he turned to the stage, watching as Alexa waited for the music to play. A couple of guys in the front were eyeing her in appreciation, and he had the absurd urge to get up and shield her from their view. But that made no sense, the desire less so, and instead he kept looking at Alexa.

She looked comfortable there, her clothing still strange, still chic. She'd tied her hair up again, but it was higher than it had been in the morning, piled onto the top of her head as if she'd put it there and forgotten about it. The waves refused to be tamed that way, though, and they fell over her forehead, created the shortest and strangest fringe he'd ever seen. It was also the cutest. Hell, she was cute. And sexy, and enticing, and he was pretty sure he had a problem.

Then she started to sing and he stopped thinking about that altogether.

Her voice was smooth and clear. Perfectly pitched on the higher notes; soulfully deep on the lower notes. She swayed in time to the beat, slowly, smiling when the lyrics were saucy or snarky.

'You've got to be kidding me,' Cherise said somewhere halfway into the song. 'She sings like it's what she does for a living.'

He agreed, but he was too enamoured to respond. He couldn't take his eyes off her, his ears thanked him profusely, and his mind was incredibly glad he hadn't spoiled this with his own voice, which was comparable to a cat's on a good day. When she was done, the entire room exploded with applause. Everyone was looking at her in appreciation now. She smiled brightly, happily, and he couldn't quite believe she was the same woman who could skin him and lay the spoils on the floor as she walked over them.

Damn if that brightness, that happiness didn't draw him in as much as her sharp wit.

'Stop looking at me like that,' Alexa said as soon as Cherise got into the taxi she'd called. Cherise was having her brother use her spare key to pick up her car, since she wasn't in any condition to drive. 'It's unnerving.'

'I just… I can't believe you've been hiding that voice away.'

'I wasn't hiding it away.' She hoped to heaven her skin wasn't glowing at the compliment the way her stupid heart was. 'It's never come up. Why would I bring it up?'

'Because it sounded like *that*?' He gestured with a thumb to the bar behind them. 'I'm still trying to figure out how you managed to do that.'

'Easy. I opened my mouth, and instead of speaking, I sang.'

'Like an angel.' She laughed. 'I'm not even mad you're being snarky,' he said, his voice filled with wonder. 'You should be singing.'

'Do you know,' she said after a moment, 'I'm really good at maths? I scored in the top five per cent of the province in my final year of school. I had a couple of bursaries to study maths that were generous.'

She didn't mention that her parents had applied for all those bursaries. They'd been so disappointed when she'd chosen not to take any of them that they hadn't even cared that she'd chosen business management instead. Well, they had cared. If they hadn't, she would have gone to culinary school from the beginning.

'Congratulations?' Benjamin's voice interrupted her thoughts.

She laughed. 'My point is that just because I'm good at something doesn't mean I want to do it for a living. I love what I do. I love the challenge of running a restaurant. I love working with my chefs to make efficient meals that are delicious and new and...' She broke off, feeling heat spread over her cheeks. 'Anyway. I won't be leaving to sing any time soon.'

'A pity,' he said with a small smile. 'But I suppose, since you're good at running a business, too, the world isn't completely missing out on your talents.'

Somehow, it didn't feel like a compliment.

'I should get going. The ride back home is long.'

'Yeah.'

But he didn't let her pass him, and, since he was standing in front of her, she kind of needed him to.

'Benjamin—'

'Is there anything you aren't good at?'

And there it was.

There isn't one thing you're bad at. Nothing. You do everything well. It's annoying.

Exhausting, too, she'd wanted to tell her brother. She wouldn't call it lucky that she was good at the things her parents thought she should be good at. It was half luck, half hard work, and all exhaustion. Her parents had come to expect her to be good at everything, so she didn't think she could fail. If she did, they would care for her even less than they already did. As a kid, she couldn't bear the thought of it.

That was the one thing she wasn't good at: accepting that her family wasn't what she wanted them to be. She tried and tried to make her parents proud, but nothing she did would ever be enough. She had tried with Lee, too, because he was the only one who would understand how their parents' pressure could become unbearable. But he'd had no interest. For every outreached hand was a slap in the form of a record she'd set that he'd broken, or a mark of hers that he'd beaten. When he'd bought the building out from under her she'd finally decided to stop reaching out her hand, and hoped it would mean no more slapping.

Except it still came. And apparently through proxies now, too.

'I should really get home.'

She moved past him but he caught her wrist. She looked at him.

'You're not going to answer?'

'What would you like me to say?' She was proud of the stiffness in her voice. It meant the thickness in her throat hadn't tainted her speaking. 'Yes, I'm good at everything. Except making rational decisions, like when I pretended you were my boyfriend. If I hadn't, we wouldn't be in this position. I wouldn't be in this position.'

He frowned, and let go of her arm. 'I'm sorry. I didn't mean to…' He exhaled. 'I'm sorry,' he said again.

'Okay.' She swallowed. 'Now can I leave?'

Chapter 13

He wanted to say sorry. For acting like a jerk the day before; for making those assumptions the night before. He arrived at the Institute early in the hope of finding a moment to talk with her again before the course started. No such luck. Which wasn't a problem—until the start of the class came and both Alexa and Cherise weren't there. Cherise rushed in ten minutes late, looking like hell.

'Sorry,' she muttered. 'My car broke down on the way. And I probably drank too much last night, made a fool of myself, and I promise you it won't happen again.'

'Sorry to hear about the car,' he said. 'About last night... You don't have to apologise. You're not working for us yet.'

'But I would like to, and I seem to have handed you reasons not to hire me.'

He smiled. 'It's nice to know you actually want this.'

'I really do.' She smiled, but it faded almost immediately. 'Although I think I spoilt my chances with Alexa. I'm pretty sure I'm the reason she's sick.'

'She's sick?'

'Yeah.' She gave him a strange look. 'She didn't tell you?'

'No.' When he realised why she was so surprised, he cleared his throat. 'We're supposed to have a date after this today. I think maybe she didn't want to tell me in case I cancelled.'

'Oh, that's so sweet,' Cherise said. 'You guys are cute.'

'Thanks.'

They fell into silence as the instructor began to guide them in a brand-new decorating nightmare. He couldn't really focus. He was too busy thinking about Alexa. He stumbled his way through the class, but that was pretty usual for him. He did notice that Cherise's hangover, and the rough morning she'd had, hadn't affected her concentration. She did the work perfectly, patiently, without one mistake. Which told him she wouldn't bring personal problems into the workplace. He was almost thankful for the night they'd had before.

She seemed forgiving of his lack of decorating skills, and by the end of it he knew their one-on-one time had done wonders for their professional working relationship. He even suspected that he might have had an edge over Alexa. It made him feel guilty. Not that he had any reason to feel guilty. He hadn't orchestrated her sickness, had he? He hadn't done anything so that he could spend time with Cherise while Alexa stayed home, sick, probably unable to breathe, her nose blocked, chest phlegmy…

He grunted, got into his car, and started it. Then he grunted again, because he already knew where he was going to, even before he started driving to the pharmacy. When he got there, he started grabbing things that usually helped him when he was feeling under the weather. He walked past an aisle, paused, looked down it. Saw a bunch of pregnancy and maternity things. Vitamins, baby bottles. He looked at the things in his hands. She probably couldn't use any of this, being pregnant. He went back to the pharmacist, and got fewer things. Bought ingredients to make some good chicken soup. Some fresh bread, too.

None of that made it easier when he was finally in front of her door. He felt as though he was intruding on her space. She obviously didn't want him to know she was sick, or she would have told him. Now he was pitching up at her door, assuming that she wanted to see him? Especially after how he'd treated her the day before?

He took a deep breath and was brutally honest with himself. He'd told himself guilt was the reason he was there. Maybe it was, but not only because he got to spend time with Cherise when Alexa couldn't.

No, it was redemption. For how he had treated her the day before. To ease his conscience, or to make it up to her, he didn't know. Either way, he was there, and he was going to make sure she knew he wasn't all bad.

He knocked on the door. Again when he heard nothing inside. A long while later, he heard some shuffling. Then the door opened. He almost dropped everything in his hands.

'You're, um…you're…' He cleared his throat. He couldn't…point out what the problem was without telling her that he had looked at her chest. But not pointing it out meant he studiously had to avoid looking down. He gritted his teeth, then thought it might look intimidating and offered her a smile. 'You're okay,' he finished lamely.

She folded her arms. Doing so should have covered the flesh spilling out of the top of the loose nightgown she wore. Instead, because of the sheer generosity of her breasts, the movement pushed them together instead.

'What are you doing here?'

'I heard you're sick.'

'Yes.'

He frowned. 'I was sorry to hear that.'

'Thank you.'

He gestured to the bags in his hands. 'Do you think I could come in?'

'Why?'

'I…' Was he really this bad at showing he cared about something? 'I thought I'd make you some soup.'

She studied him, expression unreadable, though there were dark rings around her eyes. Seconds later, as if she knew he'd seen it, she sagged against the doorframe. 'It's a bad bout of nausea. I thought because things weren't so bad in my first trimester—' She shrugged. 'Apparently my babies hate me.'

'They don't hate you,' he said automatically.

'I appreciate that.' She exhaled slowly. 'You can come in. But you can't cook anything. I'm pretty sure I'd throw up if you did.' She cast a look at him. 'That's not a reflection on your cooking or anything.'

'Thanks,' he said dryly.

He followed her inside, closing the door behind him. He wasn't sure what to do now that his grand plan wouldn't work. Plus, seeing her like this was a distraction. She'd gone back to the sofa, curled up and closed her eyes, as if he weren't in her space. And he shouldn't have been.

There wasn't much he could do about morning sickness. With a cold or flu he could ply her with medication, encourage her to sleep. But constant nausea? Enough that she couldn't come in to work? What was he supposed to do about that?

Since she wasn't looking, he asked the internet that question. Then he wandered into her kitchen, set down the things he'd bought, and looked in her cupboards. They were meticulously packed. He couldn't see what order they were in, but they were definitely in order. Same with the fridge. He tried not to disturb anything as he looked for what the internet suggested. Minutes later, he walked into the kitchen, set the tea on the coffee table and crouched down in front of her.

'Alexa?' She opened one eye. Somehow, she managed a glare with it. He resisted his smile. 'Have you eaten anything today?'

'Some toast this morning.'

'This morning?'

'I haven't really had the energy for much.'

'Okay.' He frowned. 'Well, the internet said something bland would do you good.'

'Sounds amazing.'

He chuckled softly. 'How about some brown rice? Plain avocado? Or toast with peanut butter and banana? Broth?'

Her other eye opened. 'Sounds like you're trying to get nutrients into me.'

'They said it would be best if what you ate had nutrients in it.'

'They?'

He scratched the back of his head when his skin began to prickle with heat. 'The internet.'

'You went on the internet for this?'

'Did any of what I offered sound appealing to you?' he asked instead of answering.

'The toast,' she replied after a moment. 'It's not the most appealing, but it's the easiest option, which we'll both be grateful for if I end up throwing it up.'

He appreciated her logic, but he would actually feel better if he could put some more effort into whatever he made her. To assuage the guilt, he told himself. For redemption, he added. Not because he cared enough to put more effort into it.

'On it. Also, I made you some ginger tea.'

'Did the internet tell you to do that?' She was teasing him, giving him a small smile to show it.

He offered her a hand. 'If you want me to help you sit up, you won't get the answer to that.'

'It would almost be worth it.'

But she took his hand and he helped her up. Her colour didn't look good, but that made sense since she was nauseous and hadn't eaten since the morning. He handed her the tea. Her fingers brushed his as she did, and for some bizarre reason a shiver went through him. Bizarre, because things were weird with them, and she was sick, and the only reason he was in her flat was because he felt guilty. He shouldn't feel attraction in this moment—or whatever it was that caused that shiver. It also had nothing to do with her cleavage, impressive and visible as it was. It was simply her, and how much she intrigued and confused him.

He exhaled, leaving her to the tea as he went to make her toast. It was quick work. When he handed it to her, he thought he'd head back to the kitchen, start making a broth even though she didn't seem to want it. But she said, 'Wait.'

He turned. 'Yeah?'

'You didn't make yourself anything?'

His mouth curved. 'Did I make myself some peanut butter and banana toast as well? No. Surprisingly.'

'No need to be smug about your ability to eat something other than this.' But her eyes were warm. 'Thank you.'

'You don't have to thank me.'

'Why not?'

She tore a small piece off the toast and put it into her mouth, looking at him expectantly.

'Oh…er… It wasn't a big deal.'

She chewed and finished. Swallowed. 'It is to me.'

There was a brief moment where they stared at one another before he realised he'd better look away if he wanted to keep his sanity. Although deep down he knew it wasn't his sanity he was worried about.

'Will you sit down?' she asked, looking down now, too.

'Do you want me to?'

'I wouldn't have asked if I didn't want you to.'

'Good point.' He smiled at the dry tone. 'I'll just grab myself something to drink.'

'Yeah, of course. Anything in the fridge is yours.'

He went to the kitchen, got himself a sparkling water, and went back to the lounge. It didn't even occur to him to dawdle, or delay long enough that she would be done with her meal. The opposite, in fact. He wanted to sit with her, talk to her, and he didn't know what it meant.

Or he did, but he preferred not to think about it.

When he got back, he saw her toast looked the same as it had when he left.

'Feel sick?'

'Not at the moment. I'm waiting to see how my

stomach's going to react to it.' She took a slice of banana off the toast and ate it. 'It seems cruel to me that someone who enjoys food as much as I do can't eat it.'

'But it hasn't been like this your entire pregnancy, you said?'

'No, it hasn't. I have been nauseous, but it's been pretty consistently in the mornings before work and the evenings after. I thought I was lucky.' She groaned. 'Turns out my body was lulling me into a false sense of security.'

'How has today been different?'

'You mean apart from the waves of nausea all day?' She tore off another piece of toast, but didn't eat it. Instead, she patted the seat next to her. He didn't even hesitate. Just obeyed. 'I've been throwing up more, though that seems consistent with being nauseous more, doesn't it? I've also been a little dizzier, but that could be because I haven't been eating.'

'You should have been.'

'I know,' she agreed, easily enough that he knew she wasn't feeling herself. 'But it seemed like a lot of energy to go to the kitchen and get something to eat when I could lie here.'

He studied her. Took a long drink of his water to make sure he really wanted to say what he thought he wanted to say. Sighed.

'Look, you can argue with me when you have energy for it later, okay?'

Her eyebrows rose. 'A promising start to a conversation.'

'It's concern.' He paused. 'You have to look after yourself, Alexa. That's how you're looking after your babies right now. By looking after yourself.'

Her hand went to her belly, before she brought it back to the toast. She put a piece in her mouth, then opened her palm as if to agree with him. Something in the gesture made her seem so vulnerable, he wanted to pull her into his arms and comfort her. Hell, there was a part of him that wanted to do that regardless of the vulnerability.

He settled for edging closer to her.

She deserved to have people to care about her. She deserved that she care about herself, which he thought she might struggle with. He had no proof, and he wouldn't dare ask, since he was already pushing his luck with their current conversation. But something about Alexa made him think that she put others ahead of herself. Even with her pregnancy. She was trying so hard to make things with Cherise work. Not for herself, he thought, but for her restaurant.

Part of that was because Lee had taught her she couldn't let her guard down. And yes, when he'd offered Victor Fourie that job, he'd shown her that, too. Now she was terrified of going on leave because she thought it would put all she'd worked for in jeopardy.

Someone who'd grown up as she had would hate that idea. They'd hate that it might result in failure, too. He couldn't imagine how much that would mess with someone's mind. He could, however, see that he'd contributed to her fears. That his question the night before, about her being good at everything, would add to that pressure. Which would explain how tense she'd got.

He would apologise for it. Not now. Now he had a different mission.

'You're going to have to take care of yourself when they're here, too,' he said quietly. 'It's the most important thing, your health. Not only because they need you to be healthy to take care of them.'

'What else is there?'

'Your happiness. It's going to be important to them. They'll want to see you living your life as you would have even if they weren't there. That means taking care of yourself, making sure you're as important in your life as they are.'

'You speak as if you know.'

'I…do.'

It felt a little like a betrayal, admitting that. But if he had to betray his mother—just a little—to make Alexa see she was as important as her children, then so be it. Hell, he reckoned his mother might even agree. She'd called him two days after that dinner with Alexa and told him she liked his new girlfriend.

'The baby situation is complicated,' Nina had said, 'but I can see why you couldn't move on without giving things with her a try. She's refreshing.'

'You're good at it,' Alexa said, piercing through the haze of memories.

'What?'

'Caring for people.'

The words hit him in the gut. 'I've had a lot of practice.'

'With your mom? Inference,' she said when he looked at her.

'I wouldn't say I took care of her.'

'I didn't say that you did. Only that you cared for her.'

He almost laughed at how she'd caught him out. He didn't because it wasn't funny.

'She needed a lot of support with the fibromyalgia.'

'Support can sometimes mean caring for them.'

'That's not what happened with my mom,' he said tersely.

'It was a compliment, Benjamin.' Her expression was a combination of bewilderment, kindness, and...hurt? Had he hurt her? But then she clarified. 'Speaking as someone who didn't have it all that much in her life, it's certainly a compliment.'

'I'm sorry.' He stared at the bottle in his hand. 'I seem to be apologising a lot to you these days.'

She shrugged. 'It's because I rub you up the wrong way. What?' she asked with a little laugh. 'You don't think I noticed? It's kind of hard not to.'

'To be fair, I think the reverse applies, too, and yet you don't seem to apologise nearly as often as I do.'

'I'm more irreverent.' She gave him a half-smile. 'I'm definitely less in touch with my emotions. I find them—' she wrinkled her nose '—inconvenient.'

He laughed, and some of the tension in his stomach dissipated. 'I'm not much more in touch with my emotions. They're inconvenient as hell, and it's easier to ignore them.'

'The apologies tell me you don't do the easier thing,' she pointed out. 'You might not be able to deal with them very well, but you feel them. It's more than I can say for myself.'

'And why's that?'

She heaved out a sigh. 'I don't know. No, no, I do,' she interrupted herself. 'Honestly, it's just… I guess ignoring them is what I'm used to. If I had felt every little thing when I was a kid, I wouldn't function nearly as well as I do today.'

She began to eat again, slowly, and he waited until she was done to ask the questions tumbling into his head. When she was done, she set down the remaining toast on the table. Then she moved closer to him. His heart thudded, but she didn't do anything else. Not one more thing, even though his body felt as if it was bracing for impact.

'Do you want to talk about it?' he asked hoarsely.

'I don't think so.' Her expression was uncertain when she met his eyes. 'Is that okay?'

'Of course. We don't have to talk about anything you don't want to.'

'I will, someday. It seems like a lot of effort to think about it now.'

She rested her head on his shoulder. He froze— but not for long. Slowly, so he wouldn't spook her, he lifted his arm. She immediately snuggled into his chest.

It was a good thing he was sitting, or the way his knees had gone weak would have taken him to the ground.

'Tell me what your day was like?' she asked. 'Was Cherise as hungover as she should have been after last night?'

Somehow, he managed to laugh. But as he told her about his day, it felt more natural, them sitting like this, talking. He was honest about how things had gone with Cherise, and she didn't seem upset about it. She asked him questions, laughed at his description of how terribly he'd done. He kept talking when she shifted onto her side, curling into much the same position he'd found her in. Except now she was curled into his side, then lying with her head on his lap. When she faltered he lowered his voice but kept talking, since it seemed to soothe her.

She was fast asleep shortly after, but he didn't get up as he should have. He stroked her hair, which was messy and somehow beautiful. He brushed her skin, bronze and smooth. He sat there, her warmth comforting something inside him. Much too long later, he took the dishes to the kitchen and began making her something to eat for when she got up. When he was done with that, he let himself out, but not without one last look in her direction.

She looked so peaceful, lying under the blanket he'd covered her with. His heart did something in his chest. Lurched, turned over, filled—he wasn't sure of the description. He only knew that seeing her, speaking her with her, caring for her…

It had changed him. Something had changed between them, too. He wondered if she would acknowledge it. He wondered if he would.

Chapter 14

She was feeling better the next day. She hadn't thrown up the toast Benjamin made her, and she'd slept through the entire night. It didn't seem normal to feel better when the day before she'd basically been knocked out. She supposed that was pregnancy. Or she hoped it was. If it wasn't, everyone in class, including her, was going to get more than they'd bargained for.

She had a nice long shower, got dressed, and went to the kitchen. Everything was in its place; it was as if Benjamin hadn't been there. And maybe he hadn't been. It seemed consistent with the state she'd been in the day before. Maybe she'd conjured him up, and he hadn't been sweet and patient and caring.

He hadn't made her laugh, held her, stayed with her until she'd fallen asleep.

Except when she opened her fridge she found a glass container with clear broth in it and a sticky note—she had no idea where he'd found one.

In case you're feeling up to it. B.

B. B was definitely Benjamin. She couldn't deny that he'd been there any more. Him leaving food for her meant she hadn't imagined he was sweet and patient and caring either. And if that was true, she had to believe that he'd made her laugh, held her, stayed with her as she'd fallen asleep. And he'd cooked. For her.

She took a long, deep breath as she removed the broth from the fridge and heated it up. But it didn't help, and she spent the entire time eating the flavourful liquid quietly sobbing. She was certain it was pregnancy hormones. Mostly. She supposed that was the problem.

But when was the last time someone in her life had checked on her when she was ill? When was the last time she'd let someone in her life do that?

Kenya would have, if Alexa let her. She had, once upon a time. When Kenya had started working at Infinity, something had clicked between them and they'd got along well. But Alexa had confined that relationship to the restaurant. She'd thought it best, easier, better for the restaurant. Now, after the entire Benjamin debacle, Alexa wondered if it was sim-

ply better for *her*. If she didn't go out with Kenya,
she wouldn't risk getting hurt. Except by doing that,
she'd hurt Kenya. And that, by some cruel twist of
fate, had hurt her, too.

She thought about it the entire drive to the Institute. Once she got there, she made sure there wasn't
a trace of her crying on her face. She had a feeling
Benjamin would pounce on it if he saw it. Which
turned out to be a fruitless concern anyway, since
he wasn't there.

'He must have what you had,' Cherise said with a
knowing look. Alexa murmured in agreement. She
had no choice but to. She'd told Cherise she had a
twenty-four-hour bug, which seemed like a half-
truth. But she knew that what she had wasn't conta-
gious. She also knew Benjamin well enough that she
could piece together what had happened.

When he'd told her about his day the night before,
he'd been excited, but restrained. That restraint had
come through most strongly when he was relaying
the more fun parts of the day, as if he'd felt bad. The
fact that he wasn't here told her he did feel bad. It
made her think the reason he was at her place last
night had been because he'd felt bad, too.

She set it aside as she spent the day with Cherise.
At one point, her prospective chef pointed out something Alexa was doing poorly. Alexa thanked Cherise, adjusted, and realised that, while it had helped
in some ways, it hadn't in others. So she coached
Cherise through doing it her way, and Cherise was
pleased with the ending.

'Maybe we can put it together and come up with a technique that could give us the best of both worlds.'

'Yeah, that would be great,' Cherise said with a bright smile.

She smiled back, and wondered if Benjamin had felt the same glow of appreciation at connecting with Cherise. Her heart skipped at the thought. Not at its content, but that she'd thought it at all. That she'd thought about him at all. It was dangerous; more so because the thoughts were accompanied by a soft, squishy feeling in her chest that she had no name for but made her feel warm and safe.

But how could she feel safe when even feeling that told her she was in danger? It was a conundrum, one she made no effort to clarify, even when she told herself to. She set it aside again, tried to focus on the day with Cherise. She felt worn at the end of it, her legs aching and her back, too, although it was much too early for her to be feeling that way. Then again, those were normal, non-pregnancy feelings after a long day. Today had seemed long, despite the fact that it was shorter than most days for her. Maybe being pregnant meant the length of what was long would change.

It didn't bode well for all she had to do before she went on maternity leave. Or should she even go on leave at all? She'd thought it would be a good idea to get to know her babies, but now it felt as if she was leaving her first baby, her restaurant, exposed. It was her responsibility to make sure it wasn't exposed. The fact that she hadn't meant that she'd...failed.

She drove home with that troubling thought racing in her mind. When she stopped, though, she didn't find herself at her home, but at In the Rough. It was the first time she'd been there since Lee had bought the building. She'd refused to go, on principle, despite her parents calling her stubborn. But the day that she'd wanted to show them her building, and they'd told Lee about it, had changed things for her. Their disappointment no longer hurt as much as it had. Or maybe it did hurt, but it didn't cripple her any more.

She still tried with them: a phone call every couple of weeks, a dinner once a month, telling them important news. But the truth was that she didn't want them in her life as much any more. Especially when they insisted on having Lee be part of the package.

Slowly, she climbed out of the car, staring up at the sign as she did. Black lettering flickered at her against the brick façade, courtesy of a faint white light outlining the letters. The front of the restaurant itself was all glass, allowing her to see the patrons laughing and enjoying themselves.

She took a breath and walked into the restaurant. She took in the dark wooden feel of the place, noted the red-haired barperson. It was a strange experience, seeing the place done, compared to the last time she'd been there. More so comparing it to the vision of what she'd had for the space. She'd executed the idea almost identically at Infinity, but she'd had to make adjustments because it didn't fit as well in her current space as it would have there.

The disappointment of it washed over her, and she took another breath, deeper this time, before she walked to the bar.

'Do you know where I can find Benjamin?'

The woman quirked her brow. 'Who are you?'

'Oh. I'm...er...'

She didn't know what Benjamin had told his people. Of course, she knew what Lee knew, but that didn't mean he'd announced it to his entire staff. If he hadn't, she didn't want to complicate things by telling his employee she was his girlfriend. But she also didn't want him to know she was there. He'd likely pull a runner, pretend he was really sick, and she couldn't tell him he was being a jerk.

'Is he here?'

'He might be.' She tilted her head. 'You look familiar.'

'I don't think so.'

'No, you do.' The woman came closer, limping slightly as she did. 'Have you been here before?'

'Definitely not.' She tried to cover it up when she realised how that sounded. 'I mean, I haven't had the chance.'

'You're missing out.'

She took a look at the full restaurant. It was barely six in the evening and already the vibe was jovial. The patrons were pretty much as she had imagined when she'd thought about the space. Benjamin had clearly turned it into *the* place though, since it was just about bouncing with energy.

She turned back to the barperson. 'Apparently so.'

'I think, considering it's you and considering you're my main competition, that's almost a compliment.'

She was rolling her eyes before she was even facing him fully.

'Hi.'

'Hi.'

She wasn't prepared for the way he leaned in to her, or the kiss he brushed on her cheek. It wasn't a sensual greeting in theory, but the heat of it seared through her body.

'You're feeling better?'

'Much.' She started to brush her hair off her forehead, but stopped. The movement would make her look nervous. She was already feeling it; she didn't have to look it. 'Thanks for leaving me that broth.'

'Was it good?'

'You know it was,' she said with a half-smile. 'Stop looking for compliments.'

'You gave me one now, I think,' he replied with a half-smile of his own. 'But I won't push you to see if you have any more.'

'Good. You might not like what you find.'

'Mia, could you have a whiskey and—' He looked at her expectantly.

'Oh. Water.'

'And a water sent to my office, please?'

'Sure.'

Mia waved them off, but not before Alexa saw the questioning look in her eyes. Alexa couldn't blame her. A random woman comes to the bar, asking about the boss without giving any reason, and moments later the boss appears and whisks said woman into his office? It looked dodgy, even to her, and *she* was the random woman.

'Please, sit,' Benjamin said when they walked into the small space of his office.

'Thanks.'

She took the seat opposite him. The space was confined, making it big enough only for his desk, two chairs, and a cabinet.

'If you get a smaller desk, have some floating shelves installed, you could create more space for yourself.'

'Why would I want to?' he asked dryly. 'I have everything I need.'

'You're right.'

Purposefully, she swung her handbag to her lap. It knocked a pile of books off his desk. She gave him a look, then bent to pick the books up and set them back where they were.

'Why would you need more space?'

'Fine, you've proved your point.'

He was chuckling when a young man, probably early twenties, knocked on the door and set their drinks in front of them.

'Anything else?' he asked, after Benjamin thanked him.

'We're good for now,' Benjamin replied, looking at her to confirm. She nodded. 'I'll call the kitchen if I need anything else.' He waited until the man

left. 'You would have had a smaller desk and floating shelves, wouldn't you?'

'Yeah. I was going to do the shelves on that wall.'
She pointed at one wall. 'Put the desk here.' She
pointed at the opposite wall. 'I probably would have
got some fancy desk, with three sections that were
stacked on top of one another, so I could have options
to stand and have plenty of space.' She shrugged.
'I didn't need to in the end, because my current office is huge.'

'Rub it in, won't you?' But his eyes were serious.
'You really wanted this, didn't you?'

'I was going to buy it,' she said in answer. 'I had
plans for it.' She picked up her water and took a sip
to quench her suddenly dry throat. 'It taught me to
act first, dream later. An important lesson.'

There was a long silence. She resisted the urge to
fidget during it.

'He just bought this from under you?' Benjamin
asked.

'Yes.'

'Knowing you wanted it?'

'Yes.'

Another pause.

'Then he offered the space to me.'

'He's smart.'

Seconds passed.

'He was using me.'

'Weren't you using him, too?'

'I don't feel like it's the same.'

'Probably not,' she conceded. 'Don't look so sad.'

Sadness wasn't quite the emotion in his expression, but she went with it because it also wasn't *not* sadness. 'It turned out well in the end.'

'Yeah, but it's still…' He offered her a small smile. 'It's hard to wrap my head around. The man who gave me a chance did so by robbing you of something. I considered Lee to be a friend, and now I'm wondering whether I was a fool to do so.'

She thought about it. Sighed.

'This wasn't what I thought I'd be doing here, but okay.' She set her glass down. 'The Lee you know is the Lee you know. You've known him for years. You've worked with him. Have likely been through a lot with him. The way he's treated me doesn't change that.'

'It does though,' he said softly. 'He has the capacity to be cruel and—'

'Only with me,' she interrupted. 'It's part of why my parents could never understand why I had such a problem with him. They couldn't believe he was the person I was claiming he was, even though they created the environment that forced us to compete.'

'Forced…compete?' He leaned forward. 'What do you mean?'

She couldn't answer him. It would rip off the bandage that she had put over the wounds of her childhood. She'd spent her entire adult life trying to put, to keep, that bandage in place. She wouldn't remove it now because this man was asking her to.

'You, um… You don't look sick.'

He blinked. Seemingly acknowledged she didn't

want to talk about it because he didn't press. Instead he leaned back in his chair.

'I am.' He gave a very fake cough.

She rolled her eyes, but smiled. 'You're obviously not. You didn't have to do that.'

'I didn't do anything.'

'Benjamin.'

He frowned. 'Fine. But I was only making sure the playing field was level.'

'Were you?' She bit her lip as she sat back. 'Was that what last night was, too? You were making sure things were level as you spent the night with me?'

'It wasn't quite spending the night,' he protested, colour lighting his cheeks.

'Of course not.' She didn't bother hiding her smile. 'But it was guilt, wasn't it? You felt guilty about getting a day with Cherise, and you came to look after me so you could tell yourself that you tried to make things better.'

'It wasn't exactly like that.'

She lifted her brows, waiting for him to tell her what it was like. He sighed impatiently.

'Maybe there was some guilt. But it was more because I wanted to apologise for being a brute the day before yesterday.'

'What was today, then?' she asked. 'Surely you made up for it last night? More than, even. You didn't have to do it.'

'It was fair.'

'It was stupid.'

'Can you just…?' He stopped, lowering his voice

when the words came out loudly. 'Can you just say thank you?'

'No,' she said after a moment. 'I'm not going to thank you for feeling sorry for me.'

She stood, knocking over the books with her handbag again, this time unintentionally. With a sigh, she lowered to pick them up. Then found that she was stuck.

'Oh.'

'Oh.' He stood now, too. 'Oh, what?'

She tried with all her might to push up, but her balance was shot. It only ended up pushing her forward. She put a hand out in time to keep from knocking her head.

'Lex, are you okay? Are you in labour?'

'Of course I'm not in labour.' She scowled. 'I'm thirteen weeks pregnant. Of course I'm not in labour.'

'Okay.' He crouched down in front of her. 'Why are you not getting up, then?'

'Because—' she gritted her teeth '—I can't.'

'You can't get up?'

'Seems you need your core to stand up. Who knew?'

She could almost feel him laughing at her. She chose to ignore it. Largely because she really couldn't get up and the floor was surprisingly terrible to be on.

'Are you going to help me?'

'Yeah.' But she heard the click of a camera. Her head shot up.

'What did you do?'

'Nothing,' he said innocently, taking her under the arms and lifting her gently.

'Benjamin, if you took a photo of me struggling to get up, I swear I'll make you regret it.'

'Which is exactly why I need the photo. For protection.'

'Why do you need protection?'

'You're a voracious opponent.'

'Am I an opponent?' she asked lightly, though she didn't feel light. It had nothing to do with him taking a picture of her or getting stuck on the floor.

'I didn't mean it that way.'

'How did you mean it?'

'You're a sparring partner,' he said, shoving his hands into his jeans pockets. They were close enough that she could reach out and pull them out if she wanted to. 'We argue and debate. It's what we do.'

'Yeah, but all of that started because you saw me as an opponent *in that way*.' She lifted her head because, although it smarted, he was taller than her, and the lack of distance between them meant she had to. 'Something about me in class made you think of me as competition.'

'You were the best, Alexa.' He shrugged. 'People don't compete against someone in the middle. They do so with the person at the top. And you were.'

Or they compete with the only person who's there, she thought, remembering all the years her parents had encouraged her and Lee to be better than those around them. Their words weren't only for her and

Lee; *they* competed with those around them, too. Even with one another. It seemed to invigorate their marriage though, rather than cause the relationship to crumble. Sometimes Alexa wondered whether she was their child, since she was the only one in the family who hadn't been invigorated by competition. She was the odd one out. Lee had simply been following their parents' example.

It didn't make it right though. At least not for her.

'I should… I should go.'

'Alexa,' he said, reaching for her hand. She stilled when he threaded their fingers together. Let herself go to him when he pulled her in. 'I didn't mean to upset you.'

'I know.'

'But you're upset.'

She sighed. 'It's not you. Well, not you alone.' When he only looked at her, the heat of his hand pulsing into her body, landing at her heart, she sighed again. 'I spent my entire life being the person Lee had to beat. Not because I was the best, or at the top, but because I was there. My parents told us to be the best. We got rewarded with love or gifts if we were.' She closed her eyes. 'I don't… I don't want to live my entire life like that. That's why I cut Lee out of it. That's why I barely speak to my parents.'

She dropped her head. It found a soft landing, and she realised he'd moved closer so she could lean against his chest. As it had the night before, it comforted her.

'This entire thing with Cherise is a nightmare for

me,' she whispered. 'I just want it to be over. And before you say it—no, it won't be if you step back.'

'It will.'

She looked up at him. 'No, it won't. If you don't fight fairly, I'll know. More significantly, Lee will know. And he'll stop at nothing to convince Cherise to work for In the Rough, which will put me right back in the position I was in in the first place.'

She lifted a free hand and set it on his chest. Curled her fingers.

'You'll know, too. You'll know that you sacrificed this for me. I don't want that.' She beat her fist lightly against his chest. 'I want you to think of what's best for you. Fighting for this is what's best for you,' she clarified when he frowned.

His hand lifted, curled over her fist. 'I thought you didn't want us to compete.'

'I don't. But I'm not naïve enough to believe I won't encounter competition in my life. In my business. Just…' She sighed. 'Just make it a good one so we can all move forward without this haunting us.'

For some reason, she slid an arm around his waist, rested her head against his chest again. Her other hand remained in his as if they were about to dance.

'I'll be fine without you helping me, Ben. I promise.'

Chapter 15

He wanted to believe her. He really did. But how many times had his mother said she was fine, only for him to find her curled up in pain somewhere? He was tired of the people he cared about hurting. And damn it, he cared about Alexa. No matter how much he tried to use guilt, or logic, or whatever other reason he'd used in the last weeks as an excuse to see her and spend time with her. He cared about her. He wanted her to be okay. Whether that meant her health, or her restaurant.

He needed her to be okay.

The urgency of it was partly from an unknown source, partly from that caring. Hell, it was partly because she was standing in his arms, looking up at him with reassurance in her eyes. Her stomach was pressed into his, and the rounding of it—not much, but enough—sent a rush of protectiveness through him.

Feeling the rest of her body against his wasn't as harmless.

She wore another loose top, but it clung to her breasts if nothing else, as if as amazed by them as he was. He hadn't been as fascinated by this part of the body since he was a teenager discovering his sexuality. His conclusion then had been that their biological function was as important as their appearance. He'd clearly been desperate to separate himself from his physical feelings then, which was most likely a form of protection. If he wasn't into romantic relationships, he would still be able to help at home.

His opinion had somewhat changed over the years. Probably because he'd learnt how to balance things better. If he prioritised, he could enjoy his physical feelings, too. He didn't have to shun them.

Thank goodness, or he might not have appreciated Alexa's breasts in that moment. And appreciating it caused his breath to go from simply oxygenating his body to giving her a signal something had changed. Her eyes fluttered up; something on his face had them clouding with desire. Most likely his own desire, his more rapid breathing.

He could appreciate more than Alexa's breasts though. Those eyes, clouded as they were, made him feel as though he were sitting in front of a fire on a rainy day. When they sparred, her gaze handed him a glass of whiskey, warming him from the inside, too. Her lips parted, and he couldn't resist dipping his head—until he realised what he was about to do.

'I'd like to kiss you,' he whispered.

'Okay,' she whispered back. 'Do it.'

'I was asking.'

'Your hand has been pressed into the small of my back for the better part of five minutes. Seconds ago was the first time you used it to pull me in closer. Now you want to ask?'

'I did?' He had no recollection of it. 'I'm sorry. I should have—'

He broke off when she put a finger over his lips. 'You weren't doing it on purpose. I understood that. It was part of the reason I didn't knee you in the groin.'

He laughed. 'If I ever do anything that makes you uncomfortable on purpose, please feel free to do just that.'

'I didn't need your permission.' Her mouth curved up. 'But thank you, I suppose. Now, shall we get back to that kissing thing?'

He kissed her then, glad she wasn't playing games when his need seemed to consume him. He moaned in relief when their lips touched and he felt the softness of her. Their essences tangled, their souls embraced, and he would never get over the enormity of it—from just a kiss.

Her tongue slipped between his lips, and he opened for her as desire pulsed inside him. She tasted sweet—or was that the promise of her? The idea of what they could share if they ever allowed this feeling to become more than a stolen moment. It didn't matter. All that did was his heart thumping harder against his breastbone, almost as though it were hard work; almost as though there were water in his chest and his heart was thumping despite it.

If that meant he would drown, he didn't mind. He would be drowning in her. In that scent of lemon and mint that came from he had no idea where. But it radiated off her skin, from her lips, and he'd never been a lemon and mint man until now.

His fingers stroked the skin of her arms, aware of how lucky they were to touch her. He memorised the smoothness; the bump near her right elbow where something must have bitten her; the indentations below her left shoulder where she must have got her vaccinations. She shivered when he skimmed her collarbone, when his index fingers stroked her neck. He stored the knowledge away for the future, when he could seduce her more thoroughly, when his desk and his employees weren't in the way.

That didn't stop him from giving it his best effort now.

He cupped her face, angling her into a position that would deepen their kiss. He was rewarded with her hands clinging to his waist, before they drifted up and fisted his shirt. Then they were exploring his skin, flesh to flesh somehow. He didn't know how she'd managed to slip her hands under his clothing, but he was grateful for it. Even if it did mean he'd never be able to let another person touch him this way. He couldn't; not when she was claiming him.

Not when he wanted to remember her touching him. To remember how his blood seemed to follow along beneath her strokes, pulsing with need and desire, showing him what it meant to be alive. To live.

How had he not known it before?

'You're very impressive,' she said, pulling back. Her cheeks were flushed, there was a dazed half-smile on her face, and her voice was hoarse. She was the most beguiling she'd ever been. 'I don't suppose you became this way in the last few weeks?'

'I'm not sure what you mean.'

'These muscles.' She scraped her nails lightly over his skin. There was no way it would mark him, but they might as well have with the little sparks going off everywhere she touched. 'They weren't always there.'

'No,' he said slowly. 'I don't think they were when I was born. But I was an impressive toddler.' He laughed when she pinched him. 'Hey, I was using your words.'

'And being obnoxious about it.'

'I didn't want you to think I'd changed.'

Her own laugh was softer than his. Perhaps even thoughtful. 'No, I don't think you have. Even though I seem to be hoping you had. That somehow you'd become this man I'm attracted to and maybe even like in the last few weeks.' She brought her hands out from under his shirt, straightening the material as she did. 'That was what I was implying with the muscles, by the way. I know they didn't suddenly appear. I think I only just noticed them.'

Just like I only just noticed you.

She didn't have to say it. Everything she'd already said implied it. But he wanted to tell her she was wrong. He had changed. He could no longer see Lee without thinking about how Lee had used him. More importantly, what Lee had done to her. He didn't think competing with Alexa was fun any more; didn't see it as harmless. With her, he let himself be himself. He showed her that he cared for her, despite his better judgement. He let himself take care of her, was honest with her. She hadn't used those vulnerabilities against him either.

Sure, he hadn't entirely opened up to her about how he felt about his family—but then, neither had she. They were still checking one another out, tentatively testing whether they could trust the other. He thought they were there now. And he wanted to open up to her, wanted to know more about her.

'Do you want to go out with me?' he asked, desperate to do just that. 'Tonight, I mean. Do you want to go out?'

Her lips twitched; light danced in her eyes. 'Are you sure you're feeling well enough?'

'I've made a surprising recovery.'

'Must have been the same twenty-four-hour bug I had.'

'Not quite the same,' he said with a small laugh.

'Hmm. That would be slightly puzzling.'

'Only slightly.'

'Maybe you've had an elixir.'

'I have.'

He moved closer, nuzzled her neck. She angled, giving him better access.

'What are you implying?'

'You're magical.'

She laughed. Patted his chest. 'That, I know.'

'I don't doubt it.' He nipped at her lips. Then, when it felt good, kissed her again, lingering. 'Is that a yes?'

'What was the question?' she asked, voice breathy.

He chuckled. 'Can I take you somewhere?'

'I would love that.'

'I know you like kissing me—' *she hoped* '—but taking me to Lovers Lane seems like overkill.'

Benjamin laughed as he pulled into a parking space at the edge of the road. All the parking spaces on Lovers Lane were at the edge of the road. Alexa wasn't a fan of it since the road was on a cliff, which meant the edge was more dangerous than most edges. But she wasn't going to protest when Benjamin had brought her to this—admittedly—romantic place.

She also wasn't going to move.

Except to eat this broth he'd made her.

But she'd do it very, *very* slowly.

'I wanted to bring you somewhere with a nice view.'

'The quarry was nice. It didn't have such a blatant name. It was safe, too.'

'I've already taken you there.'

It was sweet enough that she leaned forward so she could see the view past his head. It looked much like the night sky itself: dark, save for the lights twinkling back at her. Those lights weren't stars, but the city of Cape Town, and they weren't demure and subtle, but brash and bright. They stretched up until the base of Table Mountain, leaving the landmark to loom over them in darkness. If the lights spoke of the city's vibrancy, its life, then the mountain anchored it. Reminded her that people had families here, careers. Generations had become stronger, less broken, more whole.

'It is pretty nice,' she said on an exhale.

He smiled.

She didn't want to be caught in it, though it was too late to be coy. She'd already given up something of herself when she'd kissed him earlier. Or had he taken it? No, she thought. The permission she'd given him meant that she'd given it willingly. It made her uncomfortable to think she had, so she was trying to blame him.

Uncomfortable didn't feel like the right word though. It was more…like she was going into a battle for the survival of the universe and she had nothing but a sword. Perhaps not even that. Uncomfortable? Sure. Dangerous? Stupid? Completely and utterly irrational? Definitely.

She took a breath and reached into the brown bag for the broth.

'Thanks for swinging by my place to get this.'

'I could have made you a fresh batch.'

'Your kitchen was busy.' She opened the container

and sighed at the aroma. 'Besides, I didn't want my first In the Rough meal to be broth.'

She closed her eyes at the first taste of it. It had been hours since she'd eaten, and because she was at the Institute, she'd settled for one slice of toast and a banana. She'd blamed it on her bug when Cherise had asked. She'd also stared longingly at the steak Cherise was eating. But there'd be plenty of steak in the future. For now, she had broth. Warm, delicious broth that wouldn't turn her stomach against her.

Was pregnancy simplifying her appetite? She hoped not.

'Technically it is your first meal from In the Rough,' he said.

'This doesn't count. It doesn't come from the restaurant.'

'Just its manager. Its once-upon-a-time head chef.'

'I forgot about that,' she said, sipping the soup. 'Did you tell me why you decided you didn't want to be head chef any more?'

'Probably not.' He paused. 'I'm happy to share. If you are.'

She frowned. 'What do you mean? I... Oh,' she said when he gestured to the brown bag that still had his food in it. 'Sorry. I got distracted.'

'Yes, I got that.' He was smiling when she handed him his food. He went to open it, but stopped himself. Opened a window instead. Looked at her. 'The smell probably wouldn't be good if you're nauseous.'

'No,' she murmured, touched. 'Thank you.'

'No problem.'

He opened her window, too, and only then dug into his food. It was lasagne, and her mind salivated over it if not her stomach. She'd steered away from rich food the last three months, with good reason, but she missed the taste of pasta and red meat and bacon. Sighing a little, she took another spoonful of broth.

'I wanted a change,' he said between bites. 'And I thought I was capable of more than being in a kitchen. The idea of running the restaurant intrigued me.'

'Did it live up to your expectations?'

'It did.' His mouth lifted on one side. 'I think I lived up to its expectations, too.'

'If that's your way of giving yourself a compliment, you didn't have to. I could have told you that you were doing a good job.'

'But would you have?'

'Maybe. After some coercing.'

'Of what kind?' His voice had dropped seductively. He leaned closer, but she pulled back. 'What's wrong?'

'I can't kiss you when you're eating that.'

'Oh.' He frowned down at the food, as if it had betrayed him. As if he couldn't believe that it had. 'I wasn't thinking.'

'You were, but not with...' She broke off with a demure smile. 'I'm not going to be crass.' She patted his cheek. 'But yes, that would have been appropriate coercion.'

'Seems a little cruel to remind me when I can't do it.'

'I can be a little cruel sometimes.'

With a small smile that seemed to say *I know*—which pleased her more than offended her—he asked, 'Why did you stop being head chef?'

'I never was. Well,' she reconsidered, 'a lot of my responsibilities blurred the lines with the position, but I knew that I wanted to have other input than in the kitchen to make Infinity the best it could be. I also wanted the business to run independently of me. Or I guess I wanted to run independently of the business.'

'So you could have a life.'

'And maybe babies.'

'You thought about babies then?'

'I suppose I did, though it wasn't "oh, I should do this to have babies".' She set the spoon against the rim of the container. 'I knew I didn't want my life to look like my parents'. Mostly business,' she clarified when she realised he wouldn't know. 'They work a lot, enjoy it, barely spend time at home. I wanted to have more than that. I wanted to have a family. I forgot about it while I tried to get Infinity up and running. Then after an employee brought her kid to work, it hit me: I wanted a home life, too. With babies.'

'That's why your place is so homey.'

'You still sound surprised.'

'Not surprised—jealous. I would love to be so intentional about…everything.' He closed the container his food was in. 'I spent a lot of my time not doing what I wanted to do. When I got to do it, I realised it wasn't really what I wanted to do.'

'But you're there now, aren't you?' she asked. 'You like running the restaurant.'

'Yeah.'

'Great. So you got there in your professional life. Just figure out how to get there in your personal life.'

'Easier said than done.'

'Of course. But you're the only one who can do it.' She closed the container her own food was in and put it in the brown bag. Did the same for his when he handed it to her. 'You can live your life doing the easy thing and going with the flow. It'll take you where you need to be, but maybe there'll be more pit stops. Maybe it'll make you feel as if you should have done more. But—' she dragged the word out '—taking the harder route and doing things intentionally will help you feel proud. Things might still take a long time, but you'll appreciate the journey more.'

She shook her head, rolled her eyes. 'I know I sound silly.'

'You don't. It's…harder, with my mom.'

'How?'

'She needs me,' he said simply. 'If I'm not around, she'll push too hard. My father would be alone to help her with it. It's how our family is.'

'Would you move out if she didn't need you?'

'I… Yeah, maybe.' His lips pursed, then parted to let an exhale through. 'Probably. I'm over thirty,' he said with a quick laugh. 'I shouldn't be living with my parents any more.'

'That's why you're taking me to Lovers Lane instead of home. Not that you should take me home.' She closed her eyes. 'I didn't mean it that way.'

'I know. But maybe that's what you get for being a little cruel.'

He laughed when she punched him lightly in the shoulder. They sat in companionable silence until he said, 'It's cool. The way you've crafted your life. Not everyone can do that.'

She leaned back against the seat. 'I have my parents to thank for that, I guess. For all their faults, they were very clear about having a plan. It was a set plan for them—school, university, work—and they weren't thrilled that mine looked a little different. But I did have one. They just didn't see it.'

She'd faltered at the end, so she shouldn't have been surprised at the hand Benjamin reached out and took hers with. Not even the way he lifted her hand to kiss it should have surprised her. Maybe it was the warmth that spread through her body because of his actions that did. The way it settled in her chest, soothing the holes in her heart her parents had created with their rigidity.

'I'm sure they're proud of you.'

'Maybe.' She reclined the seat with her free hand. Settled both their hands on her stomach. 'I guess they are now. Though they would most likely prefer me to be a business mogul like Lee is. One successful business pales in comparison to that.'

'Which is what he intended,' Benjamin said softly. When she lifted her gaze to him, the edge of his mouth lifted. 'You've told me a lot. I can piece together the rest.'

'So it seems.' She ran the index finger of the hand that wasn't tangled with his over his skin. 'Lee's ambitious. Smart. I like to think those things were the primary motivations.'

'But you know they're not.'

She couldn't admit it out loud, so she hedged. 'Our parents taught us to be the best. I took that to mean people outside of our family. Lee took it to mean…me.' She swallowed. 'But it gave us both motivation, thinking that. If I'm part of it, it's only because of that.'

He tugged at her hand. Frowning, she looked at him. His face was serious, but other than that, she couldn't read his emotion.

'What?' she asked.

'Why are you protecting him?'

'I'm not…' She broke off at his look. 'I'm his sister. His older sister. That's what I'm supposed to do.'

'By that logic, he should be looking up to you, his older sister. Not competing with you so much you've lost your ability to trust people who care about you.'

The shock had her pulling her hand out of his, grabbing a hold of her stomach with both hands. She wasn't sure whether she thought she was protecting herself, or her children. Didn't know why she thought she had to do either.

'Lex—'

'No, give me a moment.' Purposefully, she leaned back against the chair, relaxed her body. She smoothed her clothing, took a couple of deep breaths, let her mind settle. When she was ready, or as ready as she would ever be, she nodded.

'You're right. I realise this. Which is why I've chosen not to have him in my life.'

'I'm sorry. I shouldn't have said that.'

'Stop apologising, Ben,' she said softly. 'You keep doing it.'

'Because I keep messing up.'

'Being honest, caring… That's not messing up.' She bit the inside of her lip at his expression. Tried to fix it. 'Don't get me wrong, it's very inconvenient. Especially when you're trying to avoid your issues. Don't you dare apologise!' she said when he opened his mouth.

He gave her a wry grin and she laughed.

'It's like a disease with you.'

'I can't help it.'

'Sure you can. Just stop doing it.'

'I've been doing it my entire life.'

'Why?'

He didn't reply immediately, his expression contorted in confusion. 'I don't actually know.' He tried to hide the panic that answer brought by giving her a smile. She wondered if he knew how horribly he was failing.

'Okay, we're going to play a game.'

'A game?'

'It's a distraction, Foster.'

'In that case, tell me,' Benjamin said with a smile. It was more genuine now.

'Well, I'm going to try to get you to apologise to me, and you're going to resist.'

'What are you going to do?'

'Nothing specific,' she replied nonchalantly. 'You know that game where, when you're on a road trip, you pick a colour and have to count the number of cars in that colour?'

'Yeah…'

'That's how it's going to be. When the opportunity arises.' She brought a finger under her nose, pretending to stifle a sneeze. 'Oh, my sinuses are acting up.'

'Should I close the windows?'

'Just a little.' She pretended to stop another sneeze. 'Do you have tissues or something here?'

'Yeah, I do,' he said, just as she knew he would.

He reached for the pack of tissues in his door, reached out to give it to her. She held out a hand, but moved it slightly when he tried to drop the tissues into it. The pack fell between the seats.

'Oh. Sorry about that. I thought…' He broke off when he saw her shaking her head. When he saw the smile on her face, too. 'You planned that?'

'Yes. And you failed. Terribly. In the first minute of the game.'

'But that wasn't fair!'

'All's fair in love and war.' When there was an awkward silence, she wrinkled her nose. 'This is war, in case you were wondering.'

'I wasn't.'

But, if she was being honest with herself, she was.

Chapter 16

What was the saying? *Going to hell in a handbasket?* If so, that was exactly what was happening. The handbasket was filled with delicious food courtesy of Cherise, but the tying of the bow, the giving? That was all Lee.

'You invited your sister?' Benjamin hissed the moment he saw Alexa walk into the hotel ballroom.

Okay, not the moment he saw Alexa. The moment he saw Alexa he stopped, his brain stopped, and he was pretty sure his heart stopped. She looked... amazing. It was too inadequate a word, but he clung to it. The gown she wore was somewhere between coral and peach, the colour of it magnificent against the bronze of her skin. It was a halter-neck dress that clung to her chest, ending just below her breasts in a cinch, before flowing down over the rest of her. The material was pleated, and when she moved, it moved with her. When she was still, those pleats created the illusion of space. All for the benefit of hiding the bump he knew was growing by the day.

The reason he knew it was because he'd found a reason, every day since they'd been to Lovers Lane, to see her. He didn't once go to her restaurant—he worried that would be invading her personal space—but he visited her flat under the guise of bringing more food. He asked her to go out for tea under the pretence of picking her brains about something. It had been a week and a half of this, where he was clearly making up reasons to see her, but she never once called him out on it.

He told himself that if she'd wanted to, she would have. She wasn't the kind of person not to. The fact that she wasn't saying anything told him she wanted to see him, too. As did the small, private smile she smiled every time she saw him.

The days she invited him in were the ones he liked best. Her flat was fast becoming his favourite place, in no small part because they could be whoever they wanted to be there. Turned out, they wanted to be friends. The kissing that happened quite frequently—and sometimes progressed to other things, but never far enough to undermine their friendship—was merely a bonus. But things were so easy between them when they were there. He told her about how he'd grown up trying to help his parents; she told him how she'd grown up trying to make hers proud. They comforted one another, teased one another, and, yes, kissed and touched, and it was all magnificent.

And it was going to end.

'I didn't invite her,' Lee said slowly. 'She wouldn't have come if she'd known the invitation was from me.'

Benjamin resisted grabbing the man at the front of his collar. 'What did you do?' he said through his teeth.

'Used the grapevine.' Lee smirked. 'It still works.'

It took Benjamin a long time to remember what he was like when he wasn't so damn angry. Not that anger was such a bad thing. It gave him a clarity he hadn't had before. Sure, some of that clarity was also because of his conversations with Alexa, but it was clarity nevertheless. And he knew exactly what he had to do.

'I quit.'

'What?'

'Resign, effective immediately.'

'You can't do that,' Lee spluttered. 'Your contract says you have to give me at least a month's notice.'

'Then you have it.'

'What the hell?' Lee's expression was stormy. 'This is because of my sister, isn't it? She poached you.' He shook his head in disbelief. 'You let her? You let her because you're sleeping with her?'

'Lee,' he warned.

Lee took a breath, clearly trying to get hold of his emotions. 'You can't do this, man. We've been working together for years. I gave you a chance. You can't walk out on me.'

'I'm grateful for what you did for me.' And he meant it. But the weight that had lifted from his shoulders the moment he'd quit told him he'd needed to. 'Truly, I am. You're an incredible businessman. I've learnt a lot from you. I have no doubt I could have learnt more.'

'Then why are you leaving?'

'Because you used me to beat your sister.' Saying it out loud made Benjamin feel in control. As if finally, after all those people had used him, he'd regained what they'd taken from him. His pride, perhaps. Or perhaps it was that he was no longer scared of saying it. 'And you're malicious. To your own sister, who's done nothing but love you.'

'Is that what she told you?' Lee scoffed. 'She must be really good in...'

He broke off when Benjamin, quick as lightning, took his arm. 'I'm warning you about what you say next.'

Lee's chest heaved. 'Okay. I'm sorry.'

He let go. 'I appreciate that.'

'You're serious about this?'

'Deadly.' He straightened his tie. 'I respect who you are in business, but not as a man. I can't, knowing how you've treated the woman I... I love.'

He'd hesitated in speech, just as he had with his feelings. But he could see they'd been there long before the last month. The moment he'd seen her in that class, he'd tumbled. Knocked his head in the process, it seemed, because he went back to being a kid and tried to compete with her so she would notice him.

But she'd never allowed him close enough to see that she had noticed him; not in the way he'd intended. He'd reminded her of her brother, the man, he suspected, had hurt her most. She seemed to have some kind of resignation about who her parents were, but not with Lee. With Lee, she'd tried, and he'd brushed her away. When she let Benjamin in the last few weeks, he could see how much it hurt her—and how much he had hurt her, simply by acting like a teenage fool.

Now what he had seen, what she'd allowed him to see, convinced him that if he hadn't been a fool, he would have had these feelings aeons ago. She might not have iced him out, and he might have seen who she really was. That was who he was in love with. The woman who wasn't even a little cruel. Who was passionate and driven and who cared about people.

It was the biggest honour of his life that she'd chosen to open up to him. She'd let him see her vulnerable, and he hoped with all his might he'd done enough to show her she could be vulnerable with him. He knew she struggled with it, and if he had to be patient he would be, simply because she was worth it.

If he had to spend his entire lifetime proving that she could trust him, he would. Because he loved her. And she deserved it.

He had to tell her.

'Benjamin!'

The exclamation came from a short distance away. When he turned towards it, he saw Cherise.

'Thanks so much for coming,' she said, stopping in front of him. 'I thought I should show you what I can do, too, since I hope we can work together.'

It was what he'd wanted to hear most, once upon a time. Now, what he wanted to hear most was Alexa's voice, saying anything, really, but mostly talking about them sharing a future together. He turned, barely thinking about the fact that Cherise was there, waiting for an answer.

He didn't think about it at all when he saw Lee follow Alexa out of the ballroom.

The moment she saw him walking towards her she knew.

It was silly of her to think that she could walk into an event being catered by Cherise to get another opportunity to speak with her. To perhaps even see her in action. Alexa had found out about the charity event through an acquaintance, thought it would be harmless and beneficial, considering she hadn't heard from Cherise for over a week. When she saw Lee, it all fell into place: she hadn't heard from Cherise for a reason, she'd been set up, and she shouldn't have come.

She didn't give the gorgeous ballroom and its glistening lights and formal guests any more thought. She walked out, down the brick steps, past the fountain. She was on the small stretch of grass between the fountain and the car park when Lee caught up with her.

'Leaving so soon?'

She stopped. Closed her eyes. Turned to face him. 'Sorry I didn't stay for the *gotcha*. That's what you wanted to say, isn't it?'

'No one forced you to be here,' Lee said calmly. 'Although I'm surprised you didn't accompany Ben.' He pretended to think about it. 'Is it that he didn't tell you about this, or that you really are trying to keep your personal and professional lives separate?'

He hadn't told her, though she didn't need to tell Lee that. Nor did she have to figure out why Benjamin hadn't said anything. He was protecting her, or maybe himself, and though she understood it—he was so used to protecting the people in his life—it bothered her on a deep level. But that wasn't important now.

'Look, Lee, I don't want to stick around for the gloating, okay?'

'Not even your own?'

'What are you talking about?'

'Oh, you're going to pretend you didn't ask him to do it. That seems like an odd position, all things considered.'

'Tell me, or let me go,' she said sharply.

'Your boyfriend quit.'

'He what?'

His brows rose. 'Nice acting, Sis. Didn't know you had it in you.'

'He quit? Why?' She narrowed her eyes. 'What the hell did you do?'

'Absolutely nothing.' Though she could barely see it, she knew he was biting the inside of his lip. He used to do it when they were younger, on the side. 'He told me it's because of the way I've been treating you.'

She caught the swear word before it left her lips. Mentally, though, she let the curses fly. The idiot! It was fine if he kept things from her because he thought he was protecting her—okay, not fine, understandable—but this? This was stupid. This was his entire future. It was his life. And he was doing it for her! It seemed much too much for people who'd been close for less than two weeks. This felt more like a gesture; something someone did before proclaiming their love or something.

A thin thread of panic wove between the synapses in her brain. It threatened to overcome her, and for a second she thought she would fall over. But that would hurt her babies, and she had to be strong. She couldn't let them suffer for things she was responsible for.

She looked at her brother. Realised she needed to sort this out if she wanted to keep that promise to her kids.

'If I talk to him, convince him to go back to you, would you leave me alone?' She could already see, before he even said it, that he was going to make some stupid remark. 'I'm being serious. If I get Ben to go back to In the Rough, I don't want to see or hear from you again. Unless there's a family function, which, fortunately, doesn't happen often. But outside of that. No surprises. No manipulation. Nothing.'

'You really want that?'

He'd taken the stance of a victim, his voice hurt and surprised, as if he had no contribution to why she wanted this. It made her snap.

'What I want is to have a brother who doesn't make me feel as if I have to walk carefully everywhere I go in case he pulls the rug out from under me. I want to have a brother who doesn't *enjoy* pulling the rug out from under me. Who, when I fall, asks me why I'm on the ground. Who gets upset when I refuse his help.'

She'd never spent enough time with Lee to learn how his expressions revealed his emotions. Or maybe it was that the only expressions he wore around her were variations of smugness or satisfaction or a combination of the two. So she couldn't tell how he felt now, because none of that came through in his expression.

'I thought... This is what we do, Lex. We compete with one another. We make one another better.'

'What? That's what you think this is? No—*how* do you think that is what this is?' Her voice was high with disbelief. She didn't try to temper it. 'You competed with me, Lee. I *congratulated* you for beating my records, or scoring higher than me.'

'You were conceding.'

'Conceding...'

Now she recognised the look on Lee's face: bewilderment. He genuinely didn't understand why she was so upset. She nearly laughed. He was the least self-aware person she knew.

'I wasn't conceding. I was sincerely wishing you well because I was happy for you. At first. I could see competing with me made you happy and gave you purpose and I wanted you to have that.' She took a steadying breath. 'But you didn't want me to be happy. If you did, you would have supported me the way I supported you. You would have taken the hand I held out every time I asked you to go to a movie with me, or watch a show, or do whatever stupid things brothers and sisters do together. But you said no. Instead you tried to beat me at things that didn't even matter.'

She folded her arms, suddenly cold.

'And you tried to beat me at things that did matter, too.' She blinked when that made her want to cry. 'You bought the building I spent months trying to find. Months,' she said with a shake of her head. 'I did research into who I was buying the building from, into the neighbourhood, into how much it would cost to renovate, how long it would take. Then you swooped in and stole it. Just stole it.' She lifted a hand, dropped it. 'The only thing you knew about it was that I wanted it.'

'I… I didn't realise.'

'You didn't realise that you'd destroyed my dream?' she asked. 'Of both that restaurant and ever having a normal relationship with you?'

He didn't reply, though he ran his hand over his

hair a few times, lips moving without sound. He looked at her, and if she wasn't so numb by the conversation, she would have been touched by the vulnerability she saw there.

But she was numb. She had to be. If she wasn't, the reminder of all the times she'd wanted to forge a relationship with her brother would have consumed her. The hope she'd once had was enmeshed in those memories. She'd desperately wanted to shield herself against her parents, had known that if Lee was behind the shield with her she could be stronger. *They* would be stronger together. Except Lee chose to wield their parents' weapons against her, too, even when she'd surrendered.

She wasn't surrendering any more. It might have seemed as if she was by offering Lee Benjamin, but she knew she wasn't. She was lifting her shield, protecting herself once more. Because the only way she could truly do that against her brother was by coming to a truce with him. Which meant he needed to make the decision, too.

She could smell the faint smoke of guilt at using Benjamin as a pawn, but maybe he would understand. He might even be grateful that he wouldn't have to protect her any more.

'You don't, um...' Lee cleared his throat. 'You don't have to get Benjamin to work for me.'

She just studied him.

'I'll leave you alone. I didn't realise...' Now he shook his head. 'I'll leave you alone. I promise.'

She almost ran a hand over her stomach before she

remembered Lee didn't know about her pregnancy. She settled for clasping her hands over the bag she'd brought with her.

'Thank you.'

Neither of them moved. But there was a movement behind Lee. Alexa's eyes automatically shifted to it, before she realised it was Benjamin. Her body wanted to sag against something, let it hold up her weight as she prepared for another conversation that would leave her raw. It was so different to how her body had responded to Benjamin in the last weeks. With relief, excitement, attraction, desire. She'd felt safer than at any other time in her life.

This interaction with Lee seemed to prove how much safety was an illusion.

Chapter 17

'Are you okay?'

It was the first thing that came into his mind when he reached her, but he immediately realised it was a stupid question. Of course she wasn't okay. He could see it in her stance, in her eyes, in the brittle tone of her voice when she lied and told him she was. She looked broken, tired, and he hated the person who'd put that look on her face.

He turned to Lee. 'Leave.'

Lee looked at Alexa, then back at him. Uncharacteristically withdrawn, he nodded. After one last glance at Alexa, a parting of the lips that made it seem as though he wanted to say something, he turned around and walked away. Benjamin waited until he was out of sight, then turned.

'Come on, let's find somewhere to sit down.'

She didn't fight him on it, and his worry kicked up another notch. But he kept it inside long enough to find a bench. The restaurant was in a vineyard, much like most prestigious restaurants in Cape Town. But instead of looking out onto the vineyard, the restaurant looked out over the stretch of property on the opposite side of it. It was mostly grass and a long deck that went out into a pond. The pond was still, though Benjamin saw the occasional disturbance of water and the rings that resulted from that disturbance. He watched it for a long time, waiting for Alexa to recover from whatever had happened with Lee.

When he thought she might have, he asked, 'Did that go okay?'

'He agreed to leave me alone, so I guess so.'

'That's what you wanted?'

'I asked for it.'

But she didn't say it was what she wanted, and he had a feeling it wasn't. He wasn't sure if she knew that though, or if she needed to figure it out. He wasn't sure about his position in this either: Should he prod? Give her space? Point her in the right direction? None of the options seemed right. He didn't speak, crippled by the indecision.

'Did you quit your job?' she said into the silence.

'He told you?'

'Accused me,' she corrected. 'Apparently I've been using you to get to him.'

'Sounds diabolical.'

'You can't say I didn't warn you.' She opened her

palms on her lap, looking at them, not him. He should have taken it as sign, prepared himself. Because he didn't, he was completely taken aback by her next words. 'I hope you didn't do this because of me.'

'No. Of course not.'

'You didn't quit because of me?'

'No.'

'Then why did you?'

'I…couldn't work with him any more. He got you here because he wanted to…' He broke off at her look. 'Fine, maybe it had something to do with you. But it wasn't *because* of you.'

She threaded her fingers together. 'You're going to regret it.' Her voice was neutral. 'You're going to blame me when you regret it.'

'I won't.'

'You will. Unless you can tell me you're leaving because of more than just me.'

'I…want to do my own thing.'

'Liar.'

'I'm not lying,' he snapped. Took a breath. 'I shouldn't have said that. It was—' he relaxed his jaw '—uncalled for.'

'It was, especially since it's the truth.'

'It's not fair,' he replied, barely retaining control over his anger. 'It was never fair of you to expect me to work with a man I don't respect any more.'

'You shouldn't have let the way he treated me affect your working relationship.'

'He used me to get to you.' He stood now. Walked away, trying to keep that control. Came back when it didn't help him have more of it. 'Do you know how many people have used me in my life? Too many,' he answered for her. 'It was worse that he did it to get to you. It was worse that he was still so terrible to you. How can you ask me to ignore it?'

'Because of this!' she exclaimed, shifting to the edge of the bench. 'You quit your job. The one you love, at the restaurant you built. Don't you see that? Don't you see you're going to lose everything you've worked for all because of me?' She dropped her head. 'One day you'll think I used you for this, too. I almost did.' Her voice was barely above a whisper. 'I told him that if I got you to work for him again, he had to leave me alone.'

He took the time he needed to work through that.

'Because you care,' he said, crouching down so he could see her face. 'You know what the restaurant means to me.'

'Maybe. Maybe I did it because it meant getting what I want.'

Her eyes, defiant, met his.

'You're saying this to hurt me,' he said, realising it. 'You're pushing me away.'

'Yes,' she whispered. 'You deserve more than me. You deserve someone who can care as much as you do. Selflessly. I… I can't.'

He froze. Slowly, he rose. He rubbed a hand over his face. 'Why not?'

'Can't you see?' She was sitting up, spine straight. It looked so out of place against the curved back of the bench. 'You're selfless. You protect the people you care about at all costs. Even if you're lying to them.'

He could hardly deny it when that was exactly what he'd done that day.

'I've been alone most of my life. I'm used to thinking about myself. More importantly—' she took a deep breath '—I can't trust someone who won't tell me the truth. And I can't keep worrying that I'm keeping you from doing what you want to do. But if I don't, you'll keep putting yourself last.'

'It's not... I'm not...' He exhaled. 'Why don't we talk about you being unable to accept when people try to care for you?'

She bit her lip. 'Okay. What about it would you like to discuss?'

It took him a moment to get over his surprise.

'Why?'

'Why can't I accept people caring for me?' she asked. He nodded. A short moment later, she continued. 'Because it goes away. In some shape or form, I'll discover I can't trust them. It goes away, Ben.' There was a quick inhale of air. When he moved to her, she held out a hand to stop him. Sniffed. 'No, I'm okay.' But two tears streamed down each of her cheeks. She wiped at them quickly. 'I don't want to go through that.'

'It doesn't just go away.' He went to sit next to her, as far away as the bench allowed so she had her space. 'I can't care one day and stop caring the other.'

'But you can *think* you care one day and realise you don't the other.'

'Has this happened to you?'

'No. I wouldn't let it.'

'You mean you haven't let anyone close enough to allow it to happen.'

She inclined her head in acknowledgement.

'That's not healthy.'

'It's safe.'

'Safe isn't going to give you happiness.'

'Are you speaking from experience?' she asked blandly. 'You're staying at home so you can be safe, so you can protect your mother and help your father. So you don't have to face your real feelings about your family.'

He stared at her. 'There are no feelings.'

'So you're happy?' she prodded. 'You're safe and happy, the ultimate juxtaposition, according to you?'

He stood again. 'This isn't fair.'

'It is, but you don't like it.' She stood now, too. 'Which is fine. You don't have to like it.'

'You're using this as an excuse to push me away.'

'I don't need an excuse. I've told you every reason we can't continue this.' She gestured between them.

'You're really that scared of trusting someone?' he asked. 'Is being alone better than taking a chance?'

She folded her arms, the line of her mouth flat. 'Yes. I've spent my life learning that lesson. I won't let anyone hurt me the way my family has.'

'Even if it means pushing away someone who—' he swallowed. Said it anyway. Because he was a fool '—loves you?'

She blinked. Again, and again, until her lashes were fluttering like the wings of a butterfly. He tried to give her a moment to process. He couldn't.

'I haven't once let you down, Alexa. I've been there for you since this entire thing with Lee started.

I lied, yes, but I thought…' He shook his head. 'I wasn't doing it to hurt you. The very opposite, in fact.' He took a step closer. 'Trust me. Trust me because I love you, and I'll try to do better because I love you. Trust me because I've shown you that you can.'

She was shaking her head before he had finished speaking. 'You need to care about yourself, too, in order to love, Ben. I don't think you do.'

With that, she walked away.

It had not been a good week. Someone had forgotten to order the seafood for the restaurant on Monday. It meant that Alexa had to remove all relevant dishes from the menu, make thousands of apologies, and offer substitutes. Then, on Wednesday, someone had forgotten about the staff meeting, come in late, and the event that was being hosted that evening had a few hiccups because the meeting hadn't proceeded.

Everyone made mistakes. She tried to remember that on Friday evening, when she was dead on her feet and contemplating disciplinary action. It complicated things that she'd been the someone who'd forgotten and needed to be punished. Maybe she would get her staff to give her a roasting. Making fun of her would hopefully rebuild the morale that seemed to be lacking, too.

'Hey.' Kenya appeared in her doorway, leaning against the frame of it as though she'd always been there. She was holding two bottles of beer. 'I thought you could use one?'

'Thanks, but I can't drink it.'

Kenya's brow quirked. 'Since when are you this strict about alcohol on a Friday night?'

She couldn't be bothered to keep it a secret any more. She was almost sixteen weeks pregnant with twins, her body was becoming fuller by the day, her plan to have the restaurant secured before her maternity leave had imploded, and she was tired of keeping it all to herself. At least before, she'd had Benjamin to confide in. That was no longer an option. She tried not to listen to the crack of her heart at that thought.

'Since I got pregnant.'

'You're pregnant?' Kenya stepped inside the office, slammed the door, and then put both beers on Alexa's desk. 'Who do I have to kill?'

'Why are you killing someone?' Alexa asked with a laugh.

'Because they knocked you up! Unless...' She eyed Alexa suspiciously 'Did you want to be knocked up?'

'Yes.'

'Oh.' Kenya frowned. 'You trapped them.'

She chuckled again. 'I didn't trap anyone. I went to a sperm bank because your family made me remember how much I wanted my own. How soon I wanted it, too.' She shrugged and let out a small smile. 'Anyway, that's why I've been dressing like this. Trying to hide the bump.'

'I was wondering.' Kenya dropped into the chair on the visitor's side of Alexa's desk. She drank her beer. 'Honestly, I thought you were going through a boho chic period.'

'Seriously?'

'I didn't want to limit you with my expectations of who you are.' Kenya smiled, but it lacked its fire. Alexa found out why a couple of seconds later. 'Why didn't you tell me you were doing this? I could have come with you. Supported you. From what I know about the process, it isn't easy.'

'No, it isn't. And honestly? I could have used the support.' Her heart ached at the acknowledgement. 'But I'm an idiot.' She offered Kenya a small smile. 'I thought that if I let you in, you'd hurt me. I've got so used to doing things on my own, I thought I could do this.'

She wasn't talking about conceiving her children any more, and they both knew it.

'Why would you think that?' Kenya's voice was soft, and a little judgemental. Alexa smiled.

'It's what I'm used to,' she said. 'My family is messed up. And every time I thought something was going right, it was really…not.'

She should have explained it better, but it occurred to her that she hadn't told Kenya anything of her personal life. She knew that Kenya had three older brothers, seven nieces, one nephew and a daughter, and that motherhood had pushed her to finally get the therapy she thought she needed. Alexa knew all of that, but she hadn't told Kenya one thing about her family.

'It's a long story, and I should have told you more of it sooner,' she said softly.

Kenya didn't blink. 'You should have, yes.'

'I'm sorry. For all of it.'

'Good.' Kenya didn't look away as she drank from her beer. 'So, should we thank the pregnancy for this stupendous week, or the family?'

'Neither. Or maybe the family? I don't know.' It was the perfect opportunity to make things right with Kenya. Or at least to start to. 'I think it's mostly because of the fake boyfriend.'

'Explain.'

So she did. She told Kenya about her terrible brother, who'd inspired her to pretend her rival was her boyfriend. How Benjamin had gone along with it, even after he'd found out she was pregnant. She told Kenya about the twins—to which she got a colourful reply—and about how things had snowballed, but in a nice way, with Benjamin. And then how it had all melted, leaving her feeling as though she was drowning.

She ended on an apology, because she'd been a bad friend and a worse boss. She couldn't secure the restaurant before she was on maternity leave. She could probably still try, but time was running out and—

'Firstly,' Kenya interrupted, 'you've been a pretty terrible friend. There's no way you're worse as a boss.'

'Wow. Thanks.'

'Secondly,' Kenya continued with a grin, 'we

haven't had a head chef for almost four months now. I know you've been picking up a lot of the slack, but that's because you didn't trust us—' she gave Alexa a look '—to help you with it. You don't have to kill yourself to find a replacement chef before you go on leave. If you do, great, and we'll help train them. If you don't, we'll survive.'

Kenya leaned forward and rested a hand on Alexa's.

'Babe, you've built a damn good team. You've also earned our loyalty. That includes helping out when things get rough.' She squeezed. 'It includes taking care of things while you have your babies. We could probably help you get ready for the babies, too.'

'Oh, that's not—' She cut herself off. 'Thank you,' she said instead. 'That means a lot.'

'Yeah, well, it should.' Kenya softened her words with a smile. 'You mean a lot to us.'

'And you mean a lot to me.'

Kenya blinked. Then took the last swig of her beer. 'Thanks. Now, let's go tell the people out there you're having two babies.'

'Oh. Oh, yeah. Okay.'

'It's been a rough week for all of us. This would help. But only if you want to do it.'

She thought about it for a long time. Then she nodded and stood up. 'Let's go.'

The reaction was more than she could have ever anticipated or expected. A stunned silence followed her words, but after that someone began to cheer. People came forward to congratulate her, offering her words of encouragement and advice, asking how they could help.

Alexa swallowed down her emotion many times in the next hour, her eyes prickling at the support she had no idea she'd already had. When she caught Kenya's eye later, she got a wink and a knowing look in return. It made the tears she was holding back run down her cheeks, and she was immediately handed tissues from three different directions. She laughed, waved off concern, pressed the tissue to her eyes. And in that moment she realised two things:

One, she'd spent so many years afraid of opening up and trusting people. Yet despite that, she'd found the very family she'd hoped for her entire life. And they trusted her, for whatever reason. Apparently, she'd earned it. Maybe it was time that she allowed herself to see they'd earned her trust, too.

Number two was more complicated. Because the entire time she'd experienced this emotional, overwhelming thing, she'd felt as though she were missing a limb. She didn't let herself think of it until she was alone that night in her flat. When she did, she didn't like that Benjamin had wedged himself so deeply in her mind that she couldn't go through her day without thinking about him. That she couldn't have important experiences without wanting him there. Without having him there.

She settled on the sofa, but it smelled like him, so she moved. It didn't make sense—he hadn't been there in over a week and her sofas were regularly cleaned.

Except it *did* make sense. She just didn't want to face it.

At some point during the night as she tossed and turned, she realised she already had. She knew exactly what the problem was: Benjamin hadn't wedged himself in her mind; he'd wedged himself into her heart.

Chapter 18

He'd never thought his dream job would become a nightmare. But it was. Working in a place he loved but had given up for—his darkest moments in the last week had made him think—nothing. He only had himself to blame. Alexa hadn't asked him to do this, neither had Lee. He'd done it because he'd thought he was being principled.

He *was* being principled. He couldn't work for a man like Lee. Someone whose cruelty would one day be turned on Benjamin or their staff. Benjamin would have left then anyway, so he'd just hurried along the inevitable by handing in his notice.

But principles didn't pay the bills, or help the mind when dreams were dashed. The euphoria he'd felt after saying he was leaving was well and truly gone. Now he only thought of his responsibilities, of what his parents would say when he finally told them what he'd done, and how Alexa had walked away from his proclamation of love.

A knock brought him out of his thoughts.

It was Saturday night after the restaurant had already closed and most of his staff had gone home. Lee's appearance in his doorway was perplexing for more than that reason though. The very fact that he was there after a week of radio silence was troubling. So was the fact that he'd knocked, which he never had, in all the years they'd worked together, done.

'Can I come in?'

Benjamin opened a hand, gesturing to the chair opposite him. He tried not to think about how Alexa had filled it almost three weeks before. Or anything else they'd done in the office.

'I'm surprised to see you here,' Benjamin said.

'I should have come earlier.'

'Should you have?'

Lee smiled at the casual comment. Or maybe not smiled, but Benjamin didn't think there was a description for Lee simply showing his teeth.

'Yes. We should have had a meeting to discuss the implications of your resignation and the transition plans. Have you told the staff yet?'

'No.'

'Great. We'll—'

'Lee,' Benjamin interjected. 'Did you really come here this time on a Saturday night to talk business?'

'No,' he said after a moment. He leaned forward, rested his arms on his knees. 'I'm here to apologise.'

'Apologise?'

'For setting this in motion.' Now he clasped his hands. 'I always knew you were ambitious, and that In the Rough wasn't where you'd end up. But... I sped it up, by acting like a complete jerk to Alexa. And to you. I'm sorry.'

Benjamin sat back and let his mind figure out what was happening and what he should say next. 'I appreciate that. I'm more concerned about whether you're extending that apology to Alexa.'

'No.' Lee looked down. 'She doesn't want to see me. I want to respect that.'

'I bet she'd want to see you if you're intending on apologising.'

'You think?'

'You spent your life torturing her. I think an apology would be a nice change of pace.'

Lee winced, but he straightened and ran a hand over his face. 'I don't know how I didn't see how much I was hurting her.'

'We all have blind spots when it comes to family.'

It was one of the little nuggets of wisdom his brain had come up with at three or so in the morning some time in the past week.

'Yeah, but hurting her?' He shook his head. 'That's more than a blind spot. It's...' His voice faded, and for a while after, he didn't speak. 'It's not what a brother should do to his sister.'

'Agreed.'

Lee nodded. Got up. 'I don't have anything else to say right now.'

'You could talk about the transition.'

He laughed a little. 'That was me hedging so I wouldn't have to apologise.'

Benjamin chuckled, too. 'I've been there.'

Lee walked to the door but, before he left, turned back. 'We do have to talk about the transition.'

'I know.'

'Maybe we could talk about you buying this place from me.'

'What?'

'It's lost its appeal, now that I know what it did to Alexa.' He angled his head. 'This seems like a good way to restore balance.'

'You should sell it to her, then.'

'Are you kidding me? Her place is much more popular than this. It would be a downgrade.'

With a quick wink, Lee was gone.

He hadn't left things any worse than the way he'd found them. Not even his offer to sell the place to Benjamin had made much of an impact. Perhaps because Benjamin already knew the answer: he wanted In the Rough. He wanted to run the business himself, and do things the way he'd learnt to do them. He had no doubt he would make mistakes, but that was part of the package. He was very much looking forward to making mistakes, in fact.

So yeah, he'd been lying to himself when he said he didn't know why he'd decided to leave. He'd done that because he wanted something else. But he'd

also done it because he was standing up to Lee—
because he was standing up for Alexa. It smarted
that she didn't want him to do that. It hurt that he'd
offered and she'd rejected him. She couldn't see that
he wanted to do this, that he needed to, so that he
could make up for...

He paused. He didn't have to make up for anything. He'd already apologised to Alexa for what he'd
done to her before he'd known her. He'd tried his
best to show her none of that would happen again.
Why had his brain automatically gone there, then? To
make up for something, as if he were in the wrong?

Because he'd taken responsibility for her life in
some ways, he realised. He thought he could make
the hurt she'd been through better by protecting her.
But she was right: the way he'd protected her was
all wrong. He had done what he thought was best,
knowing that she wouldn't appreciate it.

Did he always do that with her? With anyone?
With his...with his mother?

Yes. He did. It was so clear to him that he could
have been staring at its physical form right in front
of him. But he didn't want to look at it by himself. He
wanted to talk to Alexa. He wanted to share it with
her; share everything with her. Because she was his
friend, and because he loved her.

He was halfway to her place when he wondered
whether it was a good idea. It was the middle of the
night on a Saturday. Not to mention the fact that she
clearly didn't consider him her friend. She certainly
didn't love him. It took the rest of the journey there

for him to realise he didn't do a good enough job of fighting for her. She might not love him, but he was sure she cared about him, and maybe they could still be friends. He'd take her friendship if he could have nothing else of her.

Then she opened her front door in her pyjamas. A cotton nightgown that dipped in the valley of her full breasts and caressed her growing stomach. He felt a lot of things in that moment. Protectiveness. Desire. Tenderness. Love. None of it inspired him to think of friendship, and he knew he'd made a mistake.

'I shouldn't have come.'

'You realised this because I opened the door?'

'Yes, actually. What were you thinking, coming to the door like this?'

'Excuse me?'

'You're wearing lingerie.'

'This is not lingerie,' she scoffed. 'It's an old cotton nightgown. My oldest, in fact, because it's the most stretched and none of the others fit me.' She frowned. 'You're one to talk.'

He looked down at his T-shirt and jeans. 'I'm perfectly respectable.'

'Except I can see your biceps and your chest muscles.'

'You can't see my chest muscles.'

'Your T-shirt is tight. I can imagine them.'

'You think I'm dressed inappropriately because of your *imagination*?'

She folded her arms. 'Isn't that what you were doing?'

'I... Well, no. Your breasts are right there.'

She looked down, as if seeing them for the first time. 'Oh. I guess this is not only stretchy around my waist.' She shrugged. 'It's not like you haven't seen this much of them before.'

He closed his eyes and prayed for patience. And maybe a douse of cold water. Maybe an ice bucket, because then he could stuff his heart that was beating with love and amusement for her in it, too.

'Do you want to come in?' she asked when he opened his eyes.

'Yes. No. Yes?' He honestly didn't know. 'I have stuff to say.'

'You don't know where you want to say them?'

'I...think I might get distracted inside.'

'Why?' She leaned against the frame. 'Never mind. It doesn't matter.' Folded her arms. 'Say the stuff.'

'You were right,' he blurted out, because he was avoiding her chest and her eyes and because it was bubbling up inside. 'I take responsibility when I don't have to. But I've been doing it my whole life. With my mom, I mean. She needed me, so I don't know if I didn't have to—'

'You didn't,' she interrupted. 'You chose to. Because she's your mother and you love her, and the way that you show you care is by helping. Doing. Protecting.'

He frowned. Her lips curved.

'Maybe I have some stuff to say, too. But please, continue.'

'Very gracious of you.' He cleared his throat. Tried to remember where he was. 'I blamed myself. For her being sick. I had no reason to. She never made me feel that way. But in my kid brain I thought that if I hadn't been there, hadn't been born, she wouldn't have got sick and—'

She'd moved forward, so when he stopped because of the pain, because he needed to, she took his hands. Slowly, she put them on the base of her waist. Cupped his face.

'Just look at me,' she said. 'Look at me and tell me what you need to say.'

She must have woven a spell on him because he said, 'I don't know why I blamed myself. Maybe because my father said we could make things easier for her. If we could make it easier, we could make it harder. Maybe I already had made it harder. Maybe I was the cause of it?'

'Oh, Ben,' she whispered, lowering her hands to his chest. 'She got sick when you were too young to understand it. Of course your father telling you to help her made you think you needed to because you contributed to it.'

'"Maybe", not "of course",' he replied, though he appreciated the understanding. 'But it happened. The responsibility of caring for her was heavy, but I got stronger. Too strong. I carried it even when she didn't want me to. She might not have wanted me to carry it at all.' He shrugged. 'I did the same with you.'

She sucked in her cheeks, releasing it before her mouth fully became a pout.

'Remember earlier, when I said I have some things to say, too?'

'You mean a few minutes ago? Yeah.'

She'd begun to walk her fingers up his chest. At his comment, she paused to pinch him.

'Okay, okay,' he said with a small laugh. 'No more wise-guy comments.'

'Good, because I need to be serious for a moment.' She took a breath. 'You need to learn how to balance it. Caring for someone, and protecting them so blindly that you do silly, unnecessary things.'

'I know. Lex—'

'Shh,' she said, putting a finger on his lips. 'I'm not done yet.'

He nodded for her to continue.

'I need to learn how to not push you away because I'm scared.' She knitted her brows. 'It might be easier for me because I'm tired of doing it. Protecting myself… It's so much work. It takes so much energy to keep up the shield and to be careful.' She leaned her head against his chest. 'And I'm tired of doing that and of being pregnant.' She lifted her head. 'Do you know how tiring it is to be pregnant? I still have five months to go. I can't do it all.'

He bit his lip to keep from laughing.

'Yeah, okay, laugh at the pregnant lady.'

'I'm not laughing at you,' he said, catching her hand and pressing it to his lips. 'I'm happy. It sounds like you're telling me you want me to do the protecting for you.'

'Did you hear nothing of what I just said?'

'Yeah, but I'm still me. I'm still going to want to protect you. But I'm going to try,' he said sincerely. 'It's not healthy. I know that. I know the situation at home with my family isn't healthy, too. It's…it's safe.'

'For them,' she said gently. 'For you, it's familiar. But it's hard. And every time you see your mother in pain, you'll think it's because of you.'

'I can't snap my fingers and have it disappear.'

'I know that. I'm not asking you to. But I am telling you to be intentional. If you want to be happy, you need to move away from safe. You need to stop taking responsibility for people and things that don't need you to do that for them. Or that, quite simply, aren't your responsibility.' She ran her hands up and down his arms. 'Your mother's illness isn't your fault. Nor is my pregnancy. Or my problems.'

He inhaled, then exhaled. Again, when the first time he did made him feel lighter. He hadn't realised until that night how much he'd blamed himself for a range of things. This conversation made him think that he'd gone along with Alexa's plan because he'd blamed himself in some way for how Lee had treated her. He wanted to make up for it, though he couldn't possibly do that when he wasn't the cause of the treatment.

He saw it now. And, as he told Alexa, it wouldn't immediately go away. Especially not with his mother, where things were more complicated. But he promised her he'd try, so he would.

'Does this mean you're not pushing me away any more?'

'What do you think?'

He smiled when she bumped her belly lightly against him, reminding him of how close they were.

'I need you to say it.'

She rolled her eyes. 'You're annoying.'

'But you love me.'

She hesitated, but her eyes were fierce and sure when she nodded. 'I do.'

Who knew such simple words could set off such intense emotion in him?

'I love you, too,' he said softly.

'I know. You've loved me from the day you first saw me.'

'An exaggeration, I think.'

'I could see it in the way you looked at me. You were such a sucker.'

They were still debating when she led him into her flat. Smiling, he closed the door.

Epilogue

Four years later

'Do you know what's worse than having twin tod-dlers?'

Benjamin didn't look over, too busy trying to get Tori, his daughter, off her brother. 'Tori, come on. You know you're bigger than Tavier.'

'Don't you dare get off your brother because you feel sorry for him,' Alexa said, kneeling on the sofa and looking over its back at them. 'He needs to learn.'

'You're encouraging this?' Benjamin asked.

'He loves it.'

Tavier gave a giggle just then. Benjamin threw up his hands. 'Honestly. I was trying to help you.'

Tavier grinned, and pulled his sister's hair. She responded by sitting on him. All things considered, they were playing fair.

'You haven't answered my question.'

He went to join her on the sofa. 'I'm too tired to pretend to remember what you asked.'

'What's worse than having twin toddlers?'

'Is this a riddle?'

He pulled her against him. Because she'd been kneeling, she had no way of resisting. Not that she would have resisted, he knew. Their marriage was a lot of debating, teasing—she was still talking about how he'd never found her handkerchief in his room—but none of it had to do with touching.

'It's not a riddle,' she said.

'A puzzle, then?'

'Same thing.'

'I don't think so.'

'Ben,' she said, taking his face in her hands. She did it whenever she was being serious with him. After four years together, two of them in marriage, it had happened all of four times. So he knew she was serious.

'What's worse than twin toddlers?' he repeated.

'I'm not sure. Our restaurants failing.'

'Our restaurants aren't failing.'

Of course they weren't, but he'd needed to say it because he needed to get over that fear. It was still there, though he'd been running In the Rough for three years now. It was still competing with Infinity, but somehow that competition didn't matter, since they were both doing what they loved. They both seemed to be good at it, too.

Of course they weren't failing.

'I give up.'

'So easily.'

'Baby.'

'Fine. What's worse than twin toddlers…is another baby.'

He blinked. 'I'm not sure I follow.'

'I'm pregnant, dummy.'

'You're…' He trailed off. Looked at the twins. 'But they're only three.'

'They'll be four when the baby gets here.'

'You're sure?'

'I'm pretty good at maths,' she said, rolling her eyes.

Now he rolled his. 'No. I meant, are you sure you're pregnant?'

'Doctor's results came back this morning.'

Because he had no words, he drew her in, holding her so damn tightly. Their lives together had been tough. Their family situations weren't easy. His father had passed away round about the same time he'd got the restaurant, but his mother had refused to live with him and Alexa. She'd found herself an assisted care facility, visited them occasionally, and Benjamin had had a tough time accepting that. Alexa had, a year after Lee had promised not to contact her, agreed to see him. It had taken them a lot of work to get to where they were now: Lee's monthly visits.

But all of that had been okay because they'd had

one another. Their family, their kids… It was a life he'd never imagined. It was better than anything Alexa had imagined, she'd told him one night after the twins were born and they were staring at them.

'I can't believe they're yours.'

'Ours,' Alexa had replied, gripping his hand. 'You were here through everything, and you know you love them as much as I do. They're ours.'

She'd changed his life. And now she was doing it again.

'You're the best thing that ever happened to me,' he whispered.

'Wait until we're outnumbered before you say that.'

But she was smiling when he pulled away.

'We're having another baby,' he said.

'We are.' She leaned forward and kissed him. 'I love you.'

'I love you.'

A vase crashed as the twins rolled against the table. He and Alexa both jumped up, but the vase had been on the kitchen table, and the twins had knocked the coffee table, which had then knocked the vase to the ground in the kitchen, away from them. Their children were unharmed. The vase? Not so much. Tori and Tavier stared at them with wide eyes.

'I guess this means they love us, too,' Alexa said when they each had a twin in their arms.

'What a life.'

'What a life,' she repeated, and kissed him again.

* * * * *

Karin Baine lives in Northern Ireland with her husband, two sons and her out-of-control notebook collection. Her mother's and her grandmother's vast collections of books inspired her love of reading and her dream of becoming a Harlequin author. Now she can tell people she has a *proper* job! You can follow Karin on Twitter, @karinbaine1, or visit her website for the latest news—karinbaine.com.

Books by Karin Baine

Harlequin Medical Romance

Pups that Make Miracles
Their One-Night Christmas Gift

Single Dad Docs
The Single Dad's Proposal

Paddington Children's Hospital
Falling for the Foster Mom

Reforming the Playboy
Their Mistletoe Baby
From Fling to Wedding Ring
Midwife Under the Mistletoe
Their One-Night Twin Surprise
Healed by Their Unexpected Family
Reunion with His Surgeon Princess

Visit the Author Profile page at Harlequin.com for more titles.

Their One-Night
Twin Surprise

KARIN BAINE

For Jane xx

Prologue

Izzy Fitzpatrick ran blindly out into the night, uncaring about the rain soaking through her clothes and bringing goosebumps out over her skin. She didn't know where she was going, only that she no longer felt safe in her own home. Her whole life as she knew it seemed to have unravelled completely over the course of the evening.

It was bad enough she was still mourning the loss of the man she'd thought she was going to marry and raise her much-longed-for family with, but to discover Gerry had sold her a lie all along was something she knew she'd never recover from.

Now she needed to be somewhere she felt protected, be with someone she could trust. It was no wonder she found herself standing outside Cal Armstrong's house. He was her friend, her colleague, and a man she knew she could turn to in a crisis.

She jabbed at the buzzer on the gate, desperate to get inside and close the door on the nightmare haunting her out here.

Eventually the voice of a sleepy-sounding Cal came over the intercom. 'Hello?'

'Cal?' The sheer relief of hearing his familiar voice was enough to completely break her and the dam broke on the tears she'd been trying to hold at bay with every revelation she'd uncovered tonight.

'Izzy, is that you? What's wrong? I'm coming down.' The gates swung open and she ran towards the house as though she was still being chased by Gerry's invisible demons.

He was pulling on a T-shirt as he opened the door and Izzy launched herself at him, making him stagger backwards into the hall. 'Oh, Cal, I didn't know where else to go, who else to turn to.'

'Calm down and tell me what's wrong. You're safe now.' He kicked the door closed behind her and she was inclined to believe him. His solid presence was just the reassurance she needed right now.

She let him hold her, enjoying being cocooned in his strong arms and the heat of his body warming hers as the cold reality of Gerry's betrayal hit home.

'There was a man at the house…he said Gerry owed him money…something to do with a card game.' Her teeth were chattering now with the shock of having a visit from the kind of people she'd thought only existed in gangster movies.

'Did he hurt you?' Cal tensed beneath her, his biceps bunching and flexing as he demanded the truth.

'No. He was just…intimidating. I told him about the accident, that Gerry had been killed, but he didn't seem to care. He wanted the debt paid. I had to give him every penny I had in the house to make him leave.' She shivered, remembering Gerry's associate standing with a foot inside her door, knowing she was there alone and terrified he'd want more than cash from her.

Cal swore and pulled her tighter into his embrace. 'You're freezing and soaking wet. Go inside and get warm by the fire. I'll get you some towels and warm clothes.'

He led her into the living room, put a blanket around her shoulders and handed her a glass of amber liquid. 'For the shock,' he said, making her drink it before he went to get her the dry clothes he'd promised.

Her throat burned as she downed the alcohol, but she was grateful as it took the chill from her very bones and warmed her from the inside out. That unpleasant house call had only been the start of unravelling Gerry's secrets and lies and now she was afraid there could be a string of debtors turning up on her doorstep looking for recompense.

'I'm sorry I didn't have more in your size,' he said with a half-grin and she appreciated he was still trying to make her laugh even at a time like this. She needed Cal's stability, this normality, to prevent her from tipping completely over the edge.

'That's fine. Thank you.' Izzy took the fresh towels and Cal-sized outfit from him, but she didn't have the energy, or the inclination, to leave the room to get changed. She simply sat and stared at the pile of laundry on her lap, unable to move.

'Let me.' Cal knelt at her feet and gently tugged off her shoes and socks, followed by her sodden trousers and blouse. He moved swiftly and efficiently to strip her of her wet things, leaving just her underwear before wrapping her in a warm, fluffy robe.

He took one of the towels, sat beside her on the sofa and began to dry her hair. She closed her eyes as he massaged her scalp, finding comfort in the intimate gesture. It had been a long time, if ever, since anyone had done that for her.

'I'm sorry for imposing on you like this. I know I'm making a habit of turning up here unannounced.'

'There's no need to apologise and as for your previous visits, I think they were more of an intervention for my benefit. If I hadn't had you chivvying me along after Janet left me I'd either still be in bed, unable to face the world again, or in rehab for jilted men whose fiancées had run off with the *actual* fathers of their babies.' Cal's dark humour failed to disguise how much Janet had really hurt him by stringing him along, pretending they were going to have a baby together.

Izzy understood his pain more than ever since Gerry had essentially done the same thing to her. He'd promised to marry her one day and give her the family she'd always dreamed of but that would never have happened.

'Well, if we're playing who had the worst relationship, I'll see your lying fiancée and raise you a gambling addict.' That was the only way she could see him now, tonight's revelations overriding everything she'd thought she knew about Gerry.

Cal's soothing hands stilled on her scalp. 'Oh, Izzy. I'm so sorry.'

She shrugged but the tears made a resurgence as she thought of all her hopes and dreams for the future that had been doomed from the first time they'd met. 'I've been mourning him for two months, but I wasted my grief on a stranger. That knock on the door tonight prompted me to finally look at all the post and paperwork he left behind. He'd taken out bank loans in my name, forged my signature on goodness knows what and racked up debt wherever he went. It's going to take ages to sort through the mess he's left behind. I just feel so alone, Cal.'

With no family to turn to and her best friend, Helen, living miles away, those old feelings of rejection were surfacing again. She was lucky she had Cal to lend her a shoulder to lean on.

'You're not alone. I'm here for you, day or night, the way you were for me.' He put his arms around her neck and kissed the top of her head.

'What did we do to deserve Janet and Gerry?' Izzy had seen him in the depths of despair where she was currently languishing, and it just didn't seem fair.

'Absolutely nothing.' He tipped her face up and

made her look at him. 'None of this is your fault. Okay?'

'I remember saying something similar to you not so long ago…' Somehow just being in Cal's company was enough for her to stop panicking and provide her with some comfort. She hoped she'd managed the same for him in the aftermath of Janet's departure, even though turning up, unwanted, with home-cooked meals and taking the beer out of his hands had seemed like a thankless task at the time.

'Well, I think I needed reminding then and now so do you. You're a good person, Izzy.' Izzy snuggled into the crook of his arm, gazing into his eyes and realising how special he really was.

She'd never looked at him in a romantic way before but now, wrapped in his embrace, her body was responding to him altogether differently from what she was used to. The comfort she'd found with him had turned into something new and thrilling, desire stealthily making itself known so she was aware of every spot where his body was pressed against hers, that tingling sensation electrifying every inch of her skin.

He was looking at her now with the same hunger in his eyes as she was currently experiencing and the atmosphere between them was suddenly crackling with sexual tension.

She tilted her head up to his, stopped when she thought it might be an unwanted advance, then rejoiced when he bent to meet her lips with his.

They sealed the strange new dynamic with an exploratory kiss that soon obliterated Izzy's doubts that he might only be offering her comfort. She could tell from the increased passionate intensity of his kisses that Cal wanted her as much as she wanted him at that moment. Their mouths were clashing together, they were tugging at each other's clothes in their frantic need to make that ultimate connection, and Izzy knew things between them would never be the same again.

Chapter 1

Three months later

The minute the call came in Izzy knew it was going to be a tough one for her.

'We have a thirty-one-year-old pregnant woman badly hurt after a car accidentally reversed through a shop window.' She paused to clear her throat before she continued relaying the harrowing details to the rest of the crew on board the air ambulance. 'The patient was shunted through the glass and has suffered severe lacerations and potential crush injuries. Her wrist and main artery have been severed but police on the scene have applied a tourniquet to her arm and require immediate medical assistance.'

'What about the driver of the car?' Cal's voice

came over the headset and she knew, as the attending doctor, he was concerned for everybody's safety at the scene.

'Superficial injuries and shock, as far as we can tell. The ambulance can take him to hospital by road, but time is of the essence for our pregnant lady.' Depending on how much blood she'd lost and how long it took for them to get her to the hospital, there was a chance both mother and baby might not make it. Unfortunately, death was a part of the job but under current circumstances this one felt a bit close to home when Izzy's hormones were already all over the place.

Once the pilot found a clear place to land they hurried towards the melee of people and flashing lights. Thankfully the police had cordoned off the area so they could get to work without interference from the general public who were watching the drama unfold.

'This is Tara Macready. She's four months pregnant and has sustained substantial wounds to her left arm. We've been applying pressure to the wound since we arrived on scene.' One of the young police officers talked them through events as his colleagues did their best to stop the patient bleeding out. With their first-aid training they'd known to elevate the arm and apply pressure to reduce the flow of blood and had probably saved her life in the process. They'd done their part and now it was up to Izzy and Cal to get her transferred to the hospital as soon as possible.

Despite the police officers' good work, the ground

was heavily stained with the scarlet evidence of the patient's trauma and Izzy had to fight against the unexpected emotions welling up inside her. 'Tara, we're with the air ambulance crew. We're going to take over now and get you transferred to the hospital.'

'What about my baby?' she mumbled, battling against unconsciousness.

'We're going to monitor you both, but we need to do a few things first, Tara. Izzy, she needs a bilateral cannula as quick as you can.' Cal set to work getting a pressure bandage on to replace the makeshift tourniquet that had been applied to Tara's arm and Izzy inserted the cannula so they could administer fluids. Once she was at the hospital they could do the blood typing necessary for a transfusion.

'I'm giving you some morphine for the pain, Tara.' With the bleeding halted Cal went ahead with pain relief. In this situation, even though they wanted to save both lives, the mother took priority.

Their portable kit enabled them to monitor Tara's blood pressure and heart rate and Izzy made sure everything was in place before they transferred her to the helicopter. They both climbed into the back with their patient so they could keep a close eye on her for the duration of the flight.

'I'm going to take a listen to your baby while the doctor checks your progress. Okay, Tara?' Izzy kept talking her through what was happening, reassuring her everything was going to be all right, even though she was slipping in and out of consciousness.

With a special stethoscope she was able to put

her ear down to Tara's belly and listen for the baby's heartbeat. Hearing that faint rhythm felt like winning the lottery and Cal mirrored her smile when he realised the baby was still hanging in there too.

'Your baby is fighting right along with you, Tara. We'll get you both to the hospital as quickly as we can.' It was all down to timing now and Izzy was taking this one more personally than anything she'd ever witnessed before. Apparently, the prospect of becoming a mother made a woman fight harder than ever and that was one symptom of pregnancy she could get on board with.

Izzy could have kissed the tarmac when the helicopter touched down back at their Belfast base after transferring their patient into the hands of the emergency staff at the hospital.

'Are you okay, Fizz? You're looking a little green around the gills there. Don't tell me you've developed a sudden fear of flying? We'd have to ground you and then who would I have to wind up on a daily basis?'

She rolled her eyes at a grinning Cal. He knew she hated that nickname he'd foisted on her when they'd first met at air ambulance training and she'd let her temper get the better of her, striving to prove she was better than any of the men there.

At least, she used to hate it. In the five years of working together it had grown on her and she'd missed it of late when things between them had become awkward, to say the least. Things weren't going to get any easier between them once he heard her news.

They'd both been hurt by people who'd purported to love them. Cal's pregnant fiancée, Janet, had run out on him with the man who was apparently the *real* father of the baby she was carrying, leaving double the void in his life and double the hurt.

Izzy knew the heart-stabbing pain of betrayal, thanks to Gerry, the man she'd thought she'd spend the rest of her life with. She'd put all her hopes and dreams into their relationship, believing he was the one who was going to give her the family and stability she'd never had growing up in the foster system, only to have everything cruelly snatched away from her when he'd been killed in a motorcycle accident.

The only thing worse than losing someone she loved had been discovering he hadn't been who she'd thought he was at all. A parade of nefarious debt collectors and loan sharks who'd bankrolled a gambling addiction she'd been oblivious to and a bank account emptied as a result of his addiction had merely fuelled the notion that she would never have anyone in her life who loved her unconditionally. The realisation that had sent her running to the one person in her life she knew she could trust.

In Cal she'd found a kindred, wounded soul and she'd needed him to comfort her. They'd shared that one incredible night together but they both knew it could never be more than that when they were too raw to even think of getting involved in any sort of relationship. It was difficult enough going back to work as though nothing had happened between them when every erotic memory of sharing his bed was still so vivid in her mind.

And that one night of seeking solace in Cal's arms had ended in the life-changing consequences she was yet to tell him about. She didn't know how he was going to react to the news he was going to become a father so soon after his break-up and, to be truthful, she didn't want to lose his friendship if he resented the fact she was pregnant with his baby instead of Janet.

'I'm perfectly fine,' she bristled, as they ducked under the still spinning blades of the air ambulance.

This pregnancy might have come as a shock, but she wasn't going to let it get in the way of doing her job. The time would come soon enough when her bump would encroach on the limited space inside the chopper and prevent her from being as physically involved in the rescues as she was used to. At which point in time she'd probably have to become more involved in ground operations and hospital transfers, but not before then.

She was sure the odd bout of nausea would pass soon now she was reaching the end of her first trimester. Although she'd been unaware of the little person growing inside her belly for most of that time. Since she and Cal had agreed to put their indiscretion behind them, it hadn't entered her head that she might be pregnant and had blamed the stress of finding out about Gerry's secret vice as the cause for her missed period. Now everything was going to change between them.

Those tears, which never seemed far away, blurred her vision once more and she rested her hand on the slight swell of her belly to reassure her little bean it still had her, even if Cal decided he didn't want to be involved. She needed to confide in someone and the closest she had to family was Helen, her childhood friend and the only person she'd had growing up who had seemed to genuinely care for her.

Helen still lived in the Donegal area, where Izzy had spent the last of her teenage years before moving to Belfast to study nursing. She was a shoulder for Izzy to lean on when she needed one and though there was a vast geographical distance between them, hearing her voice would be enough to comfort her. Once she got over the shock herself, Izzy resolved to make that phone call. There was just one other person she had to inform first.

'Seriously, though, are you sure you're all right?' Cal stepped closer, his frown wiping away all traces of joviality, his pale blue eyes full of concern.

Izzy dropped her hand, so he wouldn't guess her secret.

'Low blood sugar, I expect. I haven't eaten all day.' A complete lie. Her blood was probably ninety per cent sugar due to the number of biscuits she'd been wolfing down lately.

'Why didn't you say? I'm sure we can do better than a cup of tea and a stale bun in the canteen. After what we've just been through we could probably do with something a lot stronger. Pub?' He began to unzip his bright orange flight suit and let the sleeves drop to his waist, revealing the lean frame encased in a tight black T-shirt beneath the bulky protective layers.

Izzy told herself it was pregnancy hormones making it impossible for her to drag her eyes away. That was the bonus side of her condition, being able to blame recent impulses, including an apparent spike in her libido, on the changes going on inside her body. Although her intimate knowledge of that hard body and the pleasures it could bring a woman was making her temperature rise steadily with every flashback of that night they'd spent together.

It was a loss to womankind that because one of their sisters had been blind to what a great man he was, all the rest would be denied the privilege of getting close to him. Except her, of course, but then they'd agreed it would never happen again, no matter how physically compatible they'd turned out to be. It was ironic that they hadn't wanted to complicate their relationship by getting romantically involved when they were now going to be tied together for the rest of their lives.

Izzy watched him climb out of his suit and flash her that cheeky grin of his.

'Enjoying the view?'

'You wish,' she shot back with just as much sarcasm before he realised how true his observation had been.

Given the physical nature of their work, it was important to keep up their fitness levels, but Cal was the type who could never sit still anyway. His trim, nicely muscled physique wasn't the result of hours spent at the gym. He wasn't the slightest bit vain enough to spend time staring at himself in the mirror whilst he hoisted weights. No, this perfect specimen of the male anatomy was a pleasant result of his busy life as a doctor in the field and the manual labour he did in his vast garden in his spare time.

She shivered as some particularly erotic memories sprang to mind of this handsome man with his tan, sun-bleached mop of hair and that mischievous glint in his eye, lying naked next to her.

'Are you sure you're all right? You've got that hungry look in your eyes again.'

Izzy blinked away inappropriate thoughts and images of her colleague, her friend, and the one constant she'd had in her life here in Belfast before she'd screwed up and potentially lost him for ever too.

'Just starved.' Apparently for more than food. Not that he'd ever shown any interest in her as a woman apart from as another one of his mates until that night.

It hadn't been planned. Izzy had just needed to be with someone who cared about her. Through the tears and shared stories of heartbreak they'd found themselves kissing and searching for some feeling of peace. She didn't regret anything. It had been a beautifully raw expression of their affection and compassion for one another. They simply should have taken adequate precautions for their evening as friends with benefits.

'Let me get the paperwork out of the way and we'll head to the pub before you get hangry. I know what you're like when you're so hungry you turn into a red-headed hulk.'

If she'd had any doubts that he only saw her as a mate, they vanished. She was so completely friend zoned he didn't expect her to take offence at that comment.

'Do not,' she huffed, regardless she knew very well her fiery temper reached boiling point when there was a lack of food close to hand. He hadn't drawn a pretty picture of her when she'd created a sexy centrefold out of him. 'I'm not keen on the pub idea either.'

She worried he'd be suspicious if she sat in the bar nursing an orange juice instead of her usual glass of wine.

'Dinner at that new Italian place, then? Although it'll probably mean having to go home and get changed first. I'm not sure sweaty work clothes will fit their dress code.' He was being unnecessarily concerned. Cal always managed to smell amazing no matter how stressful their shift proved or how energetic he'd been.

'Hmm, I fancy something stodgy and greasy.' She didn't.

'I'll die of starvation if you make me go home first.' She wouldn't. However, if they went to that posh place and Cal changed the habit of a lifetime by not offering to pay the entire bill she'd be mortified because she couldn't afford it.

Even before she'd discovered there'd be a new mouth to feed in the future, she'd been struggling to cover the bills. Gerry had never officially moved in, but he'd used her place as a base when not travelling around the country as a pharmaceutical rep. It wasn't that she was missing his financial contributions to household expenses, quite the opposite. He was the reason she had no savings left to furnish her nest now.

She'd invited him into her heart and her home without the knowledge of his gambling habits. Gerry had had no family or friends either to call on for help and the cost of his funeral on top of his other financial mismanagement meant money was tight for her and nothing short of a miracle would change that now. Wages would have to stretch as far as possible and that would mean cutting back on luxuries like fancy Italian restaurants or any sort of social life.

Izzy should have known better than to think she was sitting pretty at any stage of her life and keep herself protected. Being a kid bounced around the care system had taught her never to rely on anyone except herself and never to let her guard down. Once too often she'd imagined she'd found her forever home, only to be returned like an ill-fitting shirt. Too young, too old, too opinionated, too red, she'd been a nineties Anne Shirley, without the lovable Matthew and Marilla Cuthbert giving her a happy ending at Green Gables.

Meals and board had been provided along with whatever basic material possessions she'd needed, but that all-important element had been missing, as it had for most of her life. Love wasn't something given or received easily for her, even with Gerry.

It had been a slow burn for them but eventually she'd learned to trust, to open up her heart and believe him when he'd promised her a future and a family together.

Even though Cal knew about Gerry's betrayal since it was the reason she'd been driven to his arms, the extent of her financial struggles was another secret she was keeping from someone she considered a friend. With good reason. He'd insist on riding in on his white steed, waving his fat wallet, to save her and she wasn't going to be indebted to him or anyone else. She had to get used to managing on her own when she had errands to run or do the night feeds when she was exhausted beyond belief. The stakes were too high now for her to let anyone into that armoured heart again.

'The "caff" it is, then.' Cal took the lead from Izzy's clues as to what she could afford, not necessarily what she craved. Which, at this moment, didn't go beyond a chance to kick off her shoes and sit down with a cup of builder's tea.

'Do you think they're going to be okay?' Izzy cradled the chipped mug in her hands, drawing comfort from the heat as a chill fluttered over her skin.

'Who?' Cal sawed off another chunk of sausage

and popped it into his mouth. It had become a tradition to go for a meal when their shift had ended. Not only because they'd worked up an appetite, but they needed that time to come down from the adrenaline high and process what they'd gone through at the scene of whatever medical emergency they'd just attended.

'Tara Macready and her baby—you know, the woman we just saved.' She set her tea down and poked the sausage and bacon on her plate with a fork. A fry-up was the standard fare in this particular establishment, but the smell of grease was making her feel queasy again. Rather than make him suspicious she'd ordered her usual, but she'd only managed to nibble at the toast so far.

'We did our best and they're in the best place to recover.' Cal carried on eating, but the image of the blood and knowledge of Tara's condition wouldn't leave her. Most people probably wouldn't have realised she was pregnant, but Izzy would've noticed even if it hadn't been in her notes. These days she was aware of every new change in her body and she'd recognised Tara had the same slightly swollen belly as she did.

This kind of accident wasn't an unusual sight, given the nature of their work, and it was vital they kept a certain detachment when attending these scenes. They weren't supposed to take the emotional trauma home with them and usually she didn't, other than a phone call to check up on a patient's progress.

This one was different as it was a mother and

her unborn child in jeopardy. Perhaps they'd all be different now she was going to be a mother herself. The idea of setting off in the helicopter alone was making her question her own mortality these days. Until now she'd never worried about her own safety up there, but in the not-too-distant future she was going to have someone depending on her coming home from work day after day.

The sound of cutlery clattering onto the plate made her jump and the touch of Cal's hand as he settled it on hers didn't help soothe her nerves.

'They would never have made it at all if they'd gone by road and she might lose the use of her hand but they're still alive. Now, are you going to tell me what's going on in that head of yours today? You're not yourself at all.' It wasn't that Cal didn't have sympathy for them, but he knew, as well as she did, that they had to do their job and move onto the next one without looking back in case it affected future call-outs.

That had taken some getting used to, although she'd had years of experience as a nurse in A and E. Cal too, a consultant in emergency medicine, had found those first cases difficult to walk away from at the hospital doors. They'd often talked into the wee hours about their day, much to his fiancée's annoyance.

These pregnancy hormones were making her feel as though she'd taken a step back, seeing everything in a new, terrifying light. Not that she had any intention of giving up her job. She loved being part of the team being whisked up into the air at a moment's notice to save people in trouble. This was simply a blip and one she couldn't wait to get over, along with this nausea.

'Sorry. I'm not the best company at the minute.'

He squeezed her hand. 'You know I'm here for you anytime.'

His misplaced concern caused her eyes to prickle with tears. Recently she'd suspected her eyeballs had been replaced by tiny hedgehogs, that was happening so often. He was so considerate it pained her, knowing she was about to turn his world on its head again.

'Thanks,' she said, withdrawing her hand from the safety of his. It wasn't going to do her any good to expect Cal to prop her up every time she had a wobble, no matter how comforting it was. They hadn't planned this baby and whilst she was reconciled some way to the idea of becoming a parent there was no guarantee he would. There was every chance she would end up raising their child alone and she was fine with that. If that's what Cal wanted.

'Perhaps you came back too early—you know, after Gerry,' he said softly with some hesitation, and she knew he was half expecting her to kick off at the suggestion. Which she usually did when anyone tried to tell her what to do, thinking they knew her better than she knew herself.

She didn't agree with him on this occasion either but she'd no other way to explain her current mood without spilling the beans about the baby.

'You could be right.' She pushed her plate away before she vomited.

* * *

Now Cal knew something really was wrong with Izzy. She usually fought him over the smallest difference of opinion, so daring to suggest something as huge as she'd returned to work too soon warranted all-out war.

Between that and her roller-coaster appetite he was beginning to worry about her. One minute she was eating everything in sight, including his emergency chocolate stash he kept for those occasions they didn't have time for a meal break. The next she was sitting staring at her rejected fry-up as though she was about to burst into tears at any second.

He hadn't noticed until today how emotional she'd become, having taken her stoicism and ability to bounce back from any eventuality for granted. Caught up in the sorrow of his own break-up, he hadn't seen past the front she'd been putting on since Gerry had died, accepting her assurances she was fine too easily. Probably because he didn't want to over-analyse what had happened between them that night when she'd come to his place in a state about Gerry.

He'd been committed to his relationship with Janet, even if she hadn't considered it a priority, but when Izzy had come to him seeking support and comfort, any thoughts of his ex had been obliterated by his all-consuming need for her. Once he'd tasted desire on her lips, all those suppressed feelings he'd apparently been harbouring for her had been tangled in there right along with their limbs and tongues. He never considered that she might've been down in those depths of despair all this time.

Yes, Janet had betrayed him in the worst possible way, stringing him along with that dream of his happy family, only to snatch it away for ever. It had been partly his fault, so desperate to set up a loving home like the one he'd grown up in he'd clung onto the wrong person, ignoring all her flaws in favour of the family he'd envisaged having with her. Now he was worried he'd taken advantage of Izzy when she was obviously still emotionally vulnerable.

They'd been close for years and that bond had irritated their partners at times, but they'd only crossed the line that night when their relationships had forcibly ended. Ever since they'd fallen into bed together he'd found it difficult to rein those feelings back in and pretend nothing had happened. They'd agreed that was the best course of action, but it was impossible to put their indiscretion completely out of his head when he saw her every day and was reminded how incredible that time together had been. As though they'd finally stopped pretending their chemistry was nothing more than camaraderie and had expressed their feelings for one another physically.

How was he supposed to forget something so amazingly honest after his recent experience of deceit?

'I've been a bad friend to you lately. I'm sorry.' There'd been a distance between them recently, which he'd created as a coping mechanism to protect himself, never thinking about the support Izzy needed. He thought back over these past horrendous months and thought of all the support she'd offered him after Janet had left.

Izzy had been a constant on his doorstep despite his repeated warnings he didn't want to see or talk to anyone in the aftermath of his ex's revelation. She'd been the provider of home-cooked meals when he hadn't wanted to eat and the confiscator of alcohol when all he'd wanted to do was drink. Ignoring his bad temper, she'd fought past his defences and dragged him out of the quagmire, so he'd been able to get on with his life when he'd truly believed it was over.

That was the true definition of a friend. Not someone who muttered his sympathies and accepted her grieving was over because it suited him better than having to dig beyond a fake smile and talk about feelings. Now, seeing her here, eyes glassy with unshed tears, biting her lip to keep up the façade, he wanted to finally step up and be there for her. The way she'd done for him. She was the closest thing he had to family now. The only one who'd been there with him through the darkest hours of his life, and he owed her.

'Don't be daft. Aren't you here, putting up with my mood swings?' There was that smile again that he was learning not to trust when her eyes were cloudy with uncertainty and something else he couldn't quite decipher but which made him feel guiltier than ever.

'I wasn't there for you after Gerry died.'

'Um, I think you were.'

He wasn't expecting her to reference what had happened between them but there was a suggestion of that passionate encounter flickering like erotic flames in her eyes. Rather than complicate matters more between them, Cal chose to ignore the reminder. In conversation at least. 'If something's wrong I expect you to tell me and let me help. Okay?'

'Understood. Now, shall we get the bill?' She wrestled out from his grip and waved to the waitress.

Cal sighed and pulled his credit card from his wallet. 'I'll get this. It's the least I can do.'

Izzy made her usual protests as she fished in her bag for her purse, but he grabbed the bill first. 'Let me pay my half at least.'

'You can leave a couple of pounds for the tip if you want.' It was then he caught a glimpse inside her purse to see only a few coppers resting in the lining. Rather than embarrass her further, he tossed the loose change he found in his pocket on the table and made to leave.

Something wasn't right with Izzy and he wasn't going to rest until he discovered what. And if he wasn't the friend she needed he knew how to find the one who fitted that description.

Chapter 2

'This is supposed to be fun,' Cal called back to Izzy, who was doubled over trying to get her breath back and looking as though she was hating every second of this.

'I'm sure you're enjoying yourself, but I'd rather be vegging out watching the telly on my day off.' Izzy straightened up, pulled a hairband out of her pocket and tied her wild mane of red hair away from her face. Despite her protests, he thought she looked happier than she had in days, hiking out here in the County Down countryside, in the shadow of the Mourne Mountains. To be on the safe side he'd contacted Helen, who she often talked about, and suggested she might want to check in with her friend. It hadn't been difficult to make contact when Helen's phone number was on the birth announcement she'd sent Izzy after her son was born. The picture of mother and baby with the time and date of arrival took pride of place on Izzy's desk at work.

'I think we've both done our fair share of moping around. The fresh air will do you good.' He'd been keeping a closer eye on her lately and had noticed how withdrawn she seemed to have become compared to the old, devil-may-care Fizz he'd come to know.

There was always some excuse post-shift now about why she couldn't come out for a meal or even a quick drink, and he hated to think of her shut away in that empty house with nothing but memories to keep her company. After Janet had left him he'd thought he'd never venture over the doorstep again, afraid to face the world outside. Izzy had gone through a lot and was bound to have been changed by it, but he was determined not to let her retreat from civilisation altogether.

Since she didn't seem keen on spending time in crowded places he'd gone to the other extreme and dragged her out on one of his walks in the countryside with him.

'You can sit still and enjoy the fresh air. I think they call it sunbathing.'

'With your colouring?' He snorted as she tried to convince him her pale skin did anything other than freckle and burn.

Izzy shrugged off her jacket and tied it around her waist. Although he'd been concerned she wasn't eating properly, as her white T-shirt drew taut he could see she'd filled out a bit over these past weeks. He was glad. She looked better with a little meat on her bones, healthier, and as the sun shone through her shirt, silhouetting her figure, he could see exactly which parts of her had blossomed.

'Enjoying the view?' An amused Izzy echoed the words he'd teased her with the other day and snapped Cal's attention away from the soft round breasts he so clearly remembered palming in his hands.

'I was doing this for your benefit. I prefer a hike in the mountains myself.' He dismissed her comment, instead of confirming where his gaze had been lingering.

This walk was small potatoes for him when he preferred the challenge of a hill climb, whatever the weather, where he was focused on every step lest he end up at the bottom of a ravine. It was good for him to keep busy, his mind and body too active to entertain thoughts of his broken dreams, and he wanted to do the same for her.

'Yeah, 'cause we don't see enough of this at work.' Izzy rolled her eyes and started walking again.

'Who could ever tire of this?' He held his arms aloft in celebration of today's beautiful blue skies. They weren't always blessed with such favourable weather in Northern Ireland, even during these summer months, and he was of the opinion they should enjoy every second before the rain made another appearance.

'Me. Pretty. Damn. Quickly,' she huffed out as

she climbed the slight incline of the bluebell-lined pathway, her slim legs flexing below her shorts with every step.

Cal let her reach the top first, determined to see her do this at her own pace in case he scared her off altogether. Today was about re-forging that bond between them so she'd be comfortable enough to share what was really going on in her life now, without any awkwardness coming between them.

She stood above him, hands on hips, face tilted towards the sky, eyes closed and soaking up the heat of the sun. This was what he wanted for her, to find peace and be free of the stresses she was under. Studying her from here, he could see why his ex had always seemed so threatened by her. He'd laughed off Janet's bouts of jealousy when he'd mentioned Izzy's name because at that time he'd never thought of her as anything more than a friend. Now it was difficult to think of her as anything other than someone he wanted to share his bed with again.

As he stood there, appreciating the dusting of freckles across her nose and the stunning red hair most women would pay a fortune to try and replicate, she suddenly crumpled to the ground.

'Izzy?' His heart leapt into his mouth and he sprinted towards her, their perfect day shattered at the thought of something happening to her.

She was spread-eagled on the grass, her eyes still closed.

'Izzy?' He dropped to his knees and called her name again, before throwing off his backpack in case his medical skills would be required. Perhaps he had asked too much of her in coming here when she hadn't been herself recently, but he'd wanted to do something for her since it was his fault she felt she couldn't confide in him any more. He was sure it was because she regretted sleeping with him, but he couldn't change what had happened between them, even if he'd wanted to.

He leaned over her, his face close to hers, listening for signs she was still breathing. Her chest continued to rise and fall, and he could feel her soft breath on his cheek.

Suddenly, her eyes snapped open and he was staring into the depths of those sea-green pools. In that moment he was transported back to that night-which-should-not-be-named, when they had been lying in his bed together, naked and wanting. Izzy was looking at him the same way she had then, her eyes and her body asking him to hold her, kiss her, love her. He didn't think he'd be able to resist any more now than he had then, and it was only the impact of those past actions on their relationship that made him pull back. Today was about improving relations between them, not making their working environment more awkward.

'I hope you're happy now you've almost killed me.' Izzy sat up and brushed off any suggestion that she'd ever wanted him to do anything other than feel guilty about bringing her out into the wild.

He sat back on his heels and whistled out a quivering breath. 'Don't ever do that to me again. You nearly gave me a heart attack.'

'Now you know how it feels. I'm not moving again until we've refuelled.' She rolled over onto her side and reached for the food supplies stashed in his bag.

'There are kinder ways to let me know you're hungry than fake fainting, you know!' He pulled out a bottle of water from the side pocket in the rucksack and flicked the condensation from the cold bottle at her, getting them back on the pranking friends track rather than the almost kissing past lovers one on his mind.

She let out a shriek before dissolving into a fit of adorable giggles. It was good to hear her laugh again and for him to do it with her. He realised then it had been a while since he'd found the fun in anything. Izzy in any capacity was good for his soul.

'I'll get you back for that when you least expect it,' she vowed, eyes narrowed as she took a bite of her sandwich.

Cal stretched out on the grass beside her. They did spend the majority of their time in isolated countryside, going to the rescue of those in mortal danger, but there was no time to enjoy the surroundings. It was nice to chill out here in the open and better still with company.

Izzy handed over the parcel of sandwiches she'd made. He'd suggested a pub lunch, but she'd insisted on a picnic. Come to think of it, she'd been doing a lot of that recently, bringing her own lunches, forgoing their usual coffee runs in favour of her ever-present water bottle. He harked back to that day in the café when she'd struggled to scrabble together a few pounds for a tip. The awful realisation of what was going on made it hard for him to swallow his mouthful of food.

'I hate to sound like a broken record but is there something wrong? I'd really hate to think you were suffering and hadn't come to me for help.'

He saw the flicker of anxiety on her face as she gulped at her water, but it didn't give him any pleasure to know he'd been right. That withholding of information illustrated the decline in their friendship over these past months since they'd slept together when before that they'd used to share everything going on in their lives. He'd feared the repercussions of that intimacy so much it was possible he'd created that distance between them. Worried about getting hurt again so quickly after Janet that he'd backed right out of Izzy's life when she'd needed his support most.

'I, er, I'm just having a few money troubles at the minute. The funeral and everything else has left me a bit strapped for cash, but I'll get by. I always do.' She gave him a bright smile before quickly looking away again, but he didn't believe her problems were as straightforward as she was making out.

He was grateful she'd finally confided in him because he'd never considered the financial implications of losing her partner, regardless of the gambling debts he'd apparently accrued before his death. For one thing he would've imagined Gerry had had some sort of life insurance policy in place to ensure she was protected for this kind of eventuality. Then, of course, there were the everyday practicalities of losing a second income. When Janet had moved out he'd had to cover the mortgage and household bills himself.

He might not have been great at providing Izzy with the emotional support she'd needed but this was something practical he could help with.

'There's no point worrying yourself sick or depriving yourself over the sake of a few pounds. I can give you a loan if that would help dig you out of a hole?' He'd be happier to write her a cheque with no desire to see the money returned but she would never entertain the idea. She was already shaking her head at the alternative suggestion.

'That's a very kind offer but you know I couldn't do that. Taking money from friends always gets messy and I've had enough of being in anyone's debt. Thank you but I'll get through this myself.' Izzy wrapped up the leftovers, tucked them back into the bag and got to her feet, discussion over.

Cal wasn't surprised she'd turned him down because she was notoriously as stubborn as hell but so was he. He was sure there was more to the story, more he could do to help her.

They'd often partnered up on social occasions with their significant others and he'd never believed Gerry good enough for his Fizz. Where she had been the fun and friendly half of the two, Gerry had been her complete opposite. Often sullen and reluctant to be drawn into conversation, he was a closed book and hard to like. He'd never known what Izzy had seen in him but respected her enough not to question her judgement.

Izzy was trying to pick up the fractured pieces of her life in order to move on and Cal was going to be there for her every step of the way. It was about time someone was. Now he knew there was a problem he wasn't going to rest until he knew she was going to be okay. He could be every bit as obstinate as Isobel Fitzpatrick when it came to helping a friend.

'Ten-year-old girl suffering severe burns after falling against a barbecue.' Izzy recapped the few details they'd been given on the emergency call and directed Mac, the pilot and operations manager, to a clear landing site near the address they'd been given.

Although she didn't wish harm on anyone, never mind a child, the distraction of work was good for her. She had let slip more than she'd intended about her problems to Cal but telling him her money woes was preferable to surprising him with the news he was going to be a father. They'd both messed up, and Cal had enough of his own personal issues to deal with. There was no way she was bringing a child into the world expecting to have someone bailing her out at every hint of trouble. That would be asking for more heartache. She loved him for the offer all the same.

His ex didn't know what she'd thrown away. Cal deserved someone who loved him as much as

he'd obviously loved Janet. There was nothing he
wouldn't have done for her. Including bringing up
someone else's baby as his own if she'd been honest
with him instead of stringing him along until she'd
been sure her other lover did want her after all.

If he hadn't, Izzy suspected she'd still be letting
Cal play happy families with a child who wasn't
his. He'd been broken by the betrayal, as anyone
would've been, and Izzy had been crushed on his
behalf because she knew how important family was
to him.

Izzy needed a friend right now, someone who
could provide some normality for her when her life
was falling down around her, but as soon as he found
out about the baby she knew that would change.
Things would become untenable when he'd lost the
family he'd always dreamed of, only to be left with
one he hadn't planned. It was bound to cause some
resentment or tempt Cal into interfering in some way,
directing that focus from Janet's baby onto hers. She
wasn't going to fool herself into thinking anyone had
her back any more now than they had before. If there
was one thing she excelled at it was picking herself
up and dusting herself off after being left in the lurch.

Apart from not wanting to hurt him with her
news, she also wanted to avoid him becoming over-
protective where she was concerned. When he'd discovered Janet was expecting he'd practically dressed
her in bubble wrap, afraid to let her lift a finger to
keep mum and baby as safe as possible. Janet had

been happy to put her feet up and let Cal run around after her but that was exactly what Izzy didn't want.

She intended to carry on as normal for as long as she could. Being pregnant wasn't a disability, millions of women had gone through it time and time again. Besides, she was almost at the three-month mark and out of the danger stage. If Cal had any inkling he wouldn't have suggested a country ramble, never mind let her carry on with the physical side of her job.

Fitness and strength was a huge part of being air ambulance crew and she loved her job. If nothing else, she needed every penny she could put aside before her maternity leave. She didn't want to think about the cost of childcare for the next eighteen years. From now on she was going to take one day at a time. It was the only way she'd get through these next belly-blossoming months without going doolally.

'Earth to Izzy. I asked if you were ready for this.' Cal's eyes were on her instead of the lush green scenery whizzing past below. The last thing she needed was him getting distracted on this call with her. There was no room for error when every second counted.

''Course. Why wouldn't I be?' She frowned at him, a warning to mind his own business at work. He knew better than to let personal problems encroach on this already too-small space and make it even more claustrophobic. The pile of bills he thought was her only problem was definitely not something that warranted a discussion here. Especially when she was doing her best not to think about the little bundle who was about to throw her life into more chaos.

Cal gave her the thumbs up as they landed, and she considered the matter closed for now when there was a patient needing their help.

They hiked up the street with their gear to the house with the door already lying open.

'Let's hope someone had the foresight to administer first aid.' It was Cal who said it, although Izzy was thinking the same thing. Providing that immediate care in the aftermath of a burn could make all the difference to the long-term damage.

'I'm sure the switchboard operator would've given them instructions on cooling the burn under tepid water.' They didn't know how serious the burns were but with a child involved the stakes were that much higher. Skin grafts, infection and plastic surgery were all possible, depending on the extent of the burns, and not something a parent would want their baby to go through.

'Hello. Air ambulance crew here,' Cal called into the house as they made their entry.

'We're upstairs in the bathroom.' A woman appeared at the top of the stairs and beckoned them up where there was a group of adults crowded around a sobbing child.

'Okay, could we ask everyone to give us a bit of room, please?' The bathroom was cramped enough for them to work in so Izzy needed to clear out those taking up unnecessary space. Eventually the other family members shuffled out until there was only the child and her parents remaining.

'Hi, I'm Doctor Cal. What's your name?' Cal knelt down beside the youngster, who was trembling and crying as she stood in the bath while her father was hosing her down with a shower head.

'This is Suzy,' her father volunteered, and shut off the water so they could assess her injuries.

'I hear there was an accident with a barbecue?' Although Cal took the lead, Izzy was there to back him up and give assistance where it was needed.

Dad nodded. 'The kids were running about, and she tripped and fell into the barbecue. She stuck her hand out to break the fall and I think that's where most of the damage was done.'

Whilst Cal was inspecting the upper-body burns that had left angry red marks across her chest and shoulders, Izzy gently took her hand to assess the extent of the burns.

'Where do you hurt most, Suzy?'

The child lifted her hand up and Izzy could see where it was beginning to blister.

'We're going to give you something to help with the pain, sweetheart. Cal, do you want to take a look at this?'

His brow furrowed too, and it was clear he wasn't any happier than she was at the sight. 'The chest and shoulder burns I would say are only two per cent partial thickness so we can dress those but I'd prefer a specialist to take a look at that hand. In the meantime, can we get a line in for some pain relief?'

One of the bonuses of transporting patients by helicopter was that they could take them directly to the best centre to treat their injury. In this case they could take little Suzy to the burns unit where plastic surgeons would be there to assess her injury and treat her straight away to limit permanent damage.

'Suzy, you're just going to feel a wee scratch in your hand. We need to give you something to help with the pain. Perhaps Dad can just hold you steady for me? Good girl.' Izzy administered the drugs as instructed by Cal, which would hopefully go some way to making the child comfortable again. It was difficult to watch her suffer and Izzy felt for the mother, who was standing nearby, whispering soothing words to comfort her child, though she must've been racked with guilt and anxiety herself.

Izzy understood motherhood wasn't an easy job when so many had failed her in her childhood, but she was looking forward to the challenges ahead. She wanted her child to know its mother would be there come what may and would relish that role of being needed, bringing a sense of security she'd never experienced herself.

'Dad, are you okay to carry her out to the helicopter? Then we're going to take a quick ride to the hospital. Have you ever been on a helicopter, Suzy?' Cal got them organised and on the move whilst Izzy checked in with the control room to update them on their progress and route.

'No, she hasn't, and neither have I.' Suzy's dad gave a nervous laugh.

'There's nothing to worry about. We'll be at the hospital in twenty minutes tops.' Half the time it would've taken an ambulance and it cut out all the transfers between departments. Izzy knew if it was her daughter she'd be only too glad to have Cal and the helicopter at hand to administer treatment. He was a calm, assured presence in the storm and Izzy hoped that remained true for the one he was about to enter with her.

Once they landed, Cal and Izzy worked together to unbuckle their passengers and get them out of the helicopter. They hurried with the stretcher towards the team waiting for the transfer, but the ground was greasy after the earlier downpour of rain and in Izzy's haste she slipped and landed on her back.

'Izzy, are you all right?' Cal hesitated and offered a hand to help her to her feet, but she was winded and a little disorientated.

'Go. Go.' She waved him on, their patient a priority here, but made no move to get up.

Instead, she lay back and rested her hands protectively on her belly. It was early days and she'd hit the ground hard, as indicated by the pain shooting up her spine.

Those darned hedgehogs were back, pricking her eye sockets and trying to make her cry again, as she wondered if she had been taking too many risks after all. If she hadn't been one hundred per cent sure about wanting this baby, the prospect of having harmed it confirmed it was all she wanted. She needed to know it was safe in there, protected from her stupidity and two left feet. At least she was in the best place possible to find out.

She heard a male voice utter an expletive and looked up to find Cal standing over her. 'You really hurt yourself, huh?'

He bent down and eased her up into a sitting position. That small act of support was enough to tip her emotionally over the edge. One crack in her defences and the dam broke, tears gushing down her face for the first time since Gerry's funeral.

'I'm pregnant, Cal.' She was finally admitting it now in the hope it made this baby real and lessened the possibility of something happening to it.

'Okay. Okay. We'll get you into the emergency room and I'm sure they can arrange an ultrasound for you to make sure baby's all right. How far along are you?' Cal did his best to remain calm, so he didn't freak her out more than she already was. Regardless, that was exactly what he was doing on the inside.

'Three months.'

Perhaps it was the shock of her news, but it took a moment for it all to sink in for Cal. Gerry had died over five months ago so the baby couldn't be his. On the other hand, he and Izzy had slept together more recently. Say, three months give or take a few days. His heart tried to take a flying leap out of his mouth. This was his baby. He was going to be a father.

There were a few seconds when he thought he was going to pass out from the sheer significance of what she'd told him. It was cruel timing to discover a one-night stand with his work colleague had resulted in an unplanned pregnancy so soon after the drama of his cheating fiancée and a baby that had turned out not to be his.

Not long ago this news would have made his day. He'd been looking forward to fatherhood since his own parents had died, but circumstances had changed. Along with his outlook on life. He was still reeling from Janet's abuse of his trust and he definitely wasn't ready to be thrown into another drama. Especially one as life-changing as fathering a baby.

He was still scarred by having his last family torn away from him and there was no way of telling how that could manifest itself as this pregnancy progressed. The trauma and loss wasn't something he'd get over easily and it was going to be difficult for him to get used to the idea of becoming a father again when Janet had forever tainted that picture of having a happy family.

It was important to remember this wasn't the ideal scenario for Izzy either after losing Gerry. They were going to have to work together to make sure this baby wasn't affected by the personal baggage they were both carrying from their pasts.

'I'm sorry.' As he got staff to help him transfer her to a stretcher and take her inside, she kept apologising, and he knew why. Izzy was such an empathetic person she was more worried about how the pregnancy would affect him than her.

'You have absolutely nothing to apologise for.

We both messed up. The timing isn't the greatest, and neither are the circumstances, but the damage has been done.' He thought he saw her flinch at his choice of words, but he preferred to deal in the truth these days. This wasn't exactly a joyous occasion for either of them, rather something they were going to have to learn to live with.

They didn't love each other, and all indications would suggest she'd rather forget the night they'd apparently conceived this baby. It wasn't the family he'd planned on having but it wasn't one he could pretend wasn't happening either.

Later, as they transferred for the ultrasound it struck Cal how vulnerable Izzy looked. Once he'd got over his initial shock he could see how frightened she was, tears still falling from her red-rimmed eyes and her hands wringing her handkerchief into knots. For once she was the one who needed support rather than being the one who always provided it.

He squeezed her hand as the sonographer applied gel over her stomach to let her know he was there. If she hadn't wanted him with her she would've made it clear a long time ago.

'If this baby is as tough as its mum, it's not going to be bothered by one wee fall.'

His reassurance was rewarded with a crooked smile, but she was gripping his hand like a vice, further indication that she wanted him with her. It was survival instinct that made him want to disengage her hand from his and turn his back on the epic responsibility of becoming a parent after past experiences. They weren't even in a relationship, therefore giving her more reason to walk out the door when a better option came along. In the end it was his loyalty to Izzy that saw him stick around. This was a second chance for him to be a friend to her and give her the support she needed.

She turned her head to watch the screen as the sonographer moved the Doppler over her slightly rounded belly. Cal had been blind to the obvious signs of her pregnancy, which he would've spotted if he didn't spend so much time in his own head, wallowing in the past or trying to keep her at arm's length. The sickness, the unexpected emotional displays, not to mention the recent aversion to alcohol and greasy food, were blatant clues, along with her new curves.

Watching that hazy blob on the screen come to life brought up so many emotions he had to swallow before he started wailing. It should have been such an exciting time, seeing his baby for the first time, but this was the second time he'd been here. The memories of sitting here, holding Janet's hand, were too painful for him to enjoy the moment, even when the heartbeat sounded out around the room to let them know everything was all right. He was relieved, of course, but emotionally he was just kind of numb.

Izzy's sobs let him know she would love this baby enough for the two of them if it came to it. He lifted her hand to his mouth and kissed it, so she knew he wasn't angry at the situation they'd found themselves in and pleased that the baby was going to be okay.

Then he noticed the frown on the sonographer's face and the quick movement of the Doppler further over Izzy's stomach. She hadn't missed it either.

'What's wrong? I thought the baby was okay?' Her eyes were wide with panic and she almost cut off the circulation in his fingers with her grip. Cal's own breath stilled as they waited for a reply.

'You haven't had your twelve-week scan yet?'

Izzy shook her head. 'I didn't get around to organising that yet.'

The sonographer turned the monitor around for them to see, a smile now evening out her wrinkled forehead as the heartbeat rang out loud and clear once more.

'They'll be able to give you a more accurate reading and confirm dates with you, but I do have some news I can share with you.'

'What? What is it?' It was Cal's turn to voice his concern. He hadn't remained detached from this after all as a swell of nausea rose up inside him at the thought the baby was in any sort of jeopardy.

'I was confirming a healthy heartbeat, but I've found more than one. Meet baby number two.' She turned the screen round so they could see the evidence for themselves.

'You mean...twins?' Izzy's mouth fell open in a half laugh, half sob as it was confirmed with a nod.

'Wow.' It was all he could manage in the wake of

the bombshell. Two babies at once. A ready-made family neither of them had planned.

He could see the second reality hit home for her too.

'What am I going to do, Cal?' Struggling for money and now with the prospect of having two children to support, she was turning to him for help. She wouldn't have asked unless she was desperate when she was always so single-minded about controlling her own life. It wasn't a plea he would ignore. These babies were as much his responsibility as they were hers. Neither of them had any family around, or had any intention of getting into another relationship anytime soon. It seemed to him there was only one logical solution to their current situation.

'You'll just have to move in with me.'

Chapter 3

'It wouldn't hurt to think about it. At least until you're back on your feet financially.' Cal was sitting in the chair opposite Izzy in the control room back at base with his feet on the desk, waiting for the next call and driving her to distraction in the meantime.

It was impossible for her to relax since he'd first made that ridiculous suggestion she move in with him to help solve her money problems. Of course, she'd eventually shot him down at the hospital, convinced it had been the shock talking after finding out she was expecting twins. The news had affected her so much she'd almost accepted in the heat of the moment.

It would've been easy to say yes and line up a partner to share the bills and parenting responsibilities but shacking up together for the sake of convenience wouldn't have been fair. Especially to her, when it would give her false hope they could pick up where they'd left off that night in his house. He'd made it clear that wasn't going to be an option, regardless of the new complication in their lives. Every time she thought that attraction between them was raising its head, he backed off, and she had to get it out of her head they could be anything more than friends or she'd never move on from that night.

Cal wasn't promising her that they'd live happily ever after together. In fact, he'd yet to acknowledge wanting to take on any sort of parenting role. This sounded more like offering a friend a sofa to kip on when they were down on their luck. She supposed she should be grateful for that much when he could hardly bring himself to touch her, much less declare his undying love for her, since they'd slept together.

'You know as well as I do it's a foolish notion. I'd appreciate it if you didn't bring it up at work where someone could overhear.' With sharp reflexes she shot out her hand to catch the rubber ball he was bouncing off the wall before the repetitive thud gave her a migraine. It was fair to say it didn't take a lot to rile her these days when she was so full of stress and worry.

'Uh…there's no one here. Mac's on his break.' Smartass had an answer for everything when he knew very well she didn't want him bringing this up again regardless of who was around. This wasn't a matter for gossip fodder or outlandish proposals born of a misguided sense of duty. It was her life.

Izzy unclenched her fist and the ball pinged back into shape. As it turned out, it was a pretty good stress reliever. It saved her wringing anyone's neck.

'You know what I mean. We spend half of our lives talking over headsets and I don't want anything accidentally slipping out. My private life is just that and I'll tell people about the pregnancy in my own time. As for moving in together, we're definitely keeping that between us before anyone gets carried away with the idea.' Her included.

He was saying all the right words but since finding out about Gerry's secret life she'd learned to look beyond mere lip service. Cal was the sort of man who would fulfil his obligations no matter what the personal cost was to him, but she didn't want him to feel trapped. Neither did she want someone else promising her the world and getting her hopes up about playing happy families, only to have them cruelly dashed further down the line.

Her reservations seemed justified when he wasn't giving off the same vibes he had when he'd announced Janet's pregnancy. It was understandable he wouldn't be as excited this time around after everything that had happened, but she didn't see that same desire in him to be a father any more. Her babies deserved the very best she could give them and that didn't include a reluctant dad. She knew what it was like to grow up somewhere you weren't completely wanted, and she vowed to do better by her children as a parent. Even if that meant raising them alone.

Cal's offer might be a temporary solution to her problems, but she knew it would be setting them up for future ones.

'I don't see why you're so against the idea.' He withdrew his long limbs from the desk and sat up in the chair, no longer appearing so relaxed.

'We'll start with the fact we've both recently lost the people we loved and neither of us are in the right state of mind to make a life-changing decision like this. Then there's the whole baby issue. You weren't even prepared for one baby, never mind two. Think of the disruption that's going to cause in your life on a practical level. I didn't tell you before now that I'm pregnant because I didn't want you to feel obligated. I'm not expecting anything from you.'

This wasn't about sparing his feelings, it was about keeping things real. She could raise these babies alone because she would make them her whole world. To have two children at once gave her the family she wanted, and it didn't have to include a man.

'Are you done?' He leaned forward, his face and body rigid as he stared her down, and she knew she'd dented his pride. 'Yes, I'm thinking with my head instead of my heart but the whole love thing didn't work out for me. I don't like thinking of you in that flat with goodness knows who knocking on your door in the dead of night. My house is big enough to accommodate everyone and I've already got a nursery. We might have to double up on some things but that's easily arranged. I want to be a good friend to you as well as provide a stable home for you all.'

'What happens when you meet someone else and want to set up a home with them? Where would that leave me? Alone, penniless and out on the street with two children.'

After Gerry she knew she'd find it harder than ever to trust another man get close anyway, but her babies took priority over everything. Not that she'd be a catch, broke, with two children by another man. Cal might believe that he'd never get into another relationship, but he could change his mind over time. He was handsome, smart and too caring for his own good. There was no reason he couldn't have it all if he wanted. A woman would have to be a lunatic to turn him down. Or simply trying to save him from his own sense of chivalry.

'Think about it.' He edged his chair closer to hers and her heart picked up an extra beat.

He hadn't mentioned the babies in his argument but if Izzy was to entertain the idea of moving in she'd need some sort of assurance he was going to be a father to these babies. She couldn't live with him and pretend he was nothing more than a landlord to them. It was one thing being asked to forget what had happened between them but quite another if he thought she'd overlook that. Her children deserved a father who was crazy about them, so enamoured she'd be willing to forget everything she'd gone through in the past and risk it all again for their happiness.

She'd made the mistake of believing she'd finally found a forever home with Gerry, going all in and risking her heart in the hope things would work. The crash hadn't been his fault, but the debts and the gambling had proved he'd never put her first.

She couldn't commit herself to someone else who treated her babies the same way.

'We're friends who made a mistake, Cal, let's leave it at that. I hereby relinquish you from any responsibility.' Weary from the debate going on inside and outside her head about the subject, Izzy decided to put an end to it once and for all.

'I don't think that's your call. It took two of us to make these babies. Is that what's stopping you from letting me be involved? I mean, I wouldn't force you to be a *proper* wife, if you're worried about that?' The tinge of red flushing his complexion told him exactly what part of marriage he was thinking about.

Sleeping with Cal was something she was doing her best to keep from her mind. They had much more domestic matters to discuss, but now he'd mentioned it the image of the two of them rolling around in bed was suddenly on her mind. If they got married and planned a future together then that was something they would probably succumb to again. They both had physical needs and it would be, well, convenient as well as enjoyable. The idea held definite appeal for her, but she couldn't tell him that in case he thought she'd planned the whole thing.

'A *proper* wife? You mean like having dinner waiting on the table for you coming home after work, warming your slippers by the fire and generally losing my identity to keep my man happy? I don't fancy your chances, mate.'

'You know exactly what I mean, Fizz.' The lopsided grin and darkening eyes dared her to think about it again.

Now she was more uncomfortable than ever because she was imagining Cal as a permanent feature in her bed. A hot man who was offering her a bed and who'd already proved he could make her happy in that department made for an excellent sales pitch.

'Job! RTC. Two vehicles.' That was all Mac had to say to get the crew moving.

Cal jumped in the front of the helicopter with him to direct him to the crash site and waited for Izzy to get into the back.

'Check doors and harnesses.'

'Locked and secured.' Izzy followed his cue with the safety checks and they were in the air within minutes of the emergency call coming into the control room.

'Okay, land paramedics are on the scene and have requested our attendance. Patients are currently being assessed.' It wasn't long before Cal could see the site of the accident for himself as there was such a hive of activity going on around it. The flashing lights of the ambulance and the high-visibility vests of the crews already working to free the passengers were like a beacon signalling the location.

From the air it was easy to see the car that had

taken the brunt of the damage on the passenger side. Although they wouldn't be sure what they were dealing with until they reached the ground.

The fire service on scene seemed to be concentrating their efforts on that particular vehicle as the air ambulance landed in a field nearby and Cal and Izzy went to join them. The other vehicle in the crash had damage to the front but the driver was receiving treatment in the back of the ambulance.

One of the paramedics came to update them on events and as it had appeared from the outset, the girl still trapped in the car, Stephanie, was the one they were most concerned about. He and Izzy followed him over to the patient and while Cal assessed any visible injury, Izzy made strides to comfort the young woman pinned inside the car.

'Hi, I'm Izzy, with the air ambulance. Now, the doctor's just going to take a look at your injuries before we attempt to move you, Stephanie. Okay?'

'Okay.' She didn't sound convinced, but she was conscious and was a point in her favour.

'I want you to take nice deep breaths, Stephanie.' Cal crouched down to get as close to her as he could. 'Can you tell me where the pain is?'

'My left arm and left leg. They hurt so bad.' She was crying now but it was Cal's job to determine whether that was caused by fear or injury.

'I know they do and we're going to give you some pain relief, but I can't see any blood so we're going to try and get you out of here.' He gave the fire crew the nod to start cutting the roof so they could get better access to her, but they still had to be careful. Although there was no visible bleeding, there was a chance she could be bleeding internally, and she had most likely broken her arm and leg.

'There's going to be a lot of noise and vibration while the crew work on cutting the roof of the car, Stephanie.' Izzy reached in and held her hand until the roof finally came off.

'Good girl. You're doing really well. I know it hurts, but we need to get you to the helicopter.' Izzy kept her vigil at Stephanie's side, reassuring her she would be all right and providing some comfort to the frightened girl. It struck him more in that moment than ever what a great mum she was going to make. Her compassion and nurturing side was everything a kid could want in its mother. He should know. He had his own parents to hold up as a shining example of how family life should be. It was a shame he apparently hadn't carried on that legacy when he was avoiding the subject of becoming a dad himself.

'I need some help here to get her onto the stretcher.' He concentrated on the job he was good at, administering some strong pain relief to the patient before they attempted extrication, and called the other paramedics and fire crew to assist with the transfer. 'Ready. Brace. Roll.'

They worked together to get her onto the stretcher, causing as little pain as possible in the circumstances. Izzy put a splint on Stephanie's injured arm and they put a pelvic binder around her to protect against any internal bleeding. Once she was stabilised as best they could manage, Cal again asked for assistance in carrying her over to the ambulance.

'Ready. Brace. Go.' They moved in synch, ensuring they didn't jolt her about too much, and Izzy radioed in a progress report and an ETA of their arrival at the nearest hospital.

When it came to work, and life-or-death situations, Izzy's confidence and decisiveness were exactly what was needed. In her personal life, however, that assertiveness that she could do everything on her own was ticking him off. He mightn't be the daddy-to-be she wanted for her children, but he wasn't Gerry either. Izzy should know him better than believing he'd walk away from this pregnancy because it was inconvenient. He had no intention of leaving her to pick up the pieces alone. As long as she dropped those defences enough to see the idea to move in was for her benefit, not his.

Janet had broken everything important in him beyond repair—his trust, his belief that he could replicate the happy family he'd grown up in, and, crucially, that urge in him to be a father at all. Still, she hadn't managed to take away the basic desire to be a decent human being. The mother of his future children was in trouble and he was going to do right by her.

If being broke, alone and pregnant with twins had been an illness, Izzy wouldn't have thought twice about finding a cure. Cal knew he wasn't perfect but as far as he could see he was the best option she had, and he would do his best to make her see that. They were in this together whether they liked it or not.

It was getting harder for Izzy to switch off after a shift. Stephanie was young, and she would heal with time, but that initial phone call to let Stephanie's parents know what had happened had been painful. She'd asked Izzy to make the call for her and to play down her injuries, but her mother's fear had been almost palpable. Izzy wasn't a parent yet, but this pregnancy was already changing her in ways she hadn't prepared for and she knew once the babies were here their safety would be the only thing that mattered to her. There were only six months before they arrived, and she had nothing in place for them except uncertainty.

To his credit, Cal hadn't pushed her any more on moving in with him and had been willing to talk over her concerns regarding their patient's prognosis in a debriefing session on the ride back from the handover at the hospital, leaving her free from any additional worries to keep her awake at night.

'Your usual?' Cal rested his hand on her back the second they made it back to base.

She nodded, having become accustomed to their sober chats. It wasn't as though they'd been in the habit of rolling home steaming drunk, but the nature of their relationship had changed along with their drinking habits. They'd become more than mates when she'd gone to him about the double life she'd discovered Gerry had been leading and now they had a connection that went beyond an emotional level.

Regardless of her vow to do everything single-handedly when that little blue line had appeared on the pregnancy test, Cal had made her realise how much she needed that level of support. His company alone reminded her she wasn't alone, even if she didn't intend forcing him to do it on a permanent basis.

'Tea and a chat is exactly what I need right now,' she said as she pushed open the office door.

'Good because that's exactly why I'm here.' It took a few seconds for the sight of the blonde woman standing in the room to register with Izzy, and when it did she flung herself at her childhood friend.

'Helen? What on earth are you doing here?' she managed to sob out in the midst of the bear hug.

'Your friend Calum here persuaded me to pay a visit and clearly he was right. You're not yourself. What on earth is wrong, Iz? I've never seen you like this.' Helen prised her off to take a good look at her.

Izzy glanced at a sheepish Cal. 'But how…?'

'I thought you might need a friend.'

She did but she hadn't realised he'd been taking notes when she'd mentioned Helen, never mind take the time out to track her down. He'd obviously been concerned on more than a practical level about her welfare. Simply finding out he knew that much about her life and cared enough to make that contact instantly perked up her mood. Although he hadn't been gushing about becoming a father, his actions showed he was thinking very deeply about how this was affecting her. She hoped that was a sign he'd eventually warm to the idea of being a father beyond a superficial level, but he clearly hadn't shared their most important news.

'Thank you, Cal.' Izzy gave him a swift peck on the cheek to show her appreciation for his thoughtfulness and counted herself lucky to have these two special people in her life. Her babies deserved to have the same.

'I'm so happy to see you.' Izzy turned her attention back to Helen in case effusive thanks made Cal think twice about making such gestures in the future.

'I didn't come on my own.' Helen stepped aside to reveal a gorgeous pram with an even more gorgeous bundle wrapped inside.

'Oh, my goodness, you brought him with you?' Helen had given birth six months ago, just before Gerry's accident, but with everything going on she hadn't been able to find time to go and visit the new arrival. There was also a part of her afraid to see first-hand the trials she'd yet to face as a new mum.

'We thought we'd have a day out on the train to see Auntie Isobel and let Daddy catch up on some sleep.'

The thought that her friend had trekked the whole way here with a baby to surprise her overwhelmed Izzy with the fuzzy warmth of a love she'd forgotten existed. Helen was her bestie, a sister and a mother all wrapped in one. If it hadn't been for her, Izzy wouldn't have known love existed at all. She was the one good thing Izzy had had in her childhood and the only connection from that time she didn't want to lose. They'd kept in touch, but text messages and video calls weren't the same as a much-needed hug.

'And who's this?' Cal asked, peering into the pram where the baby was grizzling.

'This is Oliver and it's nearly time for his dinner.' Helen lifted him out of the pram as he made his impatience known at having to wait another second for his next feed.

'Feel free to feed him in here. We'll make sure everyone gives you some privacy.'

'I hope I'm not putting you out, Iz, by turning up here unannounced? I just wanted to see you.' Helen slung the changing bag over her shoulder and manoeuvred baby and pram out the door Cal was holding open.

'Not at all. I'm glad you came. Our shift's over so give us a minute to get changed out of our gear then we can go somewhere for a catch-up.'

'Will you be joining us, Calum?' As subtle as ever, Helen extended the invitation, no doubt in the hope she could pair him off with Izzy. Since she'd become a happy married she'd expected Izzy to join the club with her. Perhaps it was Helen's blissful experience of marriage that had convinced Izzy to stick it out with Gerry and hope they could eventually achieve the same idyll. Izzy hadn't told her about the pregnancy but that would likely fuel her search for a hubby for her and she certainly didn't need any more encouragement where Cal Armstrong was concerned.

'Um…'

'Of course he will. You haven't got anything else to do have you, Cal?' She knew he didn't and it was important he get used to being part of her personal life.

Biology had dictated he was included in this family of hers, but she was going to make sure he was connected to these babies by more than duty to do the right thing. Love was a staple of a happy childhood and, as she knew too well, life was miserable without it. She wasn't prepared to enter into any sort of arrangement without a guarantee he was in for the long haul.

With Cal along for their coffee date she'd also be less likely to find herself telling Helen about his offer. The last thing she needed was someone egging her on to do something as outrageous as moving in with the reluctant father to her unborn children.

'Actually, I do. That's why I brought Helen here,' he answered with a scowl, dashing any hope he could be cajoled into being part of her life, or their children's.

It was typical that as soon as they got settled with coffee and cake, baby Oliver woke up from his afternoon nap. Helen was trying to soothe him with one hand pushing the pram up and down whilst trying to inject herself with caffeine with the other. However, Oliver's wails continued to disrupt the other customers.

'Can I lift him out so you can finish your coffee in peace?' Izzy was itching to get her hands on the chubby-cheeked cherub for some cuddles. She couldn't wait for the time when she could do this any time she pleased.

'Go for it.' Helen seemed glad to have an extra pair of hands so she could have a break, and Izzy knew when she had two babies to take care of she'd have her work cut out for her. But she didn't care.

Her life would finally have purpose and meaning, not to mention love.

Izzy scooped the wriggling bundle out from under his blanket cocoon and the screaming ceased once he was in the cradle of her arms.

'You just wanted to see what was going on, didn't you?' She was lost in those big blue eyes as he stared up at her, putting his trust in her to take care of him.

'Okay, now spill.' It took Helen a nanosecond to make it clear she knew there was something going on with her.

'I think someone might need a nappy change.' Izzy held Oliver out as a buffer, preventing his mother from probing for the truth.

'I changed him before we came here, so stop stalling and start talking.' Helen swatted away the feeble attempt to divert her attention.

'Huh?'

'Are you and Cal…you know?' Helen's eyes were bright with bubbling excitement at the prospect of uncovering a new romance. 'I wouldn't blame you. He's gorgeous and he was worried enough about you to phone me. It's obvious he cares about you a lot.'

'What? No. It's only been a few months since I lost Gerry.' She had to remind herself of that too since the memories of her time with him had got lost amongst recent revelations.

'You and Gerry were over a long time before he died, even if you didn't see it then. He was never going to be the man you needed.'

If Izzy had gone to Helen first when she'd discovered Gerry's betrayal she would never have found herself in this mess. It was only when things between her and Cal had subsequently become strained she'd turned to her friend about her troubles, omitting to tell her about Cal's role in her grief counselling. However, that visceral reaction to the circumstances Gerry had left her in, where she'd cursed him up and down, was ammunition Helen was sure to use against her should she believe Izzy was using his death as an excuse not to date again.

'I know there's something going on between you and Calum. I saw the looks you kept giving each other too. As though you were afraid one of you would slip up and say something you shouldn't.'

It was uncanny how well Helen still knew her, even though they only managed a meet up once or twice a year now. Unless she avoided all future contact with Helen she wasn't going to be able to keep the secret much longer. Especially when her bump had to accommodate two surprise bundles.

She put Oliver back in his pram and knocked back the remainder of her decaf coffee, wishing it was a shot of tequila or even an espresso to give her a jolt of bravado. 'I'm pregnant. With twins.'

The words burst out of her mouth before she could stop them, the pressure of keeping the secret to herself too great to hold back. The bombshell was accompanied by the appropriate sound of a crash as Helen dropped her cup on the table.

'Why have you waited this long to tell me?' She

mopped up the spilled coffee with a paper napkin, never taking her eyes off Izzy.

'I'm still trying to come to terms with it myself.'

Helen was staring at her, her mouth open about a foot wide. 'Are they—?'

'Yes, they're Cal's. Do you remember I told you about that man who came looking for Gerry? Well, I went to Cal's that night because I knew I'd feel safe there and one thing led to another…' Izzy felt the need to justify what had happened because it seemed so quick after Gerry's death. Although Helen would never have judged her.

'It's no wonder you turned to him after everything you'd been going through. You don't have to explain yourself and Cal seems like a nice guy. I'm sure he'll stand by you.'

'I'm sure he will but that's not enough for my babies. You know what my childhood was like and I want more for these two. Cal is still hesitant about the whole parenting thing and I'd rather go it alone than have him only as a financial backer.'

'Well, if anyone's strong enough to do this on their own it's you, Iz. Wow. I can't believe you're really pregnant.' Helen reached across the table to give her a hug.

'Neither can I. It's a scary prospect.'

'I take it you're, what, two or three months gone? What are the plans?' She was vastly over-estimating Izzy's ability to process the situation and come up with a solution.

'I…er…haven't actually known for that long.'

'Have you told work?'

'Not yet.'

'Booked into prenatal classes?'

'Not yet.'

'Isobel... Have you even started taking your folic acid supplements?'

'I've been busy.'

It wasn't much of an excuse when she had no life outside work any more, but Izzy's way of dealing with her shock pregnancy had been not dealing with it.

'You're going to have to get organised,' Helen scolded, and immediately started scribbling a list of things for her to do in her personal organiser.

'You know I'm bad at this kind of thing.' She wasn't the type who pinned to-do lists to her fridge, or even marked appointments on a calendar. No, Izzy was more a spur-of-the-moment kind of girl who was used to thinking only about herself and doing what suited her.

'Well, you're going to have to get good at it pretty damn quick.' Serious-Helen face stared at her across the table until Izzy hung her head in shame.

'I know, but where the hell do I start?' She was so overwhelmed by the sheer magnitude of tasks and appointments that she'd avoided dealing with anything so far.

'Start with this.' Helen ripped out the page from her planner and slid it across the table. 'Your midwife will help you devise a birth plan. You *do* have a midwife?'

'Of course.'

'Good. What about after the birth? Have you given any thought to childcare?'

If Izzy had had a proper mother, she imagined she'd have received the same grilling as her friend was giving her now. A parent who cared might have been able to help her out with childcare and hold her hand during the pregnancy. Given a chance, Helen would do the same but she lived too far away and had a family of her own to look after.

'Cal asked me to move in with him. I said no. We're just friends. That night should never have happened.'

'It's sweet that Calum wants to take care of you. If you had better taste in men you'd have snatched him up a long time ago.'

'Yes, well, I'm done trusting men. I want to do this on my own.' She didn't, not really, but it seemed to her it was the only way to protect herself and the babies from unnecessary suffering.

'Clearly you trust him, or you wouldn't have turned to him for help in the first place.'

'I trust him in *that* way, it's just…' It was difficult to put it into words when she wasn't entirely sure why his interference frightened her so much.

'You're worried he'll hurt you the same way Gerry did?'

'Yes. No. I don't know.' He could only cause her that level of pain if she saw him as more than a friend and that wasn't what he was necessarily offering. Although there had been that nod towards a physical relationship, which had shaken her to the core, but she wasn't sharing that with Helen. The reason she was holding back was because she was afraid she'd get in too deep when she had even more to lose if it all fell apart.

'There's nothing to say you have to make a commitment beyond the rent to enjoy the benefits of what he's offering.'

Izzy's mind leapt to those images of them exploring each other's bodies again, but she decided to play the innocent. 'What do you mean?'

'You could do the fun stuff that goes with being a couple without the headaches. A housemates with benefits deal. If it doesn't work out you both move on without any baggage.'

'Wouldn't it seem as though I was using Cal by doing that? Besides, he hasn't shown any interest in me in *that* way since I spent the night with him.' It sounded feasible in theory, but Izzy was worried that was only because she was becoming desperate.

Helen shrugged. 'He offered, didn't he, with no strings? Trust me, I've seen the way he looks at you and I can read between the lines…'

This outside perspective on their situation no longer made Cal's suggestion as ludicrous as she'd first thought. They might be able to make this work after all.

Chapter 4

'Can I give you a lift home?' Cal didn't want to walk away and leave Izzy at the train station alone. She'd been very quiet since they'd waved Helen and Oliver off. Although the afternoon was supposed to help lift her spirits, he suspected it had been a huge dose of reality for her, seeing her friend struggle to look after the baby on her own for the afternoon. Not that she'd struggled per se, but it was very different trying to have a coffee and a quiet chat when you had a baby in tow. Something Izzy was going to have to get used to if she kept refusing all offers of help.

'Sure.' She barely glanced his way as she led the way to the car, deep in thought about something he wasn't privy to.

They buckled up in continued silence and Cal was

afraid she was going to retreat back into her world alone. Izzy had been let down once too often and he wasn't going to add himself to that list by shirking his responsibilities.

'Helen seems lovely.'

'She is,' Izzy confirmed, her gaze fixed firmly on the road ahead. She was remarkably sullen compared to how buoyant she'd been in her friend's company and Cal knew it was probably because he'd refused to be dragged along with them. It was one thing offering her a lifeline but quite another getting involved in her personal life.

Left to his own devices, he'd batten down the hatches at home and prevent another woman from setting foot in his inner sanctum in case she broke his heart too, but these were exceptional circumstances. Given Izzy's reluctance, he knew she was every bit as wary about moving in together as he was, but they had to set their own comfort aside in favour of the babies. What they needed more than anything was a stable home environment.

'Olly's adorable too.' The baby had been a reminder of his sisters and their offspring, who were scattered across the UK now there was nowhere for them to congregate with the family home gone. He missed being an uncle. He missed being anything to anyone.

He started the engine, resigned to the fact that Izzy was never going to agree to anything unless he fully committed to parenthood. Something he wasn't ready to do and he wasn't going to make false promises.

Then she turned to him and said, 'Take me home with you, Cal.'

If she'd been any other woman and he any other man, that sentence could've been construed as a precursor to another night of passion. There was a part of him that still held a spark of hope that that was her intention, but he knew Izzy better than that. This was a sign of something other than a sudden overwhelming urge to bed him again.

He derailed the inappropriate train of thought, wondering if it was a sign he might not be able to take a vow of celibacy where Izzy was concerned after all.

'Any, um, particular reason?' He did his best to keep his voice neutral, so she didn't guess where his mind had gone to.

'If I'm going to consider your proposal seriously, I'd like to see the goods on offer. I mean, your assets…the house…you know what I mean.' Her flustering combined with her heightened colour made him think he hadn't been alone in his less-than-pure thoughts.

He resisted the obvious teasing when they were beginning to make a breakthrough. This was the first hint he'd given that she was taking his suggestion seriously, so he didn't want to scare her off by turning it into something sordid. Whatever scenario his neglected libido had been conjuring up would have to give way to more important issues.

Cal had never been the type of guy to choose one-night stands over a meaningful relationship, but this wasn't about him. Sex wasn't something he expected in return for anything but if it was something they both decided they wanted as part of the deal, he wasn't going to say no.

Although he was still wondering what had brought her round to his initial way of thinking.

'Does this sudden turnaround have something to do with Helen?' He'd be surprised if Izzy had confided in her about his idea and even more so if her friend had advised her to proceed with it. From the outside it would've sounded absurd even to him, and he got the impression Helen was protective of Izzy and probably the closest thing to family she had. Apart from him of course. If their roles had been reversed he'd have been suspicious of him and his motives too. Still, if he'd won over her friend then he wasn't going to complain. Izzy would know Helen only had her best interests at heart, even if she doubted him.

'I told her about the babies.'

'Oh, okay. How did that go down?'

Izzy smiled for the first time since they'd been alone again. 'She's over the moon and insisted on writing me a pregnancy to-do list. It felt good, though, telling someone. Other than you, I mean. It's like I'm allowed to get excited about this now.'

She rested her hand on her belly, looking more at ease with the pregnancy than he'd seen so far.

'So you should. It's a special time.' Just not especially to him when it was a reminder of all the mistakes he'd made when it came to relationships.

'I suppose we could be housemates, landlord and tenant, whatever you want to call it, but I will be contributing to the household bills.'

'If that's what you want.' It stung a little that she wasn't interested in something more, but he'd take it.

'That's what I want. At least, I think it is.'

'I know, you still want to take a peek at the goods. I guess you can't have too much of a good thing after all.' He was rewarded with a playful nudge for his teasing.

He'd wasted time in a relationship with Janet when he could've been raising a family with someone who'd wanted to be with him. The whole idea of parenting to him had entailed being an active participant. From changing nappies and doing night feeds right through to playing football or driving to dance recitals, he'd been willing to do it all. Now, though, he could see the merits of being one of those backseat dads. Izzy didn't really want to be with him either so getting attached seemed a pointless exercise, but he could offer these children a home. For however long it was needed.

He and Izzy weren't star-crossed lovers, but they had their feet on the ground and a more realistic view of life now they'd found out the hard way that love couldn't solve everything.

'I want to get a feel for the place and see if I can picture us all living there together.'

They'd be a modern family of convenience created by circumstance and friendship if not in the conventional sense.

Once Izzy saw the nursery and the potential space to raise her children he knew she'd agree to move in. His house would finally become a home. Just for someone other than him.

It wasn't that Izzy had never seen Cal's place before, they often called at each other's houses and sometimes shared a take-away, but she'd never taken much notice of the surroundings. This time she wanted to see it from a different perspective. She was viewing his house with the prospect of moving in. With him. And their babies. Possibly for ever. Well, it had to be preferable to spending the rest of her days in that poky flat at the top of a flight of stairs, which she could barely afford. If she'd ever pictured this scenario she might have chosen somewhere with access for a twin pram.

Although that would have demanded an even larger chunk of her wages to cover costs. She had to face it, no matter what decision she might have made, the minute she'd thrown in her lot with Gerry, she'd been in trouble.

It was probably a blessing that Cal had thrown her a lifeline and an opportunity to raise their children in a proper home. One she knew would be a supportive environment, even though they wouldn't be together as a couple.

As they pulled up outside the house she was already seeing the possibilities it offered in comparison to her own home. She got that fluttering in her chest as she imagined the green lawn littered with children's toys and opportunities for the babies to play outside. A garden wasn't something she'd had on her wish list when house hunting before, but now she could see how perfect it would be for family life. The detached house surrounded by trees and shrubbery with a driveway secured with high gates made it private and secure.

The size of the house, the grounds and the location made it a highly prized property but for a mother-to-be it was the scope for safe play and adventure that made it valuable. If she did a side-by-side comparison with the square of parched communal land littered with oddments of her neighbours' patio furniture Cal would have sold the whole idea to her based solely on the garden.

'Are you okay?' It was only when he spoke she realised he'd already cut the engine and had no idea how long they'd been sitting in silence whilst she plotted her imaginary playground. It explained why he suddenly sounded nervous about having her here when she hadn't showed him any sign she was happy about it.

'Yes. Sorry. I was miles away. You said something about a nursery?' She unclipped her seatbelt, keen to do her virtual interior decorating too.

Cal didn't waste any time opening up the house, probably worried she'd change her mind again. 'Obviously we'd furnished it for the babies, so you can use anything in there or you're free to put your own stamp on things.'

He led her up the stairs and she remembered the last time she'd followed him to his room at the end of the hall. That had been the moment everything had changed.

'So, er, this is the nursery,' he said, opening the door to a bright, beautiful room that took Izzy's breath away.

'Cal, it's gorgeous and bigger than my flat.' Which meant there was sufficient space for another cot to match the beautiful white cradle already there.

The white room highlighted with silver-star details mapped out an amazing bright galaxy on the walls and made a neutral space to suit any taste or gender. There were accents of pastel pinks, blues and yellows in the furnishings to break up the dazzling white, and the thick silver carpet underfoot was luxuriously expensive. Everything from the pretty star-embroidered blankets to the pine rocking chair in the corner festooned with plump cushions was tailored for comfort as well as appearance.

'I'm sure you'll want to change a few things to suit your own taste so let me know what you have in mind and I'll get on it.'

'Did you have an interior designer in to do this?' It looked as though someone had copied a page out of a magazine, everything was so perfectly matched and positioned.

Cal picked up a soft fuzzy sheep from a stack of

toys on the dresser and laid it in the crib. 'No, it's all my own work.'

Izzy took another look around and could see how much love and care had gone into making this room baby heaven. He'd been so buoyant in those early months, planning for the baby he'd thought he was going to have with Janet, and she could picture him painstakingly painting every inch of this room in preparation for its arrival.

'I should've known something was wrong when Janet was happy to let me do this alone, without her input. I thought she was simply having a hard time accepting the pregnancy. How stupid was I?' The bitter laugh he gave was directly at odds with the caring man who'd put his heart and soul into creating this loving tribute to a baby who'd never been his.

'You weren't stupid. You trusted her, you were in love with her, and she betrayed you in the worst possible way. None of it was your fault.' She rested her hand on his shoulder to show him she was on his side. Who wouldn't be when a man this endearing had been left heartbroken and bereft, essentially grieving for a baby who'd never come home with him?

'Thanks.' When he covered her hand with his, his warmth enveloping her, she knew he was grasping for that connection he'd lost with Janet. An uneasy sense that there was more behind his motives to have her here other than being a good friend began to slither beneath her skin.

'Cal, you didn't ask me to move in just to fill the

space Janet left behind, did you?' The one that had a baby-shaped void right next to it.

No amount of saving on her bills would convince her that this was a good idea if that was the reason, because she would never be a replacement for the fiancée he'd lost, and her babies weren't up for negotiation.

'Of course not.' He turned his head so violently to shoot down that theory that he jerked her hand away. 'I told you, you can do whatever you want in here. It's not some sort of shrine. I just thought it was a shame to let all of this go to waste.'

His defensive attitude suggested there might be more behind his reasons than he even realised. As long as she remembered the history here and didn't get sucked into playing the role recently vacated by his ex, they could hopefully cohabit without anyone reading something into the arrangement that wasn't there.

'It would be when I'm going to need two of everything. We could keep the furniture and redecorate, I suppose. It's beautiful, but I do think it might be better all round for something fresh. If you're on board with that?' It was a compromise intended to make things less weird.

'Does that mean you're moving in?' The Cal she recognised immediately wrapped her in a hug and Izzy let herself revel in that moment of intimacy. He was the only person who provided her with that sense of security she found in the circle of his arms.

To have someone who could do that for her on

a regular basis, and she was going to need lots of hugs for the foreseeable future, was a definite point in Cal's favour. They were friends and soon to be housemates, with no one else close enough to provide this strength they seemed to find in each other.

She was certain that tingling sensation that travelled from her head to her toes and all the extremities in between when he touched her or held her was merely residual memory of their last, more intimate contact. It was tempting to burrow into his chest like a little dormouse seeking shelter for the winter, but she managed to keep herself in check and dragged herself out of his embrace before she got too used to using him as a crutch. She had to do this on her own. Cal was her back-up. Someone to give her a boot up the backside when she needed it, just as she'd done for him.

As soon as she stepped out of his personal space the sudden sense of loss slipped out of her mouth on a sigh. 'I'll need to see the bedroom before I make a final decision.'

The corners of his mouth tilted up as he deliberately misinterpreted her comment. It hadn't escaped her notice either that he hadn't attempted to end the too-long hug. Their previous conversation about exploring all aspects of marriage sprang to mind again and her pulse rocketed. Perhaps she should avoid all *double entendres* for the sake of her blood pressure from now on.

'*My* bedroom. The room where I'll be sleeping. Alone.' The emphasis was as much for herself as Cal when it would be far too convenient to jump into bed together should the mood strike them. That sort of blurry line would make things messy when they had to work and live together. Essentially that would put them in a relationship neither of them wanted. This new set-up was supposed to avoid the emotional uncertainty that came as part of a couple package.

'Spoilsport.' The wink he gave her sent shivers through her as though he'd danced his fingers along her spine and she followed him like a devoted puppy into another bright and spacious room.

'You really should think about a sideline as an interior decorator,' she said, taking in her proposed new accommodation. It had a modern appearance but with a lovely homely feeling.

'I'll give it some consideration when I get too old and decrepit for jumping out of helicopters.' He deflected the compliment with another self-deprecating comment, but Izzy couldn't imagine him as anything other than in his prime at any age.

'You'll certainly save me a job, anyway. I won't have to redecorate or attempt to dismantle my flat-pack furniture to move in here. I assume fixtures and fittings are included?'

'Everything I have is at your disposal.' His exaggerated bow gave him the air of a handsome prince giving her the keys to his kingdom, which she liked to think included a secret library somewhere.

'In that case, I can cancel the removal van. Everything I want is right here.' She was referring to the solid pine furniture the entire contents of her flat could fit into but found herself staring at Cal instead.

'What about the bed? No one's ever used the one in here, but you might prefer to have your own.' He walked past her to sit on the end of the mattress, bouncing up and down to show her the obvious quality of the springs.

The lumpy, barely held together with chipboard thing she called a bed, which was also half the size of this sleep playground, couldn't compete.

'Are you kidding? I could live in this.' She threw herself on top of the bed so she was flat out, staring at the ceiling. Her bouncing knocked Cal off balance until he ended up lying beside her, only a hair's breadth away.

'I'm glad you're moving in.'

'I haven't agreed yet.' She was still clinging on to that one last thread of control.

'What else can I do to convince you?' Cal's husky voice was almost enough to persuade her to do anything.

That was it. The final tie to her logical brain pinged free and left her to the mercy of her hormones. They were lying so close to one another there was nowhere else to look but at his eyes, his lips... He was staring at her mouth too, clearly thinking the same thing—how nice a kiss would be right now. Breathtakingly slowly they were gravitating towards each other, closing those last few millimetres separating them from heaven, and insanity.

Izzy sat up, breaking the thrall of his hypnotic

gaze. 'I think we should get one thing straight from the beginning, Cal. I want to move in and I appreciate everything you're doing for me, but I think we should take the, er, physical side of this relationship off the cards.'

With that bombshell Cal sat up too so they were both perched uncomfortably on the end of the bed. 'Certainly. I wouldn't dream of using this arrangement to take advantage of you. We'll keep things strictly platonic.'

The longer she spent in his company the more she'd anticipate spending nights in bed with him, but she knew the novelty of having her around would wear off as it always did.

'I think it's for the best.'

'So, we're free to date other people if and when we're ready for that?'

Izzy didn't know why that question shook her when he was a hot-blooded male, not a monk. She supposed it was because she couldn't imagine getting involved in another relationship and had thought he was of the same opinion. It wasn't fair to expect him to remain celibate for ever because she'd prefer it, but the thought of him bringing other women home with him was painful. Ridiculous, when she'd been the one drawing the line in the sand and deeming her side a sex-free zone.

She knew the one flaw in this plan could be if she fell for Cal, confusing his sense of duty for something more. Something that could only ever end badly.

Chapter 5

'You should be sitting with your feet up.' Cal marked out the light switch with masking tape so it didn't get splattered with paint and made sure the dust sheet was covering the whole floor.

'Why? You're not and unless I'm mistaken we've had exactly the same workload today.' Displaying her usual obstinacy, Izzy refused to take it easy after another hectic shift.

'Yes, but I'm not carrying two extra loads with me.' He pointed his paintbrush at her belly, which was noticeably more rounded in her form-fitting grey jersey top and black leggings.

'You promised you wouldn't mollycoddle me,' she reminded him, and began rolling on the pale turquoise paint she'd chosen to cover the nursery walls.

'There's a difference between mollycoddling and doing you a favour. I'm happy to do all the grunt work here.' That way he could make sure she had some down time. So far, since moving in with him, she hadn't shown any signs of slowing down. He had managed to convince her to let him carry the few belongings she had with her but only after an exhaustive debate. Eventually she'd accepted he was merely trying to be a gentleman and not treating her as an invalid. Despite his reservations about his suitability as a parent to these babies, he was doing his best to ensure they'd want for nothing, and that included a strong, healthy mother.

'I wouldn't call painting a wall particularly taxing.' Izzy proved her point by covering most of the mid-section in just a few strokes.

'The fumes can't be good for you.' He simply wanted her to take care of herself if she wouldn't let him do it for her.

It had been a huge part of Janet's pregnancy for him, fussing around and feeling useful in some capacity when he hadn't been able to help with any of the physical toll pregnancy had taken on her.

Seeing how active and reluctant Izzy was to let her condition become an excuse to slow down made him wonder if Janet had been laughing behind his back the whole time he'd been skivvying for her. Of course she had, the baby wasn't his and while he'd been preparing to become a father she'd been planning to leave him.

Izzy wouldn't take advantage of him in that way when he'd had to work so hard to get her this far.

Despite referencing the possibility of entering into a physical relationship, he knew it would never stay solely in the bedroom and he didn't want to jeopardise what they had here. It was simply a reaction to the attraction that had sprung to life rather quickly after their respective heartaches. Besides, apart from the scars they still bore from those ill-fated relationships, they'd be too tired dealing with two small children to think about dating or anything else.

'I promise if I start to feel faint or sick I'll hang up my paint roller.' It was a concession he was willing to accept when she didn't often make them.

'Good. No stretching either. I'll get the ladder and do the top bits.' There was no need for her to overdo things when he was there to pick up the slack.

'I assume I'm allowed to do the bottom bits? I can sit on the floor to do that. You know, take it easy.' She was making fun of him, but it was better than bristling at him each time he attempted to do something nice for her.

'As long as you don't get under my feet.' She'd already worked her way over to the section he was covering so he let a blob of paint plop onto her head.

'For your sake I hope you didn't do that on purpose.' Izzy lifted her head to look at him, eyes narrowed and lips twitching.

'You know me better than that, Fizz.' He'd never been able to resist riling that temper of hers, such was their dynamic, and he was glad that spark was still there after all this time.

'Hmm.' She knew him too well and he laughed at the apparent scepticism.

Cal resumed painting his part of the wall, only realising he was in serious trouble when he saw her roller paint over the palms of her hands instead of the plasterwork. The next thing he knew those same hands were resting on his buttocks and with one squeeze he knew she'd wreaked her revenge.

'You haven't...' He tried to twist his torso around to see the evidence but the glee on Izzy's face was proof enough that she'd left two turquoise handprints on the backside of his trousers.

'You deserved it.' She was grinning up at him, her eyes full of mischief, challenging him to do something about it.

'Isobel Fitzpatrick, you are in so much trouble...'

She let out a shriek as he dropped his paintbrush and tried to wrestle the roller out of her hands, but Izzy was too quick for him. With sleight of hand she hid her weapon behind her back, forcing him to reach around her to try and get it. Her laugh at his ear made him aware of how close their bodies were, and with the slightest turn of his head his lips were dangerously close to Izzy's.

He heard the hitch in her breath as she realised it too and he wanted so badly to kiss her it took all of his physical strength to back off before he did something stupid. The chemistry was there all right, but Izzy had made it clear she didn't want to repeat past mistakes. Instead he took a sidestep away and carried on decorating as though nothing out of the ordinary had transpired.

'It's just as well these are old clothes, or we'd have people talking about us.' As if. The only people they saw were their colleagues, and the crew had hardly batted an eyelid when they'd told them they were moving in together before they'd explained it was only as housemates. Mac, when Cal had tackled him about the lack of surprise, had explained they'd all thought the two of them had been at it like rabbits for years, despite having had partners for most of that time. Cal put him straight and asked him to pass on the information. The purpose, other than saving Izzy's reputation, was his own pride. He refused to let anyone believe he'd cheated on Janet and deserved what she'd done to him in any way.

It was a conversation he hadn't relayed to Izzy for fear of upsetting her. If he was annoyed there was any suggestion he'd played away on his treacherous ex, he could only imagine the effect it would have on her. The last thing Izzy needed stressing her out was malicious gossip that she'd somehow failed Gerry.

Cal had been blaming himself for months over what had happened between him and Janet, agonising over every disagreement that could have caused her to cheat on him. Izzy might have gone through something similar, wondering what she could've done to prevent the crash from happening, and she didn't need anything more to beat herself up over. Cal would rather put a smile on her face at his expense than give her cause to feel guilty about something she'd never had the power to control. It had taken all this time for him to learn that lesson.

It was only when Izzy had agreed to move in with him that he'd stopped blaming himself for Janet leaving. In some way he'd taken it as confirmation he wasn't as bad a person as he'd begun to believe, that he must've had some redeeming qualities if she was willing to live with him at this crucial time.

'I'll just tell them you're the father of my unborn babies and I'm marking my territory,' she said, following his lead in ignoring another heated moment between them.

The doorbell rang and gave Cal an excuse to leave the room before he took her comment seriously. The thought that Izzy wanted possession of any part of his body was arousing interest in certain areas that wasn't in keeping with their platonic agreement. 'I'll get it. It's probably the grocery shopping.'

With them both working and needing double the amount of food, they'd done their shopping online and left the front gates open for the home delivery to arrive. Izzy required proper nutritious meals and his recent casual approach to cooking ready meals and a microwave was no longer going to cut it.

The buzzer went again before he made it down the stairs.

'I'm coming,' he yelled to the dark figure outlined in the frosted glass who was clearly impatient to get to the next delivery.

As he unlocked the door to the outside world

again, the person waiting for him made him want to slam the door shut and lock himself away with Izzy again.

'Hi, Cal.' That was it. With just two words Janet was back in his world, blowing it completely apart.

'Aren't you going to ask me in?' Her audacity in thinking she could smile at him as though she hadn't ripped his heart out of his chest and stomped on it rendered him speechless.

Apparently, that was invitation enough for her to push past him. Easily done with the considerable weight she was now wielding with her heavily pregnant belly. She'd be due any day now, but the thought no longer brought the same sadness it once had.

'I hope they brought those cheesy cracker things I wanted. I have a hankering for something savoury and salty.' Naturally this was the moment Izzy's pregnancy cravings kicked in and sent her foraging for goodies. She stopped dead at the bottom of the stairs and came face to face with Janet. 'What do you want?'

There was no question that his ex was only here because she wanted something from him. Under the circumstances he didn't think he should be expected to waste time on pleasantries and small talk. He had nothing to say to her.

Janet looked Izzy up and down with the same undisguised contempt she'd always done. Only now Cal could see it for what it was—jealousy. He'd loved Janet body and soul but after how she'd treated him his eyes were open to the ugliness she wore on the inside. Izzy was honest, and kind, and all those things Janet wasn't.

'I've come for the rest of my things.' She made her way past Izzy as though she was perfectly entitled to roam where she pleased.

Cal took off after her, a frown burrowing into his brow as he envisaged her rifling through Izzy's belongings and upsetting her. 'I'm pretty sure you took everything.'

It had made quite an impact to come home from work to find empty closets and drawers and spaces where some of their joint possessions had once resided. He'd been one step away from calling the police to report a burglary when he'd found her note. The one ending their relationship and destroying the dream of having a family together.

'I want the baby's things,' she insisted, and walked on into the nursery.

'You're kidding.' Did she really not think how much this would hurt him by taking away that last connection, or did she simply not care? Given her past behaviour, Cal presumed it to be the latter.

The pressure of Izzy's hand at his lower back reminded him that someone did understand the significance of this to him and cared about it. Now he just wanted Janet to take any reminder of her out of his life for good.

'There's no point in wasting all this. It's not as though you're going to need it.' She went around the room, helping herself to the toys and bits and pieces dotted around the room and tossing them into the crib.

He was close to correcting her and informing her he did have a use for it, but he glanced at Izzy, who looked as horrified as he was, and she shook her head, making it known she didn't want a protest. Though Janet didn't deserve to walk away victorious, it was clear Izzy wanted Janet out at whatever price it took, instead of prolonging his agony.

The unwanted surprise appearance did prove one thing to Cal. He didn't, couldn't love her any more and he hoped that once she'd taken every last trace of their relationship away he'd forget all about her.

'Is Darren keeping a tight hold of the purse-strings? I don't blame him.' Cal had never denied Janet anything so perhaps she was missing being that pampered princess who'd once resided here. The thought of a possible rift didn't bring him any pleasure when their relationship had come at the price of his. Although he wasn't beyond making a dig.

'No,' she snapped, much too defensively for Cal to believe her. 'These were bought for the baby so I'm taking them for the baby.'

'Chosen by me and paid for by me.' More fool him for doing it and ending up here fighting over ownership of furniture for a baby that wasn't his.

'So you don't want him to have anything?' Janet cradled her bump and played a lament on his heartstrings. She was having a boy, a child he'd once seen himself playing football with and spending that father/son bonding time together as he'd done with his dad. He'd wanted that baby to have everything but that was when Cal had believed he'd be the one to see him make use of it all.

'I didn't say that, Janet.' If she was here for an argument he wasn't going to give her one because he no longer had the passion to fight. Not with her, anyway.

'In that case, you can start dismantling everything and take it down to the car. *She* can help you.' Janet's inclusion of Izzy in her demands was where Cal drew the line.

'No, she won't. Where's Darren? He can help with the heavy lifting.' It said a lot about the man that he'd let Janet come in here alone. Darren was a coward, along with the other names Cal had assigned to him over the months for not stepping up for the woman he'd got pregnant and allowed to carry on a relationship with someone else.

'He's waiting in the van. He didn't want a scene.'

'If he wants the furniture he can get his backside in here and help. I'm not doing it on my own and Izzy's not either.' He was already on his knees, unscrewing the sides of the cot for easier removal. The purchases he'd made when he'd been so excited for the future now held nothing but resentment for him. He was only sorry he'd promised it to Izzy and had to go back on his word.

Janet glared at Izzy, who was hovering in the doorway, then at the new pots of paint and finally at Cal's bottom where Izzy had left her mark.

'Oh. My. Goodness. You two are moving in to-gether?' She laughed as she finally took in the scene.

'We are but it's not what you think.' Their set-up was none of Janet's business.

'That's priceless, making out as though I'm the bad person here when you two were carrying on behind my back the whole time. I knew there was something going on between you. Perhaps that's why I was driven to Darren.'

There was no way he was going to let her play the injured party and deflect the responsibility of her actions onto him and Izzy when they'd done nothing wrong.

'In case you've forgotten, you're the guilty one here. The decision to cheat on me and lie about the baby was entirely down to you. Now, I suggest that, to avoid any more unpleasantness, you go and wait in the van and send Darren in to collect whatever you believe you're still entitled to. After that I don't want to see or hear from either of you ever again.' He was trying to hold the emotion back and as a result he sounded menacingly in control. It was deceptive but hopefully effective because he didn't want to subject Izzy to any more of this toxicity.

Once Janet was gone they could start with a clean slate in whatever capacity she'd allow him to participate in her life. It had to be an improvement on being the sap Janet had taken him for when they were starting from a place of honesty.

This was the first time he'd had a chance to vent about what Janet had done to him and she simply puffed herself up with indignation and stomped away rather than admit to being in the wrong.

Cal set to work dismantling what was left of the nursery, so Darren could take it away without further discussion. There was nothing left to say except to apologise to Izzy for dragging her into this whole nightmare with him. His desire for a family had brought him nothing but trouble.

Izzy managed to hold her tongue until the furniture and unwanted guests had left the premises. She'd never been the woman's greatest fan but the nerve of Janet to come here and lay claim to everything ranked her the lowest of the low.

'I'm so sorry, Cal. That was just…' Heartless. Cruel. Cold. All of the above '…unbelievable.' It was heart-wrenching to see him slumped against the half-painted wall, sitting on the floor of the empty nursery. Janet's actions and manner tonight gave her some insight into how she'd treated him at the end of their relationship and it wasn't a pretty picture.

There was no justification for treating someone like Cal, who was kindness personified, in that manner. There wasn't a flicker of doubt in Izzy's mind that as a fiancé he'd been anything other than as loving and supportive as he was as a friend.

'You shouldn't have had to witness that, Iz.' He hung his head, clearly embarrassed at how things had panned out in front of her, but she was more concerned about how tonight's events had affected him.

'No, Janet should never have waltzed in here the

way she did. I can't believe she had the audacity to turn up with Darren and take what didn't belong to her.' It was rubbing salt into the deep wound she'd inflicted, as though she never wanted it to heal.

Cal picked up a soft, cuddly sheep that had been left behind. 'It does look as though I've been burgled. At least she left Lamby behind. I've had him since I was a kid.'

He gave a sad smile that demanded she immediately hug him, but he couldn't manage to hug her back.

'I think he's had a lucky escape if you ask me. Who wants to live with a horror like that? Lamby will be much happier here with us. White furniture's too impractical anyway. Give it a week or two and everything she took will be permanently stained with puke and poo. She'll regret it someday.'

Nothing she could say would ever ease his pain, but she was here if he need her to jolly him along or keep him busy if he started to dwell on things again. It would've been so much worse if he'd have been left here in this shell of a nursery alone.

'I hope you're right.' Even so close she could sense him withdrawing from her when they needed one another more than ever.

'Next time we have a day off we could go shopping. I'm past the danger stage, touch wood, and I'd like to get organised. I'd appreciate your help in pointing me in the right direction to get what we need.' It was her attempt at including him more in this pregnancy, to give him something to look forward to, but she was taking a chance her good intentions might upset him further. The last thing she wanted to do was drag him around baby shops if it was all still too raw for him.

'I do happen to know of all the best recommendations when it comes to safety and quality.'

'I don't doubt it,' she said with a small laugh. He was so meticulous and thorough in everything he did. Assessing every possible risk was part of his job.

'She dumped me with a note taped to the fridge, you know. All those years living together, making plans for the future, and I wasn't worthy of a proper conversation. No apology, no explanation. "I'm leaving you for Darren. The baby's not yours, it's his." I mean, what could I have possibly done to deserve that? I spent weeks, months racking my brain, trying to figure out what I'd done wrong. Did I neglect her, had I become too clingy? Was I too boring or working too much? I'm still none the wiser after tonight.' His eyes were glistening with unshed tears Izzy wished she could wipe away.

'If anything good can come out of this it's that you can see this is none of your fault. Janet wouldn't have hesitated in casting up your faults if she could've blamed you for her behaviour. She has no excuse. The cheating, the lies, using the baby to get what she wanted—it's all on her. You were unlucky to have ever met her.' From now on they should concentrate on the future, instead of looking back.

'It still happened and it's not something I can easily forgive or forget.'

It was so uncharacteristic of Cal to be so despondent, but she knew from experience you had to hit rock bottom before you could claw your way back up again. Surveying the abandoned nursery, surely, he'd found his.

'No one would expect you to but please don't let her continue to ruin your life. Think of this as a new start. Now you're completely free from Janet and everything associated with her. I appreciate you, even if she doesn't.' From tomorrow Izzy was going to do everything in her power to help him move on with her.

Chapter 6

'Cal, we have enough stuff to open our own shop.'
Izzy glanced around the newly refurbished nursery,
imagining their two little ones here.

They'd left it a couple of days after Janet's surprise visit before venturing out to replace the items
she'd purloined. Even then Izzy had waited until Cal
brought up the subject, instead of pushing him into a
situation that might have made him uncomfortable.
He'd been her personal shopper, pointing out the best
products to suit her requirements, and she'd chosen
the colours and theme for the room.

Unsurprisingly, Cal had insisted on paying for
everything, though she'd sworn to pay him back
somehow. Retail therapy had helped him cast off

the shadow that had fallen over him after a certain someone had briefly come back into his life.

It was important for her to include him in these decisions for the babies so he'd stop hovering on the periphery of this pregnancy and become more involved. He was good at the practical aspects, such as the redecorating, but he'd yet to express his feelings about the situation. He was bound to have doubts and fears for their future just as she had, and it wasn't going to do any good keeping them bottled up. She didn't want to find out there were problems too late, the way she had with Gerry. That had been devastating enough but now there were children to think about too.

It wasn't going to serve anyone well if Cal maintained that emotional detachment when the babies were born. Especially when Izzy knew how much love he had to give. She only had a few months to convince him she wasn't Janet and it was safe for him to open his heart again.

'We'll have to get used to it. Twins are going to come with a lot of baggage and mess.' His immaculate home was going to be disrupted by two demanding, messy little beings. She didn't want it to come as a shock after he'd spent every spare minute putting the furniture together to complete this showroom nursery of her dreams.

They'd gone for an underwater theme, the room now festooned with cartoon sea creatures featuring on matching mobiles above the cribs and on the bedding. It was the kind of lovingly put-together room she wished she'd had as a child, instead of the generic spare bedrooms she'd always been designated. When the children were old enough to choose their own décor, she'd make sure their rooms were tailor-made to suit their individual interests and personalities so they never felt like interlopers, the way she had. Their home had to be somewhere they felt safe, wanted and surrounded by people who loved them.

'You know we're going to take over this house?' She eyed the boxes containing the highchairs and baby-walkers they wouldn't use for a while but which were already taking up space.

'Trust me, I know exactly what chaos I've invited into my home.' He didn't sound completely thrilled at the prospect but the smirk ghosting on his lips suggested he'd accepted the consequences.

After Janet's stunt she wouldn't have blamed him for changing his mind about sharing his house with anyone again. In the same position she might've decided it preferable to live on her own instead of inviting another pregnant woman to stay. To Cal's credit, he hadn't waivered in his decision to have her move in. He was reliable in that way and it was part of the reason she'd made a big decision regarding the twins.

'Cal? I have something to ask you.'

'Ask away.' He'd finished installing a night light that played a lullaby and projected moving images of seahorses and jellyfish around the walls. Izzy thought she might start sleeping in here herself if he made it any more appealing.

'Feel free to say no...you're under no obligation...

but I was wondering if you'd consider being my birthing partner?' From the second that blue line had appeared on the pregnancy test she'd been determined to do it all on her own because she hadn't seen any other option. These past weeks Cal had shown her he was there for her day or night.

Although she didn't want to rely on him too heavily, with the twins on the way it was clear there were going to be more appointments, more risks involved, and these were times when it would be good to have someone holding her hand. It was also her plan to have him there to bond immediately with the babies and fall in love with them the second he saw them.

'You mean, like, be there at the birth?' Cal stopped tinkering long enough to come towards her, making her stomach flip. She couldn't tell if it was her hormones reacting to having him close or the babies letting her know they approved of the idea.

'Yeah. I thought you might like to be there.' She didn't have a partner or family member invested in her pregnancy, and Cal was the only person who had a right to be present in the delivery room with her.

'If that's what you want.' There was no indication that was what *he* wanted, but she was working on eventually teasing that information out of him.

'Just so we're clear, that doesn't entitle you to boss me about.' This role didn't give him carte blanche to interfere, and she'd remain the independent woman she'd always been.

'Okay, no pregnancy boot camp. I promise not to attempt to take over in any way. Although I hope that doesn't mean we can't discuss things like your birth plan or what sort of pain relief you'd prefer. It's good to look at all available options and work out what's best for you.'

At least he was thinking ahead on her behalf and it gave her hope that he wasn't going to leave her in the lurch when she'd need him most. Even if it was only on a practical level so far.

'You can help me draw up a suitable list of names too. Although I am putting my foot down now and saying no to suggestions of Bill and Ben, Pinky and Perky or any other such monikers.'

'I'm guessing that rules out This One and That One, too,' he said with a grin, but she knew he'd take the job seriously.

If there was one thing Izzy could guarantee her babies it was that they'd have somewhere to call home, and Cal had played a huge part in making that happen. No matter how reluctantly.

Cal walked into the office as Izzy was rubbing her hand across her chest with that pained expression on her face again. He set a tall glass of milk and a packet of antacids on the table before her. 'For the heartburn.'

She'd been getting a lot of that recently and particularly at night if the sounds of her pacing her bedroom were anything to go by.

As a result, she was becoming tired and irritable but as she refused to take time for extra rest, all they could do was wait for the symptoms to gradually ease as the pregnancy progressed.

It was difficult trying to look out for her best interests and avoid becoming a nag. There was a fine line between offering advice and interfering, and he knew he was currently straddling it. Especially since she'd asked him to be more involved as her birthing partner. She would've known he'd take that privileged position seriously and it wasn't something she'd assign to him on a whim. He was surprised when it had taken her so long to share the news about the pregnancy with him.

Cal wasn't the sort of man, or doctor, who thought pregnant women should necessarily be wrapped up in cotton wool but sometimes there was cause to be concerned. Multiple pregnancy carried a higher risk of complications anyway but as he spent the working day alongside Izzy he knew how hard she worked and the high-octane, high-stress-level environment she did it in.

'What would I do without you?' Izzy batted her eyelashes at him and accepted the prescribed treatment.

'I think you'd manage pretty well,' he muttered, refusing to get drawn back into that role of faithful servant he'd become during Janet's pregnancy. It had hurt that much more when it had all been taken away from him, knowing she'd been taking advantage of his devotion and making a fool out of him. He wasn't going to let that happen twice in his lifetime.

'It was a joke, Cal. We both know I could do this

without you.' In case he'd doubted it, Izzy emphasised the fact he was dispensable and reinforced the notion that neither of them should get too comfortable about their situation.

'Have you spoken to Mac yet?' There was no point in being bitter about things now, so he moved them on to more practical, less emotive matters.

She'd been taking her time informing their bosses about the pregnancy, probably because she was afraid they'd ground her pretty soon. Working as ground crew overseeing hospital transfers might not be the job she'd signed up for, but there were too many health and safety risks involved professionally and personally to keep it secret for much longer.

'Yes. He's leaving it down to me to make the decision regarding when to take my maternity leave. Very sneaky, I thought. That way I can't complain when I'm forced to bail out. I suppose it depends on how huge I end up too. If I'm incubating two baby elephants in here, my bulk could stop the helicopter from lifting off the ground at all.'

Mac had been smart to put the ball back in Izzy's court because she would never jeopardise the safety of her crew over her pride. At least it was out in the open now and, bless her, her 'normal' clothes already seemed to be a bit snug. Her pride or denial that she was putting on weight couldn't last for ever. Eventually she'd have to cave in and buy some maternity wear for a little comfort. It was rare for a multiple pregnancy to go to full term so there was no predicting how this one would advance or what toll it would take on her. He did know he'd be relieved when she made the decision not to go up in the air any more, for her own good and his peace of mind.

'We've got a call.' Mac sounded the alarm for the rest of the crew to get moving, everyone pulling on their flight gear as they made their way to the waiting helicopter. Izzy had that familiar rush of adrenaline that came with every call, reminding her that she had an important part to play in every one of these life-or-death calls.

'Fifty-two-year-old woman thrown from her horse. May have sustained head and neck injuries.' Cal repeated the details of the patient requiring their assistance.

'We'll need to set down somewhere close to the site. There's an empty field next to the jumps there.' He gave instructions to the pilot over the headset for a suitable green space to land, clear of buildings, people and anything else that could impede their arrival.

Izzy was trying to focus on the ground rushing up to meet them, estimating how long it would take them to reach those in danger. However, the noise and vibration of the chopper as they raced to the scene was beginning to affect her. Before the pregnancy all the shaking and shouting that went on prior to landing had served to heighten the thrill of hitting the ground running.

Today, though, her body was responding altogether differently to the experience. Every shudder, every drop in altitude had her stomach lurching. She didn't know if it was a sudden and impractical bout of travel sickness or delayed morning sickness. One thing was sure, though, these babies seemed to be protesting about the current mode of transport. Unfortunate when it was also her place of work.

Izzy would never intentionally put any patient in jeopardy due to potential personal issues. She was hoping this was a one-off. If not, she was going to have to hang up her flight suit much earlier than she'd anticipated. She could hardly go running to someone's rescue if she was going to be violently ill every time she was on a call-out.

The wind generated by the chopper blades flattened the grass around them and Izzy and Cal jumped out. She let him run on ahead in the hope he wouldn't witness her vomit stop at the hedge and pulled the water bottle from the kit on her back to wash her mouth out. Except when she was ready to carry on he was glaring back at her. He didn't have to say anything for her to know he wasn't happy she was continuing to work as usual despite her discomfort. In other circumstances she might have accused him of pregnancy discrimination but given her current state she could see he had a point.

'What? Drinking a full glass of milk before getting shaken about was never a good idea.' She had an excuse this time but the next time he'd call her bluff. He could pull rank on her and play the doctor card to force her into co-operating. Anything more serious than some nausea and she'd put herself on bed rest. She was stubborn, but she was also a mum-to-be and she was learning what that entailed.

Cal opened his mouth to say something, probably to scold her, then took off again without saying a word towards the congregation in the adjacent field. It was almost worse having understanding colleagues trusting she knew her own body well enough to make the call when it came to cutting back on work, rather than have them making decisions on her behalf. Almost. Only because she'd have no right to rant and rave at anyone when the crew took off without her.

For now, she was making the most of still having the job she was trained to do, rushing towards someone relying on her and Cal to get them safely delivered to the nearest hospital.

He introduced himself to the gentleman kneeling on the ground next to the woman who'd apparently suffered the fall. 'Can you tell me what happened?'

Izzy knelt on the wet grass beside them and began to unpack the medical equipment they were liable to require.

'I found her like this. When she didn't come home for lunch I came to look for her.' It was clear the man was trying not to panic but he'd done the right thing by not moving her and phoning for help straight away.

'She hasn't gained consciousness since?' A sign that she could have suffered a head injury from the fall or that the horse might have kicked out at her.

'She's made the odd moaning sound, but she hasn't woken up.'

That was something at least. 'How long ago did you find her?'

'About fifteen, maybe twenty minutes ago.' The man was clinging to his wife's hand and Izzy prayed this had a happy ending. Since finding out she was going to have a family of her own she'd become much more sentimental concerning the partners and children involved on the cases. Now, with the love in her heart for the babies she was carrying and having Cal there for her, she better understood the impact of illness or injury on loved ones.

'What's her name?'

'Agnes.'

'Agnes, can you hear me?' Cal tried to garner a response as Izzy set about getting her ready to be moved.

There was a faint groan to reassure them that Agnes was clinging to consciousness.

'We think you've hit your head in a fall so it's very important you stay still until we get that neck stabilised. We're going to give you some pain relief then we'll put a brace around your neck to keep you immobile. You might be uncomfortable but the sooner we can get you stable here the quicker we can get you into the helicopter and on your way to the hospital. Okay?'

She gave another groan in response and though she tried to bat them away at times they managed to get the brace and backboard on her.

'We're going to take her to the local hospital if you want to meet us there. The trauma team already knows we're on our way.' Cal relayed their intentions to the husband.

It was at least forty minutes there by road, but they could do it in less than fifteen by air. Part of the reason they'd been dispatched for this call.

When Izzy got to her feet to transport the trolley over to the helicopter she stumbled, a tad unbalanced as the world around her began to spin. Thankfully she was holding onto the side of the stretcher, which prevented her from landing in a heap in the middle of the field.

The dizzy spell passed as quickly as it had begun but she could already feel Cal's eyes burning a hole into her.

'I'm fine,' she mouthed as they rushed towards the chopper, but knew deep down this was the beginning of the end for her out in the field.

All systems were go as they hooked Agnes up to the monitors on board and radioed in their ETA.

'I've got this.' Cal nodded towards the jump seat, indicating he wanted her to sit this one out. There was nothing to be gained from arguing and detracting his attention from the patient when he was the medical lead and had the final say here.

Although she would challenge him if she categorically believed he was wrong, on this occasion she had to concede to his authority. She was no use to Cal or Agnes swaying on her feet and ready to pass out at any second.

'There's a protein bar and a juice in my bag. Take them.' Cal went back on his word not to boss her around, but she needed it. She might have been insisting she could carry on as normal, but some things had to change. Including skipping meals and risking her blood pressure dropping too low.

In the past all that had meant was having dinner later than usual. Now it could put their missions in jeopardy. They couldn't take the chance of her fainting in the middle of treating a patient or when they were in the air. From now on she was going to have to plan and prepare for all eventualities to prevent this from happening again. That was if she was ever allowed to fly again for the duration of the pregnancy when they'd have to log a record of this incident.

Regardless that she wasn't hungry or thirsty, she followed Cal's instruction so when they landed on the helipad on the hospital roof she was feeling more like herself.

'Okay, Agnes. That's us at the hospital now. The staff know we're coming so they'll be waiting for us to transfer you into their care.' It was Cal who talked her through the proceedings as she continued to drift in and out of consciousness in the hope some of the information would filter through and the change in surroundings wouldn't be too much of a shock.

Izzy took her place on the other side of the stretcher from Cal and they wheeled her out to the waiting trauma team. Cal reeled off Agnes's personal details and his observations and once they'd handed over responsibility, the air crew was able to breathe again.

Not that Cal would let her get away with having a wobble on his watch without an investigation. 'You're going home for a proper meal and complete bed rest.'

It wasn't the worst proposition she'd ever had, and it was one she'd welcome. There wasn't a choice anyway when she was living with him. He'd insist on cooking her a nutritious meal and probably escort her to her room to make sure she followed his advice this time.

'Yes, sir.' She clicked her heels together and saluted, the teasing an attempt to reassure him he could stop fretting.

It was unfortunate that the sharp, sudden movement tilted the world around her all over again. That slight spinning sensation she'd experienced earlier evolved into a vortex sucking the oxygen out of the atmosphere and drawing her into its core. She couldn't keep her focus on any one point, including Cal's concerned face.

He sounded so far away as he called out her name. Then she was drifting away, the darkness that was calling her home. She was falling, her body crumpling under her as she gave in to unconsciousness, but the last thing she remembered was Cal's arms around her and a feeling of weightlessness as she was carried off into the unknown.

Chapter 7

'Izzy? Fizz?' Cal called out to her the second he saw her wobble. He'd known something was wrong and wished he'd asked the hospital staff to send transport for her too.

He could see the unfocused gaze and reached her a millisecond before she passed out. With a volley of expletives to alert the rest of the air crew, he caught her in his arms and rushed her off in the direction the hospital staff had gone.

Everything in his training told him it was probably wasn't anything more than a faint. Nothing unusual for a pregnant woman, especially one who hadn't been eating properly and was overdoing it. It didn't prevent him from reacting on an emotional level as he witnessed her collapse. All those irrational fears that he was going to lose another loved one came rushing to the surface, making him act as though her life depended on it.

Even pregnant with twins, she seemed so fragile in his arms, completely dependent on him to get her to safety. Whatever past hurt had been preventing him from bonding with these babies was immaterial compared to what he was feeling now, faced with the possibility of losing them for ever. He was their father after all and resisting that connection was pointless when nothing in the world could alter that fact. Worry was simply a part of fatherhood he'd never outrun, and when it could all be snatched away from him at any moment he didn't know why he was trying. He should be making the most of every second of it.

By the time he'd whisked Izzy down to the emergency department she was thankfully beginning to come around.

'Sasha, I need some help here.' He commandeered an empty cubicle and called over one of the nurses he recognised from their transfers.

With a gentle hand he manoeuvred Izzy's head to rest on the hospital bed, grateful he'd caught her before she'd hit the ground and perhaps given herself a concussion on top of everything else.

'What's happened to Iz?' One of the benefits of rushing emergencies through was that at least they were familiar faces around here. Although given the capacity in which Sasha knew them she'd be forgiven for thinking some catastrophe had befallen the helicopter.

'She fainted up on the roof while we were doing a handover. I should probably tell you she's pregnant with twins, in her second trimester.' Cal could see the surprise on the nurse's face but as she didn't push any further he refrained from sharing any more of Izzy's personal information. Although he imagined people were going to find out he was the father sooner or later.

'Did she hit her head at any point?'

'No.' He was confident about that at least, thanks to his quick reflexes and the close eye he'd been keeping on her.

'Izzy? Can you hear me? It's Sasha in Accident and Emergency. It would really help us if you could open your eyes, sweetie.' Whilst she tried to rouse Izzy, Cal scooted over to the sink to wet some paper towels.

'Cal? Where's Cal?'

He heard her confused mumble and hurried back to her bedside to place the cold compress on her forehead. 'I'm here, Fizz.'

She was trying to sit up, but he placed a hand on her chest and gently eased her back. 'You fainted. We need you to rest up for a while.'

If she wouldn't listen to him, perhaps the staff here could convince her.

'The babies?' Her first thoughts went to her bump, along with her hands.

Cal understood that sense of terror, that utter feeling of dread and powerlessness because that's exactly what had happened to him when he'd seen her drop like a stone. He might not be Izzy's romantic partner, but he was still entitled to worry about all of them. It was clear he was the only one they had in their lives to rely on and he didn't want to let any of them down.

'I'm sure they're fine. You haven't been out long, and I brought you straight here.' He squeezed her hand, although he knew it wouldn't do much to reassure her in the circumstances.

Her chin began to wobble, her throat bobbed up and down each time she swallowed, and Cal could see how much she was desperately trying to hold back tears. With a cough to clear his throat he looked to Sasha for help. 'We can get an ultrasound to check everything's okay with the babies, right? Just to put Izzy's mind at ease.'

Sasha smiled at him in that way that said she knew he needed the confirmation too. 'Of course. We're going to check your blood pressure and take some bloods first, Izzy, so we can see if there's anything that caused you to faint. Have you been thirstier or needing to urinate more than usual?'

'No. Why, do you think it could be gestational diabetes?' Izzy was one step ahead of the nurse because of the symptoms she was describing, but Cal was sure it was something much simpler. Her blood sugar level was probably too low, rather than the opposite.

'We're just being thorough in our investigations

but if you haven't noticed any symptoms then it's not likely to be GD. We'll do all the tests anyway.'

'She hasn't been eating properly.' He was ready for Izzy to call him a snitch, but she was waiting for Sasha's opinion on continuing her casual attitude to mealtimes during pregnancy.

'The thing to remember, Izzy, is that during pregnancy you're sharing your blood supply with your baby, and in your case two babies. I would recommend carrying snacks with you. Going without food will affect you more now.'

'Thanks, Sasha. I guess I'm going to have to start listening to my body more,' Izzy said, looking a little more reassured that there was no reason this pregnancy shouldn't go full term without any further complications. She probably just needed some rest and TLC, which Cal was always offering to help her with.

He knew their relationship had gone far beyond friendship, despite his intention not to get too close, but he was afraid to acknowledge it. There was so much on the line he couldn't risk what they already had together. The best he could probably hope for was that she'd continue to let him play a part in her life.

The whole event had given Izzy quite a fright. If it was a sign she should take things easier she was going to make sure she took heed of it rather than go through this again. Thank goodness she'd been given another peek at her little jellybeans to make sure they hadn't suffered during her dizzy spell. She supposed it was too much to ask if they could install one of those machines at home, so she could obsessively check on them for the next few months.

'We're going to move you onto the ward for the night, Izzy. The blood tests have shown signs of anaemia so we're going to have to get you started on some iron supplements, and your blood pressure's quite low too. I suspect that's what caused the fainting today and I'd like to keep you in overnight so we can keep an eye on that.' The doctor hadn't given her any chance to disagree and though she understood the precautions she simply wanted to go home.

'Can't you wheel me out the back door and take me home with you?' she suggested to Cal as he followed her to the ward, holding her hand as the porter manoeuvred her around corridor corner.

He was pale, she'd put him through a lot today. She was sure it had been no mean feat, carrying her dead weight down from the roof, and apparently he hadn't left her side since. That solid reassurance she wasn't in this on her own was priceless and made the whole ordeal slightly less traumatic. Although he hadn't said it, he'd obviously been as worried about the babies as she had been, and she considered that progress.

'Believe me, I would if I could, Fizz, but they're better equipped to monitor you here.' So far, he hadn't scolded her or insisted she would be on bed rest for the foreseeable future, but she would accept any conditions he might impose if she could be under his care at home, instead of being here. It wasn't going to happen, not tonight, but when she thought of home now it included Cal and the warmth and comfort she associated with his house. Their house.

'You should probably go and get changed, have something to eat. I don't want you getting sick on my account.' She didn't want him to go. Even on a busy ward full of other patients and staff, she could feel herself retreating, shrinking into the corner and building up those protective walls in the event he did go and leave her here alone.

As the staff busied themselves around her bed, getting her settled for her upcoming stay, Cal remained stubbornly in place. Once they'd gone and she was successfully hooked up to the machines checking her progress, Cal leaned in and whispered, 'I have contacts.'

'What do you mean?'

He tapped the side of his nose. 'As long as I keep out of sight and promise not to get you or any of your fellow patients over-excited I've got special dispensation to stay outside visiting hours.'

Izzy knew she should be magnanimous and tell him she was fine here on her own. In truth, she was relieved to have him with her a little longer.

There was a twinge of guilt every time Izzy glanced at Cal's flight suit draped over the back of his chair when she knew if it wasn't for her he'd be at home, relaxing after his shift.

'It's not what I'd call *haute cuisine*,' she apolo-

gised as they both finished the unappetising plate
of hospital food they'd been served. It made her appreciate Cal's efforts in the kitchen every night even
more.

'I'm just thankful she took pity on me and do-
nated the unwanted meal to a good home.' He certainly hadn't turned his nose up at the free dinner
offered to him from the trolley after being rejected
by a more discerning diner. Izzy thought it was in-
dicative of how ravenous he was when she'd had to
force down every mouthful. Then again, she was too
stressed and anxious about the babies to have any
sort of appetite.

Despite the reassurances and precautions, there
was still a long way to go and plenty of time for
other, more serious complications to occur.

'Hey, don't you go getting all maudlin on me.' Cal
set his empty plate beside hers on the table across
her bed.

'Sorry, I'm not much company for you.'

'Would you prefer it if I left you alone?' The determined set of his jaw told her he seriously believed she
might be better on her own than have him with her.

'No,' she said, much too quickly, and grabbed his
hand. All that would do was make her even more
miserable and give her more time to dwell on all the
negatives of the situation when he was the only one
who could give her a much-needed boost.

'Good. Otherwise there'd be no one here to make
sure you eat up all of your fruit salad.' He lifted the
dish of chopped fruit and pulled his chair closer to

the bed. 'Now, are you going to open up or do I have to make aeroplane noises?'

When he began moving the spoon towards her mouth she complied by eating it, touched that he cared so much about her. She couldn't remember anyone nursing her when she was ill.

In the shared foster homes, the parents had been afraid of any viruses spreading to the rest of the children and at the first sign of sickness she'd been quarantined in her room. She'd thought all those images she'd seen in TV shows of worried parents mopping the brows of fevered offspring were pure fiction. Until Cal had refused to leave her bedside and she understood what she'd been missing. To have someone who cared about her well-being more than their own was alien to her but something she could easily become accustomed to.

'Do I get a prize if I finish it all?' she asked before accepting the last morsel. In normal circumstances she might have been liable to throw the food at someone trying to feed her like a baby, but Cal wasn't trying to patronise her, he was trying to lift her spirits and make sure she got some sustenance. Okay, she was enjoying the attention too.

'Why, is there something I can tempt you with?' He waggled his eyebrows suggestively at her and made her laugh. It was good to have someone around who was so good at distracting her when she needed it and, boy, was he a distraction. There had been a few moments between them when she'd been convinced they were going to give in to temptation again. She'd ached for it, but Cal was always the one to pull back from the brink. It had been on her say so, of course, one of the conditions of her moving in, but it seemed she was powerless against her own hormones.

'I want you in my bed,' she said, enjoying the shock on his face as she leaned forward and helped herself to the last spoonful of fruit.

Izzy patted the space next to her on the bed.

'The staff have been very accommodating, but I think that might be pushing things too far,' he said with a cheeky glint in his eye.

'I won't tell if you don't.'

After years of knowing and teasing each other it suddenly felt more real. As though the flirting was going to lead somewhere. It was probably because they were both exhausted mentally and physically that they were letting this spark between them flare into life again. Beyond the comfort and support Cal represented, that attraction also lingered, on her part at least, but she knew nothing could come of it.

She was sure this fancy would pass once the babies were safely here and she didn't feel so vulnerable. More than likely she was confusing his kindness for something that wasn't there but had been lacking her entire life. Love.

Cal didn't wait for a second invitation, only pausing to kick off his shoes. The instant he climbed onto the bed beside her and put his arm around her she snuggled into his chest with a sigh.

Perhaps it was because she was feeling vulnerable, or that they'd become so close lately, but Izzy felt compelled to share how important it was to have him there for her.

'You know, I usually can't bear anyone near me when I'm sick. I'm not used to it.'

'Not even Gerry?' It was probably difficult for Cal to understand when he'd been so considerate. Plus, it was his job, his duty of care to look after the sick and infirm.

Gerry wasn't a subject she liked to discuss with Cal for obvious reasons.

'He was on the road a lot and I think it was better for us both that he wasn't around if I was ill.' She gave a little laugh because she could see now how unreasonable she'd been at times. It was fine for her to lecture others on self-care when they weren't well, but she had no time for lying around feeling sorry for herself. She wouldn't have thanked Gerry for pandering to her either, thinking he'd have an ulterior motive for keeping on her good side. That was on top of her already ingrained need to contain the possible spread of infection.

Now Cal had shown her the sort of nurturing she'd been missing out on since the day she'd been born, and she swore her own children would know what it was to be loved and cherished every day of their lives.

'That's one of the many things I miss about not having my mum around.' Cal was absent-mindedly stroking her hair and Izzy closed her eyes, gave herself over to his tender touch.

'If I was sick she'd give up her whole day, no matter what she'd been doing beforehand, to spend it looking after me. She made the best chicken soup and brought it to me in bed. Nothing was too much trouble and she'd spend hours reading to me or playing board games with me. Even when I left home she'd rush over a pot of soup at the first sign of a sniffle. I guess you could say I was spoiled.' He gave a self-deprecating laugh but the picture he painted was more about a very special mother and son bond than an over-indulged brat.

'More loved, I'd say. Your mum sounds as though she was a lovely person.' It was easy to understand where he got his loving nature from and Izzy wasn't jealous of his idyllic-sounding upbringing.

'She was, as was Dad. Nothing was ever the same after they died. There was no one there to keep the rest of us together and it felt as though I'd lost the rest of my family along with them. My sisters moved away with their husbands and children and suddenly I was no longer a son, a brother or an uncle. I lost my sense of identity along with them. When Janet told me she was pregnant I had a role again. I was going to be a husband and father, that's why the loss was so great when she left. I lost myself along with her and the baby and it took me a long time to rediscover my identity as just Cal. I think that's why I'm finding it difficult relating to the role of being a father again. I don't want it to completely define who I am.'

The sadness in his voice made Izzy reach out and wrap her arms around his waist. It was clear he was afraid of committing again in case she took it all away from him again, the way Janet had.

'I know the Cal you were before all this happened and I promise I won't let you get cast adrift in all the excitement. I want you very much to be a part of everything.'

He gave a brief nod before changing the subject. 'What about you? You don't say much about your foster parents except that they live some distance away.'

'I've never been able to think of them as Mum and Dad, although they were the last couple to assume the roles. I never knew my birth parents and I was passed around a series of foster homes until I was old enough to go it alone. Some of the foster parents genuinely wanted to help kids in the system, others you could tell were only in it for the money, and more than a few simply weren't equipped to deal with those of us who had serious issues about our start in life. I know I acted up, pushing the boundaries to test how willing they were to keep me, and as a result I never stayed in one place too long. Theory proved.

'Meeting Helen changed things for me. She lived next door and became a real friend, the first I'd ever had. I was welcomed into her home as part of the family and I probably spent more time there, eating their food and talking over my problems with her, than in any one of my foster homes. I think that's why having my own family is so important to me. I want my children to have that love and stability I'd never had. While I'm grateful to those people who did take me in, I was never treated as a *proper* daughter. There was no real affection there and I knew it when I saw how Helen's parents interacted with her. I didn't have anyone who cared when I was sick, and I'm not used to having it now. I guess that's why I get cranky around people when I'm ill.'

'My poor Izzy. Yet you're willing to put up with me. I'm honoured.' He dropped a kiss on her head and Izzy wanted to remain cocooned here in this cubicle with him for ever.

'You're different. I'm—' She stopped herself just in time before the words *I'm in love with you* caught them both by surprise. 'I'm used to you.' She managed to cover her back before she spoiled the moment by saying something daft enough to lose him, her home and her future when he'd admitted he didn't feel the same way.

'That's good to know.' He chuckled, the vibration of his chest beneath her cheek having the opposite effect on her from the judder of the helicopter. Instead of upsetting her stomach, it was comforting.

They settled into an easy silence but that thinking time soon led her into more anxiety.

'Cal? I'm scared.' She shared her fears, watching for reassurance even when she knew he'd never abandon her or lie to her the way everyone else in her life had done. He'd shown her that today and every day since he'd found out about the babies, when most would have run from the responsibility.

He leaned down until they were nose to nose and she could see the sincerity in his eyes. 'I will never let anything happen to you. You mean too much to me.'

She was tired of fighting this thing between them. When he was looking at her with such adoration and longing she no longer knew why she was resisting the inevitable. Especially when she knew how good it felt to give in to those impulses.

She closed her eyes and tilted her chin up, inviting him to make that final decision and seal their fate. Only a second later she felt that soft pressure of his lips on hers bringing her whole body back to life. For once she was being true to herself and to her feelings and could only pray Cal was doing the same.

There was the worry he was only kissing her to comfort her but as he tangled his hand in her hair and strengthened that physical connection between them she knew better than to doubt his intentions. He'd opened up to her emotionally about his childhood and his fears and he wouldn't have done that unless he was thinking seriously about their future. Cal wanted her. All of her.

Izzy freed her mind from everything except how good it felt to be touching him again. Everything she wanted was there in his kiss—comfort, security, but most of all the intense passion she'd convinced herself had only existed in that one night. How wrong she'd been when he was pulling her close to his body, telling her how much he wanted her without saying a word. His lips captured hers again and again, his tongue teased hers until she thought she'd expire if he didn't give her more.

It also sent her heart monitor into overdrive, so he knew exactly what effect he was having on her. She felt his smile against her lips before he pulled away from her again.

'I should probably go before the nurses throw me out.' His voice was thick with desire as he shifted his weight on the mattress, but Izzy wasn't ready for him to leave apparently any more than he was.

'Can't you stay a little bit longer?' It was unlike her to be needy, but she was done with being alone when she could be in Cal's arms.

'You need your sleep. I'm keeping you awake.'

'In the best possible way. There's plenty of room for two.' She tried to convince him, though it was doubtful whether either of them would have a comfortable night with four of them essentially packed into one single bed.

'Nice try.' He sat up and arranged the pillows for her to lie down.

'I'll stay here until you fall asleep,' he whispered into her ear, spooning against her with his arm draped so casually across her waist one might've believed this was a nightly occurrence. It was a pleasant thought, even though she wanted more.

Izzy closed her eyes, a smile on her lips as exhaustion claimed her. She hadn't realised how much she needed or wanted Cal in her life until she couldn't imagine one without him in it.

Chapter 8

Cal had been like a kid on Christmas Eve, unable to settle, waiting for the call to go and pick Izzy up from the hospital. He'd ignored the cramp in his limbs, which had set in as he'd been lying on that hospital bed with her because he hadn't wanted to swap it for the luxury of his spacious king-size bed.

Home offered him peace, space and comfort in comparison but without Izzy it was hard to find any of that. He'd have happily slept all night with her pressed against his chest, dead arm and all, just to be close to her a while longer. That's when he knew he was in way over his head.

This was supposed to have been a gesture that he was committed to raising the babies with Izzy. Moving in together was never meant to have been more than a favour. He'd certainly never intended to get as close to Izzy as he'd apparently become. It left him open to the same kind of emotional hurt he'd been through once too often. With her determination to include him every step of the way through this pregnancy she'd broken through those defences he'd imagined would keep his heart protected. When he thought losing her or the babies was a possibility he knew he'd become completely attached to the idea of their little family.

Yesterday had been stressful for them both but it must have taken a particular toll on Izzy for her to let him so close and to want him to stay. She'd always been a firecracker and independent to the point of being obstreperous, so it was an indication of just how much turmoil she'd been in for her to let him hold her.

Then there was the kiss. He'd been so overcome with compassion for her situation, gratitude for having her in his life and, well, love, there was nothing he could've done to prevent it from happening. When Izzy had kissed him back his whole body had sung out with sheer happiness that she'd wanted him too. It was only the rise in her blood pressure that had reminded him she was vulnerable, and he hadn't wanted to take advantage of that when he was the only person she had in her life. It would confuse her at a time when her whole world was in chaos and what she needed from him more was a sense of security and stability. Something she'd apparently been missing out on for some time.

She didn't have friends or family around and it was natural she should reach out for the nearest available substitute. He'd do well to remember that's all he was in the picture.

'Would you like me to hunt down a wheelchair to get you to the car?' Cal waited patiently as Izzy packed her newly prescribed medication and toiletries into the bag he'd brought for her.

She gave him a sidelong look. 'Would you like me to get a wheelchair to take *you* to the car?'

'Okay, okay. I was only trying to save you a walk.' He held his hands up in surrender. Secretly, he was pleased she was back to her fighting best. For him it was a better sign she was on the mend than her improved blood pressure and blood test results. Even if he'd miss his temporary position as chief handholder.

'I've been cooped up in bed too long. I need the exercise and some fresh air. Not to mention something to eat that doesn't resemble baby food. Can we stop somewhere on the way home?' She whispered the request, presumably to prevent offending anyone from hospital catering if they overheard.

'I can do better than that. I've stocked up on fresh fruit and vegetables and I'm going to cook you a veritable welcome-home feast. Anything your heart desires.' Cal bowed and grabbed her luggage before she insisted on carrying it herself.

From now on, he intended to provide her with wholesome, nutritious meals to ensure she wouldn't be lacking in any more essential vitamins or minerals. Avoiding any further upsetting overnight hospital stays.

'For now, I'd be happy if you took me home and put the kettle on.' Izzy softened a little towards him, slipping her arm through his and leaning against him for the duration of the short walk to the car.

'I think I can manage that.' He had worried that her defences had reassembled during the time since she'd last seen him and that she might have regretted their cosy bedtime cuddle session. On his return home, Cal's bed had suddenly seemed so vast and empty compared to that hospital trolley. Even more so than after Janet had left him. It was only with some considerable thought, comparing that one spooning session with Izzy against years of sharing a bed with Janet, he realised proximity to someone didn't actually constitute the nature of a close relationship.

They'd gone through the motions together as a couple, but they'd never had that bond he had with Izzy. Which was probably why Janet had never approved of their friendship.

Yesterday, experiencing that pain and worry together and finally expressing some of the emotions they'd tried to keep locked down, had finally cemented their bond. Their only worry now should be making sure these babies were safely delivered into the world.

He unlocked the car, which he'd parked as close to the entrance as he dared, risking a fine to save Izzy an uphill walk to the car park. Instead of climbing into the passenger seat, as he'd expected, Izzy suddenly turned around and said, 'Thank you for everything, Calum,' and kissed him full on the lips.

He drove on autopilot, in a loved-up haze, back to the home they shared. The only place he knew both of them wanted to be, where they could close the door and re-create that cocoon. Where all they needed was each other.

Izzy had spent the rest of the week under house arrest as per Cal's orders. She knew it wasn't a control issue, she'd worked alongside Cal long enough to know he wasn't the kind of guy who needed to exert his authority every second of the day. However, he was compassionate and well mannered. Not usually qualities a woman would find irritating unless she was used to being fiercely independent.

She was going stir crazy forced to stay in one place for so long, not permitted to lift a finger to do anything. It was alien to her, being so cosseted that she didn't know how to deal with it. So she'd gone back to being her bolshie self, giving Cal a hard time and accusing him of suffocating her because deep down she was afraid of jumping his bones for paying her a bit of attention.

Not that he'd have let her expend that sort of energy, even if he had reciprocated these new feelings she'd been harbouring towards him. She'd thought that night in the hospital and that wonderful sensation of falling asleep in his arms had been the start of something more between them. Except he'd turned into her carer since then with no inclination towards anything other than nursing her.

He hadn't reacted to the kiss she'd given him when they'd left the hospital and so she'd consigned it to the list of bad decisions she'd made regarding suitable men. She'd taken his kindness and understanding and tried to sabotage the relationship they did have by taking it somewhere he might not have wanted it to go. What else could Cal have done when she'd made him get into her bed and poured her heart except to make her feel better? She'd provided the awkward element by attempting to extend that moment beyond the hospital walls.

Unfortunately, this imposed relaxation was having the opposite effect it was supposed to have on her. Instead of keeping her calm and chilled out, it was giving her too much time to obsess about everything that had happened recently or could happen in the near future.

She'd tried everything to distract her thoughts from Cal and what he was doing without her at work. Including watching so much trashy daytime television she wanted to scratch her eyes out. Taking up knitting hadn't helped either. There were so many holes in the simple squares she'd attempted to piece into a blanket it looked more like crochet.

Izzy lit on him the second she heard the key in the lock, desperate for some human company instead of the virtual kind. 'You should have texted to let me know you were on your way home. I could have had dinner in the oven for you.'

She felt like a nineteen-fifties housewife, waiting barefoot and pregnant for the centre of her universe to come home from work and give her life some meaning. She really needed to get back to work and do something useful. Never in a million years could she have pictured herself in the role of the happy housewife because she'd never imagined it existed. Although she'd go mad if she spent every day tied to the kitchen sink with no outside interests, she had to admit there was a certain appeal in sharing dinner and chores with a man who would happily put her on a pedestal.

'I wouldn't expect you to do that. You're supposed to be taking it easy.' Cal hung up his jacket and rolled up his shirtsleeves, preparing to go into the kitchen and start making dinner. He was one in a million and easy to take advantage of if you were an unscrupulous user like his ex. On the other hand, this total pampering deal made her feel uncomfortable because she didn't know what to do with herself.

'Cal, I've been taking it so easy I'm practically comatose. I'm fine. The midwife confirmed that at my last appointment. My blood pressure is where it should be, as are my iron levels. Besides, you've cooked and labelled enough food to see out the entire pregnancy. All I'd have to do is microwave it.' Given his history it was no wonder he was used to doing his Florence Nightingale bit, but he couldn't carry on in this vein or she'd burst a blood vessel from pent-up frustration.

'You say that as though it's a bad thing.'

'It's not that I don't appreciate all your effort to take care of me, Cal. I'm simply not used to it. You know I'm not the type to sit on my backside and let everyone run around after me, no matter what the circumstances. I'm going back to work on Monday and before you say anything I'll make sure it's as ground crew only.' Then she wouldn't get in anyone's way and could still remain part of the team. She wasn't asking his permission, but she did respect him enough to inform him of her decision.

He nodded. 'It's one hundred per cent your choice, Iz. All I wanted to do was fulfil my promise to take care of you and the babies.'

'I know.' And she loved him for it. If only his actions were based on more than a misplaced sense of duty.

'Look, why don't we go out for a meal?'

Izzy was tempted to ask if he meant as a date, but it was more likely to be a compromise, so she had to dampen down her initial excitement that they were making progress on their personal relationship.

'It would be nice to leave these four walls and pay a visit into civilisation.' Izzy also realised it would be the first time they'd gone out to a restaurant as anything other than work colleagues. She couldn't help but hope for the day when they did it as a couple, or even a family.

'It's a date, then. Give me ten minutes to shower and change and we'll hit the town.' Cal bounded up the stairs to freshen up, while Izzy did her best to get her fluttering pulse back under control.

* * *

'I get the impression our waiter thinks we're having some sort of clandestine affair,' Izzy whispered across the secluded, candlelit table, which had obviously been set to create a romantic scene.

Cal grinned at her, clearly amused by being ushered towards the dark corner with her, away from businessmen and noisy young families.

'Then maybe we should give him something to talk about.' He took her hand and lifted it to his mouth, brushing his lips across her fingers and making shivers dance their way across her skin. Her brain might have decided one or two kisses were probably best forgotten, but her body was keen to remind her of the intensity of sensations his touch alone could cause.

Whilst she tried to get her thoughts and rogue body parts under control, she noticed he'd gone quiet too. It really was time they were honest about what was happening between them on an emotional level.

'Cal, I think it's us who have something to talk about.'

For once he didn't pull away from her when they were veering towards the important issues affecting their relationship and held her hand fast in his.

'I know. We've kind of let things run away from us.' He was smiling, so it seemed he didn't totally regret those flashes of passion which kept flaring up between them.

'I just want to know where I stand. Where we stand, Cal.' She was putting everything they did have on the line by asking for that clarification, but they couldn't go on pretending they were able to suppress those urges for ever. The next time they gave in to them she knew she wouldn't be able to go back to being just friends. Not now love had become part of the equation for her.

It had come slowly, creeping in along with the friendship and passion they'd cultivated over time, but as she'd learned, ignoring her feelings didn't make them go away. If anything, it simply left them to spin out of control and with time running out before the babies came along, it was more important than ever to get some clarity on their relationship. She wanted to put down roots for her family but only if there was a strong, stable foundation available for them.

Of course, their waiter arrived back with their meals at the most inconvenient time, forcing them to break apart and lose that physical connection.

'Thanks.' Cal smiled politely at their server while Izzy did her best to hold her tongue until he left.

'I mean, we're going to be a family, whether you like it or not.' Weeks of pussy-footing around him in case she frightened him off by making him face the truth finally caught up with her and she ignored her delicious plate of Cajun chicken pasta to confront this head on.

Cal hung his head and sighed. 'I'll be the first to admit I haven't been the most excited father-to-be, but after Janet I'm a bit more cautious about the idea of family.'

'No kidding.' Izzy speared a piece of pasta and

cursed that woman for making their lives more complicated than they needed to be. If it hadn't been for her cruel treatment of such a wonderful man, she and Cal might have settled down together by now and be looking forward to the birth of their children. Not fearing the event would trigger more betrayal or heartbreak.

They both ate in silence, but Izzy couldn't enjoy her dinner when it was overpowered by the taste of bitterness in her mouth.

Eventually Cal broke first, giving her some insight to the workings of his troubled mind. 'I did want it all at one time. You know, the wife and kids and the white picket fence. After my parents died all I wanted was to re-create that feeling of having my family around me.'

'And now? That's what's available to you but you're pushing us all away.' Izzy was tired of paying for someone else's mistakes. She and the babies deserved more than that.

'At first I was afraid you regretted our night together, that there was no real future for us. I tried to fight those feelings I had for you, which were about more than getting you back into bed again.' He grinned at her and she didn't know what had shaken her more, that smile, him opening up to her, or finally telling her he thought about her as more than a convenience. Whatever it was, she wanted more of it.

'I thought I could separate our relationship from the babies. A stupid notion, I know, but in my head, loving them could be my ultimate downfall. You never gave me any indication you wanted anything serious between us and I thought if you decided someday you could do better than me, I'd lose these babies the same way I lost the last one.' That pain was still so obvious in his eyes and in his quivering voice Izzy could understand why he was still trying to protect himself, even if it came at the price of her peace of mind.

'These are your babies too. I would never take them away from you. A family means more to me than anything because, unlike you, I've never had one, Cal. You don't know what it's like to grow up knowing your own parents didn't want you and people had to be paid to take you in. I've had so many foster parents I don't remember all of their names. I want better for my children. I need them to know they're loved every day of their lives. That means growing up in a house with a father who shows them that and, let's be honest, you haven't been thrilled at the prospect of becoming a dad, have you?'

If they were sweeping away the debris from the past to clear the path for a happy future together then they needed to be completely honest with each other.

'I've told you why I've been holding back. I'm sorry I can't give you more than that.' He was leaving it up to her to decide if she was willing to risk her heart again on a future with someone who couldn't commit one hundred per cent to her.

'I appreciate your honesty, but I need someone who's going to put me first, to make my children his priority. It might seem selfish, but after Gerry I'm done with being second best.' There was every chance

Cal could tell her to get lost with her demands, but it was better to know now if she was asking too much from him than finding out when it was too late.

'Hey, I'm not Gerry.' He sounded angry at the comparison and it was no wonder after everything he'd heard about his predecessor, but this wasn't about soothing his ego. It was about protecting her babies.

'Was everything okay for you?' Their waiter with the bad sense of timing arrived back at the table, staring pointedly at the discarded plates still laden with food.

'Fine, thanks.' Izzy didn't mean to snap but she wanted to finish this conversation before Cal shut her out again and left her guessing about where they stood as a couple or as a family.

Suitably cowed, he cleared the table without further comment. Cal waited until he was completely out of earshot before he continued his defence.

'Gerry was selfish, not thinking of anyone but himself in the decisions he made. I like to think I'm doing the opposite. I want to take my time and make sure everything I'm doing is for the right reasons. I won't apologise for wanting to do right by all of us.' With that logic Izzy couldn't fault him. Perhaps it was a lot to expect him to outline all his plans for the future, including how he was going to feel about the babies once they got here, when it was clear he was still trying to adjust to the idea of being a father.

Cal got up to pay the bill, not waiting for it to be brought to the table, and Izzy had to hurry to catch him as he exited the restaurant without her. He was angry at having to justify himself to her yet again and she realised she had to make some concessions for the way he had let her stay with him in the first place, despite his reservations.

'Cal, stop. Please.' This evening could've been a chance for a romantic evening together, strengthening that connection she so desperately wanted. Instead she was in danger of pushing him away for ever by asking so much of him.

'It's just… I don't know what I'd do without you, Cal. I'm afraid of losing you.' Standing there in the street, with Cal refusing to even look at her, was sufficient to make her teary. She'd done the unthinkable and fallen for him somewhere along the way. It wasn't simply that she'd become accustomed to him being there for her, providing for her every need, but he'd become part of her life, part of her. Without him she knew she couldn't function properly and that wasn't a position she'd ever intended to let herself get into again when it meant depending on one person for her happiness.

He came back to her in a heartbeat, sliding his hands around her waist and rubbing his nose against hers. 'I'm not going anywhere without you, Fizz, unless you ask me to.'

It wasn't a declaration of undying love, but she was sure it was there in his kiss as he claimed her mouth once more. He was tender and loving, as he was in all things, but Izzy demanded proof this time that this was more than him simply comforting or placating her.

She weaved her fingers into his mop of unruly hair and pulled him in deeper, seeking to find if the true nature of his affections transcended mere emotions. There was no mistaking the extent of his loyalty to her but she didn't want either of them to confuse it for something else that might never have been there in the first place.

She needn't have worried. Once she gave the green light that this was what she wanted from him, Cal pulled her hard against him, his passion leaving her legs weak at the knees.

Her skin prickled with awareness and the hairs on the back of her neck stood to attention as he showered her with kiss after kiss. He sought her with his bold tongue and teased her with little licks and flicks until she was grinding against him with longing.

Eventually they remembered to breathe, and she was glad to find she wasn't the only one panting after the unexpected encounter.

'We should probably go home,' he said half-heartedly, making no attempt to release her from his grasp.

'Mmm.'

Izzy was happy where she was but excited about moving their relationship forward. Cal had been as straightforward as he could be with her and it was up to her to decide if that was enough to base her future on. She had to ask herself if he was worth the gamble with her heart when there was no guarantee it was all going to work out this time either. Despite her whole body screaming, *Yes!*

Chapter 9

The journey home had given Cal some time to cool his ardour and think about more than what his libido was demanding. Izzy had told him in no uncertain terms what having a family meant to her, but he wasn't completely sure he felt the same as he once had about the idea. It wasn't fair to bed her and give her false hope that they were going to live happily ever after.

She deserved a partner who was totally committed to her and the babies, with no doubts about what he wanted. Until he found that certainty for himself he thought it best to cool things down between them again.

When they got back to the house he left her at the bottom of the stairs with, 'Goodnight, Izzy.'

This time his mouth barely grazed her cheek as he kissed her before going to bed. Alone. He hoped she understood he wasn't rejecting her on a personal level but taking precautions for both of their sakes.

There was a very real chance they'd both be lying awake tonight on either side of the wall separating their bedrooms, replaying the passion they'd given in to completely. He'd been doing that anyway since the very first time he'd laid his lips on her.

So much for taking a step back and focusing on being a support to Izzy rather than being further cause for stress. She was vulnerable after her scare and didn't need him making a move on her when her hormones and emotions were all over the place. As were his. Especially since she'd kissed him back, her eyes and her body asking him for more.

Cal groaned, lifted the book he'd been reading from his nightstand in deference to the sleep that had been eluding him recently.

He managed a page or two before he realised not a single word had registered He was listening out for the sound of Izzy coming upstairs to bed.

'This is insane,' he confided to the fluffy sheep Izzy had made him keep on his bed. It was impossible to concentrate on anything but the creak of the floorboards as she crossed to her room and the thought of her getting undressed for bed. Despite only wearing his boxers, Cal was beginning to sweat.

He tossed the book back onto his nightstand, not even bothering to mark his place, and turned the bedside light off. Eyes closed, he tried to force himself into slumber, knowing tomorrow at work would be as physically demanding as ever. Gone were the nights when he'd slept fitfully on the sofa because his bed held such painful connotations of the woman who'd broken his heart. Only for them to be replaced with lustful thoughts of the woman who'd been right by his side for years.

In the too-quiet darkness he thought he could hear her tossing and turning on her mattress. If he was being kept awake by thoughts of how that bubbling chemistry between them was threatening to explode again, perhaps she was too. Or, as he'd predicted all along, was she too confused after Gerry's death and their twin surprise she didn't know what she was doing?

'Cal?' Suddenly Izzy's soft voice called to him in the darkness. At first he thought he'd imagined it, then he heard her footsteps cross his floor. He'd been so lost in his own head he hadn't realised she'd left her own room.

'Izzy? What's wrong?' By the time he managed to turn the bedside lamp on again she was sitting on the bed beside him. His brain was working overtime, trying to figure out what could possibly be wrong with her when she looked so calm. If there had been an issue with the babies she would've been in full panic mode by now.

Instead, she curled up in the foetal position beside him so their heads were side by side on his pillows. 'I don't want to sleep alone, Cal.'

She didn't appear to be in a hurry to go anywhere

so he snuggled down beside her and pulled the covers over them. His heart was beating just as fast as it had when they'd kissed but he was doing his best not to misinterpret her meaning.

He couldn't help but reach out and touch her, brush the russet tresses off her shoulder to reveal the porcelain skin beneath.

'Are you sure you don't want to make the most of the peace while you've got it?' Cal tried to conceal his optimism that she was here for more than company with a lame attempt at humour. However, when she rested a hand possessively on his hip, the lower half of his body jerked wide awake.

'Don't make me beg, Cal. You know neither of us would venture into this lightly, but we don't seem to be able to stop it happening either. I don't want to stop it.'

Lying in his own bed, with Izzy saying everything he wanted to hear, touching him with confidence that he was hers, Cal was completely undone.

Izzy was putting everything on the line by being here. By climbing into Cal's bed, not only was she risking further rejection but if he kicked her out now the last of her dignity would slink out the door with her.

An evening unsuccessfully dodging the sexual tension arcing between them, on top of the close relationship they already had, had been sufficient for her to act on. She knew he'd turned away from her tonight because he didn't want her to read more into his actions than he was offering.

For now, she'd be happy for him to acknowledge the attraction with more than a passionate kiss. It wasn't in her nature to throw herself at a man, but she knew Cal better than most. He wouldn't take advantage of her, quite the opposite. It wasn't difficult to tell he'd been holding back for her sake. If there was one thing preventing them from moving their relationship on to the next level it was liable to be because he was afraid of her getting hurt somewhere along the way. He'd already voiced his fears to that effect but as far as she could see it was too late, the kisses they'd shared were proof they were powerless to stop this runaway train anyway.

She ran her hand down his corded thigh, his skin hot enough beneath her fingertips for her to suggest he take off the last of his clothes.

His mouth kicked up at the corners, his eyes darkened and then his mouth was on hers, no longer constrained by concerns for her welfare.

Unleashed by his conscience, it seemed Cal was as eager to explore this evolving dynamic as Izzy. He took command of her lips, moulding them to fit his. His hand was in her hair, drawing her closer, unashamed to let her know how his body was responding to her touch.

With her eyes closed, giving herself over to the sensation of his hands and lips sweeping over her, she was already drifting away on a cloud of pleasure. Only the pure need for him she experienced when he slipped the strap of her night dress down her shoulder and cupped her naked breast grounded her again.

He brushed his thumb lightly over her nipple and she jerked back into her body with the sudden rush of arousal in response. Her reaction to that brief, intimate contact spurred him on to extract more of it from her. Cal moved his hungry mouth from hers, sucking and tasting her skin as he moved to her neck, her collarbone, and—*oh, yes*—her breast.

She sucked in a shaky breath of arousal as he slid the other strap down to follow its neighbour and flicked her nipple with the tip of his tongue. Izzy clutched his shoulders, arched her body further against his and demanded more. The first swell of ecstasy began to build inside her once he drew the responsive nub into his mouth. She'd forgotten how good it was to simply let herself go, enjoying the moment with him.

Cal grazed his teeth over her sensitive skin and sucked hard, ripping a cry of pure ecstasy from deep inside her very core. This time she didn't even waste time on the niceties of inviting him to undress, letting her hands do the work until he was fully naked beneath her fingertips. He did the same for her, sliding the rest of her nightdress excruciatingly slowly down her body and kissing every newly exposed inch of her skin until she was completely naked, and he was kneeling at her feet.

'You're beautiful,' he said, and though she felt a little bashful, with nowhere to hide her blossoming body under the glare of the bedside light, Cal's obvious appreciation was there for her to see.

'So are you.' She repaid the compliment with as much sincerity as it had been given to her. The nature of their relationship in the past, and up until recently, meant she'd tried not to recall what he looked like out of the padded flight suit. Now she was free to let her eyes feast once more on his impressive, solid physique and the majesty of his arousal.

Cal's smile was so big it crinkled the skin at the corners of his eyes and made him even more devilishly delicious as he covered her body with his. Her limbs were trembling with anticipation she wanted him so badly. With him nibbling the skin at her neck, his erection intimately teasing her, she was on the edge of flipping him over onto his back and climbing on top of him. Just when she thought his restraint was proving greater than hers he nudged her thighs apart and groaned a satisfied 'Oh…' as he entered her.

It was a moment of perfect joy and peace for her as they were finally joined together in body as well as soul. He paused, his eyes searching her face, and she could tell he was waiting for confirmation she was okay. She didn't want her condition or his fierce desire to protect her at all costs to inhibit this pivotal, much-longed-for moment in their partnership. They had to learn to trust each other's instincts as well as their own if they were going to have a future together.

'I need you, Cal.' She needed all of him with no

holding back because she wanted to give him everything of herself in return.

Her plea, her surrender freed them both from the last threads of restraint and let them search together for that ultimate pleasure goal.

'My Isobel…' His husky voice in her ear, the sweet affection and the delicious fullness of having him inside her was too much for her to bear. She was at breaking point, desperately clinging on to prolong this feeling of ecstasy as long as possible.

With every grind of his hips, every thrust and using every trick he had in his locker to drive her wild, he made her cries more frequent, higher pitched until she was sure she'd shatter every window in the house.

Then the world was spinning somewhere far below her as she soared with one last push from her equally vocal partner.

They clung together for as long as their limbs held out, panting and grinning at each other like loons.

Izzy was so elated, if it wasn't for the obvious, one would've been forgiven for thinking this was her first time and she'd given herself to her first love. She'd had good sex before, and with him, but they were looking at each other with a certain smugness that said they'd both achieved a new level together.

'Why didn't we want to do this again?' Cal asked as he lay down beside her, still caressing her naked body and sending aftershocks of her climax rippling through her again and again.

'I think we were worried we'd burn each other

out.' To illustrate the point that they'd have trouble keeping their hands off each other, she cupped his backside and squeezed.

The truth, they both knew, was much more complicated and painful than that. Although she couldn't speak for him, Izzy couldn't regret that time when it had given her so much to look forward to now and had brought her and Cal closer than they'd ever been.

'Hmm, I hope this isn't simply your way of guaranteeing the babies get a room each.'

It didn't escape her notice he was avoiding talking seriously about their future as a couple but as long as he continued to think of this as a permanent arrangement they were good.

As for Izzy, she knew she was in love with him and their epic lovemaking had confirmed it. Hopefully in time he'd come to feel the same, but it was too much to ask for now when the wounds Janet had inflicted were still raw. It was different for her when she and Gerry had had definitive closure. The same couldn't be said for Janet, who'd made her presence known so recently it still pained Izzy to think about it. With no discernible conscience about what she'd done, Izzy wouldn't put it past her to keep turning up like the proverbial bad penny.

That left a smidgen of doubt that Cal would remain committed to her should Janet decide she preferred his attentions and wanted him back. They had a long history together, Janet had been someone Cal had imagined having a family with, and that wasn't a thought easily dismissed. She, though, was always getting carried away on dreams of the family they could make once the twins were born.

'Just wait until I try to talk you into installing a swimming pool.' This wasn't the time for deep and meaningful conversations or displays of jealousy and insecurity. She wanted to keep things fun and flirty, not to mention irresistible, so he'd come back for more. 'I won't let you get out of bed until you agree to my every demand.'

'Do your worst,' he said, lying spread-eagled on the bed, his body ready to be persuaded by anything she said or did.

Always keen to show she was every bit as physically capable as the next person, Izzy rose to the challenge and took charge.

'Are you ready to go?' Izzy peeped her head around the bedroom door, but Cal simply pulled the covers back up over his head.

'No.'

She chuckled and plonked herself down on the bed beside him. 'You can't stay in there all day.'

'Why not? It sounds like a good idea to me.'

Izzy shrieked as he reached for her and tried to pull her under the covers with him. It was very tempting to climb back in with him when his bedhead hair and morning stubble made him look even more handsome than usual.

Now they knew how phenomenal they were together in all aspects of their relationship she could happily spend the day here with him making up for lost time. She'd heard an increased libido could happen at any stage of pregnancy, but she reckoned he'd have had this effect on her every time he touched her, long after her body was her own again.

'I. Would. Love. To,' she said, through his kisses along her collarbone, and he palmed her breast through her blouse to illustrate how keen he was for her to get naked with him again. 'But we have an appointment to get to.'

'We do?'

It wasn't fair to tease her like this, awakening that ache for him inside her when they couldn't do anything about it.

'I booked us into a practical parenting class.'

'Isn't it a little early for that? I thought antenatal classes were for much later in pregnancy.' Cal frowned and seemed to withdraw to the far side of the bed. Obviously, they still had some work to do when it came to his role as a hands-on dad.

'True, but this isn't any ordinary class. It's a private course focused on parenting twins, and I hear it's very popular, so it books up early. I thought we could both use some tips.' She wanted them to be the best parents they could be for the children.

'I'll need all the help I can get,' he muttered as he pulled the duvet away.

'Cal? Are you sure you want to be my birthing partner? I don't want to force you into it if you really don't want to be there.' There was only so much she could do if he genuinely didn't want to be involved.

She wanted nothing more than to have him coaching her through her contractions as their babies were delivered into the world. Although they both had baggage they were dealing with, these babies represented their future together. She wouldn't have asked him to be part of the birth if she wasn't thinking of him as her real-life partner and the family they were going to make together.

Cal took both her hands in his and looked her deep in the eyes. 'It would be a privilege to be there for you.'

If Izzy could only believe his devotion extended to the little people they'd created together, everything would be just perfect.

Chapter 10

'Hi, everyone. I'm Sharon. Help yourselves to tea and biscuits and make yourselves comfortable.' The woman holding the practical parenting class directed the anxious-looking couples huddled by the door towards the refreshments table.

Cal poured out two cups of tea and watched Izzy load a plate with enough chocolate biscuits to see them through the whole day. At last she was heeding the snacking advice. With any luck they'd get through this class without any fainting incidents. He hadn't been thrilled by the idea of coming here today but he supposed it would be useful to pick up some practical tips today on living with twins.

Janet hadn't even wanted him to attend the scans with her and she'd probably had Darren accompany her to the antenatal classes when the time had come. It no longer bothered him. He was just grateful Izzy was making such an effort to get him involved and feel part of this pregnancy.

They were embarking on an exciting new chapter of their lives, not only as a couple but they were about to be thrown into the deep end with the arrival of the twins too. Izzy had accepted him as her partner and that was enough for him. It meant he could be here to support her when she didn't have any family around to help. Cal hoped that through these classes he'd see exactly what he could do to make life easier for her. Even if it was just being there to mop her brow or have his fingers crushed during labour. It was better for Izzy's well-being to know she had someone who'd be by her side throughout this journey.

He glanced around the room at the other couples. There were married pairs, mothers and daughters and best friends. Every couple was different, but the common theme was that loving bond like the one he had with Izzy. It would've been tough for Izzy to have come here on her own and tougher for him if he had missed out. Some things a person could never get back and thankfully he'd realised that before he'd missed out on any more of their babies' important milestones.

The presentation began with a talk on what made multiple birth pregnancies different from single pregnancies. A lot of which he and Izzy were already aware of due to their medical experience but hearing there was a higher risk of complications and need for more health professionals at the birth was different when you were preparing for real.

There were plenty of helpful tips for them to take some of the stress out of coping with more than one baby. Including bathtimes and having all necessary supplies at hand before attempting to bath the babies, one at a time. A lot of the general advice was focused on support and making sure there was more than one pair of hands available when possible. Something he intended to do. In fact, he was looking forward to sharing the bathing and feeding with Izzy and forging a bond with their babies.

They were given a couple of dolls to practise changing nappies on and Sharon came to supervise their attempts.

'I can see Dad has done this before. Well done.'

There was a good reason he had his baby doll changed in seconds whilst Izzy was still grappling with the tapes on her twin's nappy. He'd had a lot of experience when his nephews and nieces had been young. Back then, when they'd all come together at his parents' house for special occasions, he'd made the most of his precious uncle time. As far as he'd been concerned, it was practice for the family he'd always expected to have, and his sisters had been over the moon when he'd volunteered for changing duty.

This practical lesson should have been overwhelming to someone who'd been doing his best not to get too involved beyond providing practical support, but it reminded him of the joy he'd once experienced being around children. Before life with Janet had attached negative connotations with the idea of being a father. Now he and Izzy were making moves towards being a real couple it was about time he stopped catastrophising, imagining the worst outcome, and enjoyed every moment life together would bring them.

He looked around at the other couples all mucking in together to change their pretend babies whilst he was standing back watching Izzy struggle do it alone.

'Let me help, Iz. We're a team, remember?' She gave him a wary look, and he knew it was going to take time to convince her he meant every word, but he had months left to prove himself. He was going to be the best father Izzy could ever wish to have for her children.

As they arrived back at the car after the class Cal caught sight of a couple exiting the maternity wing with their newborn in one of those carriers he'd had to buy for the twins. The pair were obviously new parents, that glow of unconditional love for the life they'd just created lighting them up like Christmas trees. Cal smiled, anticipating the day he and Izzy would experience walking out that door as first-time parents too.

The little family stepped out into the sunshine and it was then everything hit home. These weren't just random strangers he was watching start a new chapter of their lives together, it was Janet and Darren and the baby he'd been father to for its first weeks of existence.

They were oblivious to anyone's presence, in their little bubble of pure joy, and it was like a kick in the gut for Cal. Not because he was jealous of Darren but because he'd never seen Janet look so at peace. Leaving him had obviously been the best thing she could have done. He would never have made her this happy. Blinded by his desire for a family at any cost, he hadn't seen the flaws in their relationship at the time, but it was obvious now he'd never loved her the way he loved Izzy.

They'd never had the same connection or interests and, looking back, something had always been lacking in their relationship. It must have been for Janet to go looking for more with another man and for Cal to be happy for them walking away as a family. Izzy was the best thing to have ever happened to him and this encounter proved it.

'Is everything all right?' Izzy was sitting in the car, waiting for Cal to get in. His attention was elsewhere, and it hadn't taken long for her to figure out why. Janet was like a dead weight around her neck, dragging her down every time she thought she was making progress with Cal.

'Fine.' He got in and closed the door, making no mention of the scene across the road. If it didn't bother him he would've referenced the couple exiting the hospital with their new bundle of joy but clearly it was still hurting that he was no longer part of it.

It was difficult not to take that personally and have it pierce her heart until it felt as though her life blood was draining slowly and painfully away every time she thought of the longing on his face. He wanted his ex and her baby over Izzy and his own children. That was the family he was supposed to have, and they were simply the imposters he'd been landed with.

It wasn't fair to carry on pretending this was going to work out when she'd been forcing him into this relationship every step of the way. Perhaps she'd been trying to convince herself he only needed time to learn to love her and the babies because deep down she was afraid of doing this alone. She'd been out of her depth in that class even with their fake twins whilst Cal had been the calm, capable one. It was in that moment, holding that doll, not even knowing how to change a nappy properly, that it had hit home what a huge undertaking motherhood was going to be for her. There were going to be two precious mites totally dependent on her to protect and provide for them as well as guide them through life. Difficult to do when she hadn't had any role models who'd done the same for her. What if she couldn't handle it like all of those who were supposed to have parented her?

She didn't want to have children who resented her and rejected a relationship with her once they were old enough to leave home. Although she hadn't realised it, she'd been acting the role of parent as much as Cal. If they carried on pretending they knew what they were getting into they were going to end up resenting each other for getting trapped in a situation that would be much harder to get out of once the twins arrived.

They'd be taking a huge gamble on the future if they stayed together and she wasn't prepared to do that again. Cal deserved that same level of happiness he'd witnessed in Janet and she wasn't convinced she could give him that. Izzy didn't want either of them settling for second best.

So much for putting her mind at ease. Regardless of the information leaflets she had tucked in her bag and all the stress-relieving tips they'd been given, Izzy was more wound up than ever by the time they got home.

She'd been so caught up in that idea of her happy family coming together that she'd only today realised something capable of bringing her back down to earth with a thump. No amount of cajoling was going to make Cal love these babies.

Her crush and her bond with Cal had, on her part at least, evolved into real love. She was grateful to him for providing a roof for her and she wanted him to be part of her babies' lives but not if he didn't love these babies the way she loved them.

'Have you taken your supplements today?' It was a simple enough question but now when she was analysing every conversation Cal's focus on the pregnancy only ever seemed to centre around her health. His interest seemed limited to that of a doctor rather than a prospective father.

'Yes. You don't have to keep reminding me.' Now she was becoming vexed on behalf of her unborn children, memories of her own childhood made her snappy with him.

Those big eyes full of hurt at her tone might have made her feel as though she'd just kicked a puppy, but she'd fallen for that guilt trick too many times with Gerry. Time and again she'd been promised a life of her dreams only to find it was nothing more than an illusion. Foster families, her parents, even Gerry had conned her into thinking she'd found security, only to snatch it away again when they discovered life with her lacking in some way.

The circumstances might be different with Cal but they were also scarily similar. Despite promises to herself not to get too invested in a relationship again, or rely on any one person solely for support, she'd left her home and jumped into bed with him. If he didn't want this family as much as she did, wasn't completely and madly in love with all three of them, then her future was as rocky as ever.

With sleepless nights and double the mess a newborn usually brought, Cal would tire quickly of them all invading his space. Izzy wasn't prepared to expose her children to the same uncertainty she'd grown up in.

'What's wrong? Please don't feel too overwhelmed by it all. We can go through those information leaflets together later and work on your birth plan if you like.'

'As a matter of fact, I have been thinking about

the birth. I'm wondering if it's a good idea for you to be there after all.' It hurt to say it, even more to see him flinch as though she'd punched him in the gut. But theirs was a complicated relationship created mostly through circumstances. They needed some way to separate those feelings encompassing friendship, love and loyalty.

'I thought we'd already discussed this?'

After a brief lapse Izzy's barriers were back up, protecting her, and she needed the truth, not some fantastic version of it, before she'd let him bypass them again. In the long run, telling her only what he thought she wanted to hear now would cause greater distress later when it turned out not to be true. Her heart bore the scars of experience.

'Do you want these babies, or just me?' Cal had never made a declaration of love to her, never mind the babies, and it should be a requirement for a man who expected to be in their lives.

'Can't I have both?' He genuinely didn't appear to understand her concerns but that was half of the problem. If he had that nursery filled and someone in his bed, he'd be content to coast along. Whereas she wasn't prepared to let her family merely exist.

'You've done so much, Cal, but I worry you only want us to replace everything Janet took from you. I'm not getting any real emotional connection between you and the babies.' It was harsh, but she needed to figure out his true intentions. If this wasn't going to work out she'd have to make alternative accommodation arrangements and time was running out before the twins arrived. Izzy couldn't bring them back from the hospital to a house that was full of tension because she was afraid to trust the man they were supposed to live with.

He was pacing the room, hands on his hips, nostrils flaring—all the symptoms of someone trying not to lose their cool. Hardly surprising, she supposed, when it would seem as though she was turning on him after all he'd done for her. She should be jumping at the chance of having someone like that in her life but the string of liars she'd endured over the years had left her suspicious, even of a good man like Cal.

'You really think that of me? That I would offer you everything I had, make love to you, provide a home for you and our babies, all so I could pick up where I left off with a woman who'd clearly never loved me?' His gasp of disbelief did make her falter in her assumptions. He made it, her, sound crazy, but she'd been able to twist all his good intentions to fit some darker purpose because it suited her better than risking her heart again.

Izzy threw her hands up. 'I don't know any more.'

'You don't know any more…' His mumbling was punctuated with soulless laughter as he scrubbed his hands through his hair. The display of frustration at her lack of faith in him was as effective as if he'd burst into tears and she hated herself for putting him through this necessary test of his devotion.

'Don't get cross with me, Cal. Everything's just so…confusing.' Her head was beginning to hurt with all the back and forth going on in there. Everything in her heart wanted to believe they were going to have their happy ending but her head knew better and was working overtime to remind her of everything that could potentially go wrong.

He stopped pacing like a caged bear and came to stand in front of her, resting his hands on her shoulders and imploring her to look him in the eye. 'Why? I've been honest with you from the start about only wanting to do right by you. I never expected to fall in love with you. I know it's complicated things, but I thought we'd be able to work things out.'

He loved her, and she wished that was all she'd needed to hear from him. Wished that it made every misgiving she had about their future flap its wings and take flight.

'I'm sorry but it's not enough for me.'

'What have I done wrong?' In truth he'd been the perfect partner in every way imaginable. It was his potential as a father that made her wary of continuing their relationship if his heart lay elsewhere. The babies were never going to be good enough for him, just as she'd never been good enough for anyone in her life.

'Family is everything to me, Cal, but we both know this one doesn't include you.'

'I can only give you what I can but if it's not enough...' He faltered then, his hands falling from her shoulders as he let his true pain at the situation show. She'd been so selfish, thinking only of how she was affected by these great life-changing moments. Cal was every bit as insecure and damaged by his past as she was.

Izzy suddenly realised he was right, she was the one in the wrong here. He'd been bending over backwards to make her life easier, to make her feel wanted, and all this time she'd been looking for excuses as to why things couldn't work between them.

'I know. I'm so sorry.' It was a mess and all she'd done was destroy a relationship that could have stood a chance.

Izzy tried to reach out to him and he physically shrank away from her touch as though he couldn't bear her to touch him. She wanted to vomit.

'I told you everything Janet had put me through, you don't think that was humiliating enough for me?' It had taken him so long to open up to her again, Izzy knew how hurt and embarrassed he'd been by Janet's betrayal.

Arms folded, lips drawn into a thin line, his body seemed to close in on itself as he physically and emotionally withdrew from her, and Izzy realised she was about to lose everything.

'You saved me, Cal, and now I don't know what I, what we, would do without you.' The babies kicked her as though to remind her she was coming close to stuffing things up for all of them. In trying to protect herself from a man who'd never put her first, she'd lost sight of the man who always did.

Cal couldn't keep track of the emotional rollercoaster he'd been strapped into since last night when

Izzy had climbed into his bed. He'd been delighted to jump on board then for the ride of his life. With her in his arms all night he'd believed it was the start of their rest of their life together. Now? It was like finding that note pinned to the fridge all over again.

'Yeah. I'm always good for picking up the pieces of the mess other men have left behind.' Janet had used him as some sort of back-up when Darren hadn't immediately stepped forward to be the father of her baby. She'd taken advantage of his desire to be part of a family again and milked him for everything he was worth in terms of money, love and attention. He'd never expected Izzy to do the same.

When someone, or something, better came along, she'd dump him quicker than a dirty nappy. It was his fault for getting into exactly the same situation again after vowing never to let any woman play him the way Janet had done. This was worse. Izzy had been his friend and confidante long before he'd fallen in love with her. Another one-sided love affair doomed to end in heartache for him.

After Janet, he hadn't thought he had anything left to lose. Now he was back in that same position with his heart, his home and his future on the line, and he had to take back some control. In another few months the babies would be here and there would be no going back.

'At the minute I feel as though I've been drafted in as a last-minute substitute to save the day, rather than someone you'd planned to be with for the rest of your life.' He was too angry, too hurt to hold back and save her feelings. He'd been doing that for too long with too many people and it was about time he was able to say what he really thought. Except getting it off his chest was doing nothing to make this any easier.

'To be fair, neither of us had planned for this to happen, Cal, and I'm sorry if you think I somehow tricked my way into your affections. If you knew me the way I thought you did, you'd realise I'm not that devious.'

'I'm beginning to think I don't know you at all.'

'So, what are you saying? That you want to put an end to this now? Do you want me to move out?' With her arms folded Izzy challenged him directly, instead of skirting around the problem the way he and Janet obviously had. If he'd known then what the problem between them had been, he wouldn't have hesitated in ending their relationship himself, but this situation with Izzy wasn't so clear cut.

He didn't want to act in the heat of the moment in case he'd come to regret it. 'I need some time to think things through.'

'I—I'll pack a bag.' Izzy didn't argue, cry, shout or do anything to show she had any passion about what they did next and that made Cal question the whole nature of their relationship when his heart was breaking. He didn't want to split now with no way back until he had some space away from the situation to see it from a different perspective, but he wasn't sure Izzy was of the same opinion.

'No, I'll go.'

He wouldn't ask her to move out unless he was one hundred per cent sure that was what they both thought was for the best. With children involved they couldn't be that sort of couple who split and got back together whenever the mood took them. Stability was the keyword in a child's life and in that of a man who'd been burned once too many times.

'No matter what you think of me, I wouldn't ask you to move out of your own house.'

'You're not. It's my decision.' It was the last vestige of control he apparently had in this relationship. This time, if things were ending he wanted it to be on his terms.

Chapter 11

When Cal had left, Izzy had thought she'd never stop crying. Somehow she'd managed to throw away her one chance of a real family. Her own damn insecurities and inability to trust had caused him to cast her in the same mould as Janet. She couldn't blame him when he'd given her everything and all she'd done was take. The irony was that the second he walked out the door she knew exactly what she wanted. Cal. The babies. A family.

The only ember of hope she had left that that could still be a possibility was that he hadn't thrown her out on the street. It was typical of Cal to let her stay in his house and make himself temporarily homeless, even when he was mad at her. She didn't know why she'd ever doubted his integrity. Oh, wait, it probably had something to do with a series of unreliable guardians and one flaky boyfriend. Things that had absolutely nothing to do with Cal and everything to do with her personal baggage.

It had been days now since he'd walked out, and she felt every second of it. She'd grieved more over losing Cal than she had for Gerry. Which highlighted the differences between the two relationships and the two men involved. Not to mention the strength of the love in her heart for one over the other.

The relief and renewed sense of purpose she'd expected on her return to work had been overshadowed by the sadness at seeing Cal there, not being able to touch him or tell him how much she loved him. She didn't even know where he'd been staying because he hadn't stopped long enough to utter more than two words to her. He could barely look at her and she didn't know what she could do to fix everything she'd broken.

Every time she tried to initiate a conversation he'd simply say, 'Not here, not now,' and expect her to back off without complaint, and she had done until now.

They couldn't carry on avoiding each other for ever. She cornered him in the staffroom, which he had a habit of retreating into so he could avoid her in the radio room. One of her dagger looks in the direction of the other crew members he was using as cover and they scurried off, knowing where they weren't wanted.

Izzy stood in the doorway, blocking Cal's escape

route, so he had no choice but to acknowledge her or attempt to push past her, and he was too much of a gentleman to do that.

'Cal, please talk to me. Shout at me, tell me to get out of your house or kiss me senseless and tell me we can work this out. Anything has to be better than this limbo we're in.' Okay, that last one was more of a fantasy than an option, but she'd spent these last days running through every scenario and that was the one she preferred.

'This isn't—'

'Don't tell me this isn't the time or the place when you haven't given me any choice. You can't stay away from your own house indefinitely and we can't go on ignoring each other at work. It's killing me.' It wasn't fair to leave her wondering if they still had a chance if he'd already made his mind up it was over. If they couldn't resolve the issues she'd caused she'd have to do something drastic, like leave her job rather than seeing him every day and realising what she'd thrown away. With the babies coming, job security wasn't something she took lightly but there was no way she could carry on here with a reminder of everything she'd lost staring her in the face every day.

'You don't think those things you said to me didn't almost destroy me? I don't think it's too much to ask for a little time out when you accused me of being some sort of conman simply because I loved you?'

He tossed the newspaper he'd been reading onto the chair as he got to his feet and slammed his coffee cup on the table, sloshing the contents everywhere. Cal had every reason to be angry and Izzy was almost grateful to see this blazing fire in his eyes that said all might not be lost after all. He'd said he'd loved her and that wasn't something a person could turn on and off at will. Whilst she was still able to rouse such a passionate display of emotion in him there was hope he hadn't stopped loving her altogether.

'I was scared, Cal, afraid history was going to repeat itself. That my dream of my little family was going to be taken from me again.' Her voice was cracking with the threat of tears, not at the memory of how people had treated her in the past but because she'd got it so wrong this time. She'd let the past steal away the one person who had actually loved her.

Cal took a step forward and for a moment she almost believed he was going to take her into his arms and tell her everything would be all right. Then the alarm rang out for all standby crew to head to the hangar and any notion of a reconciliation vanished.

'I have to go.'

There was never any doubt a call would take priority over Izzy, but she didn't want to let him go without some assurance that they'd made some progress today after she'd opened her heart to him. 'But you'll come and see me when you get back, yes?'

He looked as though he was about to refuse her, and she had to swallow the ball of disappointment lodged in her throat. Then he gave a quick nod before disappearing out the door.

That one spark of hope that she could salvage

her relationship with Cal, along with the future for her and her children she'd been afraid was too good to be true, let her breathe again. Suddenly all that pent-up tension and worry ebbed away, taking with it what little energy she had and leaving her doubled over like a ragdoll.

Pain zipped across her belly, along with the feeling of being caught in a vice. Contractions weren't to be expected at this stage, it was too early. She tried to call out for Cal, but another sharp pain stole her breath away. Tears blurred her vision as she staggered over to grip the chair he'd vacated only moments earlier. Another spike of agony and with it a trickle of fluid running down the inside of her leg. Her waters had broken.

This was everything she'd feared come true. The twins wouldn't survive being born now and she was frightened and alone. She needed Cal.

'Isobel Fitzpatrick. Where is she?' Cal knew he'd probably broken all kind of rules in his desperate hurry to get to the hospital, but he didn't care about anything other than getting to Izzy.

'Are you her partner?' The woman at the desk didn't seem to understand the urgency of the matter as she kept tip-tapping away at the computer instead of immediately whisking him through to Izzy's bedside.

He leaned on the desk, trying not to act on the impulse to swipe everything on the floor. 'Yes. Her waters have broken.' *Get me to her now!*

Saying the words made his stomach roll again the way it had been doing since Mac had broken the news to him that she'd been taken to hospital. As soon as he'd heard that on his arrival back at base, he'd jumped to his car and high-tailed it to the hospital, cursing himself for not staying with her earlier. If he'd stayed to have that talk with her he would've been there for her. He would've been the one to get her the help she needed and comfort her when she would've been frightened about what was going to happen to the babies.

Then again, if he hadn't moved out in the first place he might've seen the signs something was wrong earlier, but he'd been too busy licking his wounds in a budget hotel for the past few days to notice. He hadn't even taken the time to check in with her at work to make sure she was eating properly and looking after herself because of his damn pride.

Yes, she'd questioned his commitment to their family, as he had done during his time out, but he hadn't stopped loving her. He wanted the best for her and the babies and should have prioritised their welfare over his bruised ego. Now the stress he'd put her through, thinking he was going to leave her, had probably caused her to miscarry, as the babies wouldn't be considered viable at this stage and there would be no medical intervention to strengthen their lungs. They were already so precious to him and Izzy. If it wasn't for those babies the two of them would never have realised how much they loved one another.

'Are you Cal?' A nurse at the desk seemed to take more interest in his arrival than the woman he was talking to.

'Yes. I'm looking for Isobel Fitzpatrick. I was told she'd been brought here.' If someone didn't take him to her soon he was going to do a loop of the corridors yelling her name until she answered him back.

'She's been asking for you. Come with me.' The nurse exchanged a few words with the receptionist before marching him down towards one of the wards.

The fact Izzy hadn't sent out an alert to the staff, banning him from the premises, was promising that she was willing to forgive him for walking out on her the way he had. Although that could change if the babies came early and suffered as a consequence. He would never forgive himself if the worst happened so he wouldn't blame her if she never wanted to see him again in those circumstances.

'How is she?' He was running after the nurse, begging for more information like any other anxious partner or father-to-be.

'Frightened, tearful, and stubbornly refusing to let these babies come early.' The half-smile gave him an idea of how hard Izzy was fighting to stay in control of this pregnancy.

Good.

'That's my Iz.' Those babies needed to hold on as long as possible. If they couldn't stop the labour the babies wouldn't survive, and it would be the same outcome if too much amniotic fluid had been lost. It was simply too early to do anything other than wait. There were so many things that could go wrong at this stage, but he knew everyone here would be keeping Izzy calm and comfortable until they had a clearer picture of what was going on.

'In here.' The nurse opened the door and led him into a side room where Izzy was lying on the bed. As soon as she saw him she burst into floods of tears as though she'd been holding them back all this time, waiting for him to come and be strong for her.

'Oh, Fizz, sweetheart.' He was on the verge of breaking down himself, seeing her lying there vulnerable and helpless and so unlike the woman he knew and loved.

'Cal? I'm so glad you're here…' She stretched her hand out toward him before lapsing into more sobs. He took the seat by the bed and smoothed her hair back from her forehead.

'Shh. It's all right. Everything's going to be okay.' It had to be.

'This is my fault. You told me I was overdoing it and I wouldn't listen. I'm just too damn stubborn for my own good and now we're going to lose the babies.'

'Now, if anyone's to blame, it's me. I shouldn't have left you on your own. I'm so sorry.' He kissed her forehead, refusing to let her feel guilty when he'd been the one who'd made her worry she might have to find somewhere else to live with their two children before they'd even been born. Now he'd happily hand over the keys to his house for ever if it would ease her mind and stop this nightmare.

'We've already talked about this, Isobel. This isn't anyone's fault. It happens. Now, the scan showed that both heartbeats are strong and though baby number two is surrounded by less amniotic fluid than baby number one, there's still plenty there. We'll keep an eye on that but hopefully, if there's no further leak and no sign of infection, we'll be able to send you home soon.' The midwife did her best to comfort them, but Cal knew that was a lot of ifs. The statistics weren't in their favour for survival when the amniotic sac had ruptured this early, but Izzy Fitzpatrick was much more than a statistic.

'Thank you.' He was grateful they'd been here for Izzy when he hadn't, and luckily Mac had been the one to convince her to get to the hospital without delay. It meant they had every chance of getting the right outcome for Izzy and the babies.

'I'll leave her in your capable hands while I go and see about these test results and getting some antibiotics. Press this buzzer if you need any assistance in the meantime.' The attentive midwife unhooked the buzzer from behind the bed and left it on the bed for Izzy. It was a moment of privacy and a chance for a conversation he was no longer willing to avoid.

'Thank you for coming, Cal—'

'I'm so sorry for everything, Izzy—'

Their words tumbled over each other and he knew it was because of the seriousness of the situation. All the stuff that had caused the rift between them no longer mattered. They smiled at each other and she reached for his hand again.

'I thought I'd lost you.'

'Never. I was hurt but I meant it when I told you I'd never abandon you, Izzy. I love you. I don't care if you don't feel the same way about me, I just want to know you're all okay.' He was willing to put his feelings aside if that's what she wanted, if it meant he could remain in her life.

'Of course I love you, but I saw the way you looked at Janet with the baby. I thought you'd still rather be with them than us.'

He shook his head vigorously, unable to believe she could ever think that when everything he'd ever wanted was right here. 'Seeing them made me realise how lucky I was to have *you*. I never loved her the way I love you, Izzy. I can't wait to raise our family together.'

'Does this mean you'll move back home?' She was smiling now, those worry lines having faded away along with her tears.

'Is that what you want?' He daren't hope for anything beyond her health and happiness but it would be a relief if she genuinely wanted him with her after these past days convincing himself otherwise.

'Yes.' What Izzy wanted more than anything was to have her babies safely delivered at the right time and to go home, with Cal. She was grateful that Mac had been there at the base to make sure she'd got to hospital as soon as he had, but Cal was the only one she'd wanted.

Gone were the days when she'd expected to battle

these difficult times alone. They were a team and if it hadn't been for their wobble after the parenting class he would never have moved out. She didn't want to go through any of this without him.

'Good.' He gave her an adorable half-smile that made her fall for him all over again. She knew she was in love with him, that was the reason she'd been so scared they weren't together for the right reasons. Now, having him here after everything she'd accused him of, she knew he was committed to this family. He'd told her he loved her, and this was the proof her twice-burned, baggage-carrying self had demanded before giving herself one hundred per cent to another man.

'I've missed you.' In case he didn't already know how much he meant to her, she was going to make sure to clarify things before they left this building. The time had passed for misunderstandings and skating around important issues. They needed to be a cohesive unit to face whatever the future held for them and the babies. Their babies.

'I've missed you too.' His voice cracked a little and he gave an embarrassed cough to clear his throat, but it was an emotional time for both of them. She could see he shared her worries about the twins and how close they'd come to losing everything.

'I'm sorry for questioning your motives for being with me. I guess I'm just wary of anyone who claims to love me but that's not your fault. You've done nothing but show me what true love is.' She'd pre-empted a disastrous relationship and almost willed it into existence because of her past experiences but all that had to change for the sake of her family. As long as Cal still thought she was worth the effort.

'I had a part to play in this whole mess too, thinking I could never make you truly happy and someday you'd walk out on me too. That's why I was afraid to let myself get close to the babies, thinking I'd never recover if you took them away from me. I guess it's too late for that anyway. The second I knew you were here I knew I loved you all, wanted to keep you all safe. I'm sorry it took so long for me to work it out, but I know my place is here, with you and the babies.'

That was everything she wanted to hear, and she could almost feel her body settling down to see out the rest of this pregnancy with him, free from further drama. 'Well, I'd prefer if we could do that doting partner thing at home.'

'You won't be allowed to lift a finger, you know. Do you think you can manage that?' His teasing came with a hint of genuine concern and it was little wonder when she'd been so difficult thus far, but she'd learned her lesson and hoped she'd get a second chance at this whole pampered pregnant lady thing. This time she'd take full advantage of everything Cal was offering.

'Complete bed rest. I swear.' She crossed her heart and promised to let him fuss over her. After these past days, wandering around that big house on her own, she didn't know why she'd resisted it this far. It was nice having someone worry about her and want to take care of her for once. A shame it had taken almost losing everything for her to appreciate that instead of fearing it.

'And after the babies are here? What happens then?' It was clear he was asking in terms of their relationship what would happen next, and though no one could predict the future she could be honest about her hopes for the future.

'I am hoping we live happily ever after. I love you, Cal, and I'm sure the babies will love you too. Can we think of this as our new start, our little family finally coming together?' It was something they'd both been missing out on and this pregnancy was a gift, giving them everything they'd dreamed about. With Cal in her corner she was optimistic they could persuade these babies to stay put until they were out of the danger zone.

A smile slowly crept over his face until he was positively beaming. 'You've never said that before.'

'What? That I love you? I think I was afraid to say it out loud and acknowledge those feelings myself. Now I've said it out loud, I can't take it back.' She gave a little laugh, still nervous about entering into another serious relationship, especially when there were going to be two more wee people affected by her every future decision, but leaping into the unknown with Cal was preferable to a lonely life without him.

'No, you can't, and I for one will never get sick of hearing you say it. Along with that "our family", thing you casually tossed in there. You don't know how happy that makes me, knowing that I'm going to be part of this.' He rested his hand on her bump and she couldn't imagine anyone else she would rather spend the rest of her life with, raising these precious babies. It was important he knew that because she didn't intend wasting any more of her life regretting things she did or didn't say.

'You're very much part of this, daddy Cal, and once we know for sure these two are going to behave and stay where they are until we're ready for them, I want to make it official. Calum Armstrong, will you marry us?' She hadn't known she was going to ask him until the words came out of her mouth, but it felt so right for all of them to make this relationship as solid as possible.

It was the first time she'd ever seen him lost for words as his jaw flopped open and shut without him making a sound. If he hadn't looked so utterly thrilled by the proposal she would've worried he was searching for the words to let her down gently.

'Is that a yes?'

'That's a yes to being your husband, yes to being daddy Cal and yes to spending every day of the rest of my life with you. On one condition.' His forehead crinkled and turned his handsome face serious again.

Izzy swallowed, concerned that he might impose some impossible demands, but had to trust that belief she had in him that he would never do anything to hurt her.

'Name it,' she said, feigning a bravery she would need to see her through the next months.

'You get some rest.' He kissed her all too fleetingly on the lips.

Now, that she could do. She snuggled down into the bed, exhaustion washing over her in waves now she'd laid herself bare emotionally, but knowing Cal was sticking with her gave her enough comfort to give in to slumber.

'Where will you be when I wake up?' she mumbled, refusing to let go of his hand as she drifted off to sleep.

'Where I belong. Right here beside you.'

She smiled with the soft pressure of his lips against her cheek and knew everything would turn out fine when she woke up because now she had a future with Cal to look forward to. This family of convenience had become one she was going to cherish for ever.

Epilogue

'I now pronounce you husband and wife.'

The registrar legally confirmed their commitment to one another, although Cal and Izzy had done that almost a year ago in the hospital.

'I can kiss the bride now, right?'

As if he would've let anyone stop him. Izzy would never tire of letting him either. Being able to kiss Cal any time she pleased was one of the many good things to come her way.

The registrar nodded her approval as Cal dipped his new bride back for a true Hollywood-romance-style kiss, which still had the ability to make Izzy spend the rest of the day walking around in a daze.

A chorus of whoops and cheers rang out from the congregated guests as they finally made their relationship official. They had planned an altogether different wedding from the one currently taking place, but seeing the sea of smiling faces cheering them down the aisle, Izzy was grateful at how things had turned out.

Originally, she'd envisaged a quick, quiet ceremony with no fuss so the twins would be born into a stable relationship but, as Cal had pointed out, they were going to have that regardless of a piece of paper. They'd also decided they didn't need the extra stress of wedding preparations when she already had an increased risk of going into premature labour.

She'd been true to her word and stuck to complete bed rest and Cal had gone above and beyond the duties of a loving partner and father-to-be. He'd taken time off work to play nursemaid as well as crawl into bed to watch movies with her and cook every meal for her to make sure she didn't die of boredom or malnutrition in the run-up to the birth.

That time together had been precious for them as a couple, getting to know each other again minus their baggage. She believed it was a major contributing factor to the babies hanging on until her thirty-fourth week. The amniotic sac had resealed itself after that terrifying episode and, although a little on the small side, their girls had been born healthy and able to come home after just a few days. Then the fun had really started, and those quiet moments together had become few and far between. There was never a dull moment in the Armstrong household now and she was thankful for it.

The extra time since the birth and announcing their intention to get married had given them a chance to share their special day with the important people in their lives. Mac and the guys from work were here to celebrate with them and Cal's sisters had travelled with their families to be with them. Perhaps it wasn't too late for any of them to be a real family.

'I love you, Mrs Armstrong, but I hate to break it to you: I'm leaving you for the other two special girls in my life.' Cal stopped halfway down the aisle and let go of her hand to reach for the beauties who'd caught his eye on the way past.

'Oh, well. It was fun while it lasted.' Izzy knew she could never compare to the other important people in this marriage but for once she was happy to come second in Cal's affections when she was equally enamoured with their daughters.

'Come here, Nelly Belly.' Cal reached for the cute bundle trying to wriggle out of Helen's arms to reach her daddy and Izzy did the same with Nell's sister, Rae. She had her best friend and her husband to thank for the twins' still pristine flower girl outfits as they'd juggled the childcare duties during the ceremony. But neither she nor Cal would be parted from them for longer than necessary. They'd named the girls after Cal's parents, Ray and Eleanor, and Cal was the most devoted father anyone could ever wish for. These girls would be as spoiled and happy as she was with him in their lives.

'Well, husband, I think it's time this family really got the party started. Everyone back to our place for champagne and cake.' Their home was their favourite place in the world and the natural choice for a venue in which to celebrate their big day with friends and family. On this occasion Cal had delegated the cooking to caterers so he could spend as much quality time with her and the girls as possible.

Izzy's heart was so full of love for this man she knew it wouldn't be long before the Armstrong family would be growing again...

* * * * *

SPECIAL EXCERPT FROM

HARLEQUIN
SPECIAL EDITION

*Skylar Davis is grateful to have her late husband's dog.
But the struggling widow can barely keep her three
daughters fed, much less a hungry canine. Kyle Mitchell
was her husband's best friend and he can't stop himself
from rescuing them. But will his exposed secrets ruin
any chance they have at building a family?*

Read on for a sneak peek at
Their Rancher Protector,
*the latest book in the Texas Cowboys & K-9s miniseries
by* USA TODAY *bestselling author Sasha Summers!*

"Even the strongest people need a break now and then. It's
not a sign of being weak—it's part of being human," he
murmured against her temple. "As far as I'm concerned,
you're a badass."

She shook her head but didn't say anything.

"Look at your girls," he insisted. "You put those smiles
on their faces. You found a way to keep them entertained
and positive and with enough imagination to turn that
leaning wooden shack into a playhouse—"

"Hey," she interrupted, peering up at him with red-
rimmed eyes.

"I was teasing." He smiled. "You're missing the point
here."

"Oh?" She didn't seem fazed by the fact that she was still holding on to him—or that there was barely any space between them.

But he was. And it had him reeling. The moment her gaze met his, the tightness and pressure in his chest gave way. And having Skylar in his arms, soft and warm and all woman, was something he hadn't prepared himself for.

Focus. Not on the unnerving reaction Skylar was causing, but on being here for Skylar and the girls. *Focus on honoring Chad's last request.* Chad—who'd expected him to take care of the family he'd left behind, not get blindsided and want more than he should. How could he not? Skylar was a strong, beautiful woman who had his heart thumping in a way he didn't recognize.

"Thank you, again." Her gaze swept over his face before she rose on tiptoe and kissed his cheek. "You're a good man, Kyle Mitchell."

Don't miss
Their Rancher Protector *by Sasha Summers,*
available August 2021 wherever
Harlequin Special Edition books and ebooks are sold.

Harlequin.com

Copyright © 2021 by Sasha Best

HSEEXP0721